FORMULA Love

M.L. Miller

Formula Love

Copyright © 2024 by ML Miller

All rights reserved. No part of this book may be used or reproduced in any manner whatsoever without written permission except in the case of brief quotations for reviews.

Formula Love is a work of fiction. As such, the story is ...wait for it ... made up, and the characters and their statements, beliefs, actions, and experiences should not be confused with, or assumed to represent, the author's. Names, characters, businesses, places, historical events, and situations are a product of the author's imagination or used fictitiously. Any similarity to real people living or dead, organizations, or incidents is entirely coincidental.

Without in any way limiting the author's exclusive rights under copyright, any use of this publication to "train" generative artificial intelligence (AI) technologies to generate text is expressly prohibited. The author reserves all rights to license uses of this work for generative AI training and development of learning language models.

ISBN: 979-8-9917880-2-1 (paperback)
ISBN: 979-8-9917880-1-4 (ebook)

Cover Design: ML Miller

Editing: EJL Editing

Proofreading: Brandee Paschall Books LLC

Formatting: EJL Editing

To all the girls who've known a love worth fighting for.

CHAPTER 1

GATEKEEPER

"I DON'T KNOW THAT I'll ever get the feeling back in my feet," Ella says. "The *least* they can do is give us more sensible shoes."

I stop mid sip—*you can still feel your feet?*

"Sounds like you need another drink!" Carmen spouts, her black ringlets bouncing.

Her eyes light up as Oliver's voice comes through the microphone announcing his latest track. The crowd in the pit below roars to life as the first few beats hit. I fear I'm too inadequate to be standing front row amongst the *it-crowd* in the VIP section. *Cheers to mighty friends.*

The bass vibrates the soles of my feet. The oscillations travel up my legs and shake the beads on the red crop top the brand selected for me. *Maybe* the wedge sandals were not the best footwear choice for a music festival. But who am I to complain? I'm being *paid* to wear this outfit, which is still a foreign concept to me. I was beside myself when I saw the proposal: wear *these outfits* and attend *these parties* in exchange for posting and tagging. Ella reserves the right of feedback given her status as a top influencer boasting just over 1.1 million followers. *Influencing* was the last opportunity on my radar. I was desperate for a fresh start, and Ella convinced her agency to take a chance on me. Sure, I could let my dad bankroll my life, but the ounce of fight left in me isn't ready to give up quite yet. Besides, Mallorca isn't a bad *"work"* trip locale.

"Are you getting another drink?" Ella asks.

"Unless you want to carry me out of here, I'm okay for a bit."

"You're right, we've got to make it to the after-party."

I scoop my tangled locks off the back of my neck and let the dark brown waves cascade over the front of my shoulder. Moisture from my sweaty glass drips onto my toes as I slurp down the last of my margarita until only watery ice chips lie at the bottom. I despise the taste, but it does its job. The tequila's added another layer to my buzzed, euphoric, sun-drunk bliss. I set the glass down on the railing and put my moist fingers to the heat on the apples of my cheeks. My heart sprints as Oliver transitions to our favorite song.

"He promised me he'd play it!" Carmen shrieks, wearing her proudest girlfriend smile.

Oliver waves at us from behind his tables. I throw my hands in the air and bounce up and down with Ella. It wasn't long ago I couldn't be convinced I'd ever get back on my feet. Not after my career and the only man I've ever loved slipped through my fingers. I'm forever grateful for these girls pulling me from my lowest of lows.

Ella giggles; the rush in my head moderates my bouncing to a mellow sway. I lower my hands to my hip bones; the fabric of the flowy gauze trousers brushing against my shins. My heart pulses, absorbing every beat of the song. *Remember?* This *is what happiness feels like.* If happy is possible, maybe there's hope for getting back the confidence I once had. Fingertips land on my back as a smooth voice pours out from behind my ear.

"You having fun?"

I follow the voice over my left shoulder. My eyes land on his mouth, the sheen on his lips, then travel up and lock with his smiling eyes.

My word.

"I'm Beck," he says, holding out a hand.

I'm—*stuck.*

Is the golden sunset distorting my vision? I've never seen eyes that smiled and sparkled so brilliantly. If my eyes are a bitter espresso, his are the color of the sweetest Cadbury milk chocolate. Beck.

Snap out of it. I have a name too. I blink quickly, attempting to focus. I lift my hand and remember how to give someone a proper handshake.

"Sophie," I say, looking up at him.

Our hands linger for several seconds, bobbing up and down.

Ella barges in, bringing me back down to earth.

"I'm Ella!" she squeals, grabbing Beck's hand. I watch her eyes dart from Beck to the tattooed bloke behind him.

Her eyes grow as her pupils morph into hearts. "And who do we have here?" She scurries past us.

Beck runs his fingers through his chunky brown hair. *Are these other DJs?*

Ella's degree of excitement leads me to believe they must be worth some level of fuss.

Beck steps in closer. Even in my wedges he towers over me. The music is loud, but is it loud enough to warrant how close he's standing?

"Are you friends of Oliver's?" he asks.

"*Er*—Carmen." I point. "She's the reason why we're up here." *As if I must give him an explanation.* Carmen turns, glancing at me, then does a double take, her eyes wide. Oliver peers over and points in our direction. Beck gives him an exaggerated nod before his eyes slowly drift back down to mine.

"I see." He nods. "And will you girls be going to the after-party?"

"Yes, we plan to head there when his set is over."

"Good." He pauses. "I'll find you."

I nod. Then keep nodding because I don't know what else to do.

He hasn't stopped with that smile—with that *stare*. Finally, he breaks, retreating to his friend, who is still being dazzled by Ella.

Her eyes shoot to me as the men disappear into the pool of people behind us as quickly as they'd arrived.

"Sophie!" Ella shrieks. "Do you have any idea who that was?"

I scan the crowd behind us until I see him emerge, climbing up the stairs, heading backstage with his friend.

"Sophie!" she says again.

He's gone.

Ella grabs my shoulders, jolting me back to reality.

I narrow my eyes. *Hmm... I'd remember that face if I'd seen it before.*

"That's Beckham Wright!" Ella exclaims.

Who? Still nothing from my brain.

"The Formula One driver!" she says.

I nod. "Like *racecars?*"

"And Tommy Young!" a stranger next to us pipes in. "The tan one!"

Carmen turns to us. "What on earth are they doing here?"

"Oliver must know them?" Ella says. Carmen shrugs.

"I'll be having a word with him! What else is he gatekeeping?" Ella cries.

Neither one of their names rings any bells. I would buy Oliver knowing them. He is certainly making a name for himself. I've heard of Formula One, though I can't claim to know much about it. I don't care *what* he is; I need to lay my eyes on him again.

"What did he say to you?" Ella presses.

"Nothing really. Just…"

"Sophie! The man made a beeline to you. Please tell me you got more out than your name."

I bite my bottom lip, trying to recall what he'd said. *I was quite preoccupied with his eyes.* Ella smiles and shakes her head.

Oh! I remember.

A smile grows across my face. "He said he'd find me at the after-party."

CHAPTER 2
I Hate Tequila

THERE'S NO WAY THIS club isn't over capacity. Although it'd take some form of light to count the bodies stuffed in here. The music is bumping, and the air conditioning is having trouble keeping up. If Beck's actually coming, he'll have no issue protecting his anonymity. My stomach flutters. I need a drink.

"Alright, girls, follow me," Ella yells.

I lock elbows with Carmen and grip Ella's arm as she pushes into the crowd. With Ella in front, the crowd gracefully parts when they see her approach. Soft neon's glow under liquor packed shelves behind the bar. Having a blonde bombshell best friend has its perks. Ella's given immediate attention from a bartender. She puts her elbows on the bar and leans forward—the guy drops everything he was doing to wait on her. The bartender nods and grabs three rocks glasses.

Ella turns to us. "I'm thinking shots too?"

I exchange a look with Carmen. That wasn't a question, it was a warning. The bartender turns and grabs a skinny bottle off a high shelf, flips it in the air and catches it upside down. Ella claps her hands. *Show off.* The liquor elevates the ice in the glasses. He splashes a dash of yellow juice on top, then scoots the drinks our way. He places a straw in each glass, and Ella leans forward again. She slips him money across the counter, which he pushes back. Ella grabs the bills and tucks them into his front pocket. He smirks, then turns to fulfill her latest request. Ella passes me a glass; the gold drink glows in the neon lights.

"Here's to...getting paid to party in Mallorca!" Ella giggles.

I take the straw between my lips. It's sweet—pineapple and rum maybe? Whatever it is, I need another sip.

The bartender is back with three shot glasses topped with a lime wedge. I shudder, anticipating the taste, but then again, he probably poured her only the best top shelf tequila.

"There she is!"

A chill zings down my spine. It's the voice. *It's him.*

I turn around and try to focus on anything but his eyes.

"Beck, was it?" I ask.

He smiles, his eyes narrowing playfully. *I've failed.*

The friend leans in. "I'm Tommy. Nice to meet you."

I shake his hand. *An Aussie.* Now I understand what made Ella so giddy. She's taken notice of their arrival; the bartender's pouring additional shots. I set my drink on the bar. Beck releases Carmen's hand and shifts to face me. I panic and grab two of the shot glasses, extending one to him. I can almost taste it already. Oh well, *liquid confidence.* I take the lime off the top and raise the shot glass to eye level.

"To making a new friend."

Beck's eyes sear into me.

"New friends." He nods.

Our glasses meet, and I bravely throw the shot back. The heat travels down my throat into my chest. It's smooth, *top shelf*, but that doesn't change what it is. I quickly pull the lime to my mouth and bite into it.

"I *hate* tequila," I giggle.

Beck smiles through an equally sour face.

Carmen grabs my arm. "Come, you two! Let's sit!" I drop the lime in the glass and put it on the bar and step in line behind Carmen. Tommy and Ella lead the way, cutting through the crowd. Beck's fingertips meet my back for half a second. He's so close I can *feel* his body behind me.

A gap opens. Tea lights bounce and flicker off waiting champagne glasses at a private table in the back corner of the club.

I sink down on the end of a low couch. Beck sits down next to me and puts his arm behind me along the back of the sofa. An ice bucket holding three bottles of champagne arrives at the table. Carmen steps up on the opposing couch, clapping wildly. *My word. Please behave, Carmen.* Tommy grabs a bottle and yells as he pops the cork with his thumb. He nods at Beck before his focus returns to Ella. She's certainly met her match; Tommy almost has her beat in the volume department. She holds out four glasses while Tommy pours the champagne. Carmen bounces up and down on the couch. Oh dear, manners are out the window.

Beck doesn't seem to mind; he appears entertained. I didn't notice before, but now seated next to him, I can't keep my eyes from tracing along his rigid jawline.

"Where's Oliver?" He smiles.

"He'll be on his way," I giggle. *Then it will only get rowdier.*

Beck scooches to the edge of the couch retrieving two filled champagne glasses. He hands one to me and sits back. His arm reclaims its place around me. This time, his fingers rest against the bare skin of my left shoulder. I try to slow my breathing, clinking my glass with his. The bubbles dance in the glass, and the champagne sizzles as it hits the back of my throat.

"You're from England?"

The dull roar of the club might be louder in this corner than it was at the bar. Beck moves closer.

"London." Smiling, I nod at Ella and Carmen. "But we're staying in Paris this year."

"Destined friends." He winks. "I grew up in Surrey, but I'm living in London now."

I take another long draw of my champagne.

"Tommy and I are drivers here on holiday. Our season's on break. It picks back up in a few weeks."

"I was informed of that—after you left—sorry I didn't know…"

His eyes twinkle. "I like that you didn't know."

I fold my lips together. *You like that I'm an uninformed idiot?*

"Well, I'm glad one of us in this *friendship* can drive!" I joke.

I can't remember the last time I even drove Dad's car.

"I'll be your driver," he says bewitchingly.

Gah! His eyes. The matching grin. *Breathe.*

"Have you ever been to a race?" he asks.

"I haven't—I'm afraid I don't know anything about—"

His smile gets even bigger. *My God, this is embarrassing. Think, Sophie!*

I glance at Tommy, then back to him.

"So you two race each other?"

"Yes." He confirms, amused.

Lord, could I have asked a dumber question?

"I drive for Furio, Tommy's with MACH—our teams are probably the biggest rivalry on the grid this year."

"Friends close, enemies closer?"

He smiles wickedly. "No one is your friend when you get in the car."

His words ripple through me. *Fuck,* he's intriguing.

"Sophie!" Ella yells.

Her phone's pointed toward us. Beck's arm scoops around my shoulder, bringing me even closer. I muster up a nervous smile as she clicks a photo of us. Beck relaxes back into the couch. I watch her tap away at the screen. *Ella, where is that photo going?* She grabs Tommy around the neck and holds the phone out in front of them for a selfie.

"We're here for a few events representing brands. Half work, half play," I say. "Our hotel's up in town. It's a shame—we've hardly made it down to the beach yet."

Beck looks gobsmacked. "You haven't been to the beach?"

"We barely touched the sand!" I giggle. "We tried to walk from our place, but it took us awfully long; we had to turn around just as we made it there."

His arm leaves my shoulder. Beck leans forward and sets his glass down. He stands up quickly and holds his hand out.

"Come with me," he says.

I glance at his hand and hesitate. *Come? With you?* My gaze trails up his arm and meets his eyes. I place my hand in his. He whisks me up to my feet. I down the last sip of my champagne then set it on the table. He grips my hand and starts to pull me away. I look back—my eyes dart from Carmen's bewildered face to Ella's.

My heart races. Beck's determined, pushing back into the crowd. Behind him, I wiggle through the horde. *Can he feel how much my hand is sweating?* If he can, he doesn't let go, even when we've reached our target. He slows his pace, pushing through the final mass surrounding the door. The warm, fresh air is a welcome exchange from the stuffy club. Beck releases a deep exhale and smiles. My hearing adjusts to the chatter coming from the queue waiting to get inside. A girl in the queue shrieks as she points in our direction. The friends around her turn and stare.

Beck drops my hand and puts his arm around my waist. He pulls me close and turns on his heels.

"This way," he says.

We take a quick left then cross the street.

"Where are we going?" I ask nervously.

Beck stops at the top of the alley stairs and reaches for my hand.

"Careful, these steps are steep," he says.

I take his hand and lower down to the first stone step.

Steep, yes, but also dark and narrow. *Hold on a second*, am I really leaving my friends? Venturing off alone with a guy I've just met in a foreign country?

I take three more steps down.

Yes, Sophie, you are indeed.

Was it the tequila shot or the champagne doing the reassuring? Maybe it's his eyes. Whatever it is, I cannot escape the allure of the aura orbiting around him. Oliver's a stand-up guy; there must be only a few degrees of separation between them. *Besides, what have I got to lose?*

"Where are we going, Beck?" I ask again.

"Don't worry. Friends don't kidnap friends." He smiles. "I'm taking you to the beach."

In the middle of the night? I tuck my chin to hide my excitement and avoid falling on my face.

"Apologies for leaving rather quick. I've had enough of the crowds and chaos," he adds.

We turn right at the bottom of the stairs; our shadows move along the walls of the alley. *Do friends hold hands?* He didn't let go at the bottom of the stairs.

"You know where you're going?"

"We're almost there."

The ocean must be close—the noise from the city nightlife is distant. Now, our footsteps are the only sound bouncing off the narrow passage walls between the buildings. My heart rate picks up as we reach a *T* in the footpath. Beck stops in front of a tall iron gate. Through the iron bars, the path inside is dimly lit and surrounded by tall shrubbery on both sides. He punches in a code on the keypad and pushes the gate open.

"Is this some secret beach?" I giggle.

I step inside, and he closes the gate securely behind us. He smiles and retakes my hand.

"*Top* secret." He winks.

The steep path curves to the left. As we round the corner, the path widens, and I spot the sand. My stomach flutters. *What is this place?* The path dumps out onto a small private beach. The water is calm; it reflects the glowing string lights hung in the trees. A jetty protects the sand. Light and music pour out of a villa set back from the water. It's magical—the kind of retreat you'd see in a honeymoon advertisement.

"Is this where you're staying?" I ask.

Beck nods. "No one's here. The staff have gone home for the night."

The staff?

"Let me get your shoes," he says, crouching down. I lift my foot up and try to balance. He slides one wedge off my foot, then the other. I step down and stretch my arches in the cool moisture of the sand.

"This feels *amazing*."

He pulls off his socks, then begins rolling up the bottoms of his trousers.

"I love it out here at night."

Beck scoops up our shoes and steps into the sand. I follow him to the water and stop at the loungers sitting at the water's edge. He sets our shoes down and walks in ankle deep without hesitating. Down the beach, a wooden dock juts out into the water. Waves crash into the other side of the jetty, but here in front of us, the water rocks more like a gentle lake.

I lift the legs of my trousers and shriek, taking a step into the water. I quickly back up.

Beck turns around, grinning. "Don't be scared."

But I am. I dig my toes into the sand.

Beck gets a wild look in his eye. He grabs the bottom of his shirt and lifts it over his head. My mouth falls open.

His stomach muscles flex as he walks out of the water fiddling with the button on his trousers. He throws his shirt to a lounger then pulls the top of his trousers down. I gulp. Stepping on the bottoms; he pulls his feet free. His trousers join his shirt on the chair; only his briefs remain. He hasn't taken his eyes off me.

My heart slams in my chest. I toss my bag to the chair. I touch the beads on the bottom of my crop top. I follow his lead and pull my top over my head. *My bralette is staying on.* I drop my flowy trousers, thanking myself for choosing panties over a thong this morning. His eyes burn into me. I toss my things to the chair then cross my arms, covering as much as possible. Beck steps forward and reaches for my hand.

When the water reaches past my calves, I stop. It's bathwater, but chills soar up my legs.

"*I've got you.*"

I don't budge. Beck steps back to me and leans down. In one swift motion, he sweeps my legs out from under me and picks me up.

"*Beck*!" I shriek.

"*Shh,*" he whispers.

I cling to him for dear life as he walks deeper into the water.

"Okay, that's far enough!" I say frantically.

He takes one more step then carefully lowers onto his knees. I tense as my body dips into the water. Adrenaline pulses through me. My knees meet the sandy bottom, and he releases me. The ends of my hair submerge. Water soaks through my bralette, hardening my nipples.

"Are you scared?" he asks.

"A little," I lie. *This is terrifying.*

Beck's hands reach around my back, he pulls my body closer through the water. I stare at his lips—is *he going to kiss me?* He sits back on his heels. I gasp as he puts his hands around the back of my legs and pulls me into his lap. He rests his hands on the top of my thighs now on either side of him. A fire sets ablaze inside me.

"That's better," he says softly.

A magnetic field buzzes around us. I try to slow my breathing; I can't hold his gaze any longer. I peer down at the lonely centimeters of water between us. His hand leaves my thigh and emerges from the water. He lifts my chin with his finger. His eyes are intense.

"You're beautiful, Sophie."

I don't have time to respond before his lips meet mine, sending shockwaves through my veins. The world around me falls away. His welcome tongue invades my mouth. I throw my arms around the back of his neck. His fingers grip into the back of my hair. I thrust my chest against his. I'm panting, but he doesn't pull away and neither do I.

"Ow! Ow!"

I jerk my head back, snapping back into reality. I glance over Beck's shoulder—the cat calls are coming from the villa.

"Tommy's home." He smirks.

Oh my God, this isn't happening.

It's not only Tommy. Ella's standing next to him on the patio.

"Sophie Collins, are you mad?!" she yells.

I scoot off Beck's lap and duck further down into the water. Surely they can't see anything out here, right?

"Let's go," he says.

"I can't get out like this!"

He looks back at the villa then stands up.

"They've gone back inside."

Beck holds his hands out, his biceps flexing as he helps me to my feet. I wrap my arms around my body, trotting out of the water.

He retrieves a towel from a basket next to the lounge chair holding our clothes. He unrolls it then throws it around my back. Keeping hold of the ends, he pulls me into him. I put my palms against the muscles on his damp chest.

"There," he murmurs. "Now you've been to the beach."

I clasp onto the ends of the towel. He steps back and grabs another towel for himself, wrapping it around his waist.

I step up onto the wooden patio, gripping my clothes and the towel around me. Ella and Tommy are standing inside an open sliding door.

"I can't believe you are in the ocean at this hour!" Ella says.

Ha! Like I had a choice.

"You can't keep Beck out of the water," Tommy says.

Beck hops up the stairs behind me. "I kept her perfectly safe."

I step inside the villa's bright living room. Beck heads for a door on the right.

Ella's glaring at me. *Not now.*

"Where's Carmen?" I ask, avoiding her questioning eyes.

"Some of Ollie's friends showed up, so Carmen stayed at the club. I got a ride here with Tommy." She smirks.

Tommy stretches his arms out. "Welcome to the honeymoon cabin!"

Beck reappears in a fresh T-shirt and shorts. He nods at the door. "There's a bathroom in here, Sophie."

Perfect. This towel dress isn't going to cut it. I slide past him in the doorway. He grabs the handle and pulls the door closed behind him, leaving it open a crack. The bedroom is a crisp, blinding white. French doors are open to another patio, its sheer curtains moving gently in the breeze. *His room?* I flip the light on in the bathroom and take inventory. I certainly put on a new layer of color today. I run my fingers through the bottom of my hair, attempting to brush it out. I dry off as well as I can and drop my towel on top of his on the floor.

I slip my trousers and crop top over my damp undergarments. I stare at the towel pile and replay the last ten minutes. *Did that just happen?*

Beck and Tommy sit on either side of Ella on the couch. She points to her phone. "This is the Australian brand I was telling you about; we're wearing their pieces to a pool party Sunday," Ella says.

Beck glances up as I walk out into the living room.

"Wait, the *Trofeo* party?" Tommy asks.

"Yeah, the tequila?" she says.

Tommy lights up. "We're going to that!"

My cheeks flush. *We'll be meeting again?*

"But I suppose you girls will be *working* not partying," Tommy jokes.

"*Working!*" I giggle and sit down next to Beck.

"Yes, Sophie, it counts as *working*," Ella scolds.

Beck appears confused.

"Sorry." I shake my head. "That was rude. Influencing isn't really my thing."

"Soph's a finance girlie, but I'll make an influencer of her yet," Ella says.

I shouldn't talk. I see how hard Ella works. She puts in more hours than a regular *nine-to-fiver* keeping engaged with her followers twenty-four seven.

"So, you're a numbers girl?" Beck asks. "Was" I clarify. "Private equity." *The numbers I'm to monitor now look much different.*

"We joke all the time that when we're not driving, we're basically influencers. Working with brands is a huge part of the job," Tommy says.

Beck nods. "The whole car's covered in branding. Then the minute we step out it's *put on this watch, wear this hat, hold this drink.*"

"It has its perks." Tommy smiles. "It got us a ride here. Beck has a sponsorship with a private jet company."

Ella's jaw drops.

A private jet collab? Ella doesn't even get those calls. I shake my head. "Can't say any private jet collabs have come across my desk."

Ella busts out laughing.

"Why did you leave finance?" Beck asks.

My stomach drops.

"Because she's way too cute to be hidden in an office all day," Ella says quickly.

God, she's fast. I swallow, relief flooding over me. She saved me from surely tripping over my words. Now's not the time to delve into the fallout of my former life.

Ella leans forward. "Ivan should be here soon, Soph."

We're leaving?

"Who's Ivan?" Beck asks.

"Ella's got the driver of the hotel shuttle on speed dial," I laugh.

"We better get walking then," Tommy says.

Ella's face drops. "Oh God, the way we came in?"

The path from the villa's front door up to the road is a winding switchback of stairs.

"The side gate is kinder, but the only road is out front," Beck says.

Ella and Tommy start the climb. Soft lights glow on the narrow stone steps. I stop at the second landing to catch my breath.

"You don't have to walk us all the way up..." Beck stops next to me on the landing.

"Of course we do!" he says. "But yes, it's more fun coming than going."

I exhale and look up at the next landing. Beck reaches for my hand and takes the first step up the next flight. *That's not going to help my heartrate.*

Ella cheers. Beck and I turn for the final switchback; there's noise from the street. Tommy opens the gate at the top of the stairs. My heart races faster. Partly from the booty burner hike and partly because it's time to say goodbye. Beck stops before the last few steps and turns to me.

His chest rises and falls. "I'll see you Sunday at the pool party then?"

I smile through my huffing and puffing. "*I'll find you.*"

His eyes gleam; he steps forward and presses his lips against my forehead.

"Goodnight, Miss Sophie."

I turn and float up the last steps on my way to the car.

"Sorry Ivan—bit of a hike," Ella says, climbing into the shuttle.

I shut the door and discreetly glance out the window. Through the gate, the back of their heads descend the stairs as the shuttle pulls away from the sidewalk.

"Sophie Collins kisses an F1 driver...did *not* have that on my radar for this trip."

I roll my eyes.

"That's one way to get your confidence back! What a rebound!"

I glare at her.

"What? I'm proud of you," she says, pulling her phone out.

Phone. Wow. I haven't checked mine in hours. I open my bag and click the text notification from our *Roomie Trio* group chat.

> Where are you going?

> Are you alone? WITH HIM?!

Ha! These came in during the kidnapping. Ella's speed typing; I lean over and watch her save a phone number—*Tommy Young*.

"Of course you got his number."

"It's called *networking,* Sophie—besides, I wouldn't mind laying out on their private beach."

My hand buzzes. A text from an unknown number pops up on my screen. My heart backflips. I stare down at the message in disbelief.

> Sophie, it's Beck. It was a pleasure meeting you tonight.

I swallow. "Did you give Beck my number?"

"He asked for it. When you were putting your clothes *back on*," she winks.

"I had clothes on!"

"*Barely*," she teases.

I reread the text again. And again. I hand my phone to Ella. "Maybe their beach is a more likely scenario than not."

She scans the screen, and her mouth drops open. "Sophie Collins! He's smitten!"

"*Nahh,*" I say, grabbing the phone back. I open Instagram and click the notification.

Ella_Humphrey mentioned you in their story.

I click Ella's face to relive the day through her Instagram story.

It seems like it was yesterday when we'd left the hotel; I tap through photos from the music festival and *Ollie Godd's* set, our pictures with Oliver backstage, then our voyage to the club. My heart trips. *There it is.* Beck and I on the couch at the after-party—on display for Ella's million followers.

"You two look awfully good together," Ella says, watching me.

For being out in the sun dancing and sweating all day, *it's a great photo.* Even in a picture Beck's eyes twinkle. His lips have a perfect sheen—*I kissed those lips.* His fingers are gripping my sun kissed shoulder. *Those fingers were in my hair.* Reality creeps in. *What am I doing?* This man is several calibers out of my league. I screenshot the photo. It might bring me a laugh a month from now.

CHAPTER 3

MYSTERY GIRL

IT'S BRIGHT. I SHUT my eyes and attempt to force myself back into the dream I was having. But my mind becomes lucid. My eyelids flip back open and my heart rate spikes. *Did that truly happen last night?* Carmen's bed is still made—she must have spent the night with Oliver. By some miracle, I was able to fall asleep. I rollover, and find Ella sitting up next to me on her phone. She moves her glasses from her nose to the top of her head and peers down at me.

"You're causing quite a tussle Soph—you and *Mr. Racing Royalty.*" She turns her phone to me.

I squint at the screen. I blink rapidly to wake my eyes up, realizing what I'm seeing. It's the photo from last night of *me* with *him.* The photo is real. Beck is real. My eyes widen. *This isn't Ella's story.* It's a gossip account's Instagram page.

Beckham Wright spotted at a Mallorca Club, cuddled up with mystery girl.

What on earth? Below the photo, there are thousands of likes. I lift my finger from under the covers and tap the screen to expand the comments.

Who is she?
Noooo!!!
Beck & Sab forever!!

I pull my hand back and pull the comforter over my face. *This is too much.*

"Who is Sab?" Ella asks the blankets.

As if I would know?

"Oh my God!" she shrieks. "He used to date Sabrina Kaufmann!"

The singer? As if I didn't already know that he's out of my league. A popstar is a much more appropriate match. Ella pats the comforter.

"Is that supposed to make me feel better?" I say from under the covers.

"I think you should know who you are dealing with, dear." She sounds like a concerned parent. I throw back the comforter to get another look. Oh, kill me, *she's Googling this man?*

"It seems like they broke up last year. There's no mention of him dating anyone else...*Tommy* on the other hand—there's no shortage of pictures of him with this model or that model."

"So, he is the male version of you?" I tease.

She narrows her eyes at me.

Sabrina's a shock. Ella's failure to find Beck photographed with a slew of other women is *comforting.*

There's commotion at the door. Carmen stumbles into our room. She lights up, locking eyes with me.

"Spill!" she says, jumping onto her bed.

Carmen claps her hands at the conclusion of my post after-party recap.

"Now for the bad news." I pause. "Someone ripped off Ella's story and posted our picture on some gossip account."

Carmen's jaw drops.

"And that is why you both will now refer to me as *mystery girl*."

"I'm obsessed with all of this," Carmen says.

"Same. I can't stop reading!" Ella exclaims. "Beckham Wright is a twenty-five-year-old British Formula One driver in his third year driving for team Furio."

Only a year older. That's a little surprising—he seemed quite mature.

Ella continues reading. "Wright has been with Furio since his rookie season. He spent one year as the team's reserve driver, stepping in for F1 legend, Franco Morelli, for the final race of the season before Morelli's retirement. Wright was awarded the Furio seat after his shocking debut fifth place finish at the Abu Dhabi Grand Prix. Beckham Wright now sits alongside veteran teammate, Luca Lombardo."

My mind races.

"Oliver said he met Beck and Tommy at an event he played at in March." Carmen raises her eyebrows. "According to Oliver, Beck's a great guy."

"Soph, take a page out of my book and *go for it*," Ella says.

I roll my eyes; *there's nothing to go for, Ella.*

"Great guy or not, none of this matters. I will *never* hear from this man again."

"They *said* they were going to the party tomorrow," Ella scolds. "And he texted you after we left last night! My mother is going to drop dead when she hears about this."

Hears how I kissed some Formula One driver then never heard from him again? *What a great story.* How can I end this conversation?

"I'm famished," I say, climbing out of bed. "Can we go out and find some food?"

"*Please!*" Carmen groans.

"Wear the activewear sets—we can get some cute pictures while we're out," Ella instructs.

<hr>

Thankfully, the brunch conversation rerouted the focus from me to Ella and Carmen's packed fall schedules. Fashion weeks have both their calendars full of events, shows and exhibitions. Ella's massive audience landed her a coveted invite to *NYFW*. I'll ride her coat tails to an event here and there back home and in Paris. Meanwhile, Carmen was asked to be a fashion correspondent at the *European Open*.

Too bad I can't backtrack on the favor I was signed up for without my consent. *Thanks Ella.* It was her mum, Alice, who came up with the idea to have a couple of influencers walk among the model mix in the *Eden Eves* show. Her designer best friend, Evelyn Edwards, heads the small London-based label. Ella's an obvious choice, with her long legs and her following. I don't think three thousand followers classify me as an influencer, and I certainly don't meet the height requirement of a real model. To say I'm petrified is an understatement.

Ella leans back in her chair, eyeing the boutiques across the street. "You know, this might be the only day we can do some shopping."

"You don't have to talk me into it," Carmen says.

The third boutique we're lured into is a gold mine. I add another hanger to the two already on my arm before I've made it to the middle of the shop. My phone buzzes in my leggings pocket. I slide it halfway out to peek if it's worthy of answering. It's a FaceTime. I nearly jump out of my skin. It's the unknown London number.

Beck is FaceTiming me.

My heart jumps to my throat. I hang my finds on a random rack. Dashing for the door, I accept the call, and Beck's smile fills the screen.

"There you are!" he says.

I gulp. *The call was on purpose.*

I smile nervously and push the door open. "Hello there." I step out into the beaming sun. He's outside too, on the move, squinting when he glances up every few seconds.

"What are you up to?" he asks.

Me? Never expecting to hear from you again!

"I'm out shopping with the girls." I lean against the side of the building. "Where are you heading?"

"Just finished lunch in town. I remember you said you were staying up here somewhere…" He pauses. "And I don't want to wait for tomorrow to see you again."

My cheeks catch fire. I glance down at my feet to ensure they're still touching the ground. My white trainers throw me a bone. *Go for it.*

"Do you have trainers on?"

Beck narrows his eyes. "I do."

He sounds interested. My heart flutters.

"I've been wanting to walk out to that old watch tower… the girls haven't been overly enthused with that idea…"

His smile grows. "Well, I can't let you walk out there alone, can I?"

I pull my bottom lip between my teeth.

"Where are you?" he asks. "I'll come meet you."

I already decided *if* I happened to see Beck at the pool party, he would have long forgotten about me. Several seconds go by before I realize I'm still outside, smiling down at my blank phone screen. *Get it together*

Sophie. I grab the door handle and head back inside. He was only a few blocks away.

The girls have moved to the fitting rooms in the back of the store. I pass by the rack holding my abandoned items. *I can live without them.*

I catch Ella's eyes in the mirror outside the fitting rooms. She turns side to side, admiring a white set she's tried on. I fold my lips to contain my untamable smile.

"Who was that?" she inquires.

"Beck is on his way here." I announce. "We are going to hike out to that tower."

Carmen jerks open the drape of her fitting room. She exchanges a look with Ella. "This is *serious.*"

"On his way?" Ella raises an eyebrow. "*He's here, love.*"

Beck swings the shop's door open. *God damn,* what is it with men in backward hats? My heart takes off as he saunters toward us.

"Thank God, Beck, you've saved us from having to trudge out there with her," Ella says.

He chuckles, stopping next to me. "Glad I could help."

His eyes are on me, but I'm mute, *frozen.* "Well, Sophie." Ella grasps for my attention. "Don't get lost...or maybe—*get lost,*" she winks.

I flush. "Shall we?" I say, turning quickly on my heels.

"We'll send pictures of anything we can't decide on!" Carmen calls.

Beck steps in front of me to open the door. I try not to flinch when his fingertips meet my back while crossing the street.

"Where to, Sophie?"

I step up onto the sidewalk and slip my phone out of my leggings. I pull up a vague map I screenshot the other day. I pivot and point down the adjacent street. "This way...*I think.*"

I take off, and Beck keeps in line beside me.

"Did you have fun last night?" he asks.

That's a loaded question.

"I did. Thanks to you, I finally got some beach time."

"You were brave!"

Ha! *Not so much.*

"I like Tommy. Have you been friends a long time?"

"He's my best friend; we grew up karting together. Ella seemed to fancy him. They're quite similar."

"Life of the party type?"

He smiles.

I spot the trailhead sign ahead on the right, and my excitement builds.

"Ella's got a massive following," Beck says.

Crap. Did he see his feature in her story last night?

"Did she get you into working with brands?"

I nod. "I've only been doing it a few months. Ella's mum is high up in the PR world, so she has lots of connections. She actually got us booked to walk in a show at London and Paris fashion weeks." *Why am I telling him this?*

"That's big! Are you nervous?"

"*Beyond*. I'm not a model. I've never done anything like that."

"You could definitely be a model."

I giggle. "Maybe if you could stretch me another ten centimeters." We turn off the sidewalk onto a dirt trail.

I shrug. "I guess we'll see; our final fitting is Friday in London."

"You're going back to London?" he asks. "For a few days. We bounce back and forth a lot. We keep the *Eurostar* in business." "I know the nomad life." He concurs. "You still have a place in London?"

"My dad keeps a flat in Mayfair where the girls and I stay. He's in Kensington—in the same house I grew up in."

"Wow, he's done well for himself," he says. "I'm across the bridge near the Power Station."

My, the world is small. A trail offshoot on the left tests me, but I continue straight. Tall grasses along the trail whip in the breeze blowing off the ocean. On the horizon, the water becomes visible.

"I'm hardly ever home though. I'm always traveling or in Italy at headquarters."

"Have you not been convinced to move to Italy?" I ask.

Beck laughs. "I'll have to see if my contract's extended. That might convince me to move there or Monaco. For now, the team has a place for me when I'm visiting. It would be hard not to have a place close to my family. They're outside Ottershaw."

"Are you close with them?"

"*Very.* When I'm free, I'm always out there, golfing with Dad or playing with *the kids.* My younger siblings are adopted. Mia is twelve and Louie is six. I'm going to Rome with them Friday. Louie has a football tournament."

A family man. Like my mouth needs another reason to water.

The grassy path turns and trails along a ridge overlooking the water. I stop to take in the view of the open ocean below us. Beck props his foot up on the stone barrier at the cliff's edge.

"Why are you smiling?" he asks.

"Because we're going the right way." I smirk.

I point to the crumbling tower down to our left at the end of the ridge.

"You were worried?"

"Only a little." I shrug.

I press on. *Look at me now, Ella.* The trail changes from dirt and grass to a steep section of loose rock. Suddenly, my body is set in motion as rocks slide under my feet. I hit the ground in an instant, dust kicking up around me.

Beck rushes up behind me. "Are you ok?!" His face is worried as he looks me over. My ass is numb, and my heart is pounding. All I can do is laugh. *I was doing so well.*

He grabs both of my hands and helps me to my feet. I'm shaky from the shock of the fall. I examine my legs, taking note of any damage—all superficial, it seems.

"I can't believe I just did that," I squeal.

Beck finally breaks out a smile. "Well, I'll only laugh if you're not hurt."

I turn to wipe the dust off my ass. My yellow leggings didn't fare well in the fall. I take a deep breath and meet Beck's smiling eyes.

"It's hard to watch where you're stepping when you're surrounded by so much beauty."

The statement catches me off guard. I break eye contact and cautiously continue walking.

"I'm jealous," I say, returning to the conversation. "I always wanted a sibling."

"You're an only child?"

I nod.

"Do you get on with your parents?" *I knew that was coming.*

"We actually lost my mum to cancer when I was ten."

"I'm sorry to hear that."

I smile. "Dad and I are two peas in a pod though."

The crumbly tower sits at the end of a stubby peninsula. Tall weeds surround the base, viny plants grow up the cracks in the stone walls—*it's honestly way cooler than I expected.* I walk through the arched opening and stare up at the blue sky. One lonely board remains across the top, the rest of the roof is long gone. Beck looks up. It's eerily quiet—only the two of us encircled in stone. Three openings provide picture-perfect views of the sea in each direction.

"I didn't know this was here," he says.

I rest my palms on the ledge and peer out one of the openings. Fifty meters below, waves crash at the base of the cliff.

The hair on the back of my neck stands up—Beck's behind me. His arms come around me, and his hands rest on the ledge outside mine. *There it is again.* A field of energy buzzing around us.

"Thank you," I say. "for coming out here with me."

Beck pushes back from the ledge; I turn around to face him. His eyes burn into me. *He's going to kiss me again.* He leans forward, wrapping his arms around the back of my thighs. I shriek as my feet leave the ground. My bum meets stone as he sets me on the ledge. I cling to the stone edges of the opening. Beck wraps his arms around my back, staying between my legs. I glance back at the drop behind me.

"I've got you," he whispers.

His fingers splay on my back. He already had my heart racing; it might just stop now that he's perched me on the edge of this cliff.

I slowly let go of my death grip on the stone. One by one, I bring my arms to rest around the back of his neck.

"There you go," he says.

The smile he's wearing isn't calming me down, it's only building the heat in my chest. My gaze lingers on his mouth.

"You make me nervous," I say.

"Now, why would I make you nervous?"

Isn't it obvious?

Beck closes in. The pressure cooker inside me reaches its limit. I can't take it anymore—I pull him into me, and our lips meet furiously. His tongue masterfully entangles with mine. All the worry melts away. If last night's kiss was a shock to the system, this kiss has both jumper cables hooked on, bringing my body back to life.

Beck pulls back, and I try to steady my breathing. His eyes stay glued to my lips.

"I want to take you to the party tomorrow," he says.

I smile. *This can't be real.* "I would like that very much."

His eyes flash up to mine. "Now hold on. Let me get your picture, that way the girls can see what they missed."

I move my hands back to the stone. Beck backs up and takes his phone out of his pocket. He holds it up and focuses on the screen. I maintain a soft smile.

"And she says she's not a model," he says.

My cheeks flush; I launch myself off the ledge back to solid ground.

"I'm ready for ice cream," I say.

"Now you're speaking my language!"

⸺

The lift doors close. I put my finger to my bottom lip, still tingling from Beck's farewell kiss. A *very public* farewell kiss. It was hard to ignore the eyes on us at the ice cream shop. The shell-shocked faces of people passing us on the sidewalk on the way back. The people staring outside the hotel—*how do you get used to that?* Beck didn't seem to notice. He's on *holiday.* I can't imagine what it's like walking about back home. The hum of the lift stops and the doors part.

Reaching our room, I push open the door and recognize the blue glasses from the pool bar. The balcony slider is open; four feet rest on the railing.

"You made it!" Carmen yells.

I step out onto the balcony and shield my eyes.

"We were starting to worry." Ella studies me over the rim of her sunglasses.

"You missed out. It was *beautiful.*"

"Do we know his birthday yet?" Carmen asks eagerly.

"May second."

Her eyes light up. "A Taurus."

"The fact that you know that without having to look it up," I laugh. "What's the verdict then? Is there any hope?"

"Earth and fire." Carmen smiles. "It could be *quite* interesting."

Ella shakes her head. "Onto the important questions. Did you pick back up where you left off last night?"

I blush. "He asked to take me to the party tomorrow."

"Aw, Soph!" Carmen squeals. "This is exactly what you need after everything that went down with Fredrick."

The blow only that name can give hits me like a ton of bricks. It was the first time his name had crossed my mind all day. My phone pings—*it's the unknown number.* I open the message and instantly shift back to happy.

I'll pick you up tomorrow at 1.

Three dots appear as Beck types another message. My photo in the tower arrives. Beckham Wright has a picture of me in his phone. I didn't bother saving his number before, *but now it's different.*

37

CHAPTER 4
I'm Doomed

"Hurry up so we can get our photo!" Ella says.

"I'll be there soon. He's on his way."

Oliver waves from the car. Pink and yellow bikini strings hang out the back of Ella's and Carmen's cover-up dresses. The brand sent three white cover-ups and three bikinis, each a different shimmering color. Ella pulls the car door shut and blows me a kiss.

I step back under the awning in front of the hotel and stare down at my identical linen cover-up. What was it that Beck noticed about me standing next to the likes of Ella and Carmen?

A spotless pearl SUV with tinted windows pulls into the circle drive of the hotel. My breath quickens. This *must* be him. If Beck is trying to keep a low profile, this is not passing any tests. The car stops and the back door opens. *It's him.* The top few buttons of his loose cream button down are undone. Bright red swim trunks lie against his quads.

"You ready for work?" Beck calls.

I push off the sidewalk then slow down to play it cool. His sunglasses hide his eyes, but the smile on his face has me so giddy I could skip.

The driver flashes me a grin as I climb into the backseat. The SUV is empty. I plop down in the far seat by the window. Beck climbs in and removes his sunglasses. He takes the middle seat then hangs the glasses on the front pocket of his shirt.

"Where's Tommy?" I ask.

Beck winks. "I told him I found a better date for the party."

I smile. *Is this a date?* My hands fidget in my lap.

"Tommy's meeting us there."

The car pulls away from the drive, and Beck pulls my right hand into his lap. My heart responds in a way that has me questioning why his touch affects me this much.

Beck points to the driver. "Sal was impressed with our hike."

The driver nods in the rearview mirror.

"I sent your picture in the tower to Mum and Dad. My little brother wanted to know what the tower was for. So now I need to come up with a cool story."

Oh? "You sent the picture of me to *your parents?*"

Beck smiles. "When I'm on holiday with Tommy, they request more than a text for proof of life."

Ha!

His thumb slides back and forth against the back of my hand. "Your picture was the standout shot of the day."

My heart flutters.

"Maybe you should tell him it's famous for fending off some notorious pirate invasion."

"*Oh,* that's good!" Beck exclaims. "Louie will love that story."

Sal nods. "I'm going to start using that on the villa guests!"

Ten minutes out of town, Beck hasn't let go of my hand, and my heart hasn't lost any pace. It beats faster as the SUV approaches a private residence perched on the coastal cliffs.

Exotic cars are parked out front, and buttoned-up event staff stand in front of a breezeway tunnel. The car stops and I take a deep breath. *I'm about to enter a party on the arm of Beckham Wright.*

Music and laughter echo behind the house. Staff holding trays of perfectly crafted cocktails anticipate our entrance. Beck shuts the car door and reaches for my hand. I tuck my hair behind my ear then put my hand in his. It's foreign, holding hands *in public.*

With every step toward the breezeway, the more I see the stellar view we are in for. The brand hosts greet us, ensuring we don't walk by without taking a drink. Every frosty glass has a flower in it. I reach for the glass that appears most murky. *Less liquor perhaps?*

Beck makes his selection; he takes a sip then grins. "Tequila's your favorite, right?"

"Maybe this brand can be my breakthrough," I giggle.

I take the straw in my mouth and find it's surprisingly drinkable.

Beck's fingertips find my bare skin in the cutout on the back of my cover-up as we continue through the breezeway.

Lingering habits from my previous relationship have me hyper-aware of any form of PDA. Beck's hands are *constantly* on me—the first night, yesterday hiking and after when we ate ice cream. And now his hand remains at my back, walking into a party full of people.

A sparkling swimming pool sits on a massive terrace overlooking a panoramic view of the sea. We leave the shade of the breezeway—music is pumping, and gorgeous people are scattered around the pool. *What am I doing here?* I glance around nervously. Everyone looks like a celebrity with their noses slightly turned up.

"What's on the agenda for this party?" Beck asks.

"All we need is one photo." I smile. "But with Ella, it's *never* just one photo."

I scan the crowd.

"There they are!" I point across the pool. Oliver and the girls are at a group of lounge chairs.

Oliver greets Beck with the typical bro hug.

"Where's your sidekick?" Ella asks.

Beck laughs. "Tommy's on his way."

"Let's go get our photo, girls!" Ella stands up and pulls her cover-up over her head. Carmen follows suit. I set my bag and drink down, then nervously, I reach for the bottom hem of my cover-up.

The pale blue shimmer on my bikini comes to life.

Oliver peers at us over his sunglasses. "You look like Easter eggs."

Carmen smacks his arm. "Shut up, Oliver."

"What?" He smirks. "You could have passed on the pastel memo."

Beck's eyes are on me as I turn and follow the girls.

Ella stops. "Sophie, you forgot your drink!"

Oh right. Beck grabs my glass and extends it to me.

"Hurry back." He smiles.

I take a few sips of my drink to catch up—Ella and Carmen are almost finished with theirs. *Hurry back?* I take another sip. Across the pool, a photographer waits at a branded backdrop. A waitress hands us fresh drinks for the photo. Carmen and I take our places on either side of Ella. The photographer lifts his camera.

I glance at the lounge chairs; Beck's staring right at me. *Bloody hell!* My heart jumps to my throat. I jerk my head back and smile for the photo. *How long has he been watching?*

"Hold your positions!" Ella instructs.

She runs to the photographer to give the photo her stamp of approval.

My eyes drift back across the pool. Beck and Oliver have been noticed; a group of girls are enraptured, taking selfies with the pair. Carmen rolls her eyes. Beck smiles for a photo before his gaze trails right back to me.

"These are perfect!" Ella shrieks. "Can you take one with my phone please?"

Ella doesn't wait for an answer. She runs back, retaking her place. Tommy emerges through the breezeway. He's glistening, sporting a huge sweat ring around the neck of his T-shirt.

"Ella, let's be done. Tommy's here!"

"One more!" Ella pleads.

The fangirls are overjoyed with Tommy's arrival. I shift back to the photographer who's now holding Ella's phone. *We do look like Easter eggs.*

"The brand will love these," Ella says, tapping furiously on her screen. "Soph, I tagged you. Remember to repost!"

Uh-huh, sure.

I take two gulps of my drink, leading the charge back to our chairs. To my delight, the fangirls have departed.

Beck lowers his sunglasses to the tip of his nose, revealing his luxe chocolate eyes. "Did you get what you were after?"

I smile. "The work is done!"

Ella side eyes Tommy. "Why are you so sweaty?"

Tommy's out of breath. "I came on the boat and walked up from the dock," he pants. "We should take the boat back later!"

I sit back on the foot of a lounge chair. Tommy pulls his shirt over his head, unveiling his tattoo-covered, chiseled chest. I glance at Ella, who's foaming at the mouth. She moves her sunglasses over her eyes.

"Why is no one swimming? I've got to get in," Tommy says.

Without a care in the world, he dives headfirst into the pool. White uniform beach balls peacefully floating on the water's surface bounce to life. Half of the party turns, glaring in our direction. It's a pool party...*surely* they expected people to end up in the pool.

Beck unbuttons the rest of his shirt. I try my best not to stare. He throws his shirt to the head of the lounge chair and tosses his sunglasses on top. Now I *can't* not look. A wild glint fills his eyes. Beck glances at the pool then raises an eyebrow. He pushes forward, coming for me. *Oh shit.*

"Beck...*don't even think—!*"

He scoops me up from the chair into his arms. A second later, we're airborne over the pool. I take a deep breath and grab my nose. Our bodies break apart as we splash into the icy water. I push off the bottom and come up for air.

Beck slowly raises his head out of the water, wearing a cheeky grin. I kick my legs and swim toward him. Oliver belly flops onto a pool float. Ella and Carmen count back from three before jumping in. *We are the crazy kids at the adult pool party.*

I bounce off the bottom of the pool. Beck draws me closer. We're in a fishbowl surrounded by spectators.

"Do you know anyone else here?" I ask.

His eyes fall to my lips. My heart pounds as he hooks his hands around the back of my legs, pulling them around his waist.

"*No,*" he says.

He continues staring at my lips. "I don't want to know anyone else here."

Oh. His eyes flip up to mine.

"Do you want to know anyone else?" he asks.

We're still talking about the party, right? I shake my head slowly.

"*Good*," he says. My heart sprints as the remaining space between us disappears. I close my eyes as Beck's lips press into mine, center stage of the party. His lips are cold but heavenly soft. I open my eyes as he pulls back, amused. A waitress arrives at the edge of the pool with a tray of frosty shot glasses.

"Everyone has to take one!" Ella yells, swimming to the side.

I hold my breath and break away from Beck, pushing underwater. I surface and slick my hair back, bobbing up and down to the side of the pool. Ella passes me a shot. Oliver and Tommy throw theirs back and reach for another.

"Oliver's wasted," Carmen says from the lounger next to me.

I glance over at the boys, watching as Oliver grabs onto the railing of the pool steps.

"I can see him swaying from here," Ella laughs. "I love drunk Oliver."

He's wasted? *I'm wasted.* Is it acceptable to order a water? The boys pass on the tray of tapas brought by the side of the pool. The next waitress stops in front of them with a tray of four shots. She crouches down and passes them out. She holds the fourth one for herself. Beck's eyes meet mine; he returns the shot to the tray. Oliver reaches for Beck's untaken shot.

"Oh lord," Carmen says, watching Oliver.

Beck climbs the steps out of the pool. My heart thumps.

"No more shots for Oliver," Carmen warns Beck.

Beck smiles then lies back flat on the empty lounger next to me. He turns his head and rests his hand on my leg.

"I'm done too," he laughs.

"I think we've all been well served," I giggle. *Maybe over-served.*

"It's getting overcast. Can we take the boat back to the villa?" Ella asks.

Beck props up on his elbows. "That would be fun. We could even be fancy and do dinner on the beach."

"Oh, Beck!" Ella cries. "A proper idea, that is."

Beck turns to me. "What do you think, Sophie? Have you had your fill?"

I smile and nod.

Beck stands up and waves Tommy over.

I glance at Carmen. "Wait until you see this villa."

———

I push the bathroom door open. Ella's still thanking the party hosts. Beck slips into his sandals at the loungers and reaches down for his shirt. Carmen walks out of the bathroom and stops next to me.

"He's so hot, Soph."

I take a swig from the water bottle I secured. *I know.* I pass the bottle to Carmen.

Beck closes his shirt; he fastens the bottom button then reaches for the next.

Carmen takes a huge gulp then passes the bottle back. "And you're so tiny, he could fit you right in his front pocket."

"Did you see the way he kissed me? In the pool? *In front of everyone!*"

"I rather enjoyed watching him completely manhandle you jumping in."

"Carmen!" My cheeks flush.

"It was hot!" she giggles. "He's *quite* into you."

Oliver staggers toward us, and I chug the final few gulps of water.

Outside the breezeway, Tommy locks arms with Ella. "This way!" he yells.

Oliver's shirtless, blasting music on his phone for our walk. Beck takes my hand. My legs wobble, weaving down the steep path off the road. Heavy clouds have built up over the water.

Beck points to the dock below on the beach. "There's Tuck."

Tommy waves both of his hands in the air. A man on a small boat waves back. This poor captain. *He doesn't know what's headed for him.*

I hoped the water and walk would sober me up. With the slight movement on the dock, it's as if I'm twice as drunk.

"Aye, Tuck!" Tommy yells.

The captain happily waves and rushes to the edge of the bowrider. Tuck holds out his hand to help us load as the boat rocks in the waves. Oliver ignores Tuck's hand and jumps into the boat, nearly falling over the other side.

"You muppet!" Carmen yells. She gladly takes the captain's hand and gracefully steps into the boat.

It's my turn; I grab Tuck's hand and step off the dock. The bottom of my sandal slips on the seat cushion, and I fall sideways, taking Tuck down with me.

Blood rushes to my head. My legs are on the seat, the other half of my body is on the floor of the boat. Tuck jumps up quickly. Carmen and Ella erupt into laughter.

Beck jumps into the boat. "Sophie, are you okay?"

He lifts me off the floor. I'm stunned by the sudden impact but can't say I feel much. I smile.

"Good work, Soph! Get those falls out before fashion week!" Ella teases.

"I wish I could say this is the first time I've seen her fall," Beck chuckles.

Tuck studies me. "You sure you're okay?"

My heartbeat's still drumming in my ears. "Yes, I'm sorry, I'm quite clumsy." *What makes me think I'll be able to handle a runway?*

Oliver connects his phone into the boat's sound system and music bumps full blast through the boat's speakers. Ella and Carmen bounce up and down. Oliver grabs Carmen's bag and pulls out an unopened bottle of *Trofeo Tequila*. Ella cheers, seeing the party favor. *How did that make it out with us?* Oliver twists off the cap and takes a swig straight from the bottle. After what I just did, I reach for the bottle next.

Tommy pushes off the wooden post and Tuck steers the boat away from the dock. All my weight leans into Beck's chest behind me. His hands come around my waist, and he pulls me backward to the bench seat at the back of the boat. I melt into the padded seat and get hit with the first sprinkle of rain. Tuck turns the boat away from the shore.

The boat bumps through the waves, only amping up the dancing crew in the bow. Ella and Tommy pass the tequila back and forth. The sprinkles pick up, and Beck pulls my legs over his lap and puts his arm around me. His skin is warm against mine. He runs his fingertips over the chill bumps on my arm, only making the chills spread to the rest of my body. Beck reaches for a towel and wraps it around us. I huddle into him further; his face is so close all it takes is tilting my head up to meet his lips. I tighten my grip around him as his tongue dives into my mouth.

"*Oh yea!*" Carmen yells.

I pull away, embarrassed. My jaw drops—*we are not the spectacle*. Ella and Tommy are mouth to mouth, making out in the bow of the boat. Now

I *know* Ella's drunk. Tommy pulls away, laughing as Ella dances off, falling back into the bow seats.

Tommy puts his arm around Tuck behind the wheel and points to the shore. The boat takes a hard right, steering toward a beachside bar. The boat engine slows as we get closer.

Tommy turns down the music then turns to Beck. "Let's go check out this place."

Tuck pulls the boat alongside the dock that hooks up to the bar. Ella and Carmen stand up, anticipating the drop off. Tommy catches the post on the dock and jumps out. Beck doesn't budge. Tommy lifts Ella out of the boat and places her on the dock. Oliver stumbles out and pulls Carmen up.

"We're going to head back to the villa," Beck says.

Fire races through my veins. Tommy nods, and Ella and Carmen run up the dock toward the bar.

Tuck turns to Beck and me. "That should be interesting," he laughs.

The rain picks up. Beck's lips hover against my ear. "The villa's just around the corner." A new chill runs down the side of my body. The boat speeds up, bumping through the waves. The towel around us is getting heavy, and I blink through the drops hitting my face. As we round the corner, I spot the dock. Waves crash into the rocks and greenery built up on the backside of the jetty. The beach in front of the villa is entirely concealed.

Tuck slows the boat, and the nose eases down into the water. Thank God, *it's truly raining now.* Beck jumps up, he puts one knee on the bow seat on the side of the boat. Tuck pulls up along the dock and Beck catches onto a pillar.

It's pouring. I stand up, ready to make a run for it. Beck jumps onto the dock and holds his hands out to me. The boat rocks, and I take his hands, carefully stepping up onto the dock.

"Thanks, Tuck!" Beck yells, squinting in the rain.

Tuck waves before throwing the boat into gear, making a hard left away from the dock.

Beck takes my hand. "Let's go!"

I take off jogging next to him. Lights glow in the villa.

Where the dock meets the sand, Beck drops my hand and jumps down. I reach for his shoulders; he grips around my ribcage and lowers me off.

"Up here!" he yells, heading for the covered portion of the patio. I hop up the wooden steps and stop under the protection of the patio covering. I'm out of breath, my chest is thumping. Water runs down my legs, pooling around my sandals. When I look up, Beck's watching me. My cover-up is stuck to my skin, his shirt is see-through, plastered to the muscles on his chest.

Beck's smile fades, and his face turns serious. The electricity around us ignites. Beck steps toward me; his fingers run up my jawline as he cups my face in his hands. I let go of my bag, and it splats onto the porch. I hook my hands on his biceps and bring my hips against him. Beck's eyes sear into me as I push up on my toes and meet his lips. His kiss is soft but builds rapidly. His hand leaves my face, and a second later, it's pulling the tie on the back of my cover-up. I grab the material and wiggle out of it, not pulling away from his lips. The dress falls, smacking onto the wood around my feet. Beck's working his tongue in my mouth as if he was born to do it. I run my hand down the buttons on his shirt. *Too many.* I reach for the bottom. Our mouths release as I pull his shirt up over his head. *Splat!*

It joins my cover-up. I spread my fingers out on his bare chest. He's solid; his skin is moist and warm.

Beck grabs my hips, pulling us back together—his growing arousal pressed against me, constricted in his shorts. Diving back into my mouth, he guides me backward through the open doors of the villa. His fingers twist into the strings on the side of my bikini bottoms. The wood under my feet turns to cold tile, and my skin breaks out in chills. Peeking my eyes open, I recognize his room, dimly lit from the open porch doors. The backs of my legs hit the foot of the bed as his hand slowly moves from my hip, trailing low across the top of my bikini. My breath is heavy in his mouth. He slips his hand down the front of my bottoms. *Fuck! His fingers!* I gasp, causing his lips to curl into a smile. I tuck my fingertips into the top of his waistband. His other hand pulls the string tying the bikini top around my back. The knot loosens, releasing the weight of my breasts. My toes curl as his fingers move against my clit, completely undoing me. His free hand drifts up my spine to the tie around the back of my neck.

My top tumbles to the floor. Beck pulls back—he's breathing as hard as I am. His eyes are blazing.

"Are you okay with this?"

I take a deep breath. *I don't sleep around.* This is uncharted territory, *but I've never wanted anything more.* I nod then push up on my toes, back to his lips. My brain's moved to the backseat; *my body's now in charge.* Beck steps forward placing a knee onto the bed, but I'm unable to move any further, I fall back onto the comforter. His hands glide up my outer thighs until his fingers hook onto the sides of my bikini bottoms. I pull my feet out as he slips my bottoms off. He stands back, untying his swim trunks tortuously slow. The Velcro releases, and the constricted bulge finds relief as his shear length springs free. *My word.* My body's buzzing. I don't want him—*I need him.*

I reach for him as he crawls onto the bed, hovering over me. He stops at my breast, taking my nipple in his mouth. His hand dives between my legs while his tongue circles my nipple. I sink my teeth into my bottom lip. Two of his fingers press firmly, massaging my clit. I gasp when those fingers slide inside of me. Shockwaves radiate down my legs. *Fuck!* I grip the comforter; I need him *now.*

I pull his chin up, releasing his mouth from my nipple. His eyes spark and his fingers move quicker. I'm already overly slick with anticipation and he's building me up too fast. I move my hand into the back of his hair urgently needing an anchor.

"Beck!" I whimper.

His fingers slowly slip out of me, igniting my whole body. He slides his hand under my back and lines himself up. His lips hover over mine.

"I'll be slow," he promises, gently pushing into me.

I gasp as he enters gradually, stretching me further and further. My jaw drops, and my back arches, receiving him completely. I curl my hands around his shoulder blades as he slowly moves in and out of me; drawing him down until his chest meets mine. His lips trail up the side of my neck as I keep pulling him closer into me. *Deeper into me.*

***

"Sophie."

Hmm.

"Sophie."

It's his voice. His lips graze my ear.

"Sophie," he says softly.

I open my eyes; I'm warm and damp. *Oh my God, I was asleep.* But for how long?

Beck's behind me; I'm smothered in his arms. It couldn't have been that long. The room is still lit, even brighter than it was before. The villa's soundless, the birds on the beach seem loud.

Beck perches up onto his elbow. I roll onto my back. "Look outside," he says.

I prop myself up and peer out the open patio doors. The rain has stopped, and the sky is the color of a slushy orange creamsicle.

"We have to go out there," Beck says. He climbs out of bed. I'm still completely naked—I pull the comforter up under my chin. *But so is he.* He reaches for a robe hanging on the back of the bedroom door. He ties it around his waist and goes into the bathroom. He emerges and lays a second robe on the bed.

Beck pushes the porch doors open wider. I throw the robe around myself. He looks heavenly, robed and barefoot.

Our soaked garments litter the patio. *We were in a hurry.* Rings of moisture saturate the wood surrounding my bag, his shirt and my cover-up. The sky is dreamy; moody purple clouds hang in the distance. As pretty as it is, I can't keep my eyes off him. Only the second man I've ever been with, and he just blew my mind. I swallow. *What am I doing? Have I learned nothing?* Beck stares down at me, a smile growing across his face.

"Let's go swimming."

"*Ha!*" I throw my head back.

Beck turns, heading back inside. He finds his swim trunks on the floor and shrugs his robe off. *He's serious.* I spot my blue bikini at the foot of the bed.

Chills race down my arms, pulling the cold, wet fabric against my skin. I tie the strings around my back. A battle rages in my mind.

I step off the porch next to him. The sand is sticky, and the air is humid and heavy. My hair is a mess, my mind is a mess, but I feel so *alive. Isn't this what your twenties are for? Being reckless?* My heart races as I take off down the sand. *Maybe I'm not ready to learn yet.* I continue running, and when the water passes my knees, I dive in headfirst. My body crashes into the cool water. I surface and throw my head back, sinking down into the sand. Beck splashes in next to me, his arms come around me. I spin and latch onto him, wrapping my legs around his waist and resting my arms over his shoulders.

Beck's gaze melts into me.

"Where did you come from?" he whispers. He rests his forehead on mine. The surface of the water is glass. We're sitting in a mirror image of the creamsicle sky.

Somehow this tops that first night.

"I think I need Sophie in my life," he says softly.

My heart convulses. He pulls his head up, his lips trailing up the side of my neck, sending my eyes rolling to the back of my head.

"Fly back to London with me Thursday," he says stopping at the base of my ear.

"*What?*" I flip my eyes open.

Beck pulls his head back. "You said you were going back to London."

"Yes...*but.*"

"So come back with me—*on the jet.*"

I stare—stunned, tongue-tied. There's noise coming down the dock, I recognize that dominating voice instantly. Poor Tuck, he must have completed a pickup from the bar, or from the sound of it, maybe it was more than one bar.

Carmen's arms flail wildly. "Sophie!"

I stand up and wave back at her. Oliver's *smashed*. Beck's chest presses against my back.

Music bumps in the villa. I pick up my bag on the porch and fish out my phone. It's wet but somehow still working. I wring out my cover-up and hang it over the porch railing. My stomach growls. Beck shows up, holding out a white T-shirt.

"You'll drown in this, but at least it's dry," he laughs.

I slip it on over my bathing suit. It's soft, and *it smells like him.*

Oliver's face down, starfished on one couch. On the other, Ella and Carmen are bouncing in their bikinis with Tommy.

I quickly leave Beck's bedroom and head to the kitchen. Ella's tracking my every move.

"I'm starving!" I say.

"Yeah...Ollie looks like he could use some food," Tommy laughs. "I'll call the chef!"

Tommy walks out. The *chef?* I want to roll my eyes, but this crew is in no shape to go out. I didn't see anyone eat anything at the party. And they definitely didn't consume anything but more alcohol at the bar.

I open the refrigerator door—*vibrantly chef stocked.* I zero in on a bowl of shiny red cherries and bring them to the counter. I pop one into my mouth. Beck comes out of his room, shaking his head at the debauchery in the living room.

"What have you got there?" He smiles.

He stands behind me at the counter. I rip the stem off a cherry and feed it to him over my shoulder. His lips slide over my fingers as he grabs the cherry with his mouth.

"You got cherry ice cream yesterday," he says.

"*My favorite.*"

"Tomorrow's our last day!" Ella cries. "I don't want to leave!"

Oliver lifts his head from the couch. "At least you still have a day, my flight leaves at 10 a.m."

"The boy lives!" Beck laughs.

I hold another cherry over my shoulder.

"Sophie's flying home with us," Beck says.

I freeze.

Ella and Carmen stare at me, stunned. I look down into the bowl of cherries. The door opens, and Tommy walks back in with Sal and a bottle of tequila. The chef is the same smiley man who drove Beck and me to the party.

Sal prepares a full spread of food, but Ella is determined to keep the party going. I'm not sure that I ever fully sobered up from the pool party. I feel drunk almost instantly after taking the first shot she pours. We eat, *I think?* And Ella keeps refilling the shot glasses. Even Sal can't resist the shots Ella pours for him. He is a *riot.*

I remember bouncing up and down on the couch with Oliver and Carmen. I'm not sure when it was decided we were leaving, but someone calls the hotel shuttle. I remember laughing uncontrollably on the trek from the villa up to the street. It must have taken us double the time to climb the stairs as it did the first night. I remember Tommy pushing Carmen from behind to help her make it up the last flight of steps. I have flashes of kissing Beck outside the shuttle. He was urging me to stay the night. I don't remember the ride home, but Ivan got us back to the hotel. The last thing I remember is falling into bed with Ella. As soon as my head hit the pillow, I can't reopen my eyes. I remember Ella whispering, *"Sophie's in love."*

And I remember responding, *"I'm doomed."*

CHAPTER 5

BOTTLE THIS

"*Oh shit!*" OLIVER SAYS.

My eyes fly open. I'm on my stomach. I lift my head up, instantly confronted with the lingering buzz of those last shots. I squint over at Carmen's bed; *Oliver must have passed out here*. He jumps up, searching for his belongings frantically on the floor. Carmen giggles.

"I can't miss this flight. I've got to go." Oliver leans over Carmen and kisses her *Snow-White* style.

"Love you," he says sweetly.

I close my eyes again. "Bye, Ollie." My voice cracks.

"Bye, girls," he laughs. "I'll see you back in Paris." Moments later, the door slams.

"Please tell me I'm not the only one that's still drunk," Carmen says.

"Not even close," I answer. "I'm not even hungover yet."

"Speak for yourselves," Ella groans next to me.

"Get over here Carmen!"

Carmen throws back the comforter and swings her legs over the side of the bed.

"Oh my God. I'm still in my swimsuit and cover-up," she laughs.

"I slept in my contacts," Ella moans.

I turn over to my back and scoot to the middle of the bed, letting Carmen climb in next to me. I'm impressed I managed to throw on a T-shirt and panties. Wait, this isn't my T-shirt, *it's Beck's.*

"No sudden movements," Ella says, turning over onto her back.

There's no vibe comparable to waking up with your best friends after a big night, still buzzed. *Everything is funny.* Carmen is swiping through pictures from yesterday's tequila marathon.

"Remember when you fell?" Ella says.

Oh God. That's right. I slipped getting into the boat.

Carmen swipes through several photos of her and Oliver dancing in the bow. They are completely blocking the captain's view. How they managed to dodge falling while the boat crashed through waves is beyond me.

"Look at you two!" Carmen says, pointing to the background of a photo.

In the back of the boat, my legs are across Beck's lap, we're cuddled together under a towel. She swipes over and there we are again; this time we've moved to making out. I cover my eyes.

"I'm surprised there's a photo where you two *aren't* kissing," Ella teases.

"You're lucky I didn't snap a photo when you had your tongue down Tommy's throat!" Carmen snaps back.

Ha!

"Are you thinking about adding Tommy to your bench?" I pose.

"You're assuming there's room?" Ella fires back. "*Nahh.* I think we'll be *friends.*"

Carmen continues swiping.

"Beck can't keep his hands off you," Carmen says.

"Yes...he's very...*touchy*," I say.

"I haven't seen you look at anyone that way besides...."

Fredrick. It was another morning I didn't wake up thinking about him. Before last night, I hadn't been touched since he made love to me the morning of our final goodbye. Now, the only thing consuming my mind is *Beck*.

"Do you think the bar at the pool is open yet?" Carmen says. "I need a mimosa before everything hits me." She sits up and opens the bedside drawer.

"If it's not, we're raiding it," Ella says. "That might be the only thing that can save me."

Carmen pulls out the hotel booklet. *Now's my chance to spill.*

"Can you pass me my birth control, Carmen?"

Ella catapults up, and Carmen's eyes are wide. *That got their attention.*

"Let's check if the pool bar's open. Then I'll tell you what happened at the villa." I smile.

A lazy day by the pool is exactly what the doctor ordered. The bar isn't open, but Ella is able to shmooze a hotel worker into opening it early. We sip mimosas, and the girls hang on to every detail as I recount the events of last night.

As the afternoon shade arrives, we head inside to start the task we've been dreading: cleaning up the disaster that is our hotel room. The lift opens, and my phone pings.

Be ready for dinner at 8.

A second later, a winking icon comes through. My cheeks flush.

"That's him, isn't it?" Ella says.

Is it that obvious?

"He's taking me for dinner."

"He can't stand to be away from you, can he?" Carmen smiles.

No. He can't, *and neither can I.* It's as if I've been woken up. Beck is the breath of fresh air that's shaken me back to life.

The *Do Not Disturb* sign still hangs from our door. The absolute disarray of our room is so alarming we preemptively hung it before we left. *What am I going to wear?* Was Beck serious about flying back to London with him? If not, this could be the last time I see him.

The floor is covered in clothes. Ella and Carmen sit opposite each other. They begin throwing garments across the room, giggling.

"This is my pile," Ella says. She throws a dress aside. "Soph, that can be your pile."

I join the girls on the floor and start launching clothes to their adjacent piles.

Ella throws a T-shirt at Carmen. "Oliver must have left this."

Carmen catches it and holds it up.

My stomach flutters. I stand up to grab it.

"That's Beck's."

***

Our room has been mostly transformed back to a reasonable state. Heading out for dinner, I wait in the hall for the lift. The girls assembled the perfect dinner outfit. Ella's black silk midi dress impeccably hugs my hips.

The lift arrives empty, and I check my hair and makeup one more time in the mirrored panels. I've grown a fraction thanks to a pair of strappy black kitten heels.

The lift's never this slow. Finally, the ding sounds reaching the ground floor. My stomach flutters.

Beck's outside in front of the pearl SUV, engaging with a group of people. I head for the lobby doors, and as I get closer, the group moves in next to him for a photo. *Different world.* I stutter-step as Beck's eyes drift to mine.

He gives his regards to the fans, and the lobby doors part for him. He's unfairly handsome in a dress shirt and trousers. Beck's hand slides on the satin around my waist, making its way to my back.

His lips press into my temple. "Hello, beautiful."

I float out of the lobby on his arm. The fans are still lingering, watching us as we walk to the car. Their eyes follow him, and *follow me.* Beck opens the back door, and I hurry inside.

Chef Sal turns around from the driver's seat.

"Good evening," he says.

Oh, good, he's alive. *I wonder how he felt this morning.*

"Good to see you again," I giggle.

Beck climbs in next to me and takes my hand in his lap.

"Did Oliver make his flight this morning?"

"He passed out in our room and woke up in a panic. But he made it, *barely.* He called Carmen all out of breath after he boarded."

Beck pats Sal on the shoulder. "We all had a big night."

The chef nods his head and pulls out of the hotel drive.

"Sorry about that." I gulp. "Ella's relentless."

Smooth music pours out of the glowy open-air restaurant. The building looks as if it's clinging onto the side of the cliff for dear life. White tablecloths slowly dance in the breeze. *This is the perfect third date vibe.*

The host nods at Beck. "This way, Mr. Wright."

Beck's hand rests on my back as we walk into the dining room. I hesitate when the host makes a quick left toward a set of swinging double doors. The host smiles, holding the door open. Noise from a busy kitchen floods out. I glance at Beck, who appears unconcerned. I step into the madness that is a restaurant kitchen during dinner rush hour. The host leads us through the length of the kitchen and stops at a black velvet curtain. My heart thumps wildly as he draws the curtain back.

Beyond the curtain, the most breathtaking view of the city twinkles below. There, on a tiny balcony at the back of the kitchen, is a private table for two. My hand comes to my mouth. *Who is this man?* I drift into the seat the host pulls out. A single candle flickers on the table. Beck smiles, taking his seat across from me. All I can do is shake my head.

"I wanted something private," Beck says. "And I didn't want to wait another day to see you."

I flush. So he *was* serious about the jet invite.

Beck leans back in his chair. *My word* he looks edible in the candlelight. Each time the curtain's opened, noise from the kitchen pours out. Glasses are placed on the table, and a dark fruity wine is poured. The waiter disappears through the curtain, the noise from the kitchen fading once again behind its heavy fabric. It's practically silent now, and it's just us.

I pause, taking in the reality of the atmosphere before my eyes slowly drift and meet back up with Beck's gaze. "This is magical."

"I won't keep you away from the girls on your last night. But I wanted to see you again before we leave this place...*And* I promised a fancy dinner which we certainly didn't get last night."

I chuckle.

Beck lifts his wineglass. "To the beginning."

The beginning?

I meet my glass with his, despite the cryptic toast. I hold his gaze, taking a long pull of wine. I slowly draw the glass from my lips. He's staring at me with that same mesmerized look in his eye. The way he stares at me when he's about to kiss me. *The beginning?* I break as the waiter comes back through the curtain.

"Where are we visiting from?" the waiter asks.

I glance back at Beck—his eyes still smoldering.

"London," he answers without looking up.

I want to bar the doorway and have him take me right here on this balcony. The tension is heavy; the waiter must be uncomfortable at this point. I break eye contact again shifting my attention to the waiter.

"...And Paris," I say.

"*Bienvenue!*" He smiles. "Your plates will be out shortly."

The waiter splits for the curtain.

I return my focus to Beck. "*The beginning...?*"

He blinks. "I think it's obvious I'm having a hard time staying away from you. From the moment I saw you, *I...*" He smiles. "I was drawn to you."

My heart does a backflip. His words are making my hands fidget. I need to touch something; I reach for my wine glass and spin the stem between my fingers.

Beck clears his throat. "Sophie, I love that you didn't know who I was—*I could tell you didn't*. Something about you, about us, is quite genuine."

Us? I continue spinning the glass.

"*And...?*" I ask bravely.

He lights up. "*And* I don't want this to end."

I stop spinning the glass—my head's taken over the spinning. *He wants more.* I press my lips together to hold back my smile, but it's forcing its way in.

"I'm not the easiest person to date, but I want to give us a shot—*in the real world.*"

I give myself a few seconds to make sure I'm hearing him correctly. The *real world.* I don't know the first thing about dating someone like *him.*

"Then maybe we should...*try?*" I say slowly.

His smile grows. The flickering light of the candle amplifies the sparkle in his eyes.

"As much as I prefer to keep my personal life private, it is rather public."

Public like my face posted on a gossip account?

"I've noticed."

"PR can only control so much," he says.

Um...What? "You...told your PR team about us?"

"I didn't have to tell them; it's their job, Sophie."

My mind takes off. Did they see our picture? Did they say something to him?

"Racing is a dream career, but it's very fast-paced. I'm never in one place for long."

"I imagine your life takes a lot of logistics..." I hesitate before looking up at him. "*...but I can keep up.*"

His eyes ignite.

"Well, then"—he pats his palm against the table—"first order of business: our flight tomorrow. Wheels up at ten a.m. for London."

The curtain opens, and our dishes arrive with a new wine pairing.

Beck leans back in his chair, putting his hand on his stomach. He finished his entire plate and half of mine. I ate what I could, but my stomach is in jitters from the thoughts racing through my mind.

"And for dessert," the waiter says. "We have a Basque cheesecake with cherry rioja sauce."

My eyes shoot to Beck; he stares back amused.

The waiter puts down the oversized cheesecake slice with two forks. Cherry sauce oozes down the sides.

I wait for the curtain to close and shake my head. "Was this your doing?"

Beck shrugs. "You said they were your favorite." He grabs a fork and stretches it across the table. I smile and take the fork.

I cut into the cheesecake and run the bite through the cherry sauce that's collected on the plate.

Beck grabs the other fork and cuts into the cheesecake. "Sophie Collins, you are something special," he says.

I'm floating. I wish I could bottle this feeling. The setting, his words, the wine—all ingredients forming a *nothing is impossible* elixir.

The car will get us back to the hotel too soon; I'm not ready to say goodbye. I want to savor every second I can with him.

"Can we walk back?" I ask.

"Let's do it," he says. Beck opens the car door and tells Sal to meet him at the hotel.

Beck reaches down for my hand and leads me across the street. I watch our shadows move in the orange glow on the sidewalk. He turns, taking the quiet footpath between the buildings. The dark alley instantly takes me back to the first night, walking to the villa. Beck slows; my heart does the opposite. My eyes wander up to his as he stops. Beck drops my hand and backs me up against the wall; sending my heart sprinting. His hands on me felt foreign yesterday, but now my body craves them. He hovers over me, but it's not close enough. I clutch onto his dress shirt.

"Meeting you was quite the surprise," he says slowly.

You have no idea.

I open my mouth to speak but stop. *I'm done talking.* I curl my hand around the back of his neck and bring his lips to mine.

CHAPTER 6
Do You Trust Me?

Carmen hands me my backpack.

"Remember"—Ella stares intently—"*Act. Cool.*"

I nod at her instructions. I can try, but the butterflies in my stomach are sure to fail me. I hug them each once more.

"I'll see you tonight!" I shriek. I drag my roller bag out of our room. Their flight, *my abandoned flight*, doesn't leave until after lunch.

Beck's standing outside the SUV typing on his phone. He's wearing the kind of outfit that makes cuddling irresistible. The hood of his hoodie is pulled up over his head. He glances up with his infectious grin.

"There she is," he says. Beck slips his phone into his sweatpants pocket.

"Hop in." He smiles. He takes the handle of my roller bag. I climb into the backseat. Tommy is laid across the third row, passed out.

Tommy stirs. "Sophie, good morning," he groans. "Don't mind me—I didn't make it to bed last night."

"Two big nights in a row?"

"Gotta go out with a bang," Tommy laughs. He crosses his arms over his face. He and Ella are perfect for each other.

Beck shuts the door and pulls my hand to his lap. I point over my shoulder at Tommy. "Did you partake in this?"

"No," Beck says swiftly.

I glance back at the hotel one last time before the car pulls away. The sky is gray and lightly spitting mist. If not for these *circumstances,* a severe end of vacation depression would be setting in.

"You excited?" Beck asks.

I freeze and still my bouncing leg.

"I'm supposed to be acting cool." I admit. "But I've never been on a private jet before."

His eyes light up. He brings the back of my hand to his lips.

The moment Sal turned off the main departure drag for *private aviation,* I dropped the "act cool" pretenses. *This is next level.* It took all of five minutes to get inside and through security. Now we're being escorted outside where a small white jet with navy stripes waits with its stairs lowered. Five passenger windows line the body. A man's waiting for us at the foot of the stairs. He smiles and reaches for my bag. Tommy runs up the steps and ducks into the jet.

Beck hands his bag over and nods. "Up you go."

At the top of the steps, I peek around the corner into the interior. *My word, Ella must get us a private jet collab.*

Everything is white, crisp, and refined. Tommy is already reclined in the first seat on the right. Three rows of oversized captain seats sit on either side of the jet. Beck places his backpack on the front left seat and nods to the back. Before the third row, the aisle shifts to the side of the jet to account for one double seat in the last row. I set my purse on the plush white leather and sink into the seat by the window.

A monitor displays the airport code of our destination—*LCY. London City.* Shows how much I've been paying attention. I assumed we'd be going to Heathrow; *the girls will be quite jealous.* I click my seatbelt into the receiver.

Beck holds a button on the chair in front of me. He turns the seat around to face us. He takes his seat next to me and kicks his shoes off.

"Best seat in the house," Beck says, putting his feet up.

Tommy's snoring as we start to taxi. The jet merges into the traffic on the tarmac behind the main terminal. My fingers fidget. Beck returns his feet to the ground and reaches for my hand. The plane stops after rounding the final corner then lurches forward down the runway. Trails of water stream across the window as the ground flies by faster and faster. The nose of the plane picks up, and within seconds, we are in the air, pushing through the fog. I lean closer to the window and watch the land fall further away. The ground disappears as the jet soars out over the water. I peek back at the island before clouds patch over the view. The plane bumps, ascending higher. My hand is sweaty in his grip. Every movement of the jet is amplified due to its size.

Beck's fingers meet my chin; he guides my face away from the window, drawing me to his lips. I close my eyes as the plane bounces. He kisses me softly, not letting me pull away. *And that's all it takes*. I'm lost in him.

The jet flattens out, the bumpiness eases.

"That's better," he whispers, pulling away.

I open my eyes. Tommy's snoring intensifies. The seatbelt light flips off. Beck unbuckles and puts his feet back up. He reaches down, unbuckling my seatbelt, and lifts my legs over his lap. *He isn't finished*. He comes back in for more.

I run my tongue along his bottom lip. He tenses up and squeezes my leg. He pulls back quickly. "Okay, we've got to stop that."

Beck scoops my legs off his lap. He stands up in the aisle and stretches backward. The bottom of his hoodie rises above the top of his sweatpants, revealing the carved muscles around his hips.

Mhm.

Beck smiles and shakes his head. "I'll be right back."

I put my feet up on the seat and press my thighs together. Beck walks up the aisle to the front seat where he dropped his backpack. He turns around with a laptop.

Beck retakes his seat and opens the computer in his lap. *Maybe* it's time to peek back into reality. I pull my diary out of my purse and flip it open to August. Other than a fitting tomorrow and a meeting on Monday at our agency in Paris, every date square is empty. *This is embarrassing.* My old diary was chaotic. Every square was filled with endless meetings and agenda items, often spilling outside the day's border. I study the dates. *Is it the fifteenth?*

"What have we got here?" Beck says playfully. He pulls my diary into his lap.

He runs his finger along the final two weeks of this month, then pulls out the pen I have stashed in the binding.

"What are you doing?" I ask.

Beck shifts in his seat writing something, but his hand is masking the message. He flips to the next page—*September*—and scribbles something again.

He stops and turns to me. "Do you trust me?"

I don't know how to answer that. I've only known him a handful of days. His eyes smile, waiting for my answer.

"I think so—"

"Then say *yes*." Beck flips the page back to August and sets the diary back on my lap.

Italy with Beck is written on the twenty-first in scrappy handwriting.

My eyes snap up. "Are you serious?"

"I'll be in Rome with my family for Louie's tournament this weekend, but I'm sticking around and going to the coast. Meet me in Positano."

Meet me in Positano? I shake my head in disbelief. "The girls and I will be back in Paris next week."

"Bring them!" Beck says. "Tommy's coming."

"Yes! Bring the girls! Bring Oliver!" Tommy yells.

I peer over the headrest; he must have woken up.

They can't be serious. I blink quickly and flip the page. *Belgian Grand Prix* is written on the third of September. Beck points to his message on the Sunday square.

"*Spa* is the first race back after break."

I stare at him blankly.

"If I DNF you never have to speak to me again," he says candidly.

"Beck!" I giggle.

"Seriously. Think about it."

"You truly would want me there?"

"I want you everywhere."

My heart flips. How is he already so sure about me? About *us*? This is moving rather fast—but I'm intrigued. I can't imagine what seeing him behind the wheel of a racecar would do to me. He's slowly cracking away at the skeptic inside me, making me believe anything could happen, and *we were that anything.* I smile down at my diary, now grateful for all of the empty squares.

The jet descends sharply, breaking through the cloud cover over the city. We follow the Thames, directly over Canary Wharf, for arrival.

I stand next to Tommy on the sidewalk.

"Did you have a good nap?"

"Feel like a new man!" he laughs. "Wait, was I snoring?"

I smile.

"You were scaring Sophie," Beck teases.

Arriving on the jet was even easier than departing. We were reunited with our luggage and outside waiting for rides within ten minutes of landing. *What a luxury.*

"This is mine," Tommy says as a car approaches. "Hopefully, I'll see your crew next week!"

I nod. "I'll talk to the girls about it."

Tommy fist bumps Beck. "I'll miss you, mate. See you in a few days for *round two.*"

I'm still processing that this invitation is real. Tommy steps off the curb to meet his ride.

Beck puts his arm around me. "Just me and you now, kid."

He checks his phone and nods at the approaching car. "This one's ours."

Beck hands me his phone. "Where are we heading *Miss Mayfair?*" he asks. I type in my address. *Beckham Wright is coming to my flat.*

***

"Here is fine," I instruct. Beck peers up at the building from the car window. For once, I wasn't cursing the London traffic. The driver stops along the curb and flips the flashers on.

"I'll be right back," Beck informs the driver.

Wait, what? My heart sinks. I open the door and meet Beck at the back of the car. I thought he would be coming in, possibly staying for a while. Beck slams the boot and reaches for my hand, rolling my bag beside him.

The lobby is cold and quiet. So much has changed since I last walked through the front doors. We step into the lift, and I press five. I glance up to try and get a read on him, *maybe he will change his mind about staying?*

I retrieve the key from my purse and struggle to get it into the lock. I turn the nob and push the door open. The flat is dark and quiet from the shades pulled over the soaring windows. I click the button on the wall panel that draws up the window covers. Quickly, the flat is flooded with light, and the moody London sky is revealed.

Beck whistles. "Your place is *nice*," he says, stepping in.

Nicer than nice. *Thanks, Dad.* I set my keys and purse on the counter. "My dad owns it; he lets us stay here when we're in town."

Beck walks into the living room, looking around. I love this flat. It's clean and cold and modern with industrial touches. *Totally* different vibe than our place in Paris. Dad bought the two-bedroom flat for business, but he let Ella and I move in our second year at uni. After Ella met Carmen, the three of us became inseparable. She moved in a month later. By removing the table in the dining room, we pulled together a third bedroom—*Carmen's corner.*

"Our London crash pad," I say.

Beck walks back to me. I take a deep breath as he rests his hands on my hips.

"I have to get home before I head to Mum and Dad's tonight. We fly to Rome in the morning."

"I can't believe you're leaving again tomorrow."

"I know. It's my only chance to make it to one of Louie's tournaments this year." He pauses. "Will I get to see you next week?"

I bite my lip. "I'll talk to the girls and see if they can swing a quick *Italian getaway.*"

His face turns serious. "I want you to trust me," he says.

My heart thumps as I stare into his eyes. *Well, I want to show you to my bedroom.* How is he controlling himself while I'm barely hanging on?

"I'll talk to them as soon as they get in."

His face lights up. "I'll ring you."

I close my eyes as he leans down to kiss me. Our lips meet briefly before he pulls away, smiling.

Beck heads for the door, and panic runs through my body. I follow. He opens the door and turns back for a final kiss.

"I'll see you soon," he whispers against my lips.

Will you?

The door latches. The silence is deafening. I stare at the back of the door. For the first time in a week, I'm completely alone. I pace to the windows and look down at the street. I wait until Beck emerges from the building. He climbs back into the car. The flashers turn off, and the car pulls away from the curb.

I turn around to the quiet flat. *Will that be the last time I see him?* He said he *wanted me everywhere.* He presented not one but *two* invitations.

I've got to make myself busy and get out of here. The girls won't arrive for several hours. Their energy will get me out of my head. Until then, I can at least get us something for dinner. I walk to my room to change. Wandering around the market will keep me distracted—*maybe.*

***

Ella and Carmen barge through the door just before dinnertime. I have a salad I picked up plated on the counter.

"Oh, Sophie, you're a darling!" Ella says.

"Forget these bags," Carmen says, slamming the door shut. "Let's hear it then! How did you leave things?" "Well…he invited me to his race in Belgium."

Ella's jaw drops.

"Sophie that's mega! I'm so—" Carmen says.

"There's more," I cut Carmen off. "He's going to Rome with his family for the weekend. When they leave, Tommy is meeting Beck out there, and they're going to the Amalfi coast."

The girls stare, listening carefully.

I smile. "They want us to meet them in Positano."

They turn to each other.

"*What?!*" Ella shrieks.

"One of their friends dropped out—*we would just have to get there*."

So begins the mad dash through luggage to find their laptops. It's *their schedules* that will need reshuffling. I bring our salads to the bar while the girls investigate what can be rescheduled.

"*It's possible*," Ella says with a devilish grin.

Carmen nods her head, crunching her salad.

"Oliver's going to be pissed. There's no way he can get out of his events next week." "Soph, we're calling Mum in the morning—she needs to hear *all* of this," Ella says.

Yes, let's let the PR professional educate me on what I'm getting myself into.

"Have you told your dad yet?" Carmen asks.

"No." I pause. "I need to tell him in person."

CHAPTER 7

DIPPING A TOE

BECK'S TEXT IS TIME-STAMPED from an hour ago. It's a photo of seven suitcases filling an entryway wall to wall.

> Just a family of five off to the airport

I study the picture closer—*his parents' house?* I text him back:

> I spoke with the girls. If you're serious about us coming, I think we can do Thursday-Saturday.

Two words come through instantly:

> BOOK IT

My heart flutters.

Another text arrives.

> About to take off. We're staying at Villa Dallavalle.
> Get there and I have everything else taken care of.

I relax back into my pillows. I *really* want to go. Judging from the girls' reactions last night, this trip may just happen.

"Good, you're awake," Ella says the moment I open my bedroom door. "I've scheduled a call with Mum at nine. I said we have major updates, and it simply cannot wait."

I float past her to the kitchen with a ridiculous grin on my face.

"What are you smiling about?" Ella asks.

"Beck said we should book our flights."

Alice recently made VP at *Blanc & Basso,* one of the premier PR firms in France. She knows things weeks, sometimes *months,* before you will ever hear a word of it in the press. Ella and Alice are thick as thieves, meaning Alice has been a figure in my life from the day Ella and I met. I like to think Mum and I would have been as close as they are.

Ella opens her laptop on the counter bar. I pour us both a cup of coffee and take a seat next to her. The video call connects. Alice is seated behind her desk. She's typing, focused on a different monitor. She stops, puts her glasses on top of her head and turns to us.

"Okay, girls, I only have ten minutes," Alice says.

"Sophie is dating Beckham Wright, the F1 driver!" Ella blurts out.

Dating? *Hardly.* I've known the man for a week.

Alice's mouth drops open. *Of course, she knows exactly who he is.*

"And this has happened since we last spoke? I talked to you girls only a week ago!" Alice says.

Ella turns to me, giving me the floor.

I take a deep breath. "I met him Friday night. It's kind of been a whirl-wind," I say.

"The *Brit* that took Morelli's seat." Alice nods. She turns back to the other monitor and resumes typing. "Sophie, that's wonderful, dear!" She pauses then shifts back to us. "Pointing out the obvious...if this is serious, this could—this *will* accelerate your career in ways you never thought possible. This will *change your life*."

"A picture I took of her and Beck already got reposted on a gossip account," Ella says. "She's up a thousand followers since Friday!"

I am? Lord, I must get better at caring about these things.

"Alice, what do I do? He's asked me to come to the next race," I say.

"*Wow*." Alice's eyes widen. "These races, they're a whole media affair, Sophie. You *will be* photographed. They're broadcasted—you could even be on camera."

Alice crosses her arms. "The *paddock* is the red carpet of F1."

I gulp.

"Obviously, Beck has a whole PR team behind him. For you—stay aware that a camera could be on you at any time. And of course, be careful about what you say if someone was to put a microphone in your hand."

I stare blankly.

"Why would anyone put a camera *on me*?"

"The public has really taken interest in the driver's *personal lives* over the last several years. And while you girls are perfect in my eyes, I also know there are skeletons."

I cringe.

"No one will know who I am..."

Alice raises an eyebrow. "They won't know who you are—*yet*."

A pit forms in my stomach. "Maybe this is a bad idea…"

Alice smiles and shakes her head. "No, Sophie, this is the chance of a lifetime. *You can do it.*"

Ella nods excitedly.

"You have my number. Text me, ring me—Day or night. Advice, pep talk, anything, I'll be here."

"Thank you, Alice."

"And Oliver! Carmen has experience dating someone in the public eye," Alice says. "You also need to give a heads up to your agent. I'd predict they're about to become *quite busy.*"

I hadn't thought about that. They'll want some explanation of how my account grew without me doing a thing. I meet with my rep on Monday. *How am I supposed to bring this up?*

"Now, why are you girls back in London?" Alice asks.

"We have our *Eden Eves* fitting today!" Ella says.

"That's right!" Alice nods. "Send pictures and give Evelyn a kiss for me."

"We're taking the train home tomorrow." Ella pauses, turning to me. "But then we're off again."

"*To…?*" Alice inquires.

I'm still reeling in my head about the race.

Ella answers, "We've penciled in a *quick* dolce vita soiree. We're meeting up with Beck in Italy."

Alice rolls her eyes. "Absolute nomads. I've got to run. Goodbye, girls."

I wave to Alice and Ella hangs up the call.

I slap Ella's leg. "You didn't tell her about Tommy!"

Ella giggles, "There's nothing to tell—this is *your* moment, Soph."

Carmen walks out of the dining room half asleep.

"Did I hear my name?"

"Alice wants you to feed me advice for dating someone famous."

Carmen shakes her head. "Beck is an *entirely* different caliber, Sophie."

And I'm a *nobody*. Carmen already was someone when she met Oliver. Her following amassed during her tennis days in university. After she was injured, her following only grew when she became the face of a luxury activewear brand. She debuted the label's *trackside chic* collection in Centre Court at Wimbledon last year. *Wimbledon.* Last year, I was running financial models in Excel, wearing stuffy pantsuits.

Ella pushes back from the counter. "We need to leave soon. Carmen, do us a favor and pick some flights while we're out," she instructs.

Carmen comes behind my stool and wraps her arms around me.

"Oh my God, are we really doing this?" she squeals.

"We'd be *crazy* to say no," Ella says.

My excitement's been slightly clouded by the picture Alice painted. But if I want to pursue something with Beck, I need to be brave. *I need to dip a toe in*. I hook my hands onto Carmen's arms and smile.

"Let's do it."

The *Eden Eves* fitting provided an eye-opening reality check—it's truly happening. *I will be walking in a fashion show.*

"How was it?" Carmen asks excitedly.

"The looks are to die for," Ella says, closing the front door.

Carmen turns to me. "Soph?"

"*Gorgeous*—and my shoes are double the height of anyone else's."

"Don't worry, we can practice your walk in Positano." Carmen spins her laptop around. "What do you think?"

There it is—a lunchtime flight from Paris to Naples, returning forty-eight hours later. I take a deep breath. "Alright…I've got to deliver the news to Dad. If I stay the night, I'll be back before our train."

"Give George a hug for me," Carmen says.

"*Always.*"

It still amazes me how well Dad took on the role of *both* mum and dad. He brilliantly balanced a thriving career while catering to everything that comes with raising a ten-year-old girl. He never missed any of my school events or shied away from any conversation usually had between mother and daughter. Above everything, he's never once made me feel like I failed him, even after I took the career he handed me on a silver platter *and set it on fire*. Instead, he became more protective, more supportive. Dad insisted I get him set up with his own Instagram account to keep up with my new career *"venture."* He often reminds me Ella's his favorite to follow due to her nonstop posting. If I miss his call, he "checks in" by checking Ella's stories.

I hop out of the cab at the garden entrance. I punch in the code and swing open the spring-loaded gate. This has always been my preferred entrance to our house. The peaceful path runs the length of our street. I enjoy keeping tabs on what the neighbors are cultivating in the quaint rear gardens behind the uniform townhouses.

I unlatch our gate. I still think our garden is the prettiest. Mum hand-picked every plant, every flower. Dad has never let the gardeners get creative. Any withering plant gets replaced with the same species Mum planted during her final spring.

Dad's reading at the counter bar with his glasses perched on his nose. I walk up the back steps and push open the garden door into the kitchen.

"Sophie, darling," he says.

Dad.

He hops off his stool and squeezes me tight. His embrace is the best calming agent. He darts to the refrigerator. I take the stool next to his spot at the counter.

"What can I get you to drink? You probably need all the hydration you can consume," he laughs.

He returns and sets a sparkling water in front of me.

"Tell me about your trip then. I saw you girls having quite the time… I don't know when you sleep."

"Yes…it was an amazing trip." I hesitate. "…I met someone."

He raises an eyebrow and studies me over the edge of his glasses. "Is this the boy I saw you with on Ella's story?"

I smile. *The boy.*

He widens his eyes, waiting. *Bite the bullet and get it out.*

"Well…he's an F1 driver, *Beckham Wright.*"

Dad stares, stunned. He takes a large inhale then removes his glasses. "Is he older?"

The question strikes a sensitive nerve, *but it's fair.*

"*Only* a year…"

"*Hmm*…I haven't been to a race in, wow, twenty years maybe," he says, cleaning his glasses on his jumper.

"I didn't have the slightest idea who he was when he introduced himself, but Ella and Carmen recognized him right away."

"I haven't really kept up with the sport. What team is he with?"

"*Furio.*"

Dad's eyes widen, and he reaches for his tea.

My heart rate picks up, *breathe.* "It's the summer break, but he's asked me to come to his race, the Belgian Grand Prix, in two weeks."

"Are you going?" Dad asks, worried. "*Alone?*"

"I haven't given him a final answer, but I want to say yes..."

Dad nods slowly.

I'll keep the fact I flew home *alone* with Beck to myself.

"That would be quite the experience, Sophie, but I want you to be safe..."

"I'll be safe. I won't be alone next week; the girls are coming to the Amalfi coast with me. We're going to meet Beck and his friend out there."

I think Dad's in shock. He continues nodding. This went about how I expected, maybe better. He doesn't seem *too* worried, but I know my dad, he's itching to vet Beck himself.

"Well." He smiles. "You sound like you have a busy few weeks ahead!"

What is it about that comfort of home feeling? I knew I'd end up wanting to stay the night. Everything is warm and fuzzy here; I can truly *relax*. I take my bag upstairs. Outside my old bedroom, I pause at our family photo. The last Christmas with the three of us, before we were two and before Dad was all gray. Nowadays, I could pass as Mum's twin. We have the same dark eyes and hair—it even falls around my face exactly like hers. My phone buzzes, pulling my attention from the photo. I double take at the notification.

Beckham_Wright20 started following you.

I plop down on my bed and click on the notification. Beck's page loads and my stomach flips. *He is followed by 2.7 million people.* I scroll the first couple rows of his photos—all racing, all business. *My word*, he's dashing in his red racing suit. I scroll down several swipes. It practically jumps off the page—*a photo of Beck and Sabrina.* I click on the photo; they are dressed to the nines in a bowtie and gown. Her hand is on his chest. The picture has over *3 million likes.* I click his tagged photos tab. Three posts deep, sits our photo from the after-party, posted by the gossip account. *What am I getting myself into?* My thumb taps the follow button. A speck added to his 2.7 million followers. The number next to it surprises me; he only follows 300 accounts. I might be a speck, *but he was somehow interested in this speck.*

I love spending the night in my old bed. Nothing has changed in my room since the day I left for uni. The same pink quilt has been on my bed for at least ten years. It's been laundered so many times it's incredibly soft. Mum never liked that my windows faced out to the street, but the gas streetlamps always made perfect nightlights. My phone pings on my nightstand.

It's a message from Beck. *A selfie,* with a lit-up city view behind him.

> Made it!

I heart the photo and reply.

> We booked our flights.

Even in a still photo, Beck's eyes manage to twinkle, as if he's standing right in front of me. I put my phone back on the nightstand and force my eyes closed. I stare at the back of my eyelids. *Will I be able to handle getting involved with someone like him? I'm not Sabrina Kauffman, I'm a nobody.*

Beck doesn't act as if he's famous or above anyone. *It's scary,* but I don't think anything can overshadow what it feels like to be with him.

The next morning, my stomach wakes me up to the smell of breakfast, *Dad's breakfast.* The mixture of sweet and savory lures me out of bed and down the stairs. Anytime I stay here, Dad goes all out and prepares his Saturday morning spread like he did every weekend when I was little. I take my seat at the counter.

"I did some research on this boy," Dad says, turning around from the stove, turner in hand.

Oh God.

"Beck looks to be quite the driver, given it's only his third year. He's on a great team; they've got a great car."

"So, they win a lot?"

"Valor takes a lot of the wins, but Furio's been on the podium quite a lot this year. They're third in the constructor's championship."

I stare blankly at him. *The what?*

Dad walks to the counter and sets his phone in front of me.

"Depending upon what place you get in the race, the top ten positions are awarded points. The driver with the most points at the end of the season is the world champion."

"*Okay...?*"

"The team with the most points when you combine the points of *both* their drivers, wins the constructor's championship." He smiles.

Something sizzles on the stove, and he rushes away to attend to it.

I pick up Dad's phone and view the graphic on the screen. *Driver Standings*—a table of the driver's names in a current point ranking order.

1st	Leo VanBelle	*Valor Racing*
2nd	Elijah Kaplan	*Valor Racing*
3rd	Geoffrey Hahn	*Makellos*
4th	Luca Lombardo	*Furio*
5th	Ren Enatsu	*Makellos*
6th	Aleksandr Kholodov	*MACH*
7th	Beckham Wright	*Furio*
8th	Tommy Young	*MACH*
9th	Ian Matisse	*Holt Motorsport*
10th	Wit Nowak	*Noorden*
11th	Eduardo Almada	*Avanti Racing*
12th	Imre Bergmann	*Holt Motorsport*
13th	Qian Liu	*Avanti Racing*
14th	Gordon Whitlock	*Noorden*
15th	Antoine Auclair	*Trueno GP*
16th	Amir Bishara	*Force5*
17th	Sanjay Patel	*Trueno GP*
18th	Mateo Barrera	*ETHER*
19th	Julien Baker	*Force5*
20th	Cameron Christiansen	*ETHER*

I find Beck's name in bright red; Tommy's is below him in eighth. I scroll to the next graphic showing the constructor's championship standings.

"So, Beck's in seventh and his team is in third? That's pretty good." I glance up at Dad.

Dad clicks the tongs together. "It's *very* good! Beck is young—most of the grid has double the years of experience."

"His best friend is one of the MACH drivers, Tommy, he was there with us in Spain."

Hmm. The more I'm learning, the more I'm intrigued. I scroll down to the next graphic showing the season's schedule. *My word.* Beck wasn't kidding about the nomad life. These races are all over the world; some are back-to-back weekends. Halfway down the season's schedule, the Belgian Grand Prix's listed after the summer break.

"So, I should say yes to the invite then?" I ask.

Dad turns around smiling. "You'll never forget your first F1 race."

I take that as his stamp of approval.

Dad flips off the burner. "Let's eat! Then I'll drive you home."

———

Our train to Paris leaves in an hour.

"Let me know when we can do dinner. They've got a new menu at the club!" Dad says.

"Have they finally put a name placard on your favorite table?"

"If that day ever comes, then I'll *know* I've made it." Dad pulls the car to the curb. "Everything at the flat okay?"

"It's great, the lift makes me miss it."

Dad chuckles.

"Before I tell Beck yes, is there anything else I need to know?"

"You'll pick it up." Dad shifts his gaze to the steering wheel. He's running his fingers over the ridges of the stitching. Something's stewing in him, I can see it. I chew my lip and wait.

Finally, he turns to me. "Sophie, do you think you're ready to see someone again?"

The wind leaves my sails. "I won't know until I try—*right?*"

———

I call the lift and my phone buzzes—it's Beck on FaceTime. My heart takes off. I turn around and head back outside to answer.

The call connects and his smile appears.

"I've just escaped," Beck says.

"Are you having fun?"

"The most," he says, raising his eyebrows. "They won their first match, so we're in for a few more."

He's walking, and his hat is on backward. *That might be my favorite look.*

"What day are you coming in then?"

I try to refrain from squealing. "Thursday."

His smile grows. "Have you thought anymore about the race?"

I nod. "Will you show me how to get a ticket?"

"You don't need a ticket, babe; you'll be with me."

I gulp. *Babe.*

"I'll get your badges in order. My dad is coming too. You can hang out with him."

Dad? *What?*

"You fancy a ride on the jet again?"

I glance back and forth—*duh!*

"So, tell me then, how does this all work?"

"*You* come with *me*. We'll take the jet Wednesday with my trainer, Charlie, and fly back Monday."

Six days? I thought the race was Sunday? My heart thumps.

"Count me in."

"Atta girl." Beck praises.

God, I want to kiss that smile. *Shoot. Ella's calling.* "I've got to head in—we've got a train to catch." I wave goodbye. Forget dipping a toe in, I'm diving in headfirst.

Alice tipped us off to this apartment the week before her client moved out of it. A charming nineteenth-century, fully furnished three-bedroom in the sixth arrondissement. Though it lacked a TV *and a lift,* we were sold when we laid eyes on Pierre, the sassy, barely five-five concierge. Pierre perches behind the front desk, always acting like we are the biggest pains in his ass. We know in our hearts we're secretly his favorite tenants. The place was well out of our budget, but we splurged and signed a year lease.

The moment Pierre sees us coming through the door, he shakes his head. He walks out from behind the desk, flicking his hand in the air.

"Girls! Girls! This is getting out of hand!" he squawks. "I had to take the overflow to your door—you cannot take up half of the building's package room!"

"Pierre, we missed you!"

"Don't start with me, Miss Sophie," he says, unlocking the package closet.

Pierre wasn't kidding—he's pulled ten boxes of all sizes from the closet. We stack them haphazardly on our suitcases and head for the stairs. *Oh, the old-world charm.*

"Let's get this over with," Ella says, taking a breath. I pull my roller bag and four boxes on top of it up the first flight. Carmen struggles, laughing as two boxes fall off her suitcase.

My legs are on fire. Sweaty and out of breath, we bump up the last few stairs. Sure enough, a small mountain of packages is stacked at our door. PR packages are one perk that comes living with a mega influencer. The amount of clothes sent to Ella and Carmen is enough to stock the three wardrobes here and the two back at the flat. We collapse on the living room floor and unbox a week-and-a-half's worth of packages.

I've told Alice, I've told Dad, all who's left to tell is Stuart, my digital manager. He's a newer agent that manages a handful of micro-influencers and *me*. Even with the follower bump, I'm barely halfway to the micro level. Counting the two labels I wore in Spain, my brand deal grand total now clocks in a measly *three*. I know what I should be doing. *Hell,* I've been watching Ella do it for years. Maybe it's pride, hindering my drive to give influencing any energy beyond the bare minimum. I try to squash every notion telling me I'm too educated to be doing *this*. Ella and Carmen have equally impressive degrees—it's time to put my *"serious career girl"* ego aside.

Stuart is cute as a button, always wearing thick black-rimmed glasses and a colorful scarf. Each time we meet, he gives the same feedback: *post more.* I'm walking in with a few curveballs today, a new *friendship* to reveal and a big bump in my follower count.

Concluding our usual catch-up, Stuart shifts to business. "If there's nothing else, let's look at some numbers." He glances up from his notes. "You haven't done an unboxing video in a month," he says. "When you do those *and provide the links,* they do quite well." He smiles.

I nod. *One* video did well because Ella was in it. I forgot to link more than half of the items.

"I'd love to see some sort of get ready with me tutorial done this month. Those are always popular, and they get your name in front of brands."

I nod begrudgingly. Ella is the queen of *GRWM* videos.

Stuart narrows his eyes at the computer. "Your follower count had quite a jump since your trip to Spain, but you have to improve your post engagement and cadence. Ella posts ten stories to your one. You'll have a ton of fun opportunities to post from London and Paris fashion week events…" Stuart's rambling on and on. I'm half paying attention, half thinking about how to bring it up. *Now or never, Sophie.*

"Sorry, there is something else," I say, interrupting him.

"Yes?"

"I think I know—I mean, *I know* why my follower count jumped."

Stuart raises an eyebrow.

"I started seeing someone. He has quite a following of his own. I thought I would give you a heads up…"

There I did it.

"Oh? Is it someone I would know?" Stuart says, reaching for his teacup.

I gulp. Should I have run this by Beck? *Am I even allowed to be saying this? What the hell.*

"He's an F1 driver—Beck, Beckham Wright. He drives for Furio."

Stuart chokes on his tea, nearly spewing it on his desk. He clears his throat, and his eyes grow wide.

I must be the only living idiot that doesn't know F1 drivers. I continue, "I'll be doing a bit of travel before the London show. I'll also be going to Beck's race in Belgium."

Stuart's at a loss for words. He shuffles the papers around on his desk.

"Well then," he says. "That is *big news.* Obviously, post what you can, when you can. I imagine your numbers will keep on their upward trajectory."

⸻

Tomorrow will make it a week since I've seen Beck. I'm counting down the hours at this point. He's called every day since Spain, *sometimes twice a day*. And he doesn't just call, he FaceTimes, as if hearing each other's voices isn't good enough. *I adore it.* He calls when he's eating, he calls just to say hi, he calls when he could as easily text me something. He's so shockingly down to earth I forget he's who he is.

"Was that Beck again?" Ella asks.

I smile and stay quiet. *Dead giveaway.*

She shakes her head. "Lovesick puppy."

"He was at the pool. He wanted to show me what we're in for tomorrow," I say.

Ella raises her eyebrows. "One more sleep!" she says excitedly.

Yes, one more sleep. Although, I don't know if I'll be able to sleep. *Will we pick right back up where we left off in Spain?*

CHAPTER 8

CHERRY GIRL

My leg bounces the backpack in my lap. The GPS on the driver's dash says we've arrived.

"Sophie, calm down!" Carmen giggles.

I grip onto the door handle as our private transfer rounds the corner. I barely wait for the car to stop before opening the door.

"Party's here!" Tommy yells.

Ella steps out behind me and throws her arm in the air. *"Ciao bella!"*

They're outside the hotel. Beck's in blue swim trunks and a white linen button down that is *all the way unbuttoned.*

"There she is." Beck calls.

I rush into his arms, and my feet leave the ground. Suspended in his embrace, my left sandal slides off my foot.

"I missed you," Beck says.

There isn't room on my face for my smile to get any bigger. It was as if no time had passed; it's the way he stares at me. *This is the real deal.*

"What is it?"

"My shoe," I giggle. Beck sets me down and retrieves my sandal. He flips it upright and glides it back onto my foot. All the magic floods back as he takes my face in his hands and draws me to his lips.

"*Holy...*" Carmen says.

Once a private residence, now a quaint boutique hotel. The view from the picture window in the lobby draws us inside. It encases the perfect junction where the turquoise-blue water meets the sky. As we walk closer, the town unfolds beneath us. Brightly colored buildings trickle down the steep slope.

Tommy hoists our community roller bag up over his shoulder, and we follow them downstairs. Forty-eight hours didn't constitute packing a closet. We stop on the next floor. A short hallway lined with gold and blue patterned tiles holds four bright blue doors.

"We're holding down this floor—you girls are at the end here," Beck says.

He turns the knob on the door at the end of the hallway. Sunshine spills into the white and yellow room through open balcony doors.

"Down one more level, is the pool deck."

Ella and Carmen ditch their purses on the bed and are lured outside by the beaming sun.

Ella squeals, "The *content* this balcony will deliver!"

The sun blinds me as I step out behind her. The terrace is big enough to do several cartwheels. The view is spectacular—the whole of the famous Positano stack to our right, and the sea churning ahead.

I grip onto the railing; Beck's hand meets my back. A small pool glimmers below.

"That's our stuff down at the pool," Tommy says.

Carmen claps. "Let's get this party started!"

I meet Beck's eyes. "Come with me." He smiles. "I have a surprise."

I follow Tommy and Beck back into the hall. Beck stops at the first blue door before the stairs.

"We'll be right out," he says to Tommy.

Tommy takes off down the stairs, and Beck's gaze sinks into me.

"Our room is better."

My heart stutters. *Our room?*

It's a replica of the yellow room but with powder blue walls. The bed is perfectly made, and a small loveseat sits by the balcony doors. *Will I be sleeping in here?*

"Obviously, you can stay with the girls if you—"

I stop Beck mid sentence and push up to his lips. Everything my body's craved for a week ignites inside.

"I missed you," he says.

I blush. *It's the second time he's said that.*

My eyes dart to the balcony—Tommy's yelling to the girls from the pool.

"Before we go," he says. "Surprise first."

Our room wasn't the surprise? Beck walks to the bedside table and pulls a shallow white box from the shelf. I take a seat next to the box on the bed.

"I saw it in a shop window down the way."

I pull off the lid and fold back the tissue paper. A white ruffle edge bikini top sits inside. Little red cherries are embroidered all over it. My insides melt. I lift it from the box and see matching bottoms underneath.

"Do you like it?" Beck asks.

I don't have words. *"I love it."*

I jump up and hold the top against myself in front of the mirror on the wall. It even looks like it will fit. Beck comes behind me and brings his head over my shoulder. I watch his hands creep around my waist in the mirror.

"I saw it and said, '*Sophie needs that.*'"

My breath quickens, as his body presses against me. I could lose time staring at his reflection.

He brings his lips to my ear. "Now put that on and get to the pool." He steps back and lightly swats my ass. I shriek and grab the box off the bed.

"We'll be right out!"

Carmen opens the door, already in her swimsuit. Her eyes flash from the crazy smile on my face to the box in my hands. I push my way inside.

"What is that?"

"You have to see this," I say, putting the box down on the bed. I hold up the embroidered bikini top.

Carmen gushes, "I remember when Oliver used to do these things."

I slip my romper sleeves off my shoulders.

"Will Carmen and I be snuggling alone in here, Soph?" Ella asks.

I step into the bikini bottoms. *So far, so good.* I lay the top against my chest and move in front of the mirror to tie the strings behind my back.

"Afraid so." I smile. I drop my hands and turn slowly in the mirror. It's a *perfect fit.*

Carmen's flip-flops squeak on the pool deck. I move my hand to my forehead to shield my eyes from the blasting sun. Beck's in the water; his arms are stretched out, resting along the edge of the pool.

I sit down at the side of the pool and lower my legs into the water. The tile is hot beneath my cheeks. Beck pushes off the wall, moving my direction. I pull my cover-up over my head, and his eyes fixate. The red thread on the cherries radiates in the sun.

"This is heaven!" Ella sings, lying back on the chair next to Tommy.

Beck's hands slide up my thighs; his eyes slowly trail up to mine.

"It fits." He grins.

The indicative FaceTime ring sounds. Carmen holds her phone out.

"No!" Oliver yells.

Tommy sits up. "Bro, where you at?"

"Don't rub it in, mate. Tell me then, what's on the agenda?"

Carmen refers to Tommy.

"Beach club today and dinner back here at the hotel. Boat day tomorrow then dinner in the garden next door," Tommy says.

My heart flutters, and Ella kicks her feet. *The perfect forty-eight hours in paradise.*

"Miss you! Wish you were here," Carmen says, giving puppy eyes to the phone.

Beck squints up at me. "You fancy that plan?"

"I *love* that plan."

"Okay, enough pictures. Let's get in!" Carmen yells.

"A few more!" Ella pleads. "Take one of me and Tommy!"

Poor Carmen got roped into photo duty.

A short water taxi around the bend brought us to a tiny beach club carved into the bottom of the cliffs. Orange striped loungers sharply contrast the sapphire blue of the water's drop off. Chairs are scattered along the rocky edge anywhere they can fit. Beck's chest presses against my shoulder blades. His skin is warm, he rests his hands at my hips on the white ties of my cherry bikini. I close my eyes and listen. Waves crash against the rocks. The water sizzles then foams before the next wave hits. It's the kind of noise you'd play on a sound machine.

"I can't believe we're actually here."

"You're glad you said yes?" Beck asks.

I smirk at him over my shoulder. "I think I'm more excited for the race."

His eyes shine. "*Me too.* What are you most excited for?"

"Beck, I have no idea what to expect!"

"You're going to love it."

"You think?"

"No—*I know.*"

The waitress is back with a loaded tray. She moves neon yellow limoncello shots to our table then hands Beck a vibrant Aperol spritz. Four additional spritzes join the shots at the crowded side table between our chairs. The waitress picks up the last item then lowers the tray to her side.

"No way!" I squeal.

Beck smiles as she passes him a bowl of dark red shiny cherries.

"Sit down," Beck says. "I've got to get a picture of this."

My cheeks flush. Beck sits, straddling his legs over the sides of the chair. I sit before him at the end of the lounger and pull my legs under me. Beck sets the bowl of cherries in my lap.

He stares at me from behind his phone. "*Cherry girl.*"

Ella screams; I turn my head just in time to see Tommy release her flailing body. She crashes into the water, and Tommy jumps in beside her.

"*Uh-oh,*" Beck chuckles.

She is going to kill him.

I move to the chair beside Beck, sipping my spritz and keeping my eye on the ladder welded into the rocks. Ella's hands appear, and next, her enraged face pops up. Her mascara is running down her cheeks.

"I'm going to *kill* him!" Ella screams.

I wave her over. "Come here, sweetie. Have a bevvy!"

"Take my spot," Beck says, getting up. Ella wraps her sopping hair into a bun and lies back on the lounger next to me.

"I wasn't planning on going under just yet!"

I pass her a spritz as she glares over her sunglasses at Tommy, who's out in the water with Carmen. Beck takes off running then launches out over the water in perfect dive form.

"You looked like a goddess getting out, love," I lie.

Ella rolls her eyes and proceeds to slurp down half of her spritz.

My body pulses in the heat, and my skin tingles in the overbearing rays.

"Alright, I've got to get in." I sip down the last of the orange liquid in my glass.

Water streams down Beck's chest as he climbs up the ladder. He plants his feet and shakes the water out of his hair. I grip the bars and step to the first rung of the ladder.

"What do you think you're doing?" Beck says.

I freeze and pull my hands back from the hot metal.

"There's only one way to get in." He smirks.

"Sophie, jump!" Carmen yells from the water.

Ugh. "I think I'll lower in from the ladder."

Beck smiles and shakes his head slowly.

"You must run and jump. It's the rule." He raises an eyebrow. "Unless you want to be picked up again…"

I glance back at Ella on the chairs. *Why did I leave?!* My eyes dart to Carmen, bobbing in the waves with Tommy.

"Carmen, jump in with me!" I plead.

Carmen's hand is cold and pruned. We take two more steps back to get a better launch.

"Are you ready?" she asks.

"No!" I squeal. My hearts pounding.

"Now or never! One…two…*three!*"

I take off sprinting next to Carmen. On the last step, I push as hard as I can off the rocks.

I crash into the cool sapphire water. Adrenaline pumps through me as I kick my legs and surface, sucking in air. Beck and Ella applaud from the rocks.

Tommy and Ella exchange blows in the front of the water taxi, bickering back and forth like brother and sister. I'm sandwiched between the girls, and I can sense Beck's eyes burning into me from across the boat. We're supposed to go back to the hotel and freshen up for dinner. My eyes drift. I'm trying to be discreet, but I'm multiple limoncellos deep, returning *fuck me* eyes back at him. The way Beck's eyes sear back at me tells me he's having no trouble reading my mind. *There's only one thing I'm hungry for.*

Our room is half lit. Our mouths connect briefly before Beck falls back onto the loveseat. I place one knee down on the cushion and straddle his lap. His hands guide my hips as I slowly lower down onto him. Beck stares, and his mouth drops open.

"You're so tight," he pants; watching his length disappear inside of me.

All the blood rushes to my head. Every nerve ending in my body fires, as he fills me completely. I push off my knees and slowly glide up and down. I bring my lips to his, but I can't focus on kissing him—he feels *too* good. Shockwaves shoot down my legs. The faster I move, the faster I anoint every desire burning inside me. His hand slides up the back of my neck. He grips into my hair and tilts my head up. My back arches in response. The slight angle adjustment is too much. My legs tremble as everything inside me bubbles over, releasing so intensely I can't keep my voice in.

"Already?" he says, amused.

I slow to catch my breath. Fire rages in his eyes. His hands dive around the back of my legs. I fall against his chest as he stands up from the chair, holding me against him. I gasp, still reeling as my back meets the bed. Beck climbs over me and pulls one of my legs over his shoulder before he pushes back into me.

We don't make it to dinner.

I'm not sure anything could get my head off this pillow. None of this feels possible, it's as if I'm stuck, suspended in some boundless dream. Beck's eyes are heavy, he blinks slowly, staring back at me every time they reopen.

"Are you sure you don't have some boyfriend I should know about?"

I flinch. *Are we having this conversation now?* I gently shake my head side to side.

"I mean—I was with someone for a while but…it was a complicated, forbidden love type thing."

Beck perks up.

"…he was no *popstar*," I add.

"Good." He smiles. "Because I surely can't sing for you, darling."

"You don't talk to Sabrina anymore?"

"No." His fingers brush across my forehead as he moves the hair from my face.

"That ran its course. We were very different. Chasing different things."

And I'm not several universes different?

"Do you think we're random?" I ask softly.

A soft smile touches his lips. "I think we're *lucky*."

"Lucky?"

"It certainly took the perfect formula of *right place, right time* for us to meet."

"*Mhm. Perfect formula.*" I smile. "You weren't insulted that I didn't know who you were?"

"The opposite, really."

I slide my hand under the pillow.

"There are only twenty of me in the entire world. And you look at me like I'm a regular guy."

"You're not one of twenty to me; you're one of one."

He slides his hand under the pillow and interlocks his fingers with mine.

"And that's what makes us the perfect formula."

Beck's chest slowly rises and falls behind me. I stare out at the sunrise—we never closed the drapes or shutters. I was nervous about sleeping in here, yet I didn't wake up once until now. My stomach is begging for food. I wiggle my foot free from our intertwined legs then roll beneath his arm to face him. Even with his eyes closed, *my word,* he's handsome. His eyelids flutter open then fall again. My heart takes off.

"What's wrong?" Beck says softly.

"I'm starving," I giggle.

He opens his eyes and rolls onto his back, stretching his arms out. He turns his head to me and smirks. "Well, we *did* skip dinner."

Beck rolls back to his side and hovers over me. "Let's go upstairs and get some breakfast," he says. "We need our energy before we set out to sea."

I quietly knock on the girl's door.

Carmen swings the door open. "You're alive!"

I push inside; I need clothes from our community suitcase.

"How was dinner?" I ask.

"It's Italy—I don't know if a bad meal exists," Carmen says. "We missed you."

Ella throws the comforter back. "She didn't miss us!"

I deserve that.

"I was a bit *preoccupied,* but now I'm starving! Come upstairs and eat with us."

"Done," Ella says. "I'll text Tommy to meet us. That psycho went for a run."

After making our way upstairs, I sit down at the breakfast table with a bowl of fruit and yogurt.

"Sophie's quite the snuggler, isn't she Beck?" Ella asks.

Ella, shut it.

Beck smiles. "The *best.*"

"Morning sunshines!" Tommy says.

I turn in my seat as Tommy walks through the lobby with a handful of neon-orange bucket hats.

"I've got to find a way to get him back for throwing me in yesterday," Ella says under her breath. "*Start scheming.*"

"What have you got there?" Beck asks.

Tommy lays a bucket hat on Beck's head. "No one will notice us in these. I got one for everyone, and you're not allowed on the boat without it."

"You couldn't get me a red one?" Beck grins from under his hat.

"Only MACH orange, mate," Tommy says.

"No one will notice us? Are you blind?" Ella laughs.

The village is packed with summer tourists. We walked among the crowds yesterday attempting to blend in. They *almost* made it to the dock entirely unnoticed. Until we walked past a group of eagle-eyed girls at the main beach.

Carmen and I open our bucket hats and pull them on.

Ella watches. "Those are ridiculous."

"You heard the man, Ella," I say. "Rules are rules."

She sneers at Tommy. "You look like you're going fishing!

"Maybe we *will* do some fishing!" Tommy sasses.

Ella rolls her eyes and begrudgingly puts her hat on. I pick up my spoon and dive into my yogurt.

"There's no way he understands Ella," Beck laughs.

The boat captain's English is limited; he smiles and nods, but as fast as she talks, *there's no hope.*

I squeal as Beck presses his cold *Peroni* against my back. He follows as I skirt around the cabin to the front of the boat. A large, padded sundeck stretches from the cabin windows to the tip of the bow. Mounted Italian flags blow in the breeze at the nose of the boat. The padding on the sundeck is warm; tingling my bare feet. Beck takes a swig from his *Peroni* and puts his arm around my waist. Heat radiates off his skin. He's in his red swim trunks. The ones that ended up on the floor of the villa last week. I'm wearing the cherry bikini again—*how could I not?*

There's not a cloud in the sky. The view of the rocky coastline is incredible; in the distance, Capri rises out of the water. Gentle waves rock the boat. We have the tiny cove all to ourselves.

Beck sighs deeply and tilts his head back. He closes his eyes.

"What is it?"

"Just want to soak up every minute." He winks at me. "Before everything is full throttle for the next three months."

He takes another swig of his beer.

"Back to training and workouts. Back to business." He tilts his beer. "And *no drinking*."

He steps in front of me and rests his fingers on my hips. His bottle is cold against my leg.

"Should we be working out?"

He hovers over me. "*You* are my workout."

My breath quickens. He pulls his head up.

"Is there a no alcohol rule?"

"Not a rule, more something my trainer and I agree on. Of course, if I make the podium, it's *champagne showers*." He smiles wickedly.

"It helps keep my mind sharp, laser-focused, quick reactions." He pokes my stomach with his pointer fingers.

I grab for his finger, but he pulls away too quickly.

I can play.

"What's that?!" I yell, pointing behind him.

He jerks his head over his shoulder, and I *lose it*.

Slowly, he turns back, shaking his head. In a split second, he sets down his beer and scoops around the back of my legs. My feet leave the padding as I fold over his shoulder. He takes off for the nose of the boat.

"Man overboard!" he yells.

I scream midair and squeeze my eyes shut.

My mouth is open underwater, and when I surface, I hold my hands up.

"Okay, we're even!" I laugh.

Beck dives his head under, swimming toward me. *Oh shit!* I kick my legs as if my life depends on it. He chases after me, grabbing at my feet underwater. My heart races as he grips my ankle. I squeal and submit to my captor. His hands run up my body, and I cross my legs around his waist and pull his face to mine. He's breathing hard, working his tongue with mine, while keeping us both afloat.

"What are you yelling about?" Ella calls.

I open my eyes; she's leaning over the side of the boat. Beck leans back and starts to backstroke. I keep my hands hooked onto his shoulders but release my legs to help kick.

Beck delivers me to the wooden swim dock on the back of the boat. Ella's waiting with a frosty bottle of tequila.

"It's *too* quiet," Ella states.

I pull myself up the ladder onto the swim platform. "It's not the same without Oliver!"

Carmen grabs her phone. "I can fix that."

The mixture of saltwater and sun stings my cheeks. I reach for my bucket hat. Beck rests his forearms on the swim dock, still breathing heavily. I sit down on the platform and put my legs back in the water next to him.

"There, you got another workout." I wink.

Ella sits next to me and scoots the bottle closer.

"You two are behind a shot."

"Don't you have PTSD from that night at the villa?" Beck asks her.

"I never learn, Beck," she says sarcastically.

I turn and squint into the tiny cabin. Music suddenly bumps through the boat's speakers.

"DJ *Ollie Godd* here in spirit!" Tommy yells.

Carmen runs out of the cabin and launches over Ella's head, cannonballing into the water. Beck's biceps flex as he pulls himself up the ladder.

I grab the bottle to get my shot over with. The second the tequila hits my tongue, I yank the bottle from my lips. I grab Ella's beer with my other hand to chase it. I pass the bottle to Beck.

Tommy stands over Ella. "You're such a pusher!" He takes off his bucket hat and drops it on her head. She snatches the hat and chucks it off the platform. The hat flies through the air like a frisbee, then splats in the water.

"Ha!" Ella yells.

Tommy dives off the platform as the hat begins to sink.

"Got him," she snickers.

Ella lays three sundresses on the bed, tags still attached to each. I sway, looking down at them. Is it sea legs? Drinking in the sun all day?

"These were sent last month," she says. "I haven't had a chance to wear them."

"Which one do you want?" Carmen asks me.

"I'll take the pink one," I say. "It will match my sunburn." I made the wise decision and came straight back to the girl's room to get ready. *I can't risk missing our last dinner.*

My skin is crisp, and my cheeks are pink. Ella winces, running the brush over her head.

"I should have worn that damn hat," Ella giggles. "But seriously, did you get any sleep last night?"

"Surprisingly, *yes*." I lean over the sink to touch up my eyeliner.

Ella watches me in the mirror. "He *really* likes you, Sophie."

I smile. "I don't get it."

She narrows her eyes at me. "You're too hard on yourself."

I lower the eyeliner.

"Did you tell him about Fredrick?"

"Not...*everything*..." I grab the highlighter compact.

"Beck will be so good for you, Soph. He will put you on a pedestal for the world to see."

My, *would that be night and day.*

"Dad's nervous." I pause. "Do you think enough time has passed?"

"Maybe not," Ella says honestly. "But timing has always been my least favorite excuse."

Tommy yells from the pool. I lean out of the bathroom; Carmen shoots me a look and opens the balcony door.

"They sound hammered," Carmen laughs.

Stepping outside, I lean over the balcony railing. Several empty glasses sit on the table between Beck and Tommy. *They're smashed.*

Beck spots me and my heart jumps. "Soph, get down here!" he yells.

Oh boy. When did he start calling me that? Only Dad and the girls call me *Soph.*

"Five more minutes!" I shriek.

Tommy groans.

I turn from the railing. Carmen steps outside, yawning.

"I saw that!"

She slaps her cheeks. "I'm awake!"

I'm still rocking in the waves while walking out to the pool. Beck whistles.

"Took you long enough," Tommy yells.

"Oh, shut up. See how hot we look?" Ella scoffs.

"My body feels like a noodle," I announce.

Beck opens his arms for me. "Come here, noodle."

I sit next to Carmen, and across the table, Ella and Tommy argue over the wine Tommy picked.

"Are we sure these two aren't in love?" I ask Carmen.

"They're the same person," Carmen giggles.

Beck points to the menu. "Forget the wine. When the time comes, we're trying each of these desserts."

The tops of his cheeks are sunburnt, only exaggerating the glint in his eyes. He rests back into the chair and reaches for my hand across the corner of the table. Café lights crisscross overhead in the private garden.

Ella rolls her eyes, turning away from Tommy. "So, Beck, are we going to see Sophie on TV?"

Beck's zoned out staring at me.

"Beck!" Ella says.

I flinch my hand in his trying to break his daze.

He blinks quickly. "Sorry." He clears his throat and nods. "Spa will be epic. Sophie will crush her interviews; Tommy and I will make the podium."

I freeze.

He cracks into a smile. "*Kidding*. We'll ease you into it."

"Don't overwhelm the girl," Tommy says. "You can't throw her to the wolves on her first race."

"Oh, that's right! Tommy hasn't made the podium all year! It'll just be me up there." Beck winks.

Tommy wads up his napkin and throws it at Beck.

"Watch yourself. We're only twenty points behind!" Tommy says.

"Thanks to Alek," Beck teases.

I turn to Carmen and shake my head. "I need to take a crash course I'm afraid."

"Alek? I don't know that name," Ella says, pulling out her phone.

"My other half," Tommy says. "Oh, you want to check him out?"

Tommy leans closer to her and points at her screen. "He's chill."

Ella shrugs. "He's cute."

"I'm cuter." Tommy glares at her.

She narrows her eyes.

Beck squeezes my hand. "You'll get to meet Luca."

"Luca's such a boss," Tommy says.

"Luca, Furio...let's see then," Ella says. Her jaw drops and her eyes flip up. "*Oh my God,* he is hot." She turns her phone to Carmen and me.

My word.

Beck chuckles. "He's also thirty-six and *very* married."

Ella's bottle of *Chianti* arrives at the table. Oh, thank God, *here comes the food.*

It all goes by too fast. I had a feeling it would. Lying in bed, Beck pulls me closer. I move my head to his pillow. He's blinking in slow motion; his eyes must be as heavy as mine.

"Come home with me tomorrow," he says softly.

Ha! "I have to go back to Paris with the girls."

He shakes his head.

"We fly together from now on." "Deal." I smile. "I'm flying with you on Wednesday."

Beck exhales. "That's like five days." His eyes close.

"Five days," I whisper. "*Until I get to watch you fly*."

"*Mhm*." He murmurs. His eyes remain closed, and his breathing slows.

CHAPTER 9
Prep for the Paddock

"You're glowing," Carmen says, settling into the aisle seat.

I pull the sunshade beside me down. "*I'm sunburnt.*"

"No." She shakes her head. "I can tell—*Sophie's back.*"

"Back and brighter than ever," Ella sings.

I roll my eyes. "You're both still drunk."

"Let's see what we're up against," Ella says, firing up an internet search.

"What are you doing?"

"Research," she says. "We've got to get you prepped for the paddock."

Ella tilts her phone. "Look at all the cameras! Mum's right—this *is* like a red-carpet entrance."

A pit forms in my stomach.

"Look who we have here," she says, clicking on a photo.

It's Tommy, walking into the paddock, holding hands with a gorgeous blonde.

"This must be his ex," she says, swiping. "Wait, maybe *ex-ex*. This girl's different."

I squint. *Okay*, it's a different girl, but as much of a blonde bombshell as the first. Both are carbon copies of Ella.

Carmen leans in. "What are you going to wear?"

"I haven't really thought about it," I say.

"Oh, Sophie, I was afraid you'd say that," Ella says. "We'll have work to do when we get in."

Ella and Carmen shift in their seats and lay their heads back. I'm riding too high to relax. I pull the shade up and stare out the window as the plane taxis away from the terminal. *Will my picture be taken walking in with Beck?*

I take a deep breath. *What a morning.* Too many snoozes left us in a mad dash, stuffing the contents of our room into the suitcase. Beck walked us out, when I saw our airport transfer hadn't ditched us, I lingered in the comfort of my head tucked under his chin. Carmen's right: *I am back.* My body's awakened. I've shaken off the ashes left in the wake of my setback. The girl's heads rest against each other, both already look asleep. *Where would I be without them?* I lay my head back and try to relax. I fold my arms across my body and attempt to replicate the serenity of last night *in Beck's arms.*

The chaos coming out of our suitcase—it's as if an excavator collected everything off the floor, crumpled it up, then dumped it inside. Somehow, all three of our bucket hats made it back. Carmen picks up her hat and shakes it out.

"Ah! We should have worn these on the plane!"

"Zip that back up. I can't deal with that right now," Ella says. She raises an eyebrow at me. "Besides, we have something more fun to do."

I pull my legs under me on Ella's bed and click through the endless tabs she's opened on her laptop of *VIPs* in the paddock. She and Carmen begin to tear through her wardrobe.

"Did he give you any idea of what to expect?" Carmen asks.

"I'll take the train to London on Tuesday; we fly out Wednesday. We'll be at the track Thursday through Sunday and fly back Monday."

Ella's eyes widen.

I sigh. "He gave me the helpful advice to wear whatever I like."

"*Men.*" Ella rolls her eyes. "We need the perfect ensemble. Let's do a few dressier, chic looks and a few cool, casual looks."

She moves an arm's load of clothes to the bed. I shuffle through the hangers.

"Ella, have you even worn any of this?"

"Besides trying it on when it was sent—*no*. There aren't enough days in the week!"

Ella winks. "Do me a favor and tag the brand if you wear a piece."

"We must incorporate a bit of red too," Carmen adds. "Without being too obvious."

"Take that white-and-red seersucker dress!" Ella says. "It's far too short for me, but it'd be perfect on you."

I pull the dress from the pile. "I do fancy this!"

I try to picture any red in my wardrobe but come up blank. Then my brain fires.

"Wait here," I say, scooting off the bed.

I walk to my bedroom and grab the keys in the nightstand for the trunk at the foot of my bed. I open the lid and spot the duster bag. I reach in and clutch the bag to my chest. Even through the protective sleeve, the rich leather scent seeps through.

"What's that?" Ella says.

I climb back onto her bed and set the drawstring bag in my lap.

"I *do* have something red," I say, pulling the drawstrings loose. I reach in and pull out a red quilted double flap *Chanel*.

"Oh my God!" Carmen shrieks. "When did you get that?"

"It was Mum's. Dad kept it for me." I run my finger over the gold hardware.

"I've never worn it before. No occasions seemed special enough."

I turn the center clasp where the logo intersects, freeing the top flap. I hold the bag open and search for the red mark that stains the lining of the interior. *Of course, it's still there.* I noticed the spot the night Dad gave me the bag. We'd gone to dinner at the club for my eighteenth birthday. I have lots of Mum's things, but this bag was her absolute favorite. When I asked Dad if he knew what the stain was from, a lipstick maybe? Time stood still because he didn't know the answer. I would never get to ask Mum about the story behind the red mark.

"Sophie, you have to wear that," Ella says softly.

Mum and I didn't get to share many moments I remember together. It would be special to carry something of hers with me.

I blink quickly to dismiss the mist in my eyes. "Yes, I think I do."

The girls easily assembled four outfits and an emergency reserve option. Neutral tones, small pops of color, sensible shoes, all brought together by the red *Chanel*.

"I wish I could pack both of you."

"Send a photo every morning when you've picked your outfit!" Carmen says.

Of course I will.

CHAPTER 10
WELCOME TO MY WORLD

THE SAME CREW IS manning the cockpit of the jet. I'm as giddy as I was when we took the jet home from Spain. I sink into the double seat at the back and smile. *Best seat in the house.*

A man emerges through the jet stair door, on the phone. It's the man from the background of many of Beck's FaceTime calls. His trainer, *Charlie.* I follow Beck up the aisle, and Charlie hangs up the call as we approach.

"Sorry, the *wife*," he says, tossing the phone down to the seat. Charlie smiles, reaching for my hand. "And we finally meet in person."

He's older, with the build befitting a trainer.

"You see the weather?" Charlie asks Beck.

Beck rolls his eyes. "Perfect tomorrow but rain the second we get the cars out."

"A waterlogged welcome back," Charlie laughs. He sits down in the front left captain seat.

The London skyline disappears as the jet pulls into the clouds.

"There's no racing tomorrow?" I ask.

"Unfortunately, no." Beck smiles. "Media day is tomorrow. Practice Friday, qualifying Saturday, then the race on Sunday."

I stare back at him.

"I don't want to overwhelm you; it can be a lot."

I smile. "Just tell me where to be, and I'll be there."

"We'll get settled in then grab dinner with Tommy and some others. Hopefully Dad can join us too." Beck kisses the back of my hand. He hasn't let it go since we took our seats.

"Are you excited to be back?"

His eyes glimmer. "I could barely sleep. This circuit's quite beautiful but *super* challenging."

"Is it your favorite?"

Beck lights up. "That's a tough one. I have many favorites. Spa is legendary. Nothing compares to the way my stomach drops through Eau Rouge. But you can't beat the energy at the team's home race in Monza, with all the Furio fans—it's mad."

My heart flutters. The way he talks, his excitement, it's contagious.

"Did you always want to be a driver?"

"My dad put me in a go-kart for fun when I was five. That same year, he took me to Silverstone for the first time, and something sparked in my brain. It's been the dream ever since."

"That's amazing. Not many people can say their childhood dream came true."

"It was my parents; they did everything they could to help me get to Formula One. Did you always dream of handling large sums of money?"

"No," I laugh. "I wanted to work at *the zoo*."

"The zoo?" Beck chuckles.

"Finance came later. I inherited the numbers gene from my dad."

"I'm impressed. I was always bad with maths; do you think you'll ever go back to it?"

"Maybe one day, but for now, I need a bit of a break."

One day.

Joe, the team driver, opens my door. I slide out of the backseat of the team's black SUV. It's cool and foggy outside, with an overwhelming earthy scent of lush forest.

Joe watches me. "Beautiful, isn't it?"

I smile back. It's *stunning.*

When I thought *racetrack,* I didn't picture rolling hills of magnificent green forest. It's peaceful—everything is saturated, including the simple charcoal brick of the modern hotel. I meet Beck and Charlie around the back of the car.

Woah.

"Is that the track, just there?"

Beck nods, setting my suitcase next to me. Joe passes Beck and Charlie hotel keys. Beck pockets two of the key sleeves.

"That's turn one and a bit of the main straight." He points.

Alternating red and yellow paint marks the track's edge until it disappears behind the trees.

Beck grins. "The second *DRS* zone."

"The *what* zone?"

His smile grows.

"*D-R-S,*" he says slowly. "When you're within a second of the car ahead, you activate DRS. Less drag, more speed to overtake."

I nod. *Noted.*

Charlie shuts the trunk. Beck takes my hand, and the three of us head for the front door.

"We got lucky with your room," Beck says.

My heart skips. *I have my own room?*

We enter the hotel lobby and walk straight to the lift. The lounge up front is filled with color, busy hosting members of the various teams.

In the lift, Charlie presses the second- and third-floor buttons.

"We're on two; you and Dad are on the third floor."

The lift stops and Charlie steps out.

"I'll be down in a few," Beck says. "I'll take Sophie up to her room."

Charlie smiles.

The doors close, and I look up at Beck. "I have my own room?"

"You'll be glad for it. People will be in and out of mine at all hours."

Beck nods at several people walking through the hallway of the third floor. He stops at the second to last door and pulls one of the card envelopes from his pocket. He holds the keycard to the scanner and pushes the door open. The room is small and cozy. White linens are perfectly tucked around the double bed. Beck wheels my bag inside and sets his backpack on the bed. He unzips the front pocket and pulls out a pink lanyard.

"This is your pass for the weekend," Beck says. He holds open the loop of the lanyard and drapes it over my head. I stare up and drink in his eyes. His hands run down my waist stopping at my hips.

"This will get you through the swipe gates, into our suite, the garage, anywhere you want."

I'm listening, but every bit of my body is pleading for more. His hands leave my hips, and he steps back to his backpack. I exhale and blink quickly. I pick up the thick, shiny card hanging from the lanyard. *Paddock Pass.*

I turn and head for the window. I part the curtains and push them aside, flooding the room with soft, natural light.

"Will you be okay up here?" Beck asks.

The window frames the foggy, rich forest behind the hotel.

I smile. "*It will work—*"

I gasp as his body presses into my back. His arms wrap around my waist, and his lips graze over my ear. My breath quickens and chills run down my legs.

"With your own room, *we'll have a place to hide.*"

His lips move from my ear down my neck, turning my legs to Jell-O. *It's a drug.* Instantly, I crave more. I turn around to face him. He reaches over my shoulders and closes the curtains behind me.

"That was Dad—his flight's delayed. We'll meet up with him after dinner," Beck says, pocketing his phone.

"Is Tommy coming?"

"Tommy and Alek," Beck says. "Ren is coming too. He drives for Makellos."

Ren Enatsu. I remember that name from the graphic on Dad's phone.

"What about Luca? Is he coming?"

Beck smiles. "Nah, he's too cool for us. You'll get to meet Luca tomorrow."

We round the corner to a private room in the tiny restaurant. To my surprise, another girl is at the table.

"Sophie!" Tommy calls.

A familiar face! Tommy stands up from the table and pulls me in for a hug. Beck introduces me to Ren and his girlfriend, Ana. She's lovely, with blue-black hair and porcelain skin. I take my seat next to Beck. Ana moves her purse from the chair beside Ren to the empty seat beside me.

"Water is fine," I say to the waiter.

"Dirty martini please," Ana says.

Oh, I like her already.

"Is it only us?" Beck asks.

"Alek is running late," Tommy says. "Where's James?"

"Probably on the same flight as Alek," Beck laughs.

Fifteen minutes later, Ana's on her second martini, and she's ordered one for me. Beck has his hand on my thigh, giving it a gentle squeeze every so often. He's busy catching up with Ren and Tommy while Ana talks my ear off. She gets chattier with every sip. Ana's from Singapore originally, but now lives in Brackley with Ren.

She proudly watches at Ren at the end of the table. "It's in his blood. His father was a driver, and his grandfather was a driver."

"How did you meet?"

"He was moving to London for F3 and we were seated next to each other on the plane. My parents were across the aisle."

I smile. "That's romantic."

"We talked the whole flight, didn't sleep a wink. When we parted ways, *we kept talking*. Long distance only lasted a few months. Five years later, here we are."

I take a sip of my martini. *So, one can successfully date an F1 driver.*

"I can't believe it's your first race!" Ana exclaims. "Thursdays are painfully boring; we'll have to meet up in the paddock tomorrow!" She pulls her phone out of her purse.

"That would be wonderful!"

She opens a new contact page and hands me her phone. *Look at me.* I've already made a friend.

I pick out Beck's father as soon as we enter the hotel lobby. Beck may not have the belly, but I see where he gets his smiling eyes.

"James Wright," his father says, shaking my hand. "So glad to meet you, Sophie."

He's holding an almost empty pint glass, dressed in business attire and loafers.

"Beck will have to be at the track early. Would you care to join me for breakfast here in the morning?"

Beck smiles.

"*Oh, I'd love to!*"

James nods. "Let's meet down here at nine. We'll make the long journey to the track together after," he laughs, putting his arm around Beck.

"I hate to be boring, but I'm going to step outside and ring your mother then I'm off to bed." James takes the last sip of his pint and smiles at me.

"I promise I'll be more fun tomorrow!" He sets his empty glass on the bar.

"Goodnight, Sophie." James nods. "Beck, make sure you get some rest." James turns and heads for the lobby doors.

Beck shakes his head. "Look at you. You've already got a new friend *and a breakfast date.*"

I push open the door to my room.

"Sophie, what happened in here?" Beck teases.

My cheeks warm, seeing the bed disheveled from our predinner *exercise.*

"You started it," I fire back.

Beck takes my hips in his hands and pulls me close. *Oh.*

"Tomorrow, I'll be in and out of different media engagements. Call me when you and Dad get done with breakfast."

My heart sinks. "Are you leaving?"

"I wish I could stay." He pauses. "I'll try to meet you at the gates tomorrow."

"All I need is my lanyard?"

Beck nods and rests his forehead on mine. "I can't wait to show you around."

The next morning, I turn the knob on the shower and search for the latest episode of my favorite guilty pleasure podcast, *In the Know.* The voices of the two sister hosts fill the bathroom. Their repartee on the latest in pop culture will calm my nervous excitement while I get ready for my first day in the paddock. *It feels like Christmas morning.*

After Beck left last night, I hung up the outfits the girls put together. For today's warm and partly sunny forecast, I pull the seersucker dress and loafers outfit option. I leave my hair down in loose curls but grab a claw clip for my bag in case it gets unruly. The cotton dress is cute but casual and hits my thigh at the perfect length. I step into white loafers and pull the red Chanel over my shoulder. I move to the mirror and assess.

The girls put together a *fabulous outfit.* My tan from Positano makes the whole look pop. I snap a photo in the mirror and send it to our *Roomie Trio* group chat. In fact, this picture might be socials worthy. I open Instagram and add the photo to my story. *Stuart will be quite proud.* I grab the pink lanyard and put it in my bag before I head for the door.

In the dining room, James is seated at a table for two on the phone. The room is buzzing with people all sporting similar team gear in an array of colors. James spots me approaching and hurries to hang up the call.

James stands up. "Sophie! Good morning!" He quickly pockets his phone, as if I'd be offended his phone was out at the table.

"Good morning!" I smile. "Did you sleep well?" I pull out the chair across from him and take my seat.

"That was Elizabeth," he says, sinking back into the booth side of the table. "I'm alone, no kids, at a hotel—*I slept wonderfully,*" he laughs.

"She is quite jealous she can't be here this weekend with you. And Mia—*boy*, she's over the moon to meet you."

"Do they come to many races?"

"A lot more last season. Louie's quite involved in sports this year. We try to get the kids out for the closer races when we can." He smiles. "You'll meet everyone next weekend in Monza. It'll be a whole family affair."

My heart flutters. *Next weekend?*

"Now that I think about it, you'll probably want to act as if you don't know us," James laughs.

"I see where Beck gets his self-deprecating humor. When he asked me to come, he said if he DNFs I never have to speak to him again."

James laughs. "That sounds like Beck."

"I guess we'll have to wait and see if I'm still around after Sunday," I joke.

My hands fidget under the table. Beck hasn't mentioned anything about another race, and I certainly don't want to presume I'll be attending.

James couldn't be nicer. He's a talker and keeps the conversation light and flowing. He takes a long sip of his coffee.

"It's quite special you didn't know who Beck was."

I set my fork down a little too hard. *That was an unexpected shift.*

"To find someone so sincere; from how Beck talks, he's found that in you."

I retrieve my fork and push the fruit around my plate in an attempt to hide my delight. *Beck's spoken to his father about me…about us?*

"I warned him I'd need a crash course for this weekend," I say.

James laughs. "You're not to worry. I'll show you the ropes."

James reaches into his pocket and pulls out the same pink lanyard I was given.

"Thursdays are more relaxed. Really, only the teams are here," James says, striding next to me. "The rest of the weekend, the paddock will be as crowded and chaotic as a carnival."

I copy him and take the pink lanyard out of my *Chanel* and drape it over my head.

We slow in front of a large archway entrance of swipe gates. Among a fuss of other people, I spot Beck and Charlie inside, waiting just beyond the gates. My heart thumps. Beck is smashing in his collared red team polo.

James holds his badge up to the scanner. *Beep!* A green checkmark flashes on the screen.

"*Oh good, they still haven't banned me.*" James smirks.

I hold my badge up and wait. *Beep!*

"And you're in!" James says excitedly. I step through the gates and lock eyes with Beck. His eyes are smiling like I've never seen. James greets Charlie with a high five. Beck's eyes don't leave mine; he takes my hand and kisses the back of it.

"*You're gorgeous.*"

I take notice of my surroundings, *my word*. Cameramen and photographers sporting green lanyards are congregated on both sides of the walk. My heart jumps to my throat. The cameras follow us, calling Beck's name as we pass by. He smiles and nods, but we keep our pace.

Yes, Alice, this feels like a red-carpet entrance.

"What have I missed?"

"Walked a bit of the track this morning, finished a few media engagements"—Beck checks his watch—"Press conference will be in about an hour."

The footpath runs out, and a monumental thoroughfare opens to my left and right. It's a flood of color and *wealth*. Gargantuan luxury motorhomes decked out in team colors and branding dazzle in the sunshine.

Beck gives my hand a squeeze. "*Welcome to my world.*"

The sheer scale of the paddock didn't come through in the pictures Ella showed me.

"These are the hospitality suites," Beck says.

We take a left; the lane is bustling with camera crews and busy personnel adorned in team gear.

Beck points to a massive, gleaming red three-story structure ahead on our left.

"When you're not in the garage, this is where you'll hang out."

James turns around. "Our suite's the easiest to spot."

I stare up at the beaming emblem above the entrance. Massive glass panels enclose the front of the red suite.

"This is *incredible*."

Beck nods. "It travels with us to all the European races."

This colossal thing *travels?*

"If you meet up with Ana, the Makello's suite is just there." He points to a shiny black-and-green structure with glistening silver details.

A blonde woman in Furio gear approaches.

"Sophie, this is Shannon, our head press officer."

Ah, this is Beck's *Alice.*

"Come to me with any questions," she says, shaking my hand.

"I'm going to give Sophie a quick tour," Beck says.

Shannon nods. "Meet me in the media room in fifteen to prep."

"Take her in, I'll be in the garage!" James says, turning the other direction with Charlie.

Two glass panels split as we ascend the three steps into the suite. Team personnel are seated, scattered around a large, immaculate dining room. The space is lively with conversation and the clinking of plates and silverware.

I follow Beck toward a noisy kitchen in the back of the suite.

A serving counter covered with a massive display of food separates the dining area from the kitchen.

"The brunch spread is put out every morning. If you don't see something you like, ask the staff; they'll make it." He smiles.

Beck walks down the sprawling counter to the pastry display at the end. He points to a drizzled pastry oozing with chocolate from both ends.

"These," he says. "Are my absolute favorite. I've already had two, but no one needs to know that."

I'm in awe. This rivals any Parisian patisserie the girls and I frequent.

"Patrizio is our head chef, Italian, of course. No one goes hungry in our suite."

The glossy hallways on the second floor are lined with racing graphics and photos.

"This floor holds the offices for marketing, logistics, travel…"

Ha! Logistics! I can only imagine what a massive undertaking it is to move this operation around the globe.

Beck stops at the doorway of a large war room fitted with dozens of monitors.

"This is where we meet to brief before and after we take the cars out."

No penny was spared creating this suite; the tech is top of the line, and everything is done up to the nines.

He points down the hall to our right. "The bosses' offices are down that way."

We turn left. "And our driver rooms are down *this* way."

Luca Lombardo and *Beckham Wright* are displayed across two doors, sitting side by side. He grabs the handle and pushes his door open.

"If you ever need to get away, *come here*."

The room is compact and pristine. A small desk and chair, a massage table, and a private bathroom are squeezed inside.

"This is where I get suited up, do physio with Charlie, *sleep* when I can."

A red full-body racing suit hangs on a rod between tall cabinets. The team emblem breaks up the red on the chest, sponsor logos run down the sleeves. Beck opens one of the cabinet doors. "Anything you don't want to carry around, you can keep it here."

I touch the heavy fabric of the racing suit.

"I like this room." I smile.

He closes the cabinet and steps toward me. I tilt my head up in anticipation.

"I like you in here," he says over my lips.

There's noise in the hallway—his door is open.

He pulls back and smiles. "One more floor."

The third story is a large open room with light flooding through glass-paned walls.

"This is where we do media content, signings and when it's nice like today, you can sit outside on the terrace."

He rests his back on the door and pushes it open. There's a girl outside at a table with a laptop in front of her.

"Pippa, I want you to meet Sophie."

The girl reaches for the jean jacket on the table and drapes it over her arm. She pulls her arm in front of her before she stands up.

Like Ana, she's *gorgeous*. She's older and wearing a colossal diamond on her finger. *Luca's wife.*

"I'm giving her the grand tour. I'm not sure any other day you'll be able to come out here."

"That's Spa!" Pippa says, rolling her eyes.

"It's beautiful up here!"

"Yes, I'm enjoying it while I can." She smiles.

"Last stop is the garage. Have to show her where the magic happens."

"Luca should be in there. Lovely to meet you, Sophie."

Across the walk, parallel to the suite's front doors, is the entrance to the Furio garage.

At least it's obvious where I'm supposed to be.

At the end of the garage entrance, a blown up black-and-white chest up graphic of Beck and Luca stares back at me. I've never seen Beck make that face—it's intimidating and *sexy as hell*. Beck trails his fingertips along the polished walls of the garage hallway. The graphic doesn't faze him; Beck turns right and stops at an extensive display of hanging red headsets. Each has a name displayed below it. He scans the wall and rests his hand on one of the hangers.

"This is what you'll wear when you're watching in the garage," he says.

I double take. *Sophie Collins* is engraved on a placard below the headset where his hand rests. My jaw drops and his eyes light up.

He turns and continues down the hall. Every detail is *impeccable*.

The glossy hall opens to a noisy dual garage. Both doors are open out to the pit lane in front. *Luca Lombardo #3* displays above the left bay, *Beckham Wright #20* above the right. Mechanics are busy at work on either side. Both cars are covered, taking center stage in the bays. James waves to me from a center island between the cars. The man next to James turns and smiles. The center station is covered with stacked monitors.

"This is where you'll watch with Dad and Charlie," Beck says.

A series of screens on pedestal displays stand before us at the back of the garage.

"Back here, you'll have my onboard, Luca's onboard and the race broadcast," he says, pointing to the screens.

My heart flutters. "And my headset?"

"Yes." He smiles. "You'll hear the broadcast commentary and our team radio."

Team radio?

Beck points out of the front of the garage to a red station built right along the fencing.

"Across the pit lane, the *pit wall,* is where the bosses sit," he says. "And just beyond that fence is the start line."

I follow Beck to the center island of monitors. He puts his hand on the man's shoulder next to James.

"This is Richard Cooper, my race engineer."

The man turns. "Howdy!" He smiles, holding out a hand. "Call me *Coop.*"

I glitch, unsure of what to introduce myself as. "Sophie," I say, taking his hand.

"Coop's a Yankee, and even worse, he's a *Texan,* but we don't hold that against him," Beck says.

Coop throws his head back, laughing. Coop looks about Dad's age. Gray is peppered throughout his face stubble.

"This is Sophie's first race, we've got to give her a show, boss," Beck says.

"We'll give 'em hell!" Coop yells.

I like this man. Coop's demeanor is energetic and warm. How does a Texan end up as a race engineer for the highest regarded Italian racing team?

I stare up at the various charts and tables on the monitors.

"What is all of this?" I ask.

Coop steps in front of the monitors. "She signed the NDA?"

My eyes dart to Beck, who's wearing a wide grin.

"I'm joking," Coop laughs.

He waves me closer and holds his arms out. "This is all sim data. That end station there monitors all things tyres—the temperature, performance, degradation, all of it! Then we've got aerodynamics, all the performance engineering, race strategy and all the intercom panels."

Ok then!

"Clear as mud?"

I shake my head. "I'm afraid I'm a bit speechless!" I laugh. "How long have you been doing this?"

"Twenty-one years!" Coop says proudly. "And now that my daughter's become a fan, she won't even let me think about retiring."

"Neither will I," Beck adds.

"Did Beck show you the headsets?"

I nod.

"Good, those let y'all hear Beck and I yap away at each other."

Behind me, two mechanics begin rolling up the cover at the front of the car.

"And this"—Coop turns around, holding his hands out—"is the driving machine."

The fabric covering is carefully rolled back, revealing the muted luster carbon fiber front end.

"Built her all day yesterday with final touches this morning."

The brilliant red body is trimmed out with running white and carbon fiber details. A wishbone shaped bar surrounds the deep center cockpit. The covering is completely lifted off the back of the car, fully exposing the flawless rear wing showpiece. *#20 WRIGHT* is marked on the side of the car and brightly colored emblems of sponsors pepper the body.

"What do you think Sophie?" James asks.

My smile is intractable. The car is *stunning*. Every detail flows together seamlessly.

I turn to Beck; his eyes sear back into me. "I can't wait to see you drive it!" I squeal.

"She's hooked!" Coop shouts, clapping his hands.

"We're going to use Beck's car for pit stop practice in a few."

A gorgeously sun-kissed man walks through the front of the garage wearing the same collared shirt as Beck.

He looks to Beck then smiles at me.

"Luca Lombardo," he says in a thick Italian accent. "Welcome to the team." The words roll off his tongue, and I immediately remember Ella's reaction to his picture. *She would be on the floor.*

Shannon appears at the back of the garage, looking less than pleased. She signals to Beck and Luca.

"I've got to get to prep for the press conference. Do you want to stay here?" Beck asks me.

"I want to watch pit stop practice!"

"Attagirl!" Coop yells.

Several other teams' pit crews are in the pitlane performing the same exercise. One lucky mechanic is acting as Beck in the cockpit of the car. Coop has his elbow resting on a stack of thick tyres in front of the garage, stopwatch in hand. Another overseeing crew member with a stopwatch signals. Beck's car is pushed from the back and rolls toward the pit box. Twenty waiting crew members catch the car. In an instant, a jack is slid under the front. Crouched men at each corner simultaneously connect their wheel guns. *Whir! Whir!* In a flash all four tyres are ripped away immediately replaced by waiting spares. *Whir! Whir!* The car returns to the ground and the crew falls back.

"What on earth?!"

James doubles over laughing. "Don't blink! You might miss it, right?"

"It's bonkers!"

"The goal to beat is two seconds."

"3.22," the overseer calls out.

"Again!" Coop yells.

James raises his eyebrows. "See? That wasn't even a fast one!"

That wasn't fast?

———

When pit stop practice wrapped, I was glad to see a missed call from Ana. She collected me at the garage entrance and echoed Pippa's remarks about enjoying the weather while we can.

Ana's lanyard matches mine. I'm a sponge, and she's a wealth of knowledge. It's amazing to see each of the teams' hospitality suites that line the paddock—all different styles, all as *equally luxurious.*

We near one end of the paddock and Ana nods. "That's the media center."

The front door swings open, and a group of photographers step out. Ana locks her arm into mine and picks up her pace.

"Act like you're in a hurry," she says under her breath.

Huh?

Two of the photographers set their gaze on us, her arm tenses.

"Avoid eye contact," she says under her breath.

We pass by, and she exhales. "Sorry. I try to avoid the cameras when I can—*especially this week.*"

"Why's that?"

"Ren's contract negotiations were supposed to be finalized over break. Since no announcements been made, the media is stirring up rumors."

I see.

"You're lucky. They must not know who you are yet."

I pick up the pass on my lanyard. "The media is everyone with the green...?"

"Yes, *avoid the greens*," Ana says. "The blue lanyards you'll see tomorrow are for the club. Those people are *VIPs* or they coughed up several months' salary for a ticket."

Ha!

"Did you meet Pippa?"

"Briefly, yes. Are you friends with her?"

"Not really," Ana says. "You're lucky to have her though. I'm alone this year. Geoffrey usually has a girlfriend, but none of them have lasted for more than a year."

That's a high turnover...

"That's Ren's teammate," she adds. "For now."

"Is he getting a new teammate?"

"Possibly next year. It's rumored Geoff will move to another team. Ren will extend with Makellos, but he wants to wait until the ink is dry to make our big move."

"Where are you moving?"

"Monaco. It's where most drivers eventually end up. Beck will extend with Furio, right?" Ana asks.

"Oh, I don't know—"

"Surely, he will. He's been *phenomenal.*"

Beck has mentioned Monaco, and he did mention something about his contract, but I won't pretend to understand the first thing about that. Furio red does suit him well.

———

Patrizio is a gourmet chef to the masses. Every member of the team has a dinner plate fitting of a white-cloth establishment. The aromatic steam coming off my plate of lasagna is speaking directly to my soul. My phone lights up.

Ana.Wong is now following you.

I click the follow notification sending me to her profile. It's a private account, so I click the follow request button.

Beck pulls out the chair next to me.

"You and Ana really hit it off," he says.

"She's great! *Everyone* is great!" I turn my phone over.

Beck looks knackered.

"So, number twenty. Is that a number that you picked?" I ask.

He nods. "I picked it when I made it to Formula One."

"Is there some significance to it?"

He hesitates. "Yes—but it's sort of silly, I guess."

I raise my eyebrows waiting for more.

He stares back, then gives in.

"Growing up, every time I had a racing dream, I was always in a car with the number twenty on it. Strange, because twenty was never my number in karting, F3, F2—*never*. But the number always seemed to reveal itself in dreams. After so long of seeing it, finally, I searched if the number had any significant meaning."

"Does it?"

He smiles and shrugs. James and Charlie are heading our way, steaming plates in hand.

"What does it mean?" I pry.

"I read something once that it had deep meaning and represents an angel that watches over you. So ever since then, I have felt a connection to it. I mean, I need as many angels on my side as possible, right?"

I stare at him in awe. *That's deep.*

He takes my hand into his lap under the table. His eyes sear into me. *"And now I have another."*

CHAPTER 11

FLYING LAP

NEOWWW!

A flash of white flies 300 km/h down the main straight. A trail of mist is left floating beyond the pit lane fence. Now I understand Beck wanting every angel on his side that he can get. The rain yesterday during both practices didn't seem to scare anyone. The cars flew through the track at speeds over *320 km/h* down the back straight. Beck became a different person—he was intense and determined. *He was fearless.* The same person I saw this morning when he came into the garage with his racing suit unzipped, hanging around his waist. Forget the backward hat—*I have a new favorite look.*

Media day was laid back. The practice sessions were tense, but today, it's all business. *Very high stakes* business. The results from three rounds of qualifying will set the starting grid order for the race tomorrow.

I thought Ella talked fast, but the commentator on the race broadcast hardly takes a breath. He manages to keep tabs on all twenty drivers while continually spouting quick, witty banter. Between the commentary coming through the headset and James pointing things out, I think I'm understanding *half* of what's going on.

"I believe the rain is easing up," James says.

I glance at the onboard screens. A plethora of glowing buttons cover Beck's and Luca's steering wheels. The visibility from their vantage point is still horrible. It's foggy, with the added hazard of water being kicked up by the other cars on the track.

"How can they even tell where they're going?"

He laughs. "They know these tracks like the back of their hand."

NEOW! NEOWWW!

Two cars fly down the main straight. On the opposite side of the track, hundreds of fans are huddled in the covered grandstands. The broadcast fancies highlighting the hundreds of fans *without* a seat. They're as dedicated as they come, having the time of their lives in their ponchos.

"And that lap is good! Imre Bergmann clocks in eighth fastest. That'll drop Ian Matisse to P11, knocking him out in the final seconds of Q2. Qian Lui comes in twelfth fastest but will serve that five-place grid penalty tomorrow for the new gearbox."

The timer in the upper right of the broadcast flashes *0:00* in red. *BER* moves up to eighth place. *MAT* drops one position below the elimination zone line joining the four slowest drivers in this round.

The terms that fly around on the commentary—it's its own language. *Nothing* gets my attention quite like hearing Beck's voice through my headset.

"Good round, Beck! That's P6," Coop says over the radio.

"*Copy.* Coming in," Beck responds.

My heart thumps. Next to James, Charlie shifts his weight from side to side. Both Luca and Beck made it through the second round, qualifying P4 and P6, respectively. Tommy and Ren will also advance to the final round.

"Q3 is all that remains. All lap times will reset for the final ten drivers still pushing to start at the front of the grid, chasing that coveted *pole position*."

Cars grumble past our garage, coming in for the short break between sessions. Coop turns around from his station at the center island. Beck's red car pulls up, and my heart leaps. He's so close, but so far out of reach. The mechanics jack up the car and change out Beck's tyres. The noise builds as his car is rolled backward into the garage. The beaming red light on the back gets closer and closer. The car is soaked. Water droplets run down the back of his helmet. *He must be freezing.* There's commotion in both bays as Luca's car is brought in. *It's all hands on deck.* Tyre blankets are applied, and the car is wiped down. Mechanics plug numerous cables and tubes into the car. Screens are lowered in front of Beck in the cockpit.

James takes a big inhale; he pulls his headset off and rests it around his neck.

"This is it!" he says.

I pull my headset down. I *greatly* appreciate James being here—he hasn't left my side. I haven't seen Pippa all day; her headset was the only one left hanging on the rack in the hall.

"He seems to be doing well, right?"

James nods. "Given the track conditions, he's doing quite well."

The timer ticks back from twelve minutes. Multiple cars pass by in the pit lane, heading out to the track. The tyre blankets on Beck's wheels are removed, and a mechanic waves him out of the garage. The rubber squeals on the glossy floor as he pulls out into the pit lane. I lift my headset back over my ears.

> **"Finally, a break in the drizzle. But even on these out-laps you can see how much water remains on the track. DRS will remain disabled. Both Furios exit the pit lane to start their out-laps, and the Avanti of Eduardo Almada will be the first to set a lap time in Q3."**

The broadcast zooms in on the dark green Avanti, steering through turns eighteen and nineteen. A flash of deep green flies by the garage. The two navy Valor cars start their first flying laps behind Eduardo. The comparative lap time clocks roll next to each other at the bottom of the broadcast. I follow Beck's *WRI* labeled dot slowly moving along the track outline on the screen.

> **"Eduardo Almada comes across the line, setting the time to beat, but that won't hold with the flying lap coming in from the Valor of Elijah Kaplan...and it's a whole two seconds faster! It will be a fight to the end for pole. Here's his three-time world champion teammate, Leo VanBelle, coming in four-hundredths of a second faster!"**

Beck starts his flying lap with eight minutes to go. Luca flies across the line and drops Elijah to third place. Geoffrey Hahn comes in right behind him a tenth faster, taking second and dropping Luca to third. Tommy and Alek both come in ahead of Eduardo, taking fifth and sixth fastest. The broadcast pans to Beck, giving a bird's-eye view of his car.

"And here comes Beckham Wright, diving into Eau Rogue and up...*oh! He almost drops it!*"

The mechanics throw their hands to their head. The back end of Beck's car slides in the turn. James winces.

Oh shit!

The steering wheel jerks on his onboard screen then stills. Beck regains control of the car. James releases a burst of air.

"*Fuck*! I almost spun," Beck yells over the radio.

"Good save. Keep pushing," Coop replies.

Coop is cool as a cucumber, focused on the monitors at the center island.

"That complex is dangerous, *especially* when wet," James says. "He's going to want to go again. That cost him."

Beck's lap clock keeps running as he flies down the long straight along the back of the track. Ren's black Makellos is out ahead of him, also on a flying lap.

"We are hearing reports of rain in sector one. Here comes Ren across the line in that Makellos, four-tenths

slower than Elijah! And how will the Furio fare with that mistake in Eau Rouge?

"...Beck clocks in just behind Ren, staying ahead of both MACHs. They'll drop to seventh and eighth. Imre won't be happy with that first attempt. That lap puts him in ninth place behind Tommy Young."

1 VAN

2 HAH

3 LOM

4 KAP

5 ENA

6 WRI

7 KHO

8 YOU

9 BER

10 ALM

"Stay out, Beck, let's go for another," Coop instructs.

"Copy," Beck calls.

"Light rain is making an appearance once again. Several drivers have stayed out. A few have come into the pits

before another attempt. How much can these lap times improve in these final minutes of Q3?"

The camera moves from the pit lane action to Eduardo starting another flying lap. Luca's tyres screech, pulling out of his garage bay to our left.

"Here's Eduardo, hoping to improve his time, currently in tenth place. Up the hill to turn three...*And he's off!*"

Eduardo's car slides off the track and slams to a stop, crushing into the red and yellow track wall.

"*And into the wall!* The same corner Beckham Wright made his mistake and....We've got a red flag!"

The broadcast hovers over Eduardo's mangled car. He lifts himself out of the cockpit. Somehow, the man appears unharmed. The car is a mess—one of the tyres is completely detached. *Geez. That could have been Beck.*

A crew of track marshals descend onto the crash site. Beck and others pass slowly through the corner.

The radio fires up in the headset. "Is he ok?" Beck asks.

"Yes, he is up and out of the car," Coop reports.

"This could be it—with the deteriorating conditions, every driver did get at least one lap time...

"...and race control has made their call! Q3 will end here with that incident."

The mechanics stand and begin high fiving.

"Good run, Beck. They've called it. That's P6 for tomorrow," Coop says.

"*Ugh...*" Beck groans over the radio.

Luca will start in P3 and Beck in P6. I pull my headset down.

James's eyes are wide. "Beck got lucky."

"Is it over for Eduardo?"

"No, they'll get him rebuilt for tomorrow."

"They can fix that mess of a car by *tomorrow*?"

James nods. "It's amazing what they can do."

The rain's picked up. Mechanics and team personnel flow out of the garage entrance, making a run for the suite. Down the way, umbrellas are handed to drivers exiting the official's garage. Cameramen and photographers are ready and waiting with tents covering their equipment. A cold drop of rain hits my wrist, standing my arm hair up on its end.

"Let's get inside. Beck will be in after he gets through that media mob," James says.

We wait for a break in the traffic then take off for the suite. A few steps from the door, I catch the scent of something divinely sweet.

The dining room is packed with team members seeking shelter from the rain. Everyone has a cup of tea in hand and a tiny dessert plate.

James's eyes light up. "What is that smell?"

I shake my head. "I could smell it outside!"

We steer through the crowd to the source. The kitchen staff has stocked the back counter with hot tea. Beside the steaming cups, plates holding bite size Belgian waffles dusted in powdered sugar. The plates quickly disappear from the counter. We step forward, next in line. James grabs two plates and hands one to me. Only three plates remain on the counter. The little saucer warms my hands. James takes his waffle down in one bite.

"Oh *my God*," he says, chewing.

The waffle is so hot off the press the powdered sugar is melting down the ridges.

"I'll be right back," I say. "I'm going to save this for Beck."

Upstairs, his driver's room door is open. I set the waffle down on the desk and open the cabinet for my purse. Dad texted an hour ago, letting me know he's watching qualifying. I'd never seen a more jealous face than the one I got after I told him I'd be watching from the *garage*.

"What are you doing in here?!" a voice booms.

I scream and throw my hand over my mouth. I whip around to find Beck standing in the doorway. His face is red, and his hair is a mess; he's smiling ear to ear. I lower my hand to my chest and calm my breathing.

"*Not* funny!"

Beck enters; the top of his race suit hangs around his hips. The skintight underlayer grips the muscles of his chest. He puts his arms out for me. I grab the plate from the desk and quickly bring it between us.

His eyes jump from me to the waffle and back up again.

"I saved you something."

He picks the waffle up from the saucer and bites into it. His eyes close as he chews. A smile grows on his lips as he puts the last bite to his mouth.

He grabs my waist and pulls my hips to his.

I squeal and toss the plate down on the desk before his lips find mine. My mouth waters, tasting the melting sugar on his bottom lip.

He pulls back and opens his eyes. "I love having you here."

My stomach flutters. "I love *being* here."

"What's your favorite part?"

I contemplate a moment, *but the answer is easy.* "My headset."

"The headset?" He asks, surprised.

"I love that I can hear your voice."

His eyes flicker and he pulls me closer.

"I was sad I couldn't watch you go around again."

"I know, not the best qualifying. Don't worry, you'll get forty-four laps tomorrow."

I press my finger into his chest. "You gave me a scare out there."

"You didn't like my little power slide?"

I shake my head.

"Eddie didn't get away with his."

"Don't you ever get scared?"

"Scared? *Nah*, the rain only adds to the challenge." He pauses. "You know, I think you need to come back for a sunny race."

My heart jumps.

"I know you've got your show coming up, but I want to have you out next weekend to Monza."

I can't hold back my smile. *Why am I even trying?*

"It's the team's home race, *and* everyone will be there—Mum, Dad, *the kids.*"

"I wouldn't miss it."

I follow Beck down the hall. He drops my hand and leans inside one of the office doors. Two women are seated behind monitors. *Travel & Logistics* is etched into the signage outside.

"Lena?" Beck says.

The blonde woman looks up from her computer.

"Can we get Sophie setup with badges for next weekend?"

"Of course!" she says. She glances at me. "Do you need travel?"

Uh?

"No. She'll come out with me; I'll get her back home."

Lena smiles. "All the Wrights still coming, yes?"

Beck nods. "It will be a full house."

Showered and warm, I climb into bed and resume Beck's assignment. I screenshot the one-way flight home from Milan next Sunday. I'll take the jet out there with him, but he's staying the week at headquarters after the race.

I text him the flight details screenshot.

> Will this work?

> That should be perfect.

When I finish checking out through the airline app, I write him back:

> Ticket secured!

My message goes from delivered to read before he's FaceTiming me. Beck's room is dark, and he's already lying down.

"Sophie, I told you to *pick the flight,* not *buy* the flight. You should have let me do that."

Oh? No, I'm not helpless. "You're already giving me a ride there!"

He shakes his head.

"Now go to sleep." I blow him a kiss before ending the call.

I'm too excited to sleep just yet. *I must tell the girls.*

"Look where we are!" Ella shouts. The FaceTime camera flips around to a familiar, quaint dining room. It's our favorite restaurant in Le Marais. The camera flips back to Ella and Carmen's faces.

"Soph, come home! We miss you!" Carmen says.

"I miss you more…" I pause. "But it's going to be awhile before I'm home."

Their eyes grow wide.

"We fly back to London Monday, but we're leaving Wednesday for the Italian Grand Prix."

I can barely get the words out I'm smiling so hard.

Carmen's jaw drops.

"I take it things are going well, then?" Ella asks.

"It's amazing. *Beck's amazing.* I still can't believe all of this is happening."

"You deserve it," Ella says. "All of it."

"This race is going to be *big.* His whole family will be there—Mum, Dad, brother, sister."

"That says so much that he wants you there! With *them!*" Carmen says.

"I suppose...so start brainstorming. I need a whole new lineup of outfits!"

CHAPTER 12

Is That Rain? Or Champagne?

I PEEK DOWN AT my feet while passing the graphic of Beck and Luca to avoid blushing.

"Did you enjoy qualifying?" Pippa asks.

"It was intense!"

"Sorry I wasn't there; I wasn't feeling well yesterday."

We pause at the comms display in the garage hall to retrieve our headsets.

Both garage bays are empty, and the fencing between the pit lane and main straight is open. The cars are hardly visible on the starting grid due to the number of mechanics and personnel surrounding them.

"And just like that, the rain stops." I smile at James.

"Hopefully, the cork holds for the next two hours," he says.

The prerace broadcast hovers over the start line. All twenty cars are staggered in their grid positions—including Eduardo's car, *as if his wreck never happened.*

A trace of red pulls my attention away from the screen. Beck and Luca are heading our way. I swallow. *My word,* Beck looks divine all suited up and race ready. My visual feast is interrupted by a shrill screech as Pippa drags a stool to our post at the back of the garage.

"Sophie's first race." Beck winks. "You ready?"

My insides combust. I want to grab hold of the collar of his racing suit. Is it possible I have as much adrenaline running through me as he does? James leans over the monitors and pats Beck on the back before Charlie takes him aside.

Charlie places a hand on his shoulder, and Beck stays fixed on Charlie's words.

James leans down. "Final pep talk."

It's showtime. The camera pans to all twenty drivers standing shoulder to shoulder at the start line as a man belts the Belgian national anthem. Low, stormy clouds paint the backdrop in the broadcast. Maybe I'm biased, but the red of our racing suits is the standout showstopper. Thousands of fans applaud as the anthem ends, setting off a flurry of action. Masses of team members and mechanics migrate from the start line back to the garages. The camera zooms in on pole position. *Three-time world champion* displays next to Leo VanBelle's name as he pulls his helmet over his racing cap. Leo climbs into his navy Valor as the cameras move down the starting grid.

Every driver has taken their seat. The cars are fully visible, and only a handful of mechanics securing tyre blankets remain on track. My heart takes off as the camera moves to a head-on shot of Beck's car. The visor of his helmet is still open, and his eyes are focused and intense.

I pull on my headset and Coop's voice immediately fills my ears.

"Thirty second warning."

Beck flips his visor down. The broadcast hovers over the main straight. The tyre blankets are pulled. The remaining mechanics make final adjustments, fitting the cars perfectly into their grid position.

"Though the rain has stopped, the threat still looms here at Spa-Francorchamps. Each driver is starting on the intermediate tyres, but how quickly will the teams pit for slicks? It will be fascinating to see the pit stop strategies play out when the track starts to dry. Three hundred and eighty thousand in attendance for the first race, post summer break."

Three hundred and eighty *thousand?*

James leans down, and I lift my right headphone. "First, they'll do a formation lap."

I nod. A *what?*

The clock hand strikes three p.m. on the broadcast. One by one, the cars pull out of their positions, zigzagging down the main straight behind a luxury sports car. The conditions are better than qualifying, but a considerable amount of water is still being kicked up behind the cars.

Overhead, the broadcast follows the cars winding through lush hills. Bright yellow and red stripes along the track edges sharply contrast the saturated, deep green forest. Every grandstand is jam-packed. The standing spectator areas are shoulder to shoulder. It's a mix of colors, each fan decked out in their chosen team's gear. It's a welcome sight from yesterday's view of thousands of open umbrellas.

The cars pull through the tight set of corners at the end of the circuit. Final zigzags are made before they slowly pull back into their positions behind the start line.

"Final check," Coop says calmly over the radio.

I glance up at Coop, manning his station at the center island.

"Copy," Beck responds.

"Last car on the grid, Beck."

James flashes me a thumbs up. My stomach tenses. Five lights above the start line illuminate red one by one then flash off.

"And it's lights out and away we go for the Belgian Grand Prix!"

The commentator shouts frantically as the cars fly down the main straight to the hairpin of turn one.

"Great start off the line for the Furio of Luca Lombardo. He jumps ahead of Geoffrey Hahn! The MACH falls back, the Holt of Ian Matisse gains a position!"

The cars brake, bunching up as they steer into turn one, some two, and even three, cars wide. Pippa winces.

"There's contact! Between Luca Lombardo and Geoffrey Hahn!"

I search for Beck's car in the madness. *It's chaos.* The commentator's talking a mile a minute. Beck pulls through the corner; he's directly behind Ren, charging toward *Eau Rouge*.

"Valor in one-two after that contact between the Furio and Makellos. Luca's dropped to sixth—he looks to have a bit of front wing damage from that contact in

**turn one. Ren and Beck manage to steer clear, taking
third and fourth.”**

James grits his teeth. “Luca will come in.”

The mechanics jump into action, readying the spare front wing for
Luca’s car. The standings on the screen shift.

1 VAN

2 KAP

3 ENA

4 WRI

5 HAH

6 LOM

7 KHO

8 ALM

9 YOU

10 BER

**“Both Geoffrey and Luca are being called to the pits.
Luca with visible wing damage, and they have tyres
waiting as well. Are they already taking a gamble with
slicks?”**

The navy Valors roar down the main straight ahead. I watch Beck’s
onboard as he crosses the start line behind Ren. *Lap 2/44*. Luca’s and
Geoffrey’s names tumble down the standings as they enter the pit lane.

"Gap?" Beck yells.

"Ren 1.6 ahead," Coop reports.

Geoffrey's car passes in front of our garage. Our mechanics are crouched, ready and waiting with new tyres. They brace and catch Luca's car. In an instant, the car is lifted, the damaged front wing is removed and replaced while each tyre is changed out. Luca's car hits the ground and screeches off. Pippa applauds.

"That was a good one!"

James nods. "The tyres they put him on don't have tread like the intermediates, *much* faster but slippery in the wet."

I watch Luca's onboard; he exits the pit lane hot on Geoffrey's heels.

"Both teams rolling the dice early, swapping for slicks. Will they provide enough grip? They'll rejoin the track behind Qian Liu in nineteenth and twentieth. Both went for the hard tyre compound; they want the speed when the track dries, but until then, they must carefully maneuver the wetter sections of the circuit. At the front of the pack, the Valors have pulled away from Ren and Beck."

Coop comes over the radio. "Beck, we've put Luca on slicks. We'll see how they perform."

"Weather?" Beck asks.

"Rain's still hovering in the area, but we've got a good window."

"Copy. Seems it might grip up fairly quick."

The clouds that have been sitting on the trees for the past two days have lifted. For the first time, I'm seeing the track without fog or significant cloud cover. *It's almost getting sunny.*

Lap 8/44. Luca and Geoff struggled at first, but now they have the advantage on the slick tyres. Both easily pass Wit Nowak's pink Noorden, speeding over 320 km/h down the *Kemmel straight*. The spray off the back of the cars on this section of track has weakened to a slight mist. In other segments, dry lines are visible.

"Box, Beck. Box!" Coop instructs.

"Copy!" Beck yells.

"We've finally caught a break! That's the sun peeking out for the first time since Thursday! Both Valors have swapped for slicks, with several others calling to box...

"... And the call's been made: DRS will be enabled next lap."

The pit crew's assembled as Beck screeches into the pit box, and his pit stop clock takes off. His new rubber hits the pavement. *2.4 seconds.* Pure magic. I barely catch a glimpse of his helmet as he flashes by the garage. The pit stops have shuffled the standings. Beck rejoins the track in P7 just three places ahead of Luca, who's pushed back up to the midfield. The pit stops have built more separation between the twenty cars.

James points to the letters on the standings. The final *I* on the screen switches to *M*.

"Now everyone's off the *inters*. It's a mix, you see. Some teams went for the medium tyre and some went for hard. Mediums can be faster, but hards last longer."

I check the letter next to WRI and LOM—both Beck and Luca are on the hard tyres.

The Valors are unstoppable; they've retaken the lead by a considerable margin. Beck's flying on the slick tyres—he's picked his way back up to fourth place. Luca's still chasing after Geoff's Makellos.

"Furio said they were bringing upgrades to Spa, and they've delivered. Beckham Wright is having a phenomenal drive, now within DRS range of the MACH. He was strong before break—just missing out on a podium at his home race in Silverstone, but here he is today, the lead Furio, pushing the car to the limit."

The broadcast displays a head-on view of Alek's orange MACH speeding down the main straight. Directly behind him, the flap in the back wing of Beck's car opens. Beck's speed increases, and he veers left, easily overtaking Alek's MACH. The grandstands roar, and the garage crew erupts, as Beck moves up to third place with only the Valors ahead. I smile. *D-R-S*.

Lap 31 of 44. Charlie puts his arms behind his back and begins swaying side to side.

"...And Alek has been called to the pits. The whole front of the grid is still grinding away on that first set of slicks, but Elijah Kaplan is starting to struggle. Let's

see if he'll pit this lap. Most of the midfield's completed their final pit in a two-stop strategy."

"I'm losing these tyres, Coop!" Beck shouts.

"Understood. Stick with plan A for now. We'll reassess in two laps."

"Copy."

James looks worried. "They're keeping Beck out," he says. "You're required to use two tyre compounds. We used *inters*, and we're on hards, so a one stop *is* possible. Luca's a master at tyre management...Beck's not as good."

"And he does! One Valor comes in, Leo stays out. And again! Beck stays out, moving up into second place. Ren comes in as well, advancing Tommy Young to third and Imre Bergmann to fourth. Geoffrey Hahn and Luca remain out, nursing all they can get out of those thirty-lap-old hard tyres.

"...With Beck not pitting, is Furio aiming for a one stop strategy for both of their drivers? I imagine that was not initially the plan, but given Luca's early incident, they want to hold Beck's position."

1 VAN

2 WRI

3 YOU

4 BER

5 HAH

6 LOM

7 KAP – IN PIT

8 KHO – IN PIT

9 ENA – IN PIT

10 ALM

Pippa isn't fazed; she keeps her focus on Luca's onboard. The pit lane ahead is busy. James chews his lips, and Charlie folds his arms across his chest and begins swaying harder. The wear on Beck's front tyres is visible in his onboard. Speeding 150-plus km/h through corners repeatedly has eaten away at the tyres' integrity.

"Can his tyres last thirteen more laps?"

James grits his teeth.

But he's in second place!

The broadcast jumps to Tommy's car, battling the same white car he's held off for multiple laps. Side by side, they drift into the corner. The white car smacks into Tommy's, and a puff of smoke appears around the tyres.

"*There's contact!* Turn fourteen!"

The white car veers, flying off into the gravel. Tommy's car shifts side to side, losing traction but stays on track.

"We have contact! Imre Bergmann is off at *Stavelot*!"

Oh no!

A yellow flag banner appears across the screen. The garage crew springs to their feet.

"Box, Beck! Box!" Coop quickly instructs.

Everyone throws their fists in the air, James included.

Tommy's car is slightly banged up, but Imre's is beached in the gravel with a smashed front corner. Geoffrey and Luca steer through the few pieces of debris on the track.

"Look alive!" Coop shouts. "We're double-stacking this!"

James takes a massive sigh of relief. "Our *hope* strategy worked!" He says excitedly. "We just got a *free pit stop*!"

"And it will be a full safety car! Our race leader Leo dives for the pit lane. This just got interesting for team Furio—you've got both your drivers in perfect track position to take a desperately needed pit. They've got luck on their side today."

The pit crew quickly assembles outside with two sets of tyres. Leo's car passes in the pit lane. *He got lucky too.* Beck's car screeches in and is jacked up. Geoffrey's Makellos grumbles past our garage.

The broadcast hovers over the busy pit lane. Leo takes off for the pit exit. Beck's car hits the ground and takes off. The pit box immediately fills as Luca pulls in. Beck passes Geoffrey's car as it's lowered to the ground.

"Beautiful!" James yells. He high fives Charlie ecstatically.

Beck follows Leo, rejoining the track, and Luca takes off after Geoffrey. The mechanics celebrate. Pippa's all smiles. *Damn, that was impressive.*

"The first four drivers rejoin the track on *softs*. Magnificent double-pit for Furio! We've got a few more coming in under the safety car, giving themselves a chance to chase on fresh rubber."

The final few cars pass by Imre, who's still beached outside turn fourteen. A few midfield cars come in for a *third* pit stop. Others stay out and join the lineup behind the safety car. I'm understanding our luck. Most of the grid lost time pitting before the incident, *but what if the incident hadn't happened?!*

The broadcast moves to Tommy's car in the pit lane. The pit crew begins to wheel his car backward into the MACH garage.

"Devastating ending for half of team MACH, as they are forced to retire Tommy Young's car."

Poor Tommy! The broadcast replays the contact between him and Imre. Marshals have cleared the debris from the track.

A crew is at the crash site, and Imre is out of the car with his arms folded.

James leans down. "They'll drive at a reduced speed behind the safety car until Imre's car is removed. No overtaking behind the safety car."

Lap 36/44.

Imre's car is gone. The cars zigzag wildly behind the safety car. The tension's building.

Coop comes over the radio. "Safety car ending this lap, Beck."

James rubs his palms together. "They're getting the tyres warmed up again."

My heart rate spikes back up to race pace.

"In comes the safety car, and we are back! Leo will restart the race…."

Leo zigzags down the main straight then floors it, breaking away into turn one.

"…and here we go for the final eight laps of the Belgian Grand Prix!"

Beck's holding onto second place but remains outside the one second DRS window. Charlie is stone-faced—his eyes are glued to Beck's onboard. The real battle is happening behind Beck, where Luca has tried to overtake Geoffrey twice but remains in fourth.

James is sweating bullets. He repeatedly leans over, monitoring a radar screen to our right. A large green mass inches its way closer to the track on the radar.

"What's the weather doing, Coop?" Beck asks. "It's dark back here on the straight."

"Rain should be holding out for now," Coop reports.

"Copy."

My stomach tenses. The sky ahead in Beck's onboard has returned to a familiar, dark smoky gray.

"It's down to the final two laps of the Belgian Grand Prix. A quarter of the grid, who threw on softs, have got to be praying this rain holds off."

"Gap?" Beck yells.

"Leo 1.8 ahead."

"Is this everything we have?"

"Yes. Full push to the end, Beck."

"I'm trying!" Beck yells.

It's getting darker by the second. Leo and Beck rip down the main straight. James nervously sways side to side.

"We're down to the final lap! Beckham Wright is set to make his best finish of the season, still chasing the Valor of Leo VanBelle!"

My anxiety is through the roof. The broadcast moves, monitoring tight battles in the midfield. Leo's car remains just ahead in Beck's onboard.

James and Charlie start a steady bounce. The broadcast jumps as Leo and Beck speed toward the final chicane. The mechanics bolt out of the garage across the pit lane. Every fan is on their feet as Leo's car rips down the main straight. The mechanics cling onto the pit lane fencing, pumping their fists in the air.

"The chequered flag flies! Here comes your winner of this year's Belgian Grand Prix, Leo VanBelle!"

James and Charlie bounce wildly. Beck's car roars past. *It's second place!* James picks up Charlie in a bear hug.

"...and Beckham Wright crosses the line, taking second!

"Nice push Beck! P2!" Coop yells.
"*Let's go!*" Beck shouts.
Coop turns from his station and throws his hands in the air.

"But it's a battle for third! He's closed the gap—Luca's putting so much pressure on Geoff, diving into the bus stop chicane!"

Pippa's white knuckled, gripping the edge of her stool.

"*Ah!* It's a lock up! Geoff goes wide! Luca dives ahead into turn nineteen, barely avoiding contact there!"

Pippa's off her stool; one hand comes over her mouth, and she grabs my wrist with the other. *Luca's up to third!* I bounce up and down alongside her.

"Now Geoff's chasing Luca to the line! Who will take that final podium position?"

The grandstands *erupt*. The garage is a mad house of celebrations.

"Luca's got it!"

"That's a double podium, y'all!" Coop cries out.

James throws his arms around me. He removes his headset and hands it to a woman who's frantically collecting them on her arm. I pull mine off. The garage is chaos. The remaining cars soar down the main straight, finishing the race.

"This way!" James yells, taking my arm. I follow him out of the front of the garage. It's a flurry of Furio and Valor team members rushing down the pit lane. I lose Pippa.

My heart's knocking in my chest as James pulls me deeper into the crowd congregated around the fencing in front of the official's garages. Leo's car grumbles in, parking behind the first-place flag. Through the crowd, I catch a glimpse of red as Beck's and Luca's cars roll by. It's shoulder to shoulder, a sea of red high fiving James.

Leo stands up in the cockpit of his car and throws his fist in the air. The Valor crew to our left erupts. Leo jumps down. Cameras follow him as he runs to the fencing and throws his arms around his team members, celebrating his first-place finish.

I push up to my tiptoes and watch the back of Beck's helmet. He places the detached steering wheel on the front of the car and hoists himself up out of the cockpit. James pulls me to the front of the fencing between him and Coop.

"How's that for a race, Sophie?!" Coop yells, putting his arm around me. Beck jumps down beside his car, and he turns around with his visor open and scans the surrounding crowd. A shockwave ripples from my chest as I lock eyes with him and his search stops.

Beck bolts toward the fence. Time slows to a crawl as I realize he found the one thing he was looking for—*me*.

I throw my arms around Beck's neck as he catches me midair beyond the fence. Droves of hands slap the top of his helmet and shoulders. My feet return to the ground as he pulls James and Coop into a group hug around me. Releasing us, Beck continues down the line, celebrating with the other members of the team. Luca comes up behind him. They throw their arms around each other, and the team goes *absolutely bonkers*. There's no stopping the tears rolling down my face watching them celebrate. I've never witnessed anything like this—I'm completely overcome.

James's arm hugs around me. "It gets me every time," he says, wiping his eyes.

Beck pulls his helmet and cap off; his beaming face is red, sweaty and *divine*. He reaches for the hat that's been laid out for him and pulls it on over his mess of hair.

A microphone is placed in Luca's hand. A woman stands before him and the cameras surround them.

"Congratulations, Luca, on third place! Unbelievable overtake in the final chicane! You battled the entire race after that first contact and pushed your way back through the entire pack to make the podium."

Luca is beaming, nodding along to her remarks.

"I knew we had the pace. I was lucky to come out with minor damage in lap one. From there, Geoff and I were back and forth the whole time. When he went wide, I saw the opening. I made my move and somehow held onto it!"

"You held onto it! Completing a dream double podium finish for Furio! Congratulations!"

Luca hands the microphone to Beck and pats him on the back.

Beck's face lights up as he lifts the microphone.

"Beck, great race out there today! Congratulations on P2—your best ever finish in Formula One."

Beck nods proudly, his eyes absolutely sparkling.

"What were you thinking in those laps with everyone coming in for fresh tyres, and the team insisting you stay out?"

"I was struggling. But I trust this team with all my heart to make the right strategy calls, and *boy,* did we get lucky with that safety car. So incredibly proud of the team."

James and I move with the crowd beneath the podium stage, located above the garages that extends out over the pit lane. Suited trophy presenters wait on stage. Massive bottles of champagne sit at each platform. Luca and Beck walk out, glowing. They step up onto the second- and third-place platforms. The crowd goes wild as Leo walks out onto the podium, waving. He takes his place on the first-place platform in the center of the stage.

The three of them remove their hats as everyone quiets for the national anthem that plays for Leo. I stare up at Beck on the podium. This must be what Carmen feels when Oliver steps behind his decks. A drop of rain hits my eyelash, another splats on my red satin blouse. I glance at James.

"There's the rain we saw!" he whispers.

The anthem ends, and the boys pull their hats back on. The trophies are passed out, starting with Luca's. Beck shakes the presenter's hand then holds up the second-place trophy in the air. Large drops of rain start to pepper everyone in the crowd. Leo holds up his first-place trophy, and the crowd goes wild once more.

A race jingle plays over the speakers as red and yellow confetti bursts from cannons on the podium. The three of them quickly set their trophies down and reach for the champagne bottles. Beck and Luca turn to each other, shaking their bottles violently. Beck ducks his head as Luca points his champagne blast right at Beck's face. Sprays of champagne fall onto us as confetti flutters overhead. Luca brings his bottle to his lips. It's pure magic—*I'm hooked*. This is the greatest sporting event I've ever witnessed.

James shouts, "We might be able to catch Beck before the podium press conference."

We weave through the crowd and make our way back through the garage to the paddock. You can smell it back here, fresh rain absorbing into the pavement. It's a media frenzy. Twenty different camera crews are stationed in a media pen, interviewing drivers. Another mass of crews wait in front of us for the podium finishers to exit.

Leo walks out, gaining the attention of almost every camera. Beck walks out with Luca. They're both *soaked*. Shannon takes her place beside them and the remaining cameras close in on the Furio duo.

Somehow, Beck notices James's call in the madness. Beck dodges bodies, veering over to us. The traffic breaks; Beck holds his arms out and studies my chest.

"Is that rain or champagne?" he yells.

I look down at my spotted blouse. "Both!"

I jump into his arms and our lips meet. He's a bitter, salty mixture of sweat and champagne.

Rejoining Luca and Shannon, Beck scoops his arm around me and James. A mass of cameras follow us as we walk past the media pen. James holds his phone out in front of Beck, where a woman smiles on FaceTime. *Beck's mum.*

"P2!" Beck yells.

She pumps her fist, celebrating.

"Lucky charm!" Beck says, squeezing around my waist.

His mum waves fanatically. "I can't wait to meet you!"

She's beautiful.

"Next weekend!" Beck yells.

Her mouth drops open; beside her, a young girl and darling little boy wave.

"I gotta go!" Beck yells, waving at the screen.

My smile is *uncontrollable.* James pulls the phone back and steps aside.

Beck keeps his arm tight around me.

I shake my head. "I'm dating a star!"

Beck stares down at me and his eyes are wild. "We're not dating, Sophie. *You're mine.*"

Beck releases me. He breaks away, following Shannon and Luca into the media center. I stop in my tracks, and the cameras continue past me. His words repeat, echoing over and over.

CHAPTER 13

Joining the Circus

The jet lifts off the Liège airport runway. *I'll never forget my first F1 race.* I'm still staring at Beck in awe. Incredibly talented driver aside, if this weekend's shown me anything, it's shown me the kind of man he is. You'd think he'd be a cocky, arrogant asshole, but he's quite down to earth, so humble, so *normal*. I'm absolutely blown away by the whole operation. I'm not sure what I was expecting from the weekend, but it certainly wasn't this.

Ren came in sixth. Ana took me under her wing when James left for the airport last night. I stayed with her and watched the postrace interviews while Beck partook in the podium press conference.

"We haven't had a double podium since *Montreal* last year," Beck says.

He's smiling, clicking through pictures from last night on his laptop. When the press conference let out, the entire team gathered for a photo in front of the garage. Beck and Luca stood on either side of a pit board with their names, *Beck P2* and *Luca P3*.

"You said you'd show me a good race," I tease.

Across the aisle Charlie laughs. "You got it all! Rain, a safety car and a podium! We've really pulled ahead of MACH now."

"*Oh gosh*, have you spoken with Tommy?"

"He's still cursing Imre's name," Beck laughs.

"They were flying into that turn! I don't know what Imre was thinking!"

Beck smiles. "You think that was fast—wait for this weekend. *Monza* is the fastest track on the calendar."

"Faster than here?"

"They don't call it the *Temple of Speed* for nothing."

It's a whirlwind. Back to London for forty-eight hours until we're off again. One race in, and I'm already hooked.

"I can't wait. It will keep me distracted from thinking about the show."

Beck clicks the calendar icon on the task bar.

"What day is the show?"

I point to the screen. "Sunday, the seventeenth."

Beck runs the cursor over the dates, and a smile grows across his lips. "Have you ever been to Singapore?"

My heart skips.

"I know it's a lot of scheduling, but the Sunday after your show is the Singapore Grand Prix."

There's no way. I stare at him in disbelief.

Beck shrugs. "Even if you don't come for the whole stint, I'd love to have you there."

My whole body's *buzzing*. Beck moves his laptop to my lap, and I fire up a browser window. Nothing but divine intervention can explain it, but *I could pull it off*. The London show is the Sunday between Monza and Singapore. I'd have just enough time to make it back for the show in Paris.

I turn the laptop to him. "This could work!"

Beck narrows his eyes at the screen. "*Woah, woah*. That's a thirteen-hour flight," he says. "I'm not letting you sit in economy."

I gulp. *You're not?*

He picks up the laptop and moves it back to his lap. He clicks *modify*. "At least let me get you business class—you'll have your own little pod."

I'm speechless.

"You're not buying this one." Beck shakes his head.

He moves the selection from economy to business class and advances to the next screen.

My head's spinning.

Beck winks. "You're officially joining the traveling circus."

"What *exactly* did he say?" Ella asks, stabbing into her room service breakfast.

"He said, 'We're not dating. *You're mine.*'"

Carmen squeals in the three-way FaceTime.

Ella shakes her head. "This is moving quite fast."

For the first time all summer, our *Roomie Trio* is holding the fort down in three different countries. Carmen's in Paris, and Ella arrived in New York City last night for fashion week.

"I can't believe you're going to Singapore!" Carmen shrieks.

"Singapore, yes, but this week too! I am meeting the rest of his family on Saturday!"

I pull the red beaded crop top from Spain out of my wardrobe.

I flip the FaceTime camera around. "Can I wear this? I love this top."

"With some high-waisted trouser shorts, I approve!" Carmen says.

Good memories in this top. And I can surprise the brand with a photo. *Look at me being an influencer.*

Ella nods. "Check my closet, Sophie. There's a cute white sundress with tags still on it."

"*Perfect.* I think I'll have enough to cover this weekend. Then I can reup my outfits in Paris before Singapore."

"I can't believe both of you have boyfriends," Ella whines. "I'm on the hunt this week, and I'm not leaving this city without a date."

"It's New York City—it's got to be crawling with eligible businessmen," Carmen says.

Ella raises her eyebrows. "Yeah—like *Fredrick?*"

Alarm bells fire inside me.

***

Tuesday evening, I take a cab across the bridge to stay the night with Beck. We leave for Milan in the morning. He's seen my place, *for all of five minutes*, it's time to see his. I was glad to have a day at the flat to breathe and catch up with Dad. He watched the race at home but was amused at my attempt to retell and breakdown the action from my perspective.

I step out of the cab in front of the newly constructed modern mid-rise. "This is fancy!"

"*Way* too fancy for me." Beck reaches for me and brings me against his chest.

The lift opens to a short hallway with a single door at each end. Beck pushes open the tall walnut door and wheels my bag inside. My footsteps echo on the concrete floor. It's silent. The ceiling must be six meters high. Besides a couch and two stools at the counter, the ultra-modern flat is completely bare.

"What do you think?" Beck asks.

I scan the room for more; there's not a single thing on the counters in the kitchen.

"Beck, there's barely anything in here."

"I know…I have so much shopping to do." He smiles. "But I'm hardly ever here."

"It's a beautiful…*shell*."

"You have to help me!" Beck laughs.

"I can do that."

I pass the kitchen and head for the wall of black paned windows. Leaning against the wall, are three stacks of large, framed art. *Here's something.* I tilt one of the frames upright, revealing a similar piece behind it. They're blown-up prints of the tracks. Every frame is perfectly uniform.

"Mum had these done. She was horrified when she came here and the room echoed."

Should I tell him it still echoes?

I pull forward another frame to see the print behind.

"There's Spa…" he says.

Circuit de Spa-Francorchamps. I watched him trace along that outline all weekend. The shape of that track is permanently burned into my brain.

"These are great." I smile. "We must get them hung!"

I spot each corner of the room—*empty*.

"Where is your trophy?"

"The trophies go back with the team. They're put in the shrine at headquarters," he says.

Beck opens the balcony door. The nearly set sun has illuminated the underside of the sheet of clouds. I peer over the railing to the street. The balcony of the unit below is outfitted with three chairs.

Beck rests his forearms on the railing. His place is so bare it's *funny*. I can at least bring him a plant next time I'm over.

Something that can fend for itself.

"Are you all recharged to go again?" I ask.

Beck nods. "Got a few workouts in with Charlie and picked up the laundry. Also had a call with Shannon. She brought up a good point."

I wait.

"Since it's the team's home race, there will be lots of media attention around our camp. It's possible you'll be approached."

Approached by the greens?

"Are you okay with that?"

"I-I guess so," I say. "Why would they approach me?"

Beck scans me up and down. "You're quite hard to miss."

I roll my eyes.

"They no doubt saw you last weekend. They might simply ask your name."

I nod.

"Nothing crazy," he assures. "The fans on the other hand—it's like nothing you've ever seen."

"Your dad taught me quite a lot. I'm excited to meet the rest of your family—"

"Mia's the only scary one."

"The sweet girl waving in the FaceTime?"

Beck nods. "She's a *killer*. Twelve going on twenty-five."

He pushes back from the railing. "I'll finish the tour now."

Beck wheels my bag through the living room. The carpet in his bedroom dulls the echo *a bit*. It's a grand room with a huge, plushy bed.

There's a dresser and two nightstands with absolutely nothing on top. The only color in the room is a row of helmets queued up against the wall.

I set my makeup bag beside one of the double sinks in the bathroom. It could be a hotel—the bottles in the shower actually look out of place.

Beck stops in the bathroom doorway; his face is serious. "Maybe we should stay at your place..."

Oh gosh!

"Beck, your place is great! I love it! That reminds me—I have something of yours."

I walk back into the bedroom and lay my suitcase down flat. Everything but the shirt is tightly packed for the jet in the morning. I grab his white T-shirt, and I hold it out to him.

"I've had this since Spain. I'm sorry it's taken this long to get it back to you."

Beck's eyes fall to the shirt and slowly trail back up to mine. *I know that look.* His hand grips around my wrist, he pulls me under him.

"*I want you to keep it.*"

I tilt my head up, and his lips hover over mine.

My breath quickens. "You should know...it still echoes in here."

"*Well*, we'll have to keep it down, then, won't we?"

CHAPTER 14
PARTING THE RED SEA

WE'VE BEEN TRANSPORTED TO Furio land. All is red as far as the eye can see. Joe *creeps* the car through a sea of red surrounding the street into the track. Beck's arms hang out of the passenger seat window, signing anything fans hold out to him. Joe flashes me a smile in the rearview mirror. Apart from Luca, Beck is the hottest celebrity in town. This is *mad.* So much that it's a little scary.

Reprieve—the gates are ahead. One of Beck's arms comes back into the car; he waves a final time as the window rolls up. Beck snaps the cap back on the marker and tosses it into the cupholder. He turns around in the front seat.

"I warned you."

"I was waiting for someone to hold out their baby for you to sign."

Charlie and Joe laugh.

"Luca's probably done that," Beck says. He leans back and pulls his phone out of his pocket and holds it up to his ear.

"Sorry, we're pulling up now." He pauses. "We got held up *parting the red sea.*"

Beck ends the call then turns back. "Shannon." He grins. "We're *late.*"

Beep! A green message flashes behind my pass at the swipe gates. Beck reaches for my hand; I fall in line and try to keep up with his and Charlie's pace.

Beck waves quickly at the media gathered inside of the gates. We turn into the paddock, where Shannon's standing outside the Furio fortress with her hands on her hips. Luca waits next to her. *It's all here.* In a matter of days, the luxury paddock from Belgium has been magically reestablished in Italy.

Beck chuckles. "We're in trouble."

Our pace picks up.

"I've got to go—I'm sorry about the rush." He leans in and kisses my cheek.

Luca waves. I stop in front of the suite as Beck marches on. I take a deep breath; I've worked up an appetite *and a sweat.* The suite doors part, and Pippa smiles at me from a table in the dining room.

"Did you just get in?" she asks.

"We got a little *held* up on the drive in. That was *crazy.*"

Pippa laughs. "And it's only Thursday."

I hang my Chanel on the seat next to Pippa and head for the counter. *My word*, the brunch spread is as robust as last week's. I pass by the pastry presentation then back up. The pastry Beck pointed out last week stares back at me. He didn't even have time to come inside.

I spot one stuffed with ample chocolate and move it to my plate. I continue down to the fruit display.

A plump man in striped trousers and a white apron stops in the kitchen doorway. He smiles then walks out of the kitchen behind the counter.

"You are Miss Sophie, right?"

His accent is *thick.*

"*Yes…?*"

"Wait here!" He scurries back into the kitchen.

A moment later, he returns carrying a small bowl.

His face lights up. "We got these for you!"

A pyramid of perfectly stacked cherries sits in the bowl.

"Beck said they're your favorite. Would you like them now?" He extends the bowl to me.

I blush. "I would love them! Thank you!" I take the bowl off his hands. I point to the pastry on my plate. "Would you happen to have something I can put this in?"

He nods then ducks behind the counter. He pulls out a small plastic lidded container. *Perfect.*

It's obvious, but I ask anyway. "And what is your name, sir?"

"Patrizio!" He grins.

The man, the myth, the legend. One person I didn't get the chance to meet last week.

In the time I finished my juice and cherries, Pippa took one bite out of her toast before she moved her plate aside. I pull out my phone and check the photo Beck sent of his schedule today. Every fifteen minutes is outlined with where and what he's to be doing.

"Did you get that for Beck?" Pippa asks, pointing to the container.

I nod and try to hold back my smile.

"They should be wrapping up that interview. Let's go find them."

I follow Pippa down the front steps. I shield my eyes and search down the busy paddock.

"Here they come." Pippa points.

Beck and Luca are walking our way, active in conversation with *a green.* A cameraman walks backward in front of them, still shooting content.

The camera equipment lowers. The green stops and extends his hand to Beck and Luca.

Beck's eyes drift over to me.

"Soph! Come here!" He waves.

Good. I can deliver the surprise before he's off to his next obligation. I put the container behind my back. Pippa and I weave into the traffic in the walkway.

The greens are still hovering, watching as we approach. I smile nervously and come under Beck's arm.

The green nods to Pippa as she walks into the garage with Luca.

I look up at Beck. "I've got a surprise."

I pull the box from behind my back. "I grabbed your favorite from the brunch spread."

Beck's face lights up. He turns to the green still standing to his right.

"She's the best!" Beck says. "*David*, this is Sophie."

The green steps forward. "Nice to meet you, Sophie. I'm David Campbell."

I watch David's hand as I shake it. *Avoid the greens*, Ana warned me.

"I'm a photographer and *Youtuber*," David says.

My eyes dart to his sidekick, picking back up his camera.

"*Pleasure*," I say.

Behind the cameraman, Shannon walks out of the garage, summoning Beck.

Beck squeezes his arm tighter around me. "Have fun."

Comfort slips away as Beck takes the box and leaves my side.

"Would you mind if I asked you a few questions?" David says.

My heart races. *Me? Alone? Is this the moment Alice warned me about?* The moment I brushed off because I said it would never happen.

"*Sh-sure*," I say nervously.

David steps beside me, and the cameraman is back in action.

"You can speak at a normal conversational volume," he instructs.

I nod. Will the camera pick up the fact I'm shaking like a leaf?

David starts, "Sophie it's a pleasure to meet you here in Monza, and I believe you were also in Spa last week?"

"Yes..." I say, unsure if I should be looking at David or the camera. I focus on David.

"Beck told us that was your first Grand Prix?"

"It was." I nod. *That was easy—one point for Sophie!*

"Double podium for Furio. That's quite the first race experience."

"It was." I smile. *These are softballs.* "I was blown away by the whole weekend."

David grins. "And are we getting the exclusive of your *WAGs* debut?"

I stare at him blankly. The points I've scored get wiped from the scoreboard.

I raise an eyebrow. "*WAGs?* What is that?"

David chuckles. "Wives and girlfriends of the drivers."

I giggle nervously.

"Has quite a following these days," David adds.

"Oh wow, I-I suppose, *yes*? This is my *WAGs* introduction."

David turns to the camera proudly. "You've heard it here first. Sophie has officially joined the WAGs club."

What am I doing? I try to slow my breath. Beck steps out of the garage behind the cameraman, and Shannon's five steps behind him. *Oh, thank God.* David takes notice, showing excitement for more driver content.

"...And here comes Beck back from the Furio garage."

Beck retakes his place beside me and puts his arm around my waist.

I poke his chest. "You didn't tell me about *WAGs*, Beck."

He winks. "I didn't want to scare her off, did I, David?"

They exchange a laugh. Shannon stops, watching from a distance.

"How did you two meet?" David asks.

Beck stares at me. I wait for him to answer, but his mouth doesn't move. *I guess I'm to take this one.*

I glance back at David. "We met during the summer break in Spain...*not that I had any idea who he was.*"

David's eyes grow. "Really? I'm sure that was refreshing! And what is it like dating an F1 driver?"

My heart convulses.

"It's the *best.*" I smile. "We aren't very good at spending time apart, so it's amazing to get to come out for the races."

"Well, I'm sure we'll be seeing a lot more of you then! Thank you for introducing yourself, Sophie."

The cameraman flashes a thumbs up then lowers the equipment.

After thanking me a second time, David and the cameraman depart. Beck pulls me into his chest. I could leap out of my body. *I did it.* I survived my first *interview.*

"Did you eat it already?"

Beck licks his lips. "It was gone in two bites."

We set off for the suite.

"David was quite nice," I say.

"Yes," Beck agrees. "He's one of the good ones."

"You're a good one."

"Why do you say that?" he asks.

"You had Patrizio get cherries this week."

Beck smirks. "I might have mentioned it."

I stop at the suite entrance as Ana waves from down the way.

"I'll be inside—we've got to start on these signings before press conference prep."

"I'll be up in a minute."

Ana's talking with another girl in front of the Makellos suite. Ana shakes her head as I get closer. We're both wearing white eyelet sundresses.

"Did you two plan this?" the girl asks.

"You didn't get the memo?" Ana says. "Can't wear red, can you? You'll be lost in the crowd."

"Viktoria," the girl says, extending her hand. "I'm Alek's girlfriend."

"Tommy's teammate! It's a pleasure. I'm Sophie," I say.

Viktoria is a tall blonde with a model's jawline.

"Ana, I talked to a *green*," I confess.

"On camera? Which one?" Ana snaps.

"David...Campbell?"

"What was he saying?" Ana asks.

"I was just introducing myself...I probably sounded like a complete idiot though... I didn't know what *WAGs* meant."

Viktoria laughs, but Ana's eyes go wide. "David's YouTube channel is *massive*." Ana flicks her wrist. "But look at you—you should be on camera."

Should I have said no?

"When does Beck's family get in?" Ana asks.

"Saturday before qualifying."

"If you need an escape." She smiles. "You know who to call!"

I make my way upstairs; Beck's driver's room door is open. I peek inside and find him alone. For once, no one is lurking outside *or inside*.

I hop up on the massage table. "Where's Charlie?"

I scoot back and lean against the wall. Beck cranes his neck, peering outside. He walks to the door, quickly shuts it and flips the lock. He hasn't said a word, but the look in his eye sends a heat wave through my veins.

Beck stops in front of me and places his hands on my knees, parting my legs to move in closer. He leans forward and grips around my bum, sliding me toward him at the edge of the table. His gaze is fixed on my lips.

"Beck, where is everyone?"

"*Shh,*" he whispers, putting his finger to my lips.

My cheeks flush, and my heart fires on all cylinders.

"This dress..." he says, fixated.

He slowly bends his finger and pushes it into my mouth. His fingertip glides over my tongue. I curl my lips around his finger and suck it softly. His other hand slowly runs up my leg under the dress. A fire ignites between my thighs. Beck pulls his finger from my mouth; his hand comes from under my dress to the back of my head. Our lips meet, and his moistened finger runs up my inner thigh. Beneath my dress, he maneuvers my panties to the side. His lips curl into a smile. I flinch. The combination of his tongue in my mouth and his fingers moving against my clit is unbearable. I gasp as he pushes the wet finger inside of me. Quivers surge down my legs.

"*Shhh,*" Beck insists, adding another finger.

My body tenses, begging for more as his fingers slightly curl; finding the tipping point inside me. I grab for his waistband. *Fuck, I want him.*

He slowly moves his fingers, knowing damn well he's found *the spot.* "You're so wet," he whispers in my mouth.

There's a knock at the door.

My eyes flash open as my heart jumps out of my chest.

"Two minutes," Beck yells. He pulls me back to his mouth.

My hand flies for the button on his jeans. His other hand grabs my wrist. "*Mhm…* I want you for more than two minutes," he whispers.

Beck pulls his fingers from under my dress. *No, don't stop!*

He steps back, his eyes are scorching. He lifts his hand and puts both fingers into his mouth.

My jaw drops.

He grins wickedly and slowly pulls the fingers from his lips. "I love the way you taste."

Beck turns on his heels and opens the door, pulling it shut behind him. The door latches, and I realize how heavily I'm panting. *What* was that? And how dare he leave me pent up like this!

I took several minutes in silence to get my mind right. I ascend the stairs for the third-floor lounge. Hundreds of miniature helmets sit on the table in front of Beck. Pippa's on her laptop next to Luca at another table, where hundreds of hats sit waiting to be signed. Beck picks up a helmet and scribbles on it before he passes it to Shannon. He reaches for the next helmet, and his eyes flash up.

Lord help me. I set my gaze on the floor. *Was that Shannon knocking?*

Shannon doesn't look up from her binder as she continues going through press conference prep. I pause beside Beck's chair. His hand leaves the table and wraps around the back of my leg. I shudder, my skin still on heightened alert. Beck gazes up at me with a wicked smile on his face. He's not playing fair. I step away and pull out another chair at the table.

"You have to sign all of these today?" I ask.

"There are two more boxes over here," Luca says, churning through his hats.

"Every spare second," Shannon says.

I join the assembly line, handing Beck the next helmet. Shannon's rattling off interview questions as she collects the finished items.

Twenty minutes later, Shannon closes her binder.

"Alright, let's get over there," she says.

Beck and Luca gladly push back from their project and head for the stairs with Shannon. I move to Pippa's table and help her line up the next wave of hats to be signed. A moment later, Shannon pokes her head around the corner at the top of the stairs.

"*Ladies*," she waves us over.

I glance at Pippa, and she gets to her feet.

Shannon's twenty steps ahead of us in the paddock. Pippa shrugs, confused.

"This is not normal," Pippa says quietly.

Beck and Luca disappear through the front door of the media center. Shannon waits for us to catch up, holding the door open.

Inside, we pass a set of closed double doors. A *Do Not Disturb* sign hangs outside.

Shannon opens the next door and waves us in. The room is dark and filled with people taking their seats. We follow Shannon along the wall to a table in the back corner. A monitor is set up on the table, showing a livestream inside the press conference next door.

"Try to be quiet," Shannon whispers.

Pippa and I sit. Everyone in the room is wearing team gear, intently waiting with their laptops and notebooks ready.

On the livestream, microphones are handed to Beck, Luca and the three other drivers on the couch. *Beck is somehow more handsome on camera.*

The room goes silent.

After a few moments, the press conference begins.

"Starting with a few questions for team Furio, we saw huge success in Spa last weekend. Can we expect another big finish for the team here at home?"

Beck and Luca smile at each other.

"Another double podium, but this time P1 and 2," Luca answers.

Soft laughter fills the room.

"Beck, what did that podium last week mean to you?"

Beck holds up his microphone. "It meant the world. It's amazing to come back after break and have such a run."

"It was a nice show for your new audience," Luca teases.

I freeze. Pippa shakes her head.

Beck smiles. "Yes, it was my girlfriend's first race, it was nice to have her witness a podium."

My word. I've never heard him use the word *girlfriend.*

"Good luck to you this weekend, Beck! And now, Luca, to you. It's your eighth season with the team. Are you coming into this weekend any differently than your prior visits?"

"Actually, yes," Luca says. "You might have noticed something different in us. I have been given permission by my wife to announce we are expecting a baby…"

The press conference room gushes. Beck's arm comes around Luca's back, congratulating him. *So much makes sense now.*

Luca nods proudly. "Thank you, thank you. She should be the one getting the applause," he says. "But I guess I did have a part in it."

Laughter breaks out in the room. Tears roll down Pippa's face.

I put my hand on her wrist. *"Congratulations,"* I whisper.

"Fantastic news, Luca! May I ask when we are expecting the new Furio teammate?"

"In the spring...hopefully, not on a race weekend," Luca says, beaming.

My phone lights up in my lap with a text notification. I hold it further under the table. Below Dad's text, there's a tag notification from twenty minutes ago. I click the tag message. David's Instagram page opens. *It's my interview.*

Below the video, I quickly read the caption.

MONZA MIA! Had the pleasure of meeting Sophie, the newest WAG, in the paddock today here in Monza.

The air leaves my lungs; the video already has two thousand views. I click David's profile—*he has over two million followers.* My heart races. The video is already five posts deep in his grid. I hit the *follow* button and turn my phone over, returning my focus to the press conference.

***

"I was not expecting that!" Joe says from the driver's seat.

"Luca's quite nervous it's a girl," Beck laughs.

The pregnancy announcement was the talk of the paddock for the rest of the day.

Beck's fingertips slowly move in circles on my knee. *He knows what he's doing.*

I press my thighs together under my dress. *Can Joe drive any faster?* I'm still reeling from the stunt Beck pulled in his driver's room. It was torture watching him dazzle on the press conference stage. He's been dangling like a carrot in front of me all day. I better not be expected to go back to my room and what? *Sleep*?

In the hotel lobby, Beck hits the button, calling the lift.

"You can't look at me with those eyes like that," I say.

He smiles. "I'm afraid you're all they want to look at."

He impatiently hits the lift button a second time.

"Your room or mine?" He smirks.

Ding! The lift doors open.

My insides melt. He doesn't wait for my answer; he hits three. *Mine it is.* Two other guests step in, and Beck steps back pulling me back with him. He holds me firmly against him. I fold my lips together—feeling him grow hard behind me. I open my Chanel and retrieve my room key.

I shove the keycard into the reader and swing the door open. I take two steps inside before I drop my bag and spin around. The door slams shut behind Beck.

I pounce—his shoulders meet the back of the door. Our tongues intertwine, and I engage both hands, working the button at his waist.

I pull back and take his jeans and briefs down in one go; his erection springs free. I fall to my knees and take him into my mouth. He inhales sharply, gripping the back of my head. He groans as I work my mouth and hand together.

Beck grabs my arms and pulls me up from the floor. He steps onto the ankles of his jeans, pulling his feet free. I reach for the bottom of his shirt and pull it over his head. His eyes are wild as I drop his shirt to the floor. Completely naked, he backs me into my room.

"Lie down," he instructs.

I lie back on the bed. His hands rush up my thighs under my dress. With both hands, he peels my panties off. He crawls over me; eyes hungry, as his hand slowly creeps between my legs.

"For hours I've pictured making you come in this dress."

Oh?

"*Oh!*" I moan as he slips two fingers inside of me.

I tilt my hips up, reveling in the divine pressure of his palm moving against my clit. His tongue overruns my mouth while his fingers aggressively move in and out of me. I gasp, trying to kiss him back, but he's building me up too fast. He stops suddenly and his head dives. He pushes the front of my dress up as he lowers himself to the floor. He scoops his arms around the back of my legs; his breath is hot hovering over my already overstimulated clit. My head tips back as his tongue invades between my thighs.

"*Beck!*" I gasp as my body reaches its breaking point.

I grip his hair, and he doesn't stop. It's so intense and consuming I haven't fully touched back down to earth when he flips me onto my stomach. He pulls my hips up, and I push up on my hands. I cry out as he thrusts into me; my arms quake unsteadily as he builds me up *again*.

CHAPTER 15

TEMPLE OF SPEED

I BLINK QUICKLY, TAKING the last few steps out of the garage, giving my eyes time to adjust to the beaming sun in the paddock. The third practice is finished, and it's time to meet the family before qualifying.

"Sophie!"

It's *Mister YouTube*. He's solo today.

David stops in front of me and moves his sunglasses to the top of his head.

"Thank you for the interview on Thursday." He smiles. "I didn't mean to ambush you."

"Oh no, it was fun," I say. "Sorry I didn't know what a *WAG* was."

David laughs. "Are you an influencer?"

"*No...*" I stumble. "Well, *sort of.*"

"People loved your interview. It's at fifty thousand views," he says.

I gulp.

David puts his hand on the camera harness hanging from his neck. "I'm just doing some stills today; would you like a picture?"

That's tempting. A real picture sounds better than the selfie I took in the hotel room. *Trust the process.*

"That would be great—thank you!"

I take a step back. David holds his camera up and I smile.

"Perfect day for it!" he says. David takes the harness over his head and flips the screen to me.

It's a nice shot; there's not a cloud in the sky behind me. David puts the harness back around his neck and takes out his phone.

"I can send you the photo. I'll only need your number. You can share it too if you'd like. Just tag me, please."

I hesitate for a second. Should I ask Beck if this is allowed? Beck encouraged the interview. Surely this is fine. I type my number into David's phone and hand it back.

"Great. I'll send the picture shortly!" David waves and continues in the direction he was heading.

Beck's hand meets my back. David's just missed Beck and Luca, the real stars, coming out of the garage.

"They're headed here now. You ready?" Beck smiles.

If Elizabeth is anything like James, meeting his mum will be easy. Little Louie should be cake, but Mia, the spitfire sister? It might be hard to impress a twelve-year-old girl when my predecessor was a *popstar*.

Beck stops outside of the war room for practice debrief.

"I've told them to come straight here. If I don't see you, I'll see *all of you* in the garage for quali."

I climb up the stairs to the third floor. The terrace is empty; Pippa must be resting. I settle into a deck chair, the perfect place to bask in the sun. The view from the top of the suite is incredible. The days have been so clear the Alps look deceivingly close.

My phone pings; David's sent the photo. *Yup, this blows my selfie out of the water.* The red beads on my crop top catch the sun. It's perfect with the high-waisted trouser shorts Carmen suggested. The gold chain of the red *Chanel* shines on my shoulder. I create a new post on my page. I tag David's account and the clothing brand. *They'll love this.*

A ring illuminates around Ella's story icon. I tap her story to catch up on her events at NYFW. The dinners, the parties, the shows—they all look spectacular; she must be *thriving.*

A child's palm presses against the glass on the terrace door. *Here we go.*

"Run while you can!" James yells, waving his arms. Seeing him again is like seeing an old friend. Louie is bouncing up and down but stills when James releases me and ducks behind Elizabeth. *My word*, she is lovely in her blue smock dress.

"Finally, I get to properly meet you, Sophie," Elizabeth says, pulling me in, kissing my cheeks.

The little girl marches up, dragging Louie with her. "I'm Mia and this is Louie."

I smile down at Louie; he hides his bashful face.

"I've heard so much about you, Mia!"

"What can I say?" Mia shrugs.

Total diva.

"This weather, Sophie!" James says. "A little better than last week, aye?"

James takes Mia inside for the bathroom; I move to the outdoor sofa with Elizabeth and Louie, who's still attached to her hip.

Elizabeth pulls Louie under her arm. "He will warm up, I promise," she says. She places her hand on my leg. "I *love* that we could all be here together! Beck says you're living in Paris right now? I *adore* Paris."

"Yes, it's still quite new to us. The girls and I only moved there five months ago."

Or was it six at this point? Time has been flying by.

"James proposed to me in Paris." Elizabeth smiles. "At a little patisserie in the fifth *Mille Doux Baisers*. I actually looked not too long ago; the place is still there."

"We stay in the sixth—I will have to check it out!"

"Are you heading back to Paris tomorrow?"

"No, I have to go back to London for a fashion week *thing*." It makes me nervous even saying it. "I'm walking in a small show for *a friend of a friend*."

"How funny if we are on the same flight! Let me check!" Elizabeth digs through her purse next to her, but comes up empty-handed.

I open my email app and show Elizabeth my return flight from Milan.

Her mouth drops. "That's our flight! We can all leave together then! Now you must tell me more about this show you're walking in!"

I sigh. "Honestly, I couldn't be more nervous; I've *never* done any sort of modeling."

Mia pushes open the terrace door. Her eyes are glued to the phone in her hands.

"Mia, is that my phone?" Elizabeth scolds.

"Daddy needs you inside," Mia says, putting the phone behind her back.

Elizabeth gets up, and Louie follows like Velcro. "I'll be right back."

Mia takes Elizabeth's spot next to me, pulling the phone onto her lap.

"I'm not allowed to have my own phone yet," Mia says. Her eyes leave the screen, and she gives me a once over. "I like your outfit today."

"Thank you—"

"Do you have a stylist?"

Pardon? "No, no stylist. Just a pair of friends who help me pick outfits."

"I'm saving my best outfit for tomorrow in case we're on TV!" Mia says excitedly.

I'm impressed; I know for a fact I didn't know what a *stylist* was at Mia's age. *I'm sure Sabrina had one.*

Mia holds the phone out to me. "Your first interview?"

I narrow my eyes at the screen and drop dead in my skin—it is my interview. But this isn't David's page. It's an F1 gossip account.

I gulp. "It was..."

Am I about to get my ass reamed by a twelve-year-old? Mia pulls the phone back and continues scrolling down the page. "Did Beck tell you you'd be interviewed?" she asks.

Uh? "He warned me I might be approached at some point, but..."

"You did pretty well." Mia smiles.

Oh great, I've impressed a twelve-year-old; *I can die now.* How is this girl twelve? She has the demeanor of an adult. And what is she doing on social media? Let alone on a social media gossip page?

I crane my neck, trying to get a glimpse at the page name she's scrolling.

Elizabeth and Louie come back through the terrace doors. Mia quickly closes the app. Elizabeth walks over with her hand out. Mia gives up the phone.

"Let's head out to the garage! Come on, Mia," Elizabeth says.

"Perfect! I'll meet you in there."

I follow Beck's family downstairs and head for Beck's room. *Empty.* I whip my phone out and search for the gossip page. I find it uncomfortably quick. *Damn, this page is active.* My interview is already three rows deep in the grid. I click the video to open the post.

Sabrina's been replaced. Meet 'Sophie' who claims she didn't know who Beck was when they met last month.

I expand the comments:

Same girl he was spotted with in Spa last week.
Didn't see him going for a brunette...
Pass.
So, she lives under a rock? How do you not know what a WAG is?
Sabrina to *this*?
She's gorgeous!

Wait. That last account name—*it's one of Ella's finstas.* Unreal, even amid an insane week in New York, she's firing away at people in the comments. I click my profile. My heart fires. *That can't be right.* I've just passed ten thousand followers. Panic sets in. *Stay calm.* Suddenly, I'm out of my element. I almost feel homesick. *I need to see Beck.* I throw my phone in my purse and shut it in the cabinet.

I grab my headset from the display. This is why I'm here; it's time to support Beck. He's anxious about performing well for the home crowd.

The garage is rowdy. Beck is suited up and ready to go, standing next to Coop at the center island. Coop points to a spot on the monitor, and Beck nods his head slowly.

All I want to do is run to him, but I stay grounded and take my place next to James.

"Look at that crowd!" James says.

The grandstands across the main straight are completely overflowing in red. A Furio fan fills every seat. I can't imagine the pressure Beck is experiencing. Louie and Mia are already wearing their headsets—this should be entertaining. Will they last, standing here for the next hour?

Beck spins around from the engineering island. He grabs his helmet and heads our way. His smile instantly eases the pit in my stomach. *That smile is worth a thousand nasty comments.*

Beck leans over the pedestal screens in front of me, and his eyes twinkle.

"*Drive fast*," I say softly.

Beck plants a peck on my lips. Mia squeals, and Beck rolls his eyes at her and roughs up Louie's hair. Beck fist bumps James. Elizabeth kisses Beck's cheeks and holds his face in her hands. *Oh dear, my heart.*

Beck pulls on his helmet and climbs into the cockpit. Louie's face lights up, hearing the car roar to life in the bay before us. I put the headset over my ears—the rumbling of the engine drowns out the broadcast commentary.

The timer on the screen ticks back from eighteen minutes, starting the first session of qualifying. The mechanics surrounding Beck's car pull the tyre blankets and step aside. Luca's car rips out of the bay to our left, and Beck's waved out behind him.

"Green light at the end of the pitlane! Here come the Furios. First out, pushing for a clear track. Both had strong performances in practice, with Luca placing top three in each session. This duo is riding high after that double podium in Spa. They'll be on the hunt this week at the Temple of Speed for a race win in front of their home crowd. We've got a Makellos coming out, followed by Elijah Kaplan in the Valor, coming down the pit exit."

Luca's car soars down the main straight, starting his flying lap. Beck exits the final corner and takes off behind him. His onboard flashes 339 km/h before he brakes for the first chicane. *Full body chills.* Compared to Spa, the layout of this track is straight forward. It's about as flat as a pancake, unleashing the cars to push full throttle nearly the whole lap. There are a few tricky, tight chicanes. One in particular is right at the end of the main straight. That chicane was fun to watch in practice, but I can't imagine all the cars trying to fly through it at once tomorrow when it's lights out.

"And here comes the first lap times in Q1. Luca puts up the time to beat and Beck comes in six-tenths slower. Let's see if Makellos can compete...

"...and Ren comes in third fastest. The first of the Valor's clock in...Elijah in two-hundredths of a second faster than Ren."

1 LOM

2 WRI

3 KAP

4 ENA

**"Ah! And Beckham Wright's lap time has been delet-
ed for track limits."**

Coop's voice comes over the radio. "Lap deleted, Beck. Careful at turn seven."

"Ah fu—*shoot!*" Beck yells.

Louie perks up and Elizabeth's hand comes over her eyes.

"Sorry, Mum," Beck adds.

"Nice catch, Beck," Coop teases.

Beck's name falls from second place to the bottom of the board. His lap time is erased and replaced with *NO TIME*. Other laps post, shifting the standings. Coop calls Beck back to the garage.

**"Tommy Young puts up the fourth fastest lap, and
Ian Matisse's lap time also will be deleted for track
limits. All four tyres out at turn five. Luca's still holding the quickest lap, but here comes the Valor of Leo
VanBelle..."**

Ian's name joins Beck under the elimination zone line on the board with the three slowest lap times. Leo's lap time posts, knocking Luca from P1 to P2. *The clock is ticking.* After a short stint in the garage, Beck pulls out for his out lap.

Charlie takes a deep breath and starts his side-to-side sway as Beck enters the final turn. The broadcast jumps to Beck's flying lap.

"And here's Beckham Wright's second attempt. He goes a bit wide again in turn seven but managed to keep it in that time. He's got a mess ahead with cars on track through Ascari and entering Parabolica."

"Congestion ahead, Beck," Coop reports.

Beck flies past the slow cars, staying out of his way on the back straight and enters the final turn. The onboard view becomes cluttered. His momentum is interrupted in the sweeping corner as he veers, dodging multiple cars.

"This traffic!" Beck yells.

"He really had to leave the racing line there to avoid contact. Beck might be in some trouble. That's hurt his sector three pace."

Beck's car roars down the main straight in front of the garages.

"Yes, that lap from the Furio will only be good enough for P12."

Charlie folds his arms. I glance at James,

"That's not going to work," he says, pulling his headset down. "He won't be happy with that."

"Stay out, Beck. We're going for three," Coop says.

"Yeah, baby!" Beck yells.

The top three lap times are holding, and the middle of the standings shift repeatedly as more lap attempts clock in. Beck's name drops to P15. There are only two minutes left on the clock, and Beck is teetering on the drop zone. Luca's car rolls in front of the garage to pit. He now sits in P3 behind Elijah and Leo.

"This is it, Beck, full push."

"Copy."

"And here's Beckham Wright's third and final chance in the Furio. His first lap was deleted for track limits; he met a traffic jam in attempt two. Here he comes, pulling to stay in the fight and advance to Q2. This lap is crucial."

My hands fidget; I unclench my jaw, keeping my eyes glued to the screen, watching him dive through turns four and five.

"We've got Tommy coming in, with Wit just behind him, and there's the chequered flag! Beck stays on track through turn seven, sector pace improving, and he'll have no issue with traffic this time around."

I crack my knuckles. *This has got to do it.* I fan out my fingers, giving my sweaty palms some air to breathe as Beck rounds through the final sweeping turn.

NEOWWW!!!! The Furio fans jump to their feet as Beck flies over the line. My heart pounds as his name shoots up the standings.

"And he's got it! That lap puts him up to P8, knocking out Wit Nowak. And all is well as both Furios advance to the second round of qualifying."

Coop comes over the radio. "That's P8, Beck, good push."

"P8?" Beck responds. "What am I doing?"

He sounds frustrated. James takes down his headset, releasing a sharp exhale. Elizabeth points to Beck's name on the screen in front of us. Louie throws his hands in the air. *Boy*, I feel like doing the same. That was a nail biter, but onto Q2.

Pippa turns into the garage; I sense she's just woken up. She looks down the line to Elizabeth and waves.

"How's it going?" Pippa asks.

"Luca did great! P3! Beck had us a little on edge, but he made it."

Beck pulls into the pit box; his car is jacked up and backed into the garage bay before us. The mechanics hook up Beck's car and lower the monitors in front of him. *I wish I could see him.*

Louie is losing it, with only four minutes remaining in Q3. Pippa and I tried to help entertain him, but now he's attempting to climb up James's back. Mia was bored before Q2 even got underway. She's been on Elizabeth's phone ever since; I hope playing some innocent game and not social media scrolling. Session two was much smoother. Luca had the second fastest time and Beck took fourth behind Luca and both Valors.

"Currently sitting P6, Beck."

"Copy."

Luca clocks in his second flying lap and the garage erupts in a collective cheer. The grandstands roar.

"With that lap, Luca moves to P1! Will it hold for him to start pole position at his home race? And can Beck join him on the front of the grid?"

Pulling out of turn eleven, Beck starts his final flying lap attempt.

"Beck's not pushing as hard in sector two as we saw from that first lap in Q1. But he's keeping it on track, avoiding mistakes."

The pavement in Beck's onboard is a complete blur as his speedometer flies past 325 km/h. He downshifts into turn eleven, steering wide through the massive curve then floors it for the finish line.

"Great lap! And that will move him up to P4 behind the Valors. But here comes Ren Enatsu, absolutely flying in that Makellos. Where will the Japanese driver start the Italian Grand Prix? *Ah!* And he's beaten both his teammate and the Furio! Ren Enatsu takes P4!"

Beck's name falls to fifth.

1 LOM

2 VAN

3 KAP

4 ENA

5 WRI

6 HAH

7 YOU

8 MAT

9 KHO

10 BER

James nods his head. "We can work with that."

I nod. I hope Beck will be pleased. Last week he started P6 *and look what happened.*

"I'm coming down." Beck smiles. I recognize the hotel hallway behind him. He hangs up the FaceTime. I move the clothes I've folded on the bed to my suitcase. I've got on his white T-shirt and silky pajama shorts; I'm fresh out of the shower without a spot of makeup. He knocks at the door. *Oh well.*

"What a pleasant surprise..."

Beck pushes inside.

"I thought Charlie would have a strict curfew for you tonight!"

"Oh, he does—a *suggested* curfew." Beck grins.

I fold my arms across my chest—my nipples are probably showing up to the party through his shirt. Beck takes my wrists and opens my arms. He pulls me against his chest.

"I wanted to see you again. Tomorrow will be crazy and if…" He stops.

"If what?"

"*If* I happen to make the podium, it's not guaranteed that I'll get to say goodbye before you have to leave."

Oh. I hadn't thought of that.

I interlock my fingers at the back of his neck.

"Well, if that's the case," I say. "Even though it pains me to say it, *I hope I don't see you after.*"

No, please, not yet. My eyes flip open. *Wait, that's* not my alarm. I roll over and grab my phone off the nightstand. It's Ella on FaceTime. I snuggle back down into the comforter and click accept, squinting at the screen.

"Good morning, sunshine!" Ella says.

"What time is it? Have you even gone to bed yet?"

She's at least a few martinis deep—there's a little less life behind those eyes than normal.

"No, but I'm headed back to the hotel now. I missed you and had to tell you I met not one, but two, of my future husbands tonight."

"Oh?"

"I have a date with one tomorrow."

"You have time for a date?"

"No," Ella laughs. "That's why the date starts at eleven p.m."

Oh dear.

"I'm afraid I'll be keeping your white sundress."

"Crowd pleaser?" Ella asks.

I smile. "It did *something* to Beck."

"Tell me more!" Ella pleads.

My cheeks flush, I quickly change the subject. "New York looks incredible! I can't wait to hear all about it."

"Will you actually be home when I get in on Wednesday?"

"Of course I will be! I'm flying back tonight."

Ella stares at me. "Are people being nice to you?"

"Yes...I told you about Ana—"

"I mean—never mind." She smiles. "Promise me we'll plan a trip back here."

Oh, you mean the trolls in the comments?

I smile. "I promise. Goodnight, dear."

Ella blows a kiss and hangs up.

I avoided going back to the gossip page yesterday, but no, I wouldn't put the people in the comment section in the *nice* category. But here's a supportive text, just in time.

Saw your photo wearing your mother's bag. Very special, Sophie. Tell Beck good luck today! I'll be watching! Miss you. -Dad

Mia and I lean out of the front of the garage. The last words of the Italian national anthem are drowned out. The crowd roars as nine planes rip over the main straight. I stare down at the hair on my arm, standing up on its end as chills spread up to my shoulders. Mia giggles and holds up her arm for comparison.

"That shook my whole stomach!" she says.

A trail of red, white and green smoke lingers in the sky. I didn't think the crowd could get any louder, but that flyover revved everyone up another notch. Italian flags bounce, and a massive Furio flag stretches across the grandstands, covering a whole section of people.

"Alright, girls, inside!" James yells.

Mia takes off to our post at the back of the garage.

"Pretty special, huh?" James says.

"That was amazing!"

"It's here and Silverstone that guarantee the full body chills."

Silverstone. Maybe one day I will get to go to my home race. It would be quite a spectacle to see Beck on the top podium for *God Save the King*.

I tickle Louie, who's set up, sitting on a stool today. He warmed up this morning at breakfast when I started asking him about football. Elizabeth's brought an arsenal of distractions for him: a backpack full of gummy snacks, crisps and an iPad with games galore.

My heartbeat echoes in slow motion. Five lights glow Furio red above the start line, then vanish.

"And its lights out and away we go for the Italian Grand Prix! Excellent reaction speed for both Furio's off the line!"

Elizabeth tightens her squeeze on my arm. Both of us are on our toes as all twenty cars barrel down the main straight to the first tight chicane.

The entire garage tenses, watching on the edge of their seats as the pack brakes before the corner. A huge collective sigh of relief settles as every car meanders through the kink without contact.

The Temple of Speed lives up to its name. Beck's speedometer nears 340 km/h each time he passes down the main straight.

"A handful of laps to the midpoint of this race. Issues at Makellos, but it's a stellar pit for team Furio! 2.1 seconds for Beck, beating Luca's earlier pit of 2.3 seconds. Beck will rejoin the track in ninth, just behind both Holts, still riding on those original mediums."

Beck caught a break and picked up a position when Ren's pit stop went awry. Ren's car wasn't released for almost ten seconds. Tommy's in fourth but hasn't yet pitted. The Valors are *on rails*, and Luca trails behind Elijah and Leo.

1 KAP

2 VAN

3 LOM

4 YOU

5 HAH

6 KHO

7 BER

8 MAT

9 WRI

10 ENA

The front of the grid has really pulled away; a big gap exists between Geoff in fifth and Alek in sixth place.

"Tommy's built himself a great window to pit. He'll come in this lap..."

The broadcast moves to Beck's car, tailing Ian.

"And it's an easy overtake for Beck on fresh tyres in turn three!"

"Woo-hoo!" Mia yells. Beck's name moves up to eighth. Tommy's car exits the track for the pit lane.

"Ren now in Ian's slipstream, preparing the overtake in the second DRS zone. Geoffrey Hahn takes over fourth. Tommy won't get out before Alek, but he just might be able to rejoin in front of the group lead by the Holt of Imre Bergmann."

1 KAP

2 VAN

3 LOM

4 HAH

5 KHO

6 YOU – PIT EXIT

7 BER

8 WRI

9 ENA

10 MAT

Tommy's car exits the pit lane barely ahead; Imre pulls along his right, the pair fly wheel to wheel down the remainder of the main straight. *Oh shit.*

Their cars collide in the right hander of turn one. Tommy breaks away and cuts across turn two, his left tyres skidding through the grass.

"Woah!" Louie yells.

Imre's car flies into the gravel on the outside of turn two. *Not again!*

"Big contact in turn one! That is back-to-back week-ends of contact between these two!"

The yellow flag banner flashes on the screen. Beck and Ren overtake through the chicane, passing through the middle of Tommy and Imre's incident. Tommy pulls back onto the track, rejoining behind Ren. Ian and Wit pass Imre, pulling out of the gravel. The yellow banner disappears, and Imre rejoins the track in eleventh.

1 KAP

2 VAN

3 LOM

4 HAH

5 KHO

6 WRI

7 ENA

8 YOU

9 MAT

10 NOW

11 BER

The broadcast cuts to Tommy's onboard replay, flashing his team radio message.

"What the *f*** is he thinking?! Complete idiot, that one!"

Louie's hands come over his giggling mouth, and Elizabeth rolls her eyes.

"You can hear the anger in his voice! And rightfully so, Tommy was devastated after being forced to retire last week after the incident in Spa."

The camera zooms in on Tommy's car.

"Tommy might have some body damage behind that front right, but he appears to be okay. I don't know if the same can be said for Imre. He seems to be losing speed."

What's the deal? Does Imre have it out for Tommy? The broadcast cuts to Imre's car. Qian, Amir and Antoine pass by him as he slowly moves through turn eleven. Imre's name falls quickly in the standings. Alek and Ian finally pull into the pit lane, advancing Beck to fifth.

"Somehow, Imre got that car into the pit lane, avoiding a stop on track, but it will be a retirement. Holt will not be happy with back-to-back DNFs for the driver...And he's off in the gravel!"

Who? The mechanics cheer wildly. The broadcast pans to a navy Valor surrounded by a cloud of dirt, rejoining the track. Pippa's hands come to her mouth as Luca passes Leo, advancing to second. The grandstands jump to their feet for Luca.

"An uncharacteristic mistake by Leo VanBelle sends him off the track, into the gravel, at turn ten!"

Leo gets back up to speed keeping ahead of Geoffrey.

"That was a close one! Leo lost the position but…

"…Oh! He might be dealing with a puncture! He's being called to the pits! Only eight laps to go and one Valor is forced to make another pit stop."

Leo's name tumbles down the standings, and Beck moves up to fourth. James turns to me eyes and smile wide. I interlock my fingers and rest them under my chin. *Only eight more laps.*

"An unplanned pit for Leo, and he'll rejoin the track in thirteenth. But look out, that car will be flying on a speedy new set of softs. He's sure to be chasing that extra point for fastest lap. How far can he push back up through the pack?"

There's still a significant gap between Elijah and Luca at the front, but Beck has nearly closed the gap with Geoffrey.

"Alright, Beck, time to hunt. Geoff 1.4 ahead, need to get to DRS range," Coop says.

"I'm full out, mate!" Beck shouts.

The laps are running out as the cars are holding position, besides Leo. He is elbows out, *unstoppable*. He's plowed back through the grid, already up to eighth from thirteenth.

"And we are down to the final lap. Luca will not have an easy run to catch Elijah. Geoff still has Beck in his mirrors, pushing to make this a back-to-back double podium for the team. Can Beck do it? After missing a podium by a Furio last week, Geoff is hungry for it. He won't let that easily happen again. It'll come down to these final two DRS zones for Beck's best shot at an overtake.

"...Beck's managed to close the gap, finally in DRS range, but Ren will be breathing down the Furio's neck. Here's the first chance—Beck's holding right in that slipstream..."

The mechanics shout. Beck's car flies down the main straight directly in line behind Geoff's.

"No!" James shouts. He closes his eyes.

What's happening? Why isn't he trying to pass!

"That's a DRS failure," Coop reports.

"Fucking hell, Coop!" Beck shouts.

Elizabeth doesn't even notice the expletives this time while she's bouncing up and down nervously.

"Radio comms confirm DRS activation failure in the Furio. Beck will not have the speed for the overtake. But look out, Ren is in DRS range of Beck. He won't have enough straight before turn one."

Beck chases Geoff through the first chicane.

"Ren will be in DRS range again, Beck," Coop warns.

"Stop talking!" Beck yells.

Crap. He sounds panicked, and rightfully so—Ren *is right there.* Beck keeps on Geoff's tail through the sweeping right hander and into the next chicane. The next DRS zone is approaching.

My heart sinks. Ren's rear wing flap opens as he's closing in on Beck. My fists clench, my toes clench, the whole garage is on the edge of their seats.

"Crushing. Again, the DRS fails on the Furio in that final zone, but not for the Makellos of Ren Enatsu who is charging behind."

I exhale.

"But Ren does not get the overtake!

"...With such low downforce, the DRS does not always give a guarantee... And look at Beck brilliantly defend-

ing through Ascari, keeping that Makellos behind. And Valor will pick up another win. Here's your Italian Grand Prix winner, Elijah Kaplan, with Luca Lombardo bringing in P2 for the home team!"

Pippa bounces next to me. I can't look yet. It's a flurry of commotion with the grandstands roaring, and half of the garage is celebrating for Luca. The other half is still glued to Beck's onboard while the commentary is going a mile a minute.

"Leo is relentless! He's made up five positions, now storming behind the pair of MACHs. Can he make it six? And here comes Geoff, Beck then Ren out of turn eleven!"

The broadcast flips to a head on view of the cars approaching the finish. A flash of black, red then black again roars past. *Beck did it.* He held Ren off, *barely*.

"Makellos on the podium! Geoff takes third and Beck narrowly escapes with P4. And here's Leo! Wheel to wheel with Aleksandr Kholodov through the final corner... he breaks away!"

Leo's navy Valor passes the orange MACH.

**"Tommy Young takes sixth! Leo splits the MACH's at
the final moment, taking seventh place!"**

I pull down my headset and turn to James. *My word,* I need a hug.
Maybe a drink.

Charlie shakes James's hand.

"He'll be gutted, but damn, that was a fight," Charlie says.

"That was *mad*, that was scary, that was amazing—I can't decide."
James throws his head back, laughing.

Louie pulls off his headset. "Beck didn't win?"

"He got fourth!" I smile.

Louie looks confused.

"That's not winning!" Mia snaps at him.

"I need a wine!" Elizabeth giggles. She brings everyone in for a
much-needed collective hug.

The garage empties for Luca's podium. The magic feeling of last
week isn't here. Coop is visibly distraught with Beck's DRS issue.

The broadcast is playing on the screens in the paddock. Fans have
flooded the track; the podium area is *bonkers*. Massive Furio flags are
stretched out across the fans that have filled the width of the main
straight. *I hope Beck's not too upset.* Not the outcome we'd hoped for,
but it could have been much worse.

Ana exits the Makellos garage. *No hard feelings, I hope?*

"Ana!" I call.

She heads my way.

"What a battle between Beck and Ren!"

"Oh, they chase each other all the time," Ana happily dismisses.

She keeps her pace, walking away from the media mob back toward the Makellos suite. Ana turns around, continuing to walk backward. *"I'll see you in Singapore!"* she yells.

The press officers unite with the drivers exiting the garage. Out comes Tommy with a big smile on his face, and *there he is*.

"Beck! Over here!" Mia yells.

I want to run to him, but I refrain. He's animatedly talking with Ren. *Oh, good they're still friends.* Shannon hands Beck a hat. He pulls it on over his mess of sweaty helmet hair. The drivers get corralled to the postrace media pen. Multiple interviews are happening simultaneously with drivers who were quick to exit.

"I'm glad you'll be there for Beck in Singapore," Elizabeth says.

James nods.

Uh?

"Wait, you're not coming?"

James grits his teeth, shaking his head.

"But...what am I going to do without you?" I whine.

"Louie has another tourney." Mia rolls her eyes.

"You're a pro now, Sophie!" James smiles.

I don't know if I qualify as a pro just yet. Two races and I'm to be trusted in the garage alone? Who will I ask my stupid questions to? *Charlie?*

Tommy's staring down Imre, finishing his interview. The two exchange an ice-cold glare before Imre walks off with his camp. *There's some serious tension brewing there.* Shannon and Charlie swoop in beside us. Beck's handed a microphone and steps in front of the nearest camera. He pulls at the collar of his race suit, heavenly sweaty.

"Beck, well-fought race! P4 in front of the Furio home crowd. Such a shame, that DRS failure in the last lap. Do you think that cost you a podium?"

"It's hard to say." Beck shrugs. "I was ready, pushing hard for another double, but in the end, I didn't have enough to overtake."

"Chasing one Makellos and going on defense with the other in those final corners, what was going through your head?"

"A little bit of panic, to be honest. Another lap, and Ren would have gotten the overtake. But I'm over the moon for Luca and happy with the points I was able to pick up for the team."

"Furio has really started to pull away from MACH in the points. Do you expect to keep that up and put the pressure on Makellos?"

"We've got two difficult races coming up. Obviously, need to get the DRS working on my car." Beck grins. "But the car feels great, even better than it did before break. We're going to keep our focus and momentum and maximize every chance we can get for points."

Oh my God. I could listen to him speak for an hour. Beck hands the microphone off to another driver, and our eyes meet. It feels wrong to have to leave for the airport now. I can't wait any longer, I close the gap between us and throw my arms around him.

"I'm so proud of you!"

My feet lift off the ground as Beck leans backward.

"*Ughh,*" he groans. "This one hurts." He lowers me down.

I hold his face. "I'm even more impressed than I was last week!"

A sliver of a smile touches his lips. "I'm just disappointed."

"You almost had him, even without the DRS, son!" James says behind me.

Elizabeth lets go of Louie's hand, and Louie charges toward us. Beck leans down to catch him. *My heart.*

Mia gives Beck a high five. "Nice try, big bro."

Elizabeth rolls her eyes at Mia and brings Beck into her arms. Fingers tap my shoulder.

I spin around. "Tommy! Great job!" I say, giving him a hug.

"Phew," Tommy says. "Did you see that near disaster?"

"What's the deal with Imre?" I giggle.

"Oh, don't get me going. *I'm boiling.*"

"Well, you certainly won that spar!"

Tommy beats on his chest.

"My second family!" Tommy smiles, moving to hug Elizabeth.

It's the third time Elizabeth has said it: it's time to leave. *This is killing me.* Shannon takes one step closer, keeping her presence known. At least ten other interview cameras wait in the media pen behind Beck.

"You're not done, are you?" I say.

"Not even close," he says, pulling me into his chest. "I wish I could take you to the airport myself."

I squeeze him tighter. *I'd be willing to miss my flight.*

"You ring me when you get home," Beck instructs.

I nod. He glances at his family. "And don't feel obligated to sit by them!" he jokes.

Beck presses an ultra-wet kiss on my lips, pulling away too fast. I open my eyes and relish the saltiness of his taste.

My heart feels as if it's been ripped from my chest. It takes everything in me to not turn back around for another look at him. I keep one foot in front of the other, walking back to the suite with his family to retrieve our luggage.

CHAPTER 16

OUTFIT REPEATER

THOUGH STUART PREFERS TO meet in person, he's overjoyed to catch up with me over a video conference. I arrived in London late Sunday night, and Beck's parents insisted on taking me into the city to drop me off at the flat. They're incredibly kind. Both Mia and Louie were asleep the entire drive. I won't see Beck for more than a week as he prepares for the Singapore and Japanese races at headquarters. This week, it's *my turn* to perform: London fashion week is here. The *Eden Eves* show is Sunday. Ella returns from New York tonight, and Carmen gets in Saturday from Paris.

"Sophie, you've *flown* past fifteen thousand followers," Stuart says.

"I'm *finally* getting good at this," I joke.

Stuart shakes his head. I've done next to *nothing,* only posting a random story here and there. Besides David's picture I posted on Saturday, I haven't posted to my feed since the cherry bikini photo. The new followers amassed from David tagging me in the interview on his page.

"Keep riding the wave, but understand this is not how it happens. You must start posting more," Stuart says.

I know he's right—I did nothing to deserve this. Surely, I can get suitable pictures to post from the show this weekend.

"Onto the brands that have reached out. It's mostly fashion and a few beauty collections—where am I sending these packages?"

Now I feel like Ella.

"I'm coming back to Paris Monday night and leaving for Singapore from there."

"Perfect. I will get these sent to your apartment and you can take what you want for the race."

Amen. I will gladly have wardrobe duty for Singapore taken off my plate. I hope it's not too many packages, or Pierre might have words for me!

"Now, the collab I wanted to run by you," Stuart says. "It's a multi-deal opportunity. I think you should consider it, especially given your recent jet setting."

Oh?

"*RIMI* is a new luxury travel company that's sending their travel essentials kit. With all the travel you're doing, they're also interested in having you promote their new luggage line coming out for the holidays."

I glance at the front door. My beat-up roller bag is still sitting against the wall from Monza.

"I would be very interested in that."

"Great! You'll have the travel kit for the race, and I'll move forward with the luggage discussion," Stuart says, taking off his glasses. "I'll also email you the mock-ups of the luggage—it's lovely."

"Thank you, Stuart. Is that all?"

"I believe so. Please keep on top of your emails this week—especially due to the public's newfound *interest* in you."

Someone's climbing into my bed. I open my eyes and lift my head. I crash back down into my pillows. *It's only Ella and her jetlag from New York.*

"You miss me that much?"

"I can't sleep," Ella whines.

"I noticed," I say. I close my eyes and pull the comforter under my chin.

"I have so much to do, and I'm not ready to start doing any of it," Ella sighs. "I need to move. Will you come to the early class with me?"

"Only for you, and *only* if I can lay here for five more minutes."

Ella scoots to the pillows and lays her head down beside me. "Okay, deal. Plus—I have notes for you."

My eyes flip open. "*Notes?*"

"From the race."

"Oh gosh, did I do that bad?"

"*Shh*...enjoy your five minutes."

My final minutes of relaxation turned into five minutes of stewing over these *notes*. I drag myself out of bed and step into a yoga set. I half brush my hair then throw it on top of my head in a scrunchie. I finish off my look by tying a hoodie around my waist.

Ella holds the door open. *My word,* the sun hasn't even fully risen.

"I saw your interview," she says.

I pull my hoodie off my waist and shove my arms through the sleeves.

She locks her elbow into mine, and we step off the sidewalk into the street.

"You looked beautiful, *and* you came off quite charming."

I pause us for a passing car. "Is there a *but* coming?"

The studio lights flip on down the street. We continue jay walking our way across.

"Not a but, just an...*and*," she says.

We step up onto the sidewalk and I stop.

She pulls me along. "*After.*"

I lay back on my mat and stare up at the ceiling. We're so early they're still getting the studio open.

"I have a boatload of content to recap and post," Ella says, forward folding.

"You still have to give me a recap of all the dates you went on."

"Basically, two were good and one was…" She raises her eyebrow, glancing at the few more people carrying their mats in. "*Great.*"

I shake my head.

"Has Stuart become your biggest fan?" Ella asks.

"I met with him yesterday. Apparently, I have some *things* inbound for Singapore."

"Look at you!"

"Yes, now I have to keep my end of the bargain and actually start *trying.*"

Ella laughs.

It's 7:30, and we've already accomplished our workout for the day. All the suited nine-to-fivers have flooded the streets. Young professionals talk to their earbuds and carry their own coffee, while balancing a full drink caddy to please the bosses. *I remember that life.*

Ella and I grab a table by the counter at *Mayfair Brew*. I lift the lid off my latte and inhale the rich steam. Now, I'm more at peace than when we *namasted* at yoga.

"Soph, you know how much I support your relationship. But your star is rising fast. I don't want you to be caught off guard." Ella takes a sip of her latte and continues. "There are some things you need to be aware of."

She slides her phone across the table. It's open to what appears to be another "F1 gossip" account, this one called *F1_LOL*. It's a different page than the one Mia was browsing at Monza. My peace is gone.

I slide the phone back. "I know about these accounts, Ella." I take a sip of my latte.

"I even saw one of your *finstas* fighting back in the comments on some page."

She pushes the phone back toward me. "I don't think you've seen *this* account—look at the link in the bio."

I scan the bio and click the blue link. It opens to an external blog site. *Lights Out Ladies* flashes at the top of the screen. *A page dedicated to all the F1 WAG tea you can consume.*

Lord, there's that abbreviation again; a pit plants its seed in my stomach.

"These pages are normal. There's one I'm featured on all the time that's dedicated to shitting on influencers—*this one*"—she raises her eyebrows—"Carmen and I found to be particularly nasty."

I scroll the page and immediately catch my name—I read to Ella:

"Sophie Collins...What's the tea? Official rating still pending?"

Ella purses her lips. I expand the comments.

"Still working on my final score. Will be up shortly."

My heart pounds. I scroll past several posts before catching another headline bearing my name.

"Sophie Collins: newest WAG in the crosshairs?"

I scan the comments and continue reading.

"Looks like she was first spotted with Beck in Spain at the start of August."

"WOW—had classes with her at Uni. Surprised she hasn't choked on that silver spoon in her mouth. Her dad is LOADED."

"She's a nobody. Beck will be bored out of his mind in no time."

My insides collapse into the sinkhole in my stomach. How do they know anything about *my dad?* Ella grabs my wrist, seeing me spiral.

"You're anything but boring, darling. Come on," she says, snatching her phone back. Ella gets up from the table. I re-lid my latte and follow her out.

"I just want to protect you," Ella says. "I thought you ought to know this stuff exists. I've already made a username that I'll keep on standby for any counteroffensive that might be necessary."

I link into Ella's arm. I've been reunited with one of my security blankets. If only I could take her with me everywhere.

I make up an excuse to stay at the flat while Ella runs to the post office. It's quiet and my laptop is staring at me from the coffee table. *Time to dig.* I open the lid, and my heart pumps with anticipation. A black screen with a red battery symbol greets me. *Great.* I get up to find the charger in my room. That was my sign, wasn't it? I shouldn't care what a random blog site says. I rip the cord out of the wall in my bedroom. I don't need to read it, *but how can I not?*

The computer starts to fire up, but it's not fast enough. I open my phone and look up the Instagram page. *F1_LOL*—it has over 300k followers. Ella follows, and even some of the drivers follow the account. Viktoria, the girl I met with Ana, is a follower. I gulp. The page follows thousands of accounts, including mine and Beck's. Thankfully, Beck does not reciprocate the following. Avoiding the *follow* button, I begin scrolling the pictures. The drivers' photos pale in comparison to the number of photos posted of the girls. Some photos are professional, others are blurry, obviously captured by fans.

My face appears in the grid. It's the picture from the club that first night from Ella's story. The login screen shines on my laptop. I set my phone down and punch in the password. I fire up a web browser and navigate to the *Lights Out Ladies* gossip page. I dive back into the post I was reading before Ella interrupted my examination.

Looks like Sophie's BFFs with mega-influencer, Ella Humphrey, AND Oliver Goddard's girlfriend, Carmen Reyes…I assumed it was Tommy and Ella hooking up!
She's WAYYY out of her league. She doesn't even have 10k followers.

Ha! Check your facts now, less than 10k was so last week.

She's got nothing on our Queen Sabrina

A wannabe influencer trying to grow her following. She'll be more than happy to follow Beck around the world, and he'll have a pretty girl to parade around the paddock for the remainder of the season.

…fingers crossed she'll make Sabrina jealous enough to get Beck and Sab back together.

Beck and Sabrina? Why are people this hung up on a relationship that ended more than a year ago? I'll take those comments as a win. I mean, they said I was pretty. *Glass half full.* I click on a collapsed comment.

I love this. Finally, a driver dates a normie. What a dream!

The dislike button is highlighted on the comment for receiving multiple thumbs down votes. This is the kind of page where positivity goes to die. I back out to the main thread and continue scrolling. Several posts carry the same heading above a girl's photo.

OFFICIAL: Avanti Martin WAG Angelina Alvares 8.5/10
OFFICIAL: Valor WAG Eliana Hughes 7.0/10
OFFICIAL: Holt WAG Lili Horvath 7.25/10
OFFICIAL: Valor WAG Camila Rodrigues 8.25/10
OFFICIAL: MACH WAG Viktoria Martinovich 7.5/10
OFFICIAL: Trueno WAG Madi Auclair 7.5/10

What is this rating system? I open "*the official*" post for Pippa, dating back three years ago.

OFFICIAL: Furio WAG Pippa Lombardo 7.75/10
Outfit rating: 7.5/10.
First media day introduction: 8/10.

I scan the comments. According to this page, Pippa's a former model—*not surprising*, she's gorgeous.

Did you see Pippa is trying (& failing) to launch a handbag line? Bored housewife much?

Rude. I scan to the most recent comments. My eyes bulge. *Who are these sleuths?* They've known Pippa was pregnant for weeks. Well before Luca's announcement.

I scroll down and see Tommy's face—a blonde is on his arm. *Emma Trautmann,* a girl he used to date, was given a 7.0.

Model, jersey chaser, gold digger and shit for brains.

At least she has good outfits

Confirmed: Tommy and Emma have called it quits. Another one bites the dust. #exWAG

Was this Tommy's number 3 or 4? I'm losing count.

First, it was that blonde model, Bella, then there was Audrey a.k.a. Miss Tweet Scandal (also blonde model) then Emma.

I scroll further. The next photo comes up and my stomach drops. A picture of Beck and Sabrina stares back at me.

OFFICIAL: Furio WAG Sabrina Kaufmann 9.9/10

I open the post, dated from March last year.

Our queen gracing us with her presence in the paddock.

Outfit rating 9.8/10.

First media day introduction: 10/10.

It's the highest score I've seen. The photo is hard to look at. Beck's holding her hand, wearing sunglasses and a plain look on his face. Sabrina's smiling, waving to the cameras.

The comments are gushing over Sabrina. They were a fan favorite couple.

Beckham Wright & Sabrina Kaufmann split after 2.5 years.

Still holding out hope they get back together.

It can't be true! We can't lose our popstar princess of the paddock.

I think back to the outfits I wore in Belgium; will that be what I'm rated on? And my interview with David—will *that* be scrutinized? This is ridiculous. *He's only dating her so he can parade her around the paddock*—it certainly didn't feel like my experience with Beck. Sure, a few of the other drivers might have a new girl each season, *ahem—Tommy*, but Beck hasn't been with anyone since Sabrina. Ella made sure of that with the research she'd done. I scroll further before recognizing Ana's face. While the picture looks like her, she also looks quite different. Her *"official"* post is from three years ago, and there are *hundreds* of comments.

OFFICIAL: Makellos WAG Ana Wong 5.5/10
Because I'm feeling nice, I've given Ana a 5.5 out of 10 because the girl could stand to lose ten more pounds. Doesn't she know this job requires you to be size 2 skinny?
Ren drives for Makellos...he can do better.
Agreed, imagine standing next to Geoffrey's girlfriend in the garage.
The outfits could use work—but yes, the tummy could use more work.

Blood pulses in my ears. Ana is *stick thin* now—has she seen this? How can anyone have a bad thing to say about her? She's a lovely girl. I scroll down to more recent comments.

Ana went dark on social media, deleted her profiles then missed the first four races of the season. She appeared back on socials with a private account, twenty pounds lighter.
Did you notice the new nose?

A fire rages in my stomach. I can hardly believe my eyes. Why are they coming this hard for Ana? The other girls made it out relatively unscathed compared to this. *I know I shouldn't*—my brain's telling me no, but my fingers aren't obeying. They're currently typing *Sophie* into the search filter. I stab the enter key and sort the results from oldest to newest. There it is—the first post mentioning my name from three weeks ago.

Beckham Wright spotted with mystery girl in Mallorca...

Pictures from the after-party and a blurry photo taken from a distance are posted below the heading.

I did some sleuthing on the girl Beckham Wright was spotted with on holiday. She posted this picture on her feed of her and her friends at Oliver Goddard's set. Beck was in Tommy Young's story at the same music festival. Here she's pictured with Beck, wearing the same outfit—this was posted on Ella Humphrey's Instagram story later that night. And finally, here she is in Ella's story, shopping in the same yellow activewear set as the mystery girl in the pictures taken of Beck outside an ice cream shop. It appears the summer fling is Sophie Collins...a nobody, really. Typical South Ken, private school, private club snob...but she's got some powerful friends.

I expand the comments.

Another account has a hands-on photo of her and Beck at a Trofeo pool party.
As of Friday, Beck now follows her, Ella and Carmen—and he follows hardly anyone.

I scroll to the last comment.

Confirmed couple! Beck referred to Sophie as his girlfriend in the driver's press conference in Monza.

I'm speechless. Are these people private investigators? I didn't know it was that interesting. It feels violating? The blurry picture is from our ice cream date. People were following us? Taking pictures of us? Is *this* what Ana was warning me about? This must be what Alice was warning me about. I'm with Ana—can I make my Instagram private? Ella would kill me. *Stuart* would kill me, not to mention, it would also break my contract.

A balloon flashes in the corner of the page: *1 New Post.*

I stare at the balloon and fall for the bait. The new post opens.

OFFICIAL: Furio WAG Sophie Collins 5/10

David's picture of me Saturday before qualifying is below the heading.

Seems Beck has bagged a new girl over break. She was spotted in Spa last week, pictured here at the Italian Grand Prix. The score is fair. I mean, we've got to hate her, right? She's got nothing on Sab. Her outfits aren't bad, but I've already seen this top AND is this the only bag she owns? She's worn it <u>every single day</u> in the paddock for the past two races! I don't do outfit repeaters, and for that, she gets an outfit score of 4/10. Interview score 6/10. Watch for yourselves. Can we drop the sheltered Daddy's girl act? And come on, no one believes you didn't know who Beck was.

I slam the laptop lid closed. I grab my latte, and the lid pops off, splashing the hot liquid on the table. I loosen my grip around the cup and snap the lid back on. I don't give a shit about my "score" or about the comments, but Ana's? This is pure evil. Do the other girlfriends know about this page? Does *Beck* know about the page? I'm torn. I'm glad Ella brought it to my attention, but *wow.* Keys jangle outside. *That was quick.* Or have I been scrolling that long?

"Oh, good, you're still here," Ella says, coming through the door. "Are you busy?"

"No," I say, getting up quickly from the couch. "What's up?"

"You've been hired," she says, waving me to follow her.

Three full-size suitcases from New York fashion week await in her room. I welcome anything to get my mind off that horror show of a gossip page, even if it's unpacking and helping her dive into her content recap. This is a job that will last us into the evening.

A bruised apple or our takeout leftovers from last night? I grab the apple and sink my teeth into it. My ears perk up.

"Gotta go, I only have two hands."

I smile. That will be Carmen in from Paris. Finally, I'm reunited with *both of my security blankets.*

Carmen clumsily swings open the front door, dragging her luggage and balancing two bottles of champagne in her arms. I grab the door and hold it open.

"Guess what!" Carmen says, setting the bottles on the counter.

I flip the lock on the front door.

"Oliver has a show in Amsterdam the week of the Dutch Grand Prix! You'll be there, right?"

"*Oh*, I-I don't know..?" I shrug. That race is *weeks* away. I mean, I *hope* I'll be there.

"Of course you will!" Carmen yells. "We're going to the race with Oliver's producer and sitting in some suite along the track!"

"That's fabulous! I'll have to make sure Beck wants me to come to that one..." I eye the champagne. "Are we celebrating something?"

"Sophie's first fashion week!" Carmen throws her arms around me.

I squeeze her tight. *God*, I missed her.

"And it will make the vlog more enjoyable," she says, spinning around for the glass's cabinet.

"*Vlog?*"

"I haven't told her yet, Carmen!" Ella yells from her room.

Carmen presses her lips together.

Please, no. Carmen cracks a smile. I know what this means. We'll be filming the get ready process from Ella's bathroom for the next two hours. The first few times I made an appearance in the vlogs was fun, but now that I've lived through several *years* of having to participate, *I hate them.* They are always at the top of Stuart's wish list.

Fine.

I'll do it. Ella does 90 percent of the talking anyway, and it will save me from having to do one of my own. I can give Stuart a final cherry on top of his week.

Ella walks out of her room. "I haven't posted a get ready with me in over a month, and we have to get ready for the event anyway!"

"How dare you do that to your followers, Ella! They are waiting on pins and needles for this content!"

Carmen busts out laughing, and Ella flips me the finger.

Two hours and four minutes into recording the glam process, we've successfully destroyed Ella's bathroom. Every bit of the countertop is covered with pallets, makeup brushes, bottles of product and hair tools. It's as if a bomb went off in a beauty store, but we got the content Ella was after, and all three of us are ready. We're attending a store exhibition. Our grand assignment is brand awareness. Fancy term for attend the event, have fun and *post*. I'll be studying the standing fashion show during the exhibition. I need to cram as much as possible before the *Eden Eves* show tomorrow.

My phone lights up on the counter. I blow off the dusting of setting powder sprinkled on the screen before answering.

Beck's smile fills the frame. "What are you doing?"

I flip the camera around to the devastation on the bathroom counter.

"What on earth is going on there?"

I flip the camera back. "Just finished filming a *get ready with me* vlog for Ella."

"Hi, Beck!" Carmen yells, spraying her hair once more.

"Hi, girls!" Beck says.

I grab my champagne glass and leave the chaotic bathroom. "What are you up to?"

"Just finished up in the sim—tomorrow's the big day, right?"

I nod.

"You're going to do great!" he says. "Smile pretty and no falling!"

"Beck! Don't jinx me!"

He laughs. "That's right, you got your falls out. You must ring me after, I want to hear all about it."

"I will—*well,* only if I don't fall. If I do, you probably will never hear from me again."

Beck narrows his eyes. "Send pictures too."

"That I can do. My dad is coming, and I'm sure he'll be snapping away."

Beck's gaze melts into me. *"I can't wait to see you in Singapore."*

CHAPTER 17

FLY LITTLE BIRD

TWENTY MINUTES UNTIL SHOWTIME, the impostor syndrome is setting in. I wasn't expecting the day to fly by this fast. After a quick rehearsal, we were brought backstage to start the endeavor that is creating show-worthy hair and makeup.

When Ella brought me by the venue last month, it was a vast, empty ballroom. Today, it's transformed into a high fashion arena. Beautiful uplighting highlights the marble columns and soaring ceilings of the space. Rows of perfectly aligned white chairs surround the long runway that's raised only slightly above the floor. *Thank God.* It's the first time I get to see all fifteen models booked for the show. These girls are the *real deal.* Every one of them is tall, sleek and absolutely stunning. *Ella fits right in.*

"Okay, close again," my makeup artist instructs.

I peek my eyes open each time a brush leaves my face. The energy in the room is picking up by the minute. More people are added to the frenzy, rushing around in every glimpse I catch in the mirror. The army of hair, makeup and dressers, all outfitted in black, have been here for hours. Now, a force of backstage coordinators with headsets and clipboards are pacing the room. I crack my knuckles for the twentieth time. A warm chunk of my hair falls between my shoulder blades. The warmth seeps through the silk robe I was given on arrival. The next chunk is pulled through the curling iron. The heat slowly leaves the curl at my back. A brush leaves my face. My makeup artist turns around to the vanity. Ella's gabbing away with her makeup artist at her station directly behind me. I slowly inhale to soothe the knots in my stomach.

"Alright, close one more time," he instructs.

I wince from a cold dousing of setting spray. Then choke on the rosy mist infiltrating my nostrils.

"And voilà!" he says.

I open my eyes and my heart thumps. He steps aside, giving me an unobstructed view of his masterpiece.

I turn my head slowly. "*Wow.*"

My face has never had such a dewy glow. The makeup is so soft it's as if I have barely any on at all, which I know isn't true, since he's been working his voodoo for the last half hour. It's creamy and light with pops of bright pink on my cheeks and lips.

"I'm going to need you to teach me your ways!"

He studies my reflection in the mirror, pleased with his work. *I needed this confidence boost.*

The hot tools are retired to the counter of my station. The lady working the back of my head slowly brushes out my massive, bouncing curls. A rolling rack zooms behind me, parking next to my hair and makeup station. A card is fastened to the rack, reading *Model 3: Sophie Collins.* A posterboard is clipped underneath, holding polaroids of me in my first and second looks. *My,* how things have changed since those photos were taken two months ago.

A dresser unzips the first garment bag. The romantic pale pink patterned dress is pulled out. It hangs, softly swaying on the rack. The baby-blue fabric of the matching top and skirt set peeks out of the second garment bag. Another dresser unhooks the drawstring bag on my rack, pulling out the first flower-embellished heel. I shift in my seat. *Damn,* the shoes are as tall as I remember. At least the heel is more blocky than stiletto.

The hairdresser steps beside me, blocking my view.

"Okay, hold your breath," she warns.

I pull in a deep inhale before closing my mouth and eyes. The final cleansing of aerosol begins. A cloud of sticky hairspray encases my head. I let out all my air the second the hissing stops. I open my eyes as she moves pieces of the loose Hollywood curls in front of my shoulders.

I can't hold in my smile. These magicians have glammed me to the *gods.* Ella jumps out of her chair behind me. Holding her phone to her ear, she jogs to one of the side doors.

The dresser at the rack waves me over. "Let's get into your first look!"

I push up out of the chair and try to get a peek at what Ella is up to. Ella flips her head back in my direction. She frantically waves for me. *Maybe Carmen was able to make it?*

The dresser removes the pink straps from the hanger.

"I'll be right back," I say to the dresser.

She sighs, annoyed. "*Run!*"

I dash across the room to the door Ella disappeared through. I swing it open and gasp. *It's him.*

Beck's standing in the hallway, sporting his heart-stopping smile. *No. Way!*

"What are you doing here!" I squeal.

I rush through the door past Ella and throw my arms around him.

Beck catches me. "You think I would miss this?"

I pull back, shaking my head. "Aren't you in Italy?"

A voice calls out from inside. "Ten minutes, ladies!"

If I wasn't already nervous. My head is spinning. Beck takes my hands in his.

He shakes his head. "You're gorgeous."

This isn't happening—how can I back out of this?

"Mum and I are a couple rows back on the right."

What! "Your mum is here?"

He moves his hand to the back of my neck and draws me to his lips. *I can't breathe.*

Ella grabs my arm.

Beck nods at the door. "You better get going!"

I slowly back away.

"You got this, Soph!" he yells, before turning around.

Ella holds the door open. "You had no idea he was coming?"

"No! He's been at headquarters. I wasn't supposed to see him until Singapore!"

Ella shakes her head in disbelief.

I rush back to my station; my dresser is livid. She urgently disrobes me while another dresser crouches down and holds the dress open at my feet. I step into the first look and hold my arms out. The dresser rises, gliding the dress up my body. I'm lightheaded, and my heart is pumping a mile a minute—how did Beck pull this off? *How am I going to pull this off?*

The straps rest on my shoulders, and the material hugs my body as the back zipper rises, stopping a hands width above my tailbone. I trace my fingers down the deep V-cut on my chest. The dresser spins me around. The slight breeze on my ribs brings my awareness to the sheer accents on the bodice. My left foot is picked up off the ground and slid into the chunky heel. A dresser works the straps around my ankle under the dress. I step up into the other shoe, the flowy skirt of the dress perfectly lifts from the ground. My wrist is lifted, and a sheeny lotion is lathered down my arm. Clips, I didn't even know existed, are taken out of the back of my hair. A hiss sounds, and more hairspray mist lands on the exposed skin on my back. Suddenly, all the fidgeting stops. Both dressers stand up and take two steps back, giving me an up down.

The lead dresser nods. "First look's ready."

Both dressers disappear in a flash.

I step back in front of my mirror station and run my hands over the silk on my hips. The dress is something you'd wear to a dreamy garden tea party, and it *fits like a glove.*

"Five minutes ladies!"

Panic sets in. Beck being here, only adds an avalanche onto the mountain of nerves in my stomach. *I need Ella.* I turn and wave to her. She's runway ready; her dresser is taking her photo.

"*Help!*" I mouth.

Ella's blonde curls bounce in slow motion. She floats across the room smiling ear to ear in her cream Battenberg lace midi.

"Are you ready?!"

"No! I'm panicking!" I say, shaking out my sweaty hands. "I can't believe he's here. I don't think I can do this."

Ella grabs my wrists and interlocks her fingers with mine. Her eyes widen. "Sophie Collins!" she yells.

I still.

"You are smarter than half this room put together. You are *cute as hell...*" She rolls her eyes. "You are dating an F1 driver who's *enamored with you!*" She pauses, coming in closer. "For God's sake, start acting like it!"

A tepid zing ripples through me.

"You've got this," Ella says. "Once you get the first couple of steps out of the way—you will feel like *you own the world*. I promise."

Ella squeezes me tight. "Now get out there and *fly, little bird*," she whispers.

It was exactly the gut-punch, spoonful of tough love I needed. The kind that only Ella can deliver.

Makeup man is back, applying more gloss to my bottom lip in the lineup.

"Try not to lick your lips," he says.

My cheeks flush. *That was Beck, not me.*

The front of house noise dwindles. The voices backstage fade to whispers. The lights dim; only the vanity lighting glows at our stations. *Breathe.* I try to feed off the energy of the other girls in line. They are calm, loose and couldn't be more relaxed. The pusher holds a thumbs up in the air then grabs hold of the edge of the curtain. The first few beats of our music hits—a remix of a Lana Del Rey's "West Coast." The model in front of me snaps her fingers to the beat. The curtain is pulled back, and the first model disappears into a flood of light. My heart pounds, taking a step forward. I turn around one more time to glance at Ella. She blows me a kiss, seventh in the lineup. The model in front of me disappears. I step forward now at the curtain's edge. I watch model two take off from the head of the runway and disappear.

"Sophie, on deck," the mic-ed pusher reports. She nods at me, smiling. "Ready?"

I can do this, I can do this, I can do this....

I take an inhale so large the corset in the dress constricts my ribcage. Her hand comes to my back, and she sends me out. I take five steps from the dim backstage into the flood of lights before turning right. I set my gaze at the backwall beyond the end of the runway and *take off.*

My soul leaves my body, pure adrenaline carries me down the runway. Model two passes by halfway to the end.

I slow at the end of the runway and successfully turn. The bottom of the dress spins. Ella's right, *this is amazing.* I can't help it—my smile breaks as I strut back to the curtain. The intensity of the lighting nearly blocks the view of the staring audience. *Beck is out there somewhere.* I turn right and exit back through the curtain on the opposite side.

I did it! And I already want to go again! I squint, searching for Ella in the lineup. She's on deck. I want to grab her, but my dresser catches my arm. I'm rushed back to my rack, and my dress is unzipped while I walk. The dress falls to the floor, and another dresser is already holding open the mini skirt. I wiggle into the skirt and hold my arms out for the puffy cap sleeve crop top. The back of the top is tied into a sideways bow. I'm spun. The baby-blue two-piece set is shifted on my body perfectly in place. I *love* this outfit.

I step back into the lineup and the song changes. Three girls wait in front of me, giving me a moment to breathe. But that's when it hits me—everything soaks in.

I wish Mum was here to see this. I tilt my head back, stopping the tears before their arrival. She might not be here, but I can't believe Beck is here with his mum and my dad. Oh my God, *Dad. He will get to meet Beck.*

I turn down the runway, not even attempting a model *smize* on this lap. *I feel like I own the world.* I stop at the end of the runway and take it all in before turning on my heel. In an instant, *it's over.*

Relief floods over me as I step back through the curtain. *The rest is cake.* I get back in the lineup for the group finale walk. One after another, all fifteen of us walk out, making a final pass, showing the whole collection. The audience is out of their seats, clapping along. It takes everything in me not to scan the crowd for Dad and Beck.

Ella squeals, "You loved it, didn't you!"

She holds me close, rocking side to side backstage. Whistling erupts from the crowd. The designer, Evelyn, emerges from the curtain, utterly ecstatic.

"You girls were perfect!" Evelyn says, hugging Ella. Evelyn shifts to me. "What did you think?"

"I *loved* it!" I shriek. "I can't wait to do it again in Paris!"

The lobby outside the ballroom is crowded and rowdy. Dad waves excitedly. "Sophie!"

I steer through the crowd and throw my arms around him.

"You were amazing, darling!"

"I did it!"

I open my eyes, and Beck's coming up behind him.

"Dad," I say nervously. "There's someone I want you to meet."

Dad releases me and pivots.

Beck reaches his arm out and brings me under his chin. "You are stunning."

Beck holds his hand out to Dad. "Great to meet you, sir. I'm Beckham Wright."

Dad's star struck.

"George Collins," Dad manages. Their hands meet and my heart does a backflip.

"I've heard quite a lot about you, *Beck*."

"Who is this girl?" Beck says to Dad.

"I did a double-take! As soon as she walked out, I thought that can't be *my little Sophie!*" Dad whines.

Oh, Dad.

I can hear her voice before I spot her. Elizabeth holds out her hands. "You were gorgeous up there, Sophie!" Elizabeth kisses my cheeks. "When Beck said he was coming to surprise you, I said not without me, you're not!"

Elizabeth finishes taking mine and Beck's photo. The crowd's taken notice of him. He's being approached right and left. I'm still in shock that he's truly here. My smile won't be wearing off anytime soon. Beck cups my face in his hands and his eyes sparkle. "I need to get *you* out of here."

A sleek, blacked-out Range Rover pulls up to the valet stand. Beck steps ahead of me to get the door. The valet slips out of the driver's seat. I pause halfway into the car.

"You know—this is the first time you've ever driven me."

I plop down onto the quilted leather.

Beck narrows his eyes. "In that case," he says, grabbing for the seatbelt. He tugs the strap tight across my chest and clicks it into the buckle.

"Lucky for you, I don't have the Ferrari right now," he bops the tip of my nose with his finger and shuts the door. I watch him in the sideview mirror disappear behind the car. *Lucky for me?* I'm not sure I could handle myself, riding passenger in a Ferrari with him.

Beck pulls the car from the curb.

"I love a little surprise," he smirks.

"Little?"

"Though I wish you were coming with me in the morning."

His eyes flash from me, to the road, and back.

"Me too," I sigh. "One more event, and I'll be on my way."

"You're not the star of that show, are you?"

"No," I giggle.

I don't think I'll ever get over this night. The runway, Beck's surprise appearance, him meeting Dad, Dad meeting Elizabeth. *It was all too perfect.*

"I liked your dad." Beck smiles.

Ha! "He liked you..."

My heart winces. "I wish my mum could have been here. She would have loved this."

Beck reaches across the center console for my hand.

"She was there," he says. "You know she was watching, Sophie."

I nod my head gently. Beck squeezes my hand before returning to the wheel.

I replay the video clip Dad took during the show. It's my first look, and I barely recognize myself. I wasn't a deer in headlights—I was floating down the runway. Is this that moment people talk about when you can feel your life picking up and taking off? I never thought my confidence would come back, not this quick. A month ago, *before Beck,* my confidence was at ground level. Within a few weeks, it's slowly lifted off the runway. After tonight, it's fully taken flight. I swipe over to the photo Elizabeth took. I open Instagram then stop. Will this get ripped from my page and posted to the gossip site? Beck's arm is wrapped around me, hand resting on my hip. His eyes are focused on me while I smile wildly at the camera. *Here goes nothing.* I create a new post with the photo and the video clip.

Beck slows for the light before the Chelsea bridge.

"Are you going to tag me?" he asks.

My heart jumps.

"I-I don't know..." I stammer. "Is that allowed?"

Beck leans over. With his pointer finger, he hits the tag option and clicks his face. My heart flutters as he selects his name.

"That's better." He smiles.

The light changes.

I stare down at *our* photo about to be posted on my page.

I click the caption box and type out a message:

His turn to do the cheering.

CHAPTER 18

Catching Flights

My world is moving at 100 km/h. If I'm not in Paris, I'm in London. If I'm not in London, I'm jetting off to Beck's next race. I still haven't come down from the high of the fashion show. Now I'm pinching myself, thinking about the week ahead in Singapore. My first night race, and my first street circuit. It's Ana's home race, and she's already scheming an escape plan for us from the paddock. I stand up from my table at *Pret* and squint across the terminal to the signage at my gate. I check the group number on my boarding pass again, time to see this *business class pod*.

I zip my backpack and sling it around my back.

A girl stops in front of me. "You're Sophie, right?"

I freeze. "Yes...?"

The girl smiles. "I'm a huge fan of Beck."

I smile awkwardly, still completely taken off guard.

She lifts her phone. "Can I get a photo with you?"

With me?

"*O-of* course."

She steps beside me and holds the selfie camera out in front of us. I smile for her picture.

She stares proudly at our photo. "Are you on your way to the race?"

"Yes, my flight's just started boarding. Beck is already there."

"Tell him good luck this weekend!" she says.

I nod. She starts to turn away, but then backtracks and comes closer.

"I know it might not always feel this way, but a lot of people are rooting for you two."

She flashes me a reassuring grin then disappears into the flow of airport foot traffic. *Did I hear her correctly?* I didn't even get her name. I take a breath, then merge into the stream of bodies. *That was a first.*

I never wanted for anything growing up, but Dad also didn't spoil me rotten. If this is what business class looks like, what on earth do you get in first class? Up here, I do feel *like a snob*. The seat fully lays down. I lean forward to look out the not one but *two* windows in my pod. *This is too much.* I press the button beside me that raises the leg rest. I cross my legs in front of me and send a picture to Beck.

> Almost as good as the jet.

I hope that doesn't wake him—it's, what, *three a.m.* there?

I pull the *RIMI* travel essentials kit from my backpack. My first big influencing opportunity is immensely appropriate. Stuart sent the luggage briefing last night; I'll be receiving beautiful hardshell roller bags with custom engraved luggage tags. From the kit I pull out a multi-port power bank, a pair of noise canceling headphones and a luxurious black silk neck pillow with a matching eye mask. I snap a photo of the items in my lap with the swanky pod in the background. I add the photo to my story, thanking and tagging the *RIMI* account.

See you in Singapore!

A tag notification appears, the selfie with Beck's fangirl. I glance at the *add to my story* button. What would the gossip blog say if I reposted this? I hate that I'm even questioning myself. *Why do I care what internet strangers think?*

My photo from the fashion show made its way to the page rather quickly. A handful of comments were predictable.

ICYMI—Sophie thinks she's a model now.

The other comments were *vile*. The thousands of likes that were left on my Instagram post kept me buoyed. *Screw it*, I repost the selfie to my story. I'm not going to let the opinions of strangers have that kind of power over me. I pull the headphones over my ears. They're quite comfortable. Finally, I have time to catch up on episodes of *In the Know*. I tap the latest episode.

"Welcome back to In the Know! Your daily pop culture podcast to keep you up to date and in the know at the water cooler…"

I recline back and close my eyes; it's amazing the comfort a podcast can give.

Is jet lag even a thing when you've flown in your own private pod? This is bad—now that I've traveled on this level, how will I ever stand to be in coach again?

"The roads are a mess," Joe says. "It's going to take a while to get to the hotel from the road closures."

"That's okay!" I say, staring out the window. "More time for sightseeing. I might not get any further than the track while I'm here!"

"Very true," Joe laughs.

Beck arranged for Joe to collect me from the airport. Beck's tied up at an event and felt terrible he couldn't be there to retrieve me himself.

"If you have time to get out, go for it. This is my favorite city in the whole world," Joe says.

I can see why; I could have wandered *inside* of the Changi airport for hours.

A pristine-suited woman behind the reception counter smiles. "You've already been checked in, Miss Collins." She extends her hand across the counter. "Here is your key, and the elevators are just to your left. *Welcome to Singapore.*"

The weight of the keycard surprises me.

"Can we get your bags for you?"

"Oh no, I can manage. Thank you."

It's all too much. The city sparkled on the drive in. The five-story soaring hotel lobby dazzles. I drag my roller bag to the lift and stare up into the cascading crystal chandelier.

A suited man waits in the lift.

"Floor, ma'am?"

I glance at the keycard envelope. "Eighteen, please."

His white glove reaches out and presses the button. My stomach drops as the lift takes off. Moments later, it slows to a smooth stop. *Ding!*

Even the keycard is a fancy, thick metal. The green light flashes on the door's card reader. I turn the handle and push open the solid wood door. *Oh shoot!* I jump backward, the door slowly closing in my face. Personal items are strewn about the room. Perhaps I've been given the wrong key?

I catch the door just before it latches, spotting a hoodie over the back of a chair.

Slowly, I push the door open another few centimeters and peek in—*that's Beck's hoodie*. This is Beck's room. I pull my roller bag inside, and the door slams behind me. Floor to ceiling windows frame the sparkling city lights in the large living room. A purple Ferris wheel glows in the distance before the lights end at the marina's edge. A bouquet of purple and white orchids sits in the middle of a small dining table. I turn the vase to read the tag fastened to a stem. *Sophie.* It's eerily silent. I walk to the double doors across the room and push inside. Beck's things litter the floor in the separate bedroom. A wall of windows in the bedroom boasts the same phenomenal view. I peer down at the track, flooded with light. *It's right there.* You could probably watch a good portion of the race from this very hotel room.

I jump as the card reader of the door beeps. My heart pounds as I pace back to the double doors. I lean my head and peek outside.

Beck smiles. "*Surprise.*"

CHAPTER 19

Is It Always This Hot?

Best. Surprise. Ever. Beck handpicked this suite so that we could stay together. I can close the bedroom doors when Charlie or anyone else comes in. It was my idea to keep the shades open went we went to bed. Now that I've stared at the lights and stars over Singapore for what feels like hours, I need to pull the drapes.

I've been contemplating it for the last twenty minutes; I might never fall asleep if I don't. But I'm trapped. I carefully lift Beck's arm and set it behind me gently. I slowly crawl out of the bed. My feet hit the rug; I turn back to check his state. *Sound asleep.* I grab the edge of the curtain and slowly pull it across the wall of windows. The dreamy city scape glow fades to pitch black.

The next morning, Beck's ordered the whole menu for breakfast. Eight hooded plates cover the top of the service cart in the living room. I uncover several plates before finding a vibrant bowl of fruit. I grab a fork and head for the windows.

The doors creek behind me. Beck walks out of the bedroom, wearing only a towel around his waist. *My word.* Water droplets still cling to his chest. He wraps his arms around me and rests his chin on my shoulder. This is *cloud nine*.

Beck points outside to the track below. "That's sector three there."

"The track is quite narrow…"

"It is, and there's nineteen turns to maneuver."

"So slower this week? Well, slower, *relatively* speaking."

He laughs. "Yes. And if you brake half a second late, you're in the wall."

Yikes.

"I can't have mistakes in qualifying. It's quite hard to overtake. If you get pole here, you've got a good chance to win."

I stab a blueberry and hold it up over my shoulder. He bites it off the fork then pulls me to his mouth.

There's a knock at the front door. I freeze. Only a robe covers my birthday suit.

"That will be Charlie," he says. Beck slaps my bum. "Get dressed. We'll head down to the track soon."

The lobby doors part, and I pause, choking on the wave of humidity that's slapped me in the face. Beck smiles. My new blouse and shorts set instantly clings to my skin.

"Is it always this hot?" I ask. It must be over thirty degrees, and with the 80 percent humidity, it's a steam sauna.

Beck laughs and exchanges a look with Charlie.

"It cools off a *bit* at night."

Fencing and security detail hold back fan traffic on the few minutes' walk to the swipe gates. I walk slowly next to Charlie while Beck makes several stops to sign merchandise fans eagerly stretch out to him. As it looked from our windows, the track is on the hotel's doorstep. *Praise be.* I scoop my hair up, giving the back of my neck some air to breathe.

"You'll get a nice surprise in a second," Beck says. "There are massive machines that blow cold air in the paddock."

Oh? I might just have to park my ass right in front of one.

I swipe the badge on my lanyard and return to Beck's extended hand.

Beck waves to the photographers capturing arrival shots. I put on a soft smile and set my eyes on the ground ahead of me. So many of the photos on the gossip page captured this very moment: a girl walking in on the arm of a driver. It's not the photographer's eyes making me wary, it's the hundreds of eyes that will pick the photo apart if it gets posted. Ana comes to the forefront of my mind.

"Ah! There it is!" I squeal. Cold, dry air violently fights as it mixes with the searing humidity. The paddock is flourishing with palm trees and greenery. Grass breaks up the concrete paths and hot pink blooms spill over flower beds.

"It's gorgeous here!"

"It is." Beck squeezes my hand. "The suite doesn't come to the fly aways, but our hospitality is right over there," Beck points.

Shannon's waiting at the garage entrance. *Are we late again?*

"Can you take my backpack inside? My driver's room is on the main floor."

"Of course." I smile. I take one of the straps over my shoulder.

Beck turns down the garage hall then spins around. "Thanks, *love.*"

My heart jumps. I turn on my heels. *Will I ever not feel like a schoolgirl around him?*

"Sophie!"

My eyes yank up from the pavement.

"David!" I gasp.

"Apologies, I didn't mean to startle you."

I shake my head. "No, I should pay more attention to my surroundings."

David's cameraman smiles.

"Can I get a quick clip with you?" David asks.

I tense up as the comments on my last interview flash through my mind. But something ignites in me. *Do it, Sophie.* This is my time, my time to fire back and make a stand. If not for myself, for *Ana.*

"Let's do it." I nod. "Better now than before I completely melt."

I take a deep breath and pull my bag higher on my shoulder. I set Beck's backpack down next to me. Why not show off one of the cute sets I was gifted?

The cameraman holds out a thumbs up. David's eyes shift to me.

"Miss Sophie, this is the third race I've seen you carry this iconic red bag—tell me about it."

No. Way. And he said he'd start with something easy. "Yes, I am an *outfit repeater,*" I giggle. *Shots fired,* a direct hit on the gossip blog.

"It's a rather special bag, actually. My mum left it to me when she passed away."

David's eyes widen. "Oh, wow!" he says, overwhelmed. "That's *quite* special. And how fitting it being the perfect cherry-red color."

"The perfect Furio red! I can't help but think it must be something more than coincidence, you know?" I continue.

"Speaking of bags, did you know Pippa recently launched a handbag line of her own?" David lights up. "I did not."

"Absolutely gorgeous Italian leather; you've probably seen her carrying them around."

"I'm sure my wife will be more than happy to check those out!" David says.

I smile. This is *empowering*.

"It's great to see you here in lovely Singapore. Your third race in a row. How are you liking it?" he asks.

"I'm hooked! I was blown away at Spa and again last week in Monza. I've never witnessed a sport with such passion and energy, and all the teamwork—it's unbelievable."

"Monza is pretty spectacular, isn't it?"

"Incredible." I nod. "I had literal chills from the flyover. And the fans that come out bring so much electricity."

"Speaking of fans, I saw a fan caught you at the airport!"

You watch my stories?

"She was a fan of Beck's," I correct him.

"This is the first time that women make up as big a portion of the fan base as men. What do you think about that?"

My heart pounds. "I think it's...*great*..."

This is it, this is my chance. Before I'm ready, my mouth starts moving. "Obviously the fandom and fascination with the drivers I understand, but I guess I underestimated the fascination—*with us*."

David nods.

"People come for us girls pretty hard online. The things that are said about us, *assumed* about us, it's hard to see."

David continues nodding.

I shrug. "But I suppose with any massive sport fandom you expect to grow that fringe group of *toxic fandom*...that's just that—*toxic*."

David smiles. "The keyboard warriors?"

"Exactly!" I say. My lord, *he gets it.*

"Perhaps it's time to look into *getting another hobby*?"

I close my lips. I've shocked myself—that last comment completely slipped.

David laughs. "You heard her! Trolls disengage!"

He holds out his hand. "Thank you, Sophie."

There's an emboldened pep in my step after dropping off Beck's backpack. I did the right thing. Something needed to be said. Coop waves from the pit wall. I walk through the front of the garage. A posse of cameras and film equipment surround Beck and Luca in the pit lane. My phone pings, and I duck back inside the shade in the garage. *It's Ana.*

> I'm already driving Ren nuts.
> He said I can take the car, let's have a field trip!

I'm torn. I saw Beck's schedule today—booked solid, and the press conference isn't until seven.

Would he mind if I left? It's the only time I would consider leaving; he'll be in and out of media engagements all day. I'd love to see more of the city and spend time with Ana.

Beck and Luca stand up. It appears they're wrapping up. I step back in front of the garage to make my presence known. The camera posse turns, looking my direction. *Oh lord*, I take two steps back. Beck jogs over, slowing to a drool-worthy swag ten steps in front of me.

He raises an eyebrow. *"Yes?"*

My word, if I wasn't already hot and bothered.

"How did you know I needed something?"

He smiles. "I know you, Sophie Collins."

I flush.

"Would you mind if I went out with Ana for a few hours?"

Beck's smile fades. "Take me?"

Oh no!

He steps closer. "You saw my schedule today—you're making me insanely jealous."

Beck takes my face in his hands. "Go. And have fun." He stares down at me. "Be careful."

"I will," I giggle. "I'll be back before the press conference."

I could jump with excitement. Beck presses an extended kiss on my lips and leaves me coming up for air.

A team driver sits behind the wheel of a dark gray Mercedes S-Class.

"Bay South, Armand!" Ana sings. "You can't visit Singapore and not see the gardens!"

I smile.

"Besides, it's super close. I can't have the car too long."

The pictures I've seen of Gardens by the Bay don't do it justice. It's a mind-blowing oasis of botanical beauty. I walk further out on the dizzyingly elevated walkway through the tree structures. The same Ferris wheel outside our hotel windows is visible.

"I remember the first time I brought Ren here," Ana laughs. "He would barely take a photo with me at the railing—he's terrified of heights."

"Really? I figured those boys are fearless!"

She shakes her head. "Let's get our photo!"

Ana stops the next passing tourist and hands him her phone.

I put my arm around her, and we cautiously back up to the railing.

The stranger captured a magnificent shot. It would be hard to take a bad photo here. Two and a half of the vertical garden tree structures make the picture. The monstrous hotel with a ship across its towers sits behind us.

"Tag me!" Ana says.

She's posting our photo to her story.

"Yeah?" I say, a little shocked.

I open Instagram and create a new post. *She knows my profile is public, right?* I find her name and also tag the brand that gifted my outfit.

I step out of the steam sauna and into the air-conditioned café.

"Grab that table." Ana nods.

I take a seat at the cute tea and sweets shop we stopped at on the way back. I pull my phone out of my bag. *It's happened.* My screen is full of notifications. David posted the interview to his page fifteen minutes ago, and he's *tagged my account once again.*

My eyes drift to the comments.

Get this girl a muzzle!
She's got a big head for only two races in.

Crap. I roll my eyes and turn my phone over on the table. Since when does standing up for yourself equate to having a big head? Ana turns around carrying three brightly colored iced drinks.

"What's the matter?" Ana asks, scooting a drink to me.

"I might have done something stupid."

She raises an eyebrow.

"Ana, how do you deal with the crazies?"

"What do you mean?"

"These people online—*they're awful*. I was doing an interview this morning with David, and I broke. I had to say something."

Her eyes go wide. "You're brave." Ana takes a long sip from her straw. "I deal with it horribly."

Does she know about the page?

"I had such a hard time my first two years, reading things that people would comment on pictures of Ren and me, about *me*. I went on a downward spiral and lost so much weight, I had to enter a program."

My heart sinks.

"There are entire pages dedicated to bringing us down, and they succeeded with me."

"But they didn't, Ana! You're still here. *They didn't win.*"

"I suppose." Ana shrugs. "But I completely shut down. I went radio silent, turned down every picture, interview, and deleted all my social media and made private accounts." She shakes her head. "I should have warned you."

"You warned me to stay away from *the greens*, and I couldn't keep my mouth shut."

Ana laughs.

"David's a good guy, though, right?" I ask.

"He is. Maybe one day, I'll get the courage again. But the way I think about it, the less time I'm in front of a camera, the less people will have to talk about."

I nod. *It makes total sense.* Her skittishness around the media in the paddock.

"Did you tell Ren about it?"

"Ren knew everything. He's the one that got me into treatment. It was pretty dark there for a moment, but he loved me through it all."

I smile. I don't know Ren well, but that speaks volumes about his character.

"Do you think Ren is the one?"

"Oh yes! I've known for years—he's the one."

"That's so special, Ana."

She smiles. "I'm still working on my confidence. I'm not a model like you, Sophie."

I nearly spit out my bubble tea.

"*Neither am I*! You should have seen the shoes they had to put me in."

"Well, you certainly looked the part."

Ana raises an eyebrow. "What about Beck?"

I stare and stir the bubbles in my tea. "I'm crazy about him."

"The golden retriever of the grid." She grins.

"*What*?"

"I read it somewhere once." Ana shrugs. "Someone went and gave every driver some personality label. Beck's a *great* guy."

Golden retriever. That's exactly what Beck is, except perhaps in the bedroom. Our encounter in his driver's room last week will live rent free in my head for life. It's weird to think of my golden retriever dating a popstar.

Ana sips her drink while I contemplate asking my question.

"Were you friends with Sabrina?"

"No," Ana answers quickly. "Sabrina walked around with a major superiority complex. I don't think she ever tried to speak to me, and that was *before* she really blew up."

"You suit Beck much better." Ana says.

My heart flutters. *Agreed.* Hearing firsthand what Ana's been through, now I truly have *no regrets* saying what I did with David.

I point to the extra lidded to-go cup on the table.

"Is that for Ren?"

"Armand. Let's get out of here."

"Before we go, what's something sweet I can bring back for Beck?"

I turn down the hall to Beck's driver's room and spot the soles of his shoes. Charlie's leaning against the wall inside the tiny room. Shannon's hovering in the hallway. Beck lifts his head up and spots me before collapsing back down on the massage table.

"Soph," he groans. "I need you." I walk in and put my purse down. He's absolutely knackered.

"What did you do to him, Charlie?"

Charlie laughs and pushes off the wall.

"Meet me upstairs, Beck," Shannon instructs.

Beck lifts his hand in the air and makes a thumbs up. He lowers his arm and reaches his hand to me.

"Who's in your press conference this time?" Beck rolls his eyes. "Me, Qian, Sanjay, Tommy and"—he pauses—"*Imre*."

My eyes widen. "Tommy *and* Imre? Did they do that on purpose?"

"Definitely." Beck grins. "Should be entertaining."

Beck hops up and tousles his hair in the mirror. He turns to me and cups my face in his hands. "I can't wait for our bed."

CHAPTER 20
SUGAR, ICE, RUNOFF WOULD BE NICE

BECK'S ALARM HAS GONE off twice already. Both were silenced by a snooze. I keep my eyes closed; they aren't ready to open yet. This time, it's not the alarm, it's the ringer vibrating against the glass top of the bedside table. Beck shifts in bed, reaching for the phone.

"What's up," Beck says.

I peek my eyes open. He's on his back with his eyes closed, talking to the phone on the side table.

"Making sure you're up and ordered breakfast," Charlie says over the speaker phone.

Beck peeps his eyes open and smiles at me.

"We're up. We'll get to ordering some breakfast."

"Brilliant, I'll be by after."

"Sounds good."

He leans over and ends the call.

"Does he always check on you like this?"

"No," Beck chuckles. "But you're usually in your own room. He's got to make sure we didn't stay up and party all night."

I sit across Beck's lap at the breakfast table in the living room and set my yogurt down. He hooks his hand on my inner thigh as I bring up the pictures from yesterday's field trip.

"This was the coolest part!"

Beck reaches across my lap and grabs a *second* sticky raspberry pastry braid.

I raise an eyebrow.

"You're sworn to secrecy." He smirks.

"Better get rid of the evidence before Charlie comes."

He bites into the gooey pastry and I swipe to the next picture. "Look how high up the walkway is! It was gorgeous."

"Yes, you are."

I give him eyes.

"Oh yeah, the gardens are nice too." Beck points to the Ferris wheel in the photo. "There's the track!"

"I might have left, but I still had my eye on you." I wink.

Beck stops chewing, and his eyes devour me. He sets the pastry down and I quickly hop out of his lap, moving back to my own chair.

"Where do you think you're going?"

"Charlie is coming!" I squeak.

"I can be fast." He says waggling his eyebrows.

I stare into his eyes and push off the chair slowly leaning across the table. The front of my robe hangs open, exposing my bare chest. I retrieve my yogurt and return to my seat. Beck shakes his head displeased and sucks the glaze off his fingers. *My word.* I squeeze my thighs together.

Beck's phone is lying on the table; he taps the calendar app and scrolls.

"Tell me your schedule next week again."

"Our first event is Thursday evening; Friday is the show."

He twists his lips.

"Dang, I won't be able to crash that one."

His phone pings, and he lifts it off the table. I watch him scan the screen. He lets out a chuckle then slides his phone to me.

"What was this about?" he says.

It's a message from Shannon. I click the attached picture to expand it. *Oh no.*

New Furio WAG calls out "toxic fandom"

My eyes jump past the headline and my heart takes off.

Beckham Wright's new girlfriend has no problem calling out fans for what she says is 'toxic fandom.' Sophie Collins, the newest WAG in the F1 paddock, was first introduced when F1 content creator David Campbell interviewed her at the Italian Grand Prix. New to the world of F1, Sophie gushed over the sport but wasn't afraid to call out fans that have given her grief online.

I exhale. *Really?*

"I mean, that's not all I said," I huff. "Why did they only report on that?"

Shouldn't the headline be about Pippa's handbags? Or the reason I keep carrying the same bag week after week?

"That's why we have minders. Shannon records everything that way we have the whole story...Not the out of context lines the media picks and chooses to report."

"Oh well." I shrug. "I said what I said."

"Is it true? Are people coming after you?"

I bite my lip. "I mean, yeah, but it's all of us. The online bullying is a *little* out of control."

"What could people possibly be saying about you?"

Ha!

"I have one of the lowest scores, Beck."

"Scores? What are you talking about?"

I shake my head. I'm *not* about to dive down this rabbit hole.

"I couldn't care less what's said about me, but the other girls? When I saw the posts about Ana—I had to say something."

"Ana? What has Ana ever done?"

"*Exactly.*" I pause. "She looks quite different from a few years ago, wouldn't you say?" "*Eh?* I suppose?"

There's no way he understands the severity of what's being written on this forum.

"People are ruthless." I stab a raspberry.

"I remember people going pretty hard after Tommy's ex, Audrey. Some Twitter thing? Accounts she followed or something she retweeted years ago, I don't remember."

I know *exactly* what he's talking about. *Miss Tweet Scandal.* There was an entire thread on the page; they scoured the internet for her entire Tweet history. They went as far as contacting the company she worked at, trying to get her fired.

Beck smiles. "Well, good for you for saying something."

I stir the yogurt in my bowl. *What a nightmare.* David posting the interview is one thing but a tabloid headline, *really?*

"How do you deal with negative attention?"

Beck leans back in his seat and crosses his arms.

"It got me down a few times my rookie season. But for me, I had to shift it and make it my fuel. Prove them wrong, you know?"

I didn't think Beck could get more attractive.

I scoot his phone back.

Oh, I've made it my fuel, and I *will* prove them wrong.

"Speaking of Ana," Beck says, tapping on his phone. "This was announced this morning."

He sets the phone back down.

Ren Enatsu signs three-year $16 million contract extension with Makellos

My jaw drops. "Oh my God!"

"He deserves it," Beck says, picking up the phone.

I study his face; I can't discern if he's jealous or worried about his own situation, *maybe both*. I know Ana is ecstatic; she'll be moving to Monaco soon enough.

"You didn't say, how did Tommy get along with Imre in the press conference?" I ask.

"There was some back and forth. Tommy brought up Imre's penalty points then Imre called Tommy an idiot. Tommy busted out laughing—"

"Oh dear."

"Which in turn, made me laugh and half the others. Imre was about to combust."

"I'm worried about Tommy! He's got a target on his back!"

"That's motor racing, Soph."

"I don't like how close they get to the walls here!" I say.

Pippa nods. "Hardly any runoff...*wait until you see Monaco.*"

I didn't see Pippa at all yesterday, but I don't blame her. I can't imagine being in this heat and humidity *with child.*

The broadcast replays Beck coming through a turn in slow motion. His tyre is half a centimeter from skimming the wall.

There is no gravel and no grass. The white track limit lines butt up almost directly with the bounding walls for a large portion of the circuit. The top speeds aren't nearly what they were in Monza, granted, there are *nineteen* turns to navigate. It's a bit claustrophobic. There is no running wide, or you are running into the wall. My phone buzzes. The blasted thing has me on my toes lately. It's a text from James. It's midmorning in London.

Missing the garage! How is practice going?

Looking good thus far!
Wish you were here!

I reread the text and smile. I'm already on a texting basis with Beck's parents.

"Good lap, Beck. All sectors improved," Coop says over the radio. He wipes his forehead on the sleeve of his T-shirt. The A/C is trying its best, but it can't keep up with the heat rolling in through the garage doors. The sky is gold—Beck will finally get some shade on the track in these last few minutes of practice one. I don't know how they're doing it in full body race suits.

"I saw your interview with David," Pippa says. "You mentioned my bags..."

I freeze. *Did you happen to see today's tabloid headline?*

Pippa turns to me. "...You didn't have to do that."

"I know I didn't...but *I wanted to.* They're gorgeous bags." I pause. "I'm sorry. I should have asked you first."

"No, it isn't that." Pippa shakes her head. "We saw a huge uptick in visits to the site. I know your piece with David had everything to do with it."

I fold my lips together. *Maybe my big mouth did benefit someone.*

Beck's car pulls in front of the garage.

I didn't realize Beck doesn't have a shower here, another reason to miss the Furio fortress. Charlie improvised and dumped buckets of water over Beck's head before we came inside. Beck's beat, laying shirtless on the massage table. I pull his driver's room door closed behind me so he can properly rest before second practice.

"Just the person I was after!" Lena smiles.

It's the travel admin I met in Spa.

"Have you checked your email? I sent you your new flight information."

"*What* new flight?"

Her smile disappears.

"Beck asked me to move your flight Monday..."

He did?

"Right." I nod. "Thank you, Lena."

She turns away nervously. *Beck had my flight moved?* I glance back at his door. I don't want to disturb him now. I step back out into the paddock and bring up my email. It's there at the top, a rebooking confirmation. Instead of leaving Monday morning, I'm leaving that night. That should work...*but why?*

I look up, David's walking across the way, heading toward the media center. It's been brewing in me since Beck showed me the article this morning. *I owe David a thank you.* I cut across the grass to catch up to him. I want more for us girls. I want more than for us to be the F1 *wives and girlfriends* people gossip about because we *are*. His brightly colored bucket hat has a ring of moisture around it.

"Hello, Sophie!" he says with a grin.

"David, do you have a moment?"

He nods. "What can I do for you?"

"I just wanted to say how much I appreciate the segments you've done with me."

"That means a lot." David smiles. "You ladies are a big part of these drivers' lives. You all have your own voices that are worth being heard. Thank you for trusting me."

This man is a saint.

"Thank *you* for putting out the stories worth hearing. The tabloids only clip what they want to make a headline."

David rolls his eyes. "I did see the write up."

I smile. "I wish all the media was as nice as you."

Beck comes up for air through the layer of floating ice cubes taking short quick breaths. Frigid water streams down his beet-red face.

"Alright, ten minutes, Beck," Charlie instructs. "Sophie." His eyes shift to me. "You watch him!"

Beck shakes his head like a dog after a bath, sending ice-cold water flying. He wipes the water from his eyes. I've never seen athletes as spent as Beck and Luca were after second practice. Beck reclines against the back of the massive plastic bin of the makeshift ice bath. I sit beside his tub and dip my hand in the water. Instantly my hand cramps up.

"Oh, that's nice!" I whip my hand out.

Beck nods to the identical plastic bin next to him. "Hop in Luca's."

"No! He'll be out here any second!"

He gets a mischievous grin on his face. He cocks his head to the side.

"I have a surprise…" Beck says.

My heart clinches.

"I probably should have asked, but I had your flight switched to Monday evening. That will buy us a few more hours together."

The dam bursts, and the rush of a thousand butterflies propagate from my stomach.

"We don't leave for Japan until after ten," he adds. "I won't see you for a while…"

I don't have words. I open my purse and pull out the rainbow sugar-coated candies I fetched with Ana yesterday.

Beck's eyes grow wide.

"It just so happens I have a surprise for you too."

***

"That's P7 Beck," Coop reports.

"Copy," Beck groans. "Coming in."

Beck's frustrated. I could tell he was nervous for qualifying when he couldn't sit still during lunch. Luca's hung out at the top of the standings, trading fastest lap back and forth with the Valors each round of qualifying. The cars appear otherworldly flying through the floodlit track. Our red Furios look especially wicked.

"This is it," Charlie says. "It's gripped up. Lowest fuel load. Let's get it done."

I nod my head. *Yes, you can do it, Beck.*

He *must* improve. Tommy's lap time posts—it's two-hundredths faster, dropping Beck to eighth. With Luca currently holding pole position, the pressure must be crushing.

Beck's car flies down the main straight, and catches the inside kerb of turn one.

> **"Beck hasn't been able to get the results out of the Furio that we're seeing from Luca. He'll be desperately trying to put a clean lap together this go around. And there's the chequered flag! Let's see if Beck can improve on this final attempt. Elijah coming across the line...and...*will not* unseat the pole sitter! Phenomenal performance out of Luca this evening."**

Beck's car sneaks by the wall, exiting turn five and his DRS activates. The words on the signage of the tight track walls morph into stripes from the speed he's traveling. The mechanics celebrate.

> **"And how about that sector one pace! Beckham Wright's outdone both of the Valors and his own team-mate!"**

My heart takes off. *Why isn't James here?!* The standings shift in the midfield. Geoff's final hot lap moves him to fourth. Beck's rear wing flap closes at the end of the second DRS zone.

"Look at the speed he's carried into the apex at turn fourteen! Beck's done it again! Drastically improving his pace in sector two! And matches the pace of the pole sitter!"

Beck's approaching the pair of turns at the *East Coast Parkway* underpass. I wipe my palms on my shorts. Charlie rocks nervously.

"This will be close! Beck is threatening the front of the grid with this lap!"

Charlie jerks next to me.

"Oh! He's skimmed the wall there! Fighting the car on the exit of turn seventeen!"

I clench my jaw. Beck flies for the final two corners. The steering wheel jerks wildly in Beck's onboard. *No!* Charlie's hand comes over his mouth. The mechanics throw their heads back.

"*Oh!* The oversteer gets him at turn eighteen! Too much juice!"

Beck rights the car.

"*How* did he hang on to that? He was nearly sideways. *My*, he'll be kicking himself. That mistake massively cost him..."

Beck floors it out of turn nineteen when his radio comes through.

"Fuck!" he shouts. *"Why, Beck!"*

I cover my mouth. My heart breaks for him.

"You okay, Beck?" Coop asks.

"No!" Beck shouts. "Check the back right for damage."

His tone has me shaken. I pull my headset down; my chest is pounding.

Charlie shakes his head. "That would have been *pole*."

The final grid order for the race is displayed on screen. Due to that mistake, the lap doesn't beat his first attempt, he remains in eighth.

1st	Luca Lombardo
2nd	Leo VanBelle
3rd	Elijah Kaplan
4th	Geoffrey Hahn
5th	Aleksandr Kholodov
6th	Ren Enatsu
7th	Tommy Young
8th	Beckham Wright
9th	Wit Nowak
10th	Ian Matisse
11th	Eduardo Almada
12th	Gordon Whitlock
13th	Imre Bergmann
14th	Amir Bishara
15th	Sanjay Patel
16th	Qian Liu
17th	Mateo Barrera
18th	Julien Baker
19th	Antoine Auclair
20th	Cameron Christiansen

I'm nervous. *He's going to be a mess.* I know eighth won't be good enough for Beck, *but it's good enough for me.*

There's too much going on to hear any of Beck's post quali interviews, but I can read the devastation on his face. I chew my bottom lip. Even with a sullen expression, *he's cripplingly handsome.*

Beck hands the microphone off and quickly exits the media pen. *Finally.* I just want to hug him. Beck heads mine and Charlie's way, not taking his eyes off the ground. He doesn't stop or look up, but reaches out for my hand. I interlace his fingers and join his pace. My heart races. I want to be supportive, but I know he's not ready to talk. Shannon and Charlie mumble back and forth a few steps behind us.

Inside hospitality, Beck walks straight for his driver's room. He hasn't said a word. He releases my hand and immediately shuts the door behind us. I lean against the massage table; Beck stands with his back to me for several seconds. When he turns around, his eyes are closed. He puts his hands on top of his head and exhales. His silence is *killing* me. I push off the table and rest my hands on the top of his racing suit at his hips. He still hasn't looked at me. *I can't do this anymore.*

"Beck what can I do for you?" I say softly.

He opens his eyes and lowers his arms around me. He rests his sweaty forehead against mine.

"Just be with me," he says quietly.

My heart shatters.

"I can do that."

I can't make out much of what Charlie's saying to Beck in the other room. I came straight to the bedroom to give them space. Plus, I could hardly wait to peel my sweaty clothes off. Now that I'm naked, I have no desire to put anything on, *robe it is.*

I pull my hair up into a bun. It's time to wash off the makeup that didn't melt off my face.

A door slams. I turn the water off and listen. *It's silent now.* I grab the other robe off the hook and peek out the bedroom door. Beck's on the couch. His head is lying on the backrest and his eyes are staring up at the ceiling. *It's just us now.*

I push the door open. "Come here and put this on."

Beck pushes off the loveseat.

He follows me into the bedroom and sets the robe at the foot of the bed. He reaches a hand over his shoulder and pulls his shirt off over his head. *Will I ever be able to look at him without gawking?*

He pushes his arms through the sleeves of the robe and ties it at the waist. I pull my legs under me at the head of the bed and pat the comforter. He crawls up on the bed and flops onto his back. He scoots up and rests his head in my lap. *He looks pitiful.*

A smile creeps over my lips.

"Do you trust me?"

Beck closes his eyes. "Of course I do, Sophie."

"Wait right here."

I scoop up his head and gently scoot out from under him.

In the bathroom, I grab a fresh washcloth and turn the sink to hot. I move to my toiletry bag and unzip the pouch pocket. I grab the green gel face mask I packed on a whim. I glance at the faucet—*perfectly steamy.*

Beck's eyes are still closed, and I set my supplies on the nightstand. I lift his head and reclaim my place, cradling his head in my lap. I reach for the washcloth; it leaves a ring of condensation on the glass top of the nightstand. I gently drape the washcloth over his face. He doesn't flinch or say a word; he either trusts me or couldn't care less about what's currently happening. After a few seconds, I lift the washcloth and toss it back to the bedside table. I squirt a good amount of the gooey mask into my palm and begin applying the mask to his face. Beck's eyes wince, and he folds his arms over his chest. Very well. *At least he's awake.*

"Are you still thinking about qualifying?" I ask quietly.

"I seriously could have had pole—I totally screwed myself."

I take that as a *yes.*

"I've made too many mistakes in qualifying this year..." he continues.

I keep quiet, letting him get it out. I continue spreading the mask over the ridges of his face.

"I still have so much to prove. I took over the seat of a legend...I don't have a legacy backing me like Tommy does, like *Ren* does, *like most of the grid does.*"

"And you'll do it tomorrow!" I say.

Beck sighs.

"Does Ren's contract announcement have anything to do with how you're feeling?"

"How can it not?" He pauses. "I don't have a guaranteed seat next year—nothing's finalized. There's a line of drivers waiting to take my seat."

I massage the last of the mask onto his chin. *How can he be this hard on himself?* He's moved past Alek and up to sixth place in the driver's championship.

"Beck, I know I don't know anything about *anything*, but you're a phenomenal driver. The broadcast gushes over you week after week. From what I see, you're just as good as Luca."

His eyes flicker open and stare directly into my soul.

Beck swallows. "Why are you so good to me?"

Why? He's killing me!

"Because you mean *the world* to me, Beck."

I spot the slightest twinkle in his eye before he closes them. The smallest hint of a smile touches his lips.

I win.

I grab the washcloth and gently start wiping off the mask.

"*Beautiful,*" I swoon.

Beck's eyes open. "I've got to see."

He sits up quickly and heads for the bathroom. I scoot off the bed and follow. I stand in the doorway and watch.

Beck slowly turns his face side to side in the mirror then smiles.

"Do you feel a little better?"

"A little," he says. He turns away from the mirror and his eyes dive into me.

"At least I'll be shiny for interviews tomorrow."

CHAPTER 21
I Don't Sweat I Sparkle

Pippa's handheld fan just ran out of batteries. It lasted the entirety of the race. We'll have to rough it for the remainder of postrace interviews. The paddock's lit up, and the grid is sweaty and beat after a long, hard sixty-two laps.

"Pretty amazing, I haven't been around for a Singapore Grand Prix where everyone's finished!" Pippa says.

Charlie nods. "I don't know that I have either."

Is it wrong to be proud of every team? This track was *hard*. I mean, *Leo did end up lapping two drivers*, but they finished! Even Imre and Tommy managed to avoid each other!

Luca's about to lose it in the media pen. I've swapped places with Pippa tonight. She's trying to stay positive. After starting pole, Luca didn't have the best race. An unlucky lockup in turn sixteen cost him two positions in lap one. Thankfully, that turn has a bit of forgiveness on the outside and he avoided contact with the wall. *I'm most proud of Beck.* He managed not one, but two tricky overtakes. I think it's more than fair to say he turned his weekend around. P4 for Luca and P5 for Beck. Maybe it was the contract announcement giving him a boost, but Ren had the race of his life and came in second.

Coop stops beside us on his way back to the suite. He pats Charlie on the back.

"Good to see Beck smiling again," Charlie says.

"His day's coming—I can feel it." Coop smiles.

"Did Beck look more glowy than normal this morning?"

Coop narrows his eyes.

I glance at Beck and shrug. "I put an energizing mask on him last night!"

Pippa laughs.

Charlie closes his eyes and shakes his head.

"You should have stayed for masks last night, Charlie!" I tease.

"What is it with those masks?" Coop laughs. "My daughter can't get enough."

Charlie smiles. "You both are glowing!"

"*That* would be sweat," I correct him.

"Sophie doesn't sweat! She sparkles!" Coop yells.

Coop. God love that man. The moisture that's collected under my boobs for the last three hours says otherwise. I don't know why I bothered straightening my hair this morning; it frizzed up within minutes of leaving the hotel. It was a proper mess by eight p.m. when the five lights went out. Beck moves to the next interview station in the pen, and finally I can hear him.

"Beck, congratulations on P5 here in Singapore! You started eighth on the grid and had some great battles. You really kept us on our toes with those aggressive overtakes. How are you feeling about your performance?"

"Obviously not where I *wanted* to start." Beck smiles. "I think I raced a little angry, so I had my elbows out. But our strategy was good, and the pace was good. I'm happy with the ground I was able to make up."

"Are you still hung up on that mistake in qualifying?"

"That one will hurt for a while," Beck confirms. "I truly thought that could be my first pole position start. But I'm happy with what I was able to do tonight and full steam ahead for Japan!"

The next evening, I scoot to the middle in the backseat next to Beck. The extra hours flew by, but they were glorious. Between our bed and the rooftop pool, we didn't even leave the hotel; *we didn't need to*. We were perfectly content being there together.

Dusk is setting in as the magic skyline of Singapore falls further and further away. Beck yawns. I look away to avoid contagion. We might have slept in, but I never adjusted to the time difference. And here I am, throwing another wrench in my internal clock, *but my pod awaits*.

"I'm glad you came out," Beck says, pulling my hand to his lap. "This one was rough, but having you here makes it so much better."

My eyes dart to Joe and Charlie in the front seat. Can they hear him?

"It'll be weird not having anyone this week."

I give Beck puppy eyes. "You'll have Charlie."

Charlie turns in the front seat and smiles. *So he can hear us.*

Beck pats Charlie's shoulder around the headrest.

"Sophie hasn't seen Luca's jet, has she?" Charlie asks.

"Huge," Beck says. "And *he owns it*. We're flying with him to Japan then we'll take it back to headquarters."

"I wish I could be there," I say.

"Are you ready for your show?"

"Somehow, I didn't fall the first time—even after your surprise appearance in the eleventh hour. If I could handle that, this one will be easy, right?"

"You'll kill it." Beck winks.

I couldn't be more excited to walk again. The first show is a core memory I'll never forget. My feelings are conflicted. I can't wait to be back in Paris with the girls, but-I'm devastated to miss the Japanese Grand Prix. I won't see Beck for a week and a half. After Japan, he's going straight to headquarters. I'm so bound to him already. That length of time seems like *eternity*.

Beck sets his hand on my bag. "Your purse is vibrating."

I quickly free the top flap to check the caller.

"Oh, it's Ana. She's FaceTiming."

"Answer it." He smiles.

"Are you sure? I can call her back."

He continues smiling.

I swiftly pull my phone out and accept the call. *I hope everything's alright.*

Ana's eyes are wet. A drapery of purple lights twinkle in the dusk-pink sky behind her beaming face. *Wait...*

"Are you back at the gardens?" I ask.

Ana pulls her left hand over her mouth. The sparkling lights have nothing on the twinkle of the massive oval diamond that's appeared on her finger.

I gasp. "Oh my God, Ana!"

She bounces up and down, too ecstatic for words.

I turn the phone to Beck. Ana spins, and Ren waves in the background.

Beck flashes Ren a thumbs up. "Congrats, mate!"

"You're the first person we called!" Ana shouts.

"Me?"

"We were only just here! I've got to call my parents now!"

Ana waves and frantically ends the call.

"My word! I'm so happy for them!" I squeal, returning my phone to my purse.

"He's had the ring for months."

My jaw drops. "You knew he was proposing?"

Beck nods, amused.

"How funny. I asked her Thursday if he was *the one*."

"Well, I hope she said he was…"

"She did," I giggle. "Oh gosh, I won't get to see her!"

"You'll have to wait for *Zandvoort*."

The Dutch Grand Prix. It's the race Carmen's attending with Oliver. It's mind-blowing—Beck isn't even asking me to the races anymore. It's now a given I'll be going with him. From the Netherlands, it's Qatar, Portugal, then to the final race in Abu Dhabi. This year will make up for that gap year I never took.

The departure drop off is busy with lingering fans who traveled in for the race. Joe stops the car along the curb, and Charlie turns around and hands Beck a hat. Beck leans toward the rearview mirror and lowers the hat just above his eyes.

I step onto the sidewalk; the final slap of humidity is bittersweet. Beck closes the back wing of the SUV and sets my suitcase beside me.

"I can't believe they're engaged," I say quietly.

Beck cradles my head in his hands. I gaze into his eyes and take a mental picture.

"Well, when you've found *the one...*" he says, moving closer to my lips. "*Why wait?*"

My heart skips as his hands slide down my neck. Beck leans down and extends the handle on my suitcase.

"All set?" he asks.

My eyes tingle. I shove my hands in my pockets and stare down at my feet. "I suppose." *What is this lump in my throat?*

Beck lifts my chin with his finger. "Let me know you got on the plane," he says.

I nod.

He tips the bill of his hat up and hovers over my lips. "*Miss you already.*"

I join the security line and open Instagram. Ren and Ana's engagement is *everywhere*. Even the Makellos team account reposted their proposal picture from the gardens.

Big weekend for Ren Enatsu! After his contract announcement, he took second place at the Singapore Grand Prix! Ren ended the weekend an engaged man after proposing to his longtime girlfriend, Ana Wong.

My heart. They're so happy. He pulled off an epic proposal. But I can't ignore the comments directly below their blissful faces.

Gold digger!
But why? He can do better.

A claw grips in my stomach. This is the team's account; I can't imagine the commentary on the gossip site. Now that I know Ana's story, I feel protective of her. I tap the screen and add my own comment of five red heart icons.

A call notification drops down—it's Stuart. *Crap*, I've been meaning to return his calls *and emails*. It's eight p.m. here, but it's the middle of the workday in Paris.

"Hi, Stuart!"

"Sophie, I've been trying to get a hold of you!"

"I know I'm terribly—"

"I can't believe I'm saying this, but *Chanel* reached out."

"What?" I manage.

"I believe they saw your interview speaking about your mother's bag."

I beg your pardon? Chanel?

"They wanted to send something, and I wasn't entirely sure if you'd be in London or Paris next, so I had them send it here to the office."

I hand my passport and boarding pass to the security attendant.

"You're saying there is a package from Chanel at the office with *my* name on it?"

"Yes, Sophie," Stuart giggles. "Please come in and get it—it won't stop staring at me."

My passport's handed back. Who am I? *I must not leave Chanel waiting!*

"I'll be there first thing tomorrow morning! I'm at the airport for my flight home! Thank you, Stuart. I promise, I'll be better with the communication."

I yank the phone from my ear and end the call. I throw my phone into a plastic bin for the security scanner. My mind takes off. *What could they have sent?*

CHAPTER 22
TIME TRAVELER

IT'S A TIME WARP. I traipse under the Charles de Gaulle signage. How did I get here and what day is it? I slept through an entire meal service. How is the airport this chaotic? *It's seven a.m.* I pat my cheeks and head for the train. *Back to reality, Sophie*—it's Paris fashion week.

I want nothing more than to head home, but I make my way to the agency, luggage in tow. The office is never open this early. Everyone is rushing around as if they're running IV drips of espresso. I slip into Stuart's office, narrowly dodging being plowed over by a woman carrying a stack of boxes so high she can't see in front of her. My roller bag hits the back of my ankles. Stuart shoots up from his desk, clapping. There, on the meeting table in the corner, sits the chic black-and-white box.

My heart thumps.

"Should I open it now?" I ask Stuart.

"*Please.* I've been dying to see what they sent."

The lid is perfectly tight and fitted; it makes a suction noise as I lift it from the sturdy box. A note is lying on top of perfectly packed tissue paper.

Sophie-
Thank you for sharing your heart-warming story about your mother's bag. We thought you could use some treasure to put inside.

I smile.

"What does it say?!" Stuart asks.

"You're right." I hand Stuart the card. "They saw my interview—I can't believe it."

I lift the tissue paper, revealing dozens of small boxes of all shapes and sizes.

I wave Stuart closer.

Stuart gasps. "What a treat!"

Together, we unbox their entire collection of makeup, a compact mirror and a bottle of *Chanel No 5*. Finally, I open a flat box, holding a quilted red leather cardholder that perfectly matches my mother's bag.

"Please, let me know how I can send them a formal thank you."

He nods.

I balance the Chanel box on top of my suitcase. Stuart walks me to the door. "As for the communication—"

"I'm truly sorry. I was quite busy, and with the time difference, I was always wary of calling you back."

What's my excuse for the unanswered emails?

Stuart smiles. "If it's alright with you, I'm going to start texting you. You can write me back any hour of the day."

I step into the lift and text the girls.

Honey, I'm home!

Half of my hair is fastened in curlers on top of my head, the other half is being sprayed at my back. My makeup is finished. It's the same soft look from the London show. I stare at Beck in the FaceTime, *half a world away.* His room is dark as he puts his arm behind his head on the pillows.

"It's lonely here," Beck says. "I've gotten used to having you with me."

I stare at my usual spot in the nook of his arm. I can almost sense the warmth of his chest against my cheek.

"What would we be doing right now if I was there?"

Beck's eyes widen.

"I could think of a lot of *things* we would be doing." He smirks.

Heat fills my cheeks. I glance in the mirror to see if the stylist caught that. She's still in the zone, working on the next section of my hair.

I glare at Beck and shake my head.

"Ren was spilling some details in the press conference; I just sent you the clip."

"Is he as excited as Ana?"

Beck nods. His chest slowly falls as he deeply exhales.

"I'm going to try to go to sleep. Good luck out there, rockstar."

I smile. "*Goodnight.*"

Beck waves and ends the FaceTime. *I should be there.*

I open the press conference clip Beck sent.

Beck's beside Ren on the couch; his microphone is in his lap.

"Ren, let's start with you. First and foremost, congratulations are in order on your engagement."

Ren flips his microphone upright, and his face lights up. *"Thank you."*

"Obviously, that took some planning. Tell us how you pulled that off in the midst of a race weekend."

"I was a little worried in the weeks leading up, since my contract wasn't completely ironed out. I wanted to have all the pressure from that out of the way, but once the announcements were made, the plan was a go. Singapore was the perfect opportunity—it's Ana's home. As long as the race went well, I had all the arrangements to do it after."

"I'd say P2 in Singapore is a great race result."

"Agreed." Ren smiles. *"I arranged special access to the gardens and...she said yes, so it all worked out."*

The clip ends. I want to cry. Ren looks quite *proud.* I've never heard him talk that much. I set my phone in my lap. The difference I feel today from how I felt in this chair before the London show is night and day. I'm going to give my all to this runway. Beck might not be in the audience this time, but Dad got in last night, and Carmen is sitting in the front row with Alice.

A mass of red moves behind me in the mirror. *My word.* The bouquet of roses is so large, the bearer's shoulders and head are completely covered. The bouquet stops behind me, and my stylist puts down the hot iron.

A voice murmurs behind the flowers, "These just came by messenger."

My heart skips.

The stylist smiles. "They're for you, Sophie."

I hop out of the chair and extend my arms. The weight of the bundle is shocking—there must be three hundred roses. I use my knee to cradle them in one arm. I retrieve the note tucked into the ribbon around the stems.

I'm sorry I couldn't make it.
Can't wait to see you next week.
-Beck

My heart bursts. *How* does he pull these things off? Across the globe, with the busiest schedule imaginable. I reread the note again, and again *and again.* It's *incomprehensible.*

I shift my gaze to the rafters and wave the card at my eyes. I need every bit of gravity to keep the tears at bay.

"*Oh my God*!" Ella shrieks.

I hand her the notecard. The red intrusion was hard to miss backstage. Ella shakes her head then hands the card back.

"These roses, your robe, the curlers in your hair—sit down! I must get your picture!"

Ella grabs my phone from the hair and makeup chair.

I retake my seat and cradle the roses in my lap.

"Perfect!" Ella squeals.

The flowers look even more ridiculous in the photo. The arrangement hides half of my body.

The stylist puts her hand on her hip. "We've got to get back to it—are you going to keep those in your lap?"

I glance at the roses then to the table in front of me, covered in makeup palettes. She rolls her eyes and walks over to the wall. She retrieves a stool and retraces her steps, dragging it behind her.

The stylist winks. "They deserve their own chair."

Ella backs away, shaking her head. "You're as spoiled as they come."

Hands are back in my hair, removing the roller clips. I want to call Beck, but he might have truly gone to sleep. The picture is glamorous. *The roses are epic.* I send the photo to Beck.

YOU ARE CRAZY!!

I open Instagram. The roses deserve their own chair and their own spot on my feed. I tap the caption box and type out an explanation below the photo.

When your man can't make it, but sends his love 300-fold.

"Alright, close your eyes," the stylist instructs.

A cloud of sticky, fragrant mist surrounds me. When the spraying stops, I turn to the velvety red petals next to me.

"Don't worry! They're still there!" the stylist laughs.

I can't help it; I'm bubbling over the edge. I tap the screen and post the photo.

"This is the cutest picture I've ever seen of you two!" Ella says, handing my phone back.

Dad keeps his arm around me. "That deserves a spot on the desk!"

Oh dear! Dad is precious in his sweater-vest.

A FaceTime from Beck drops down; the show after-party space is loud, but I hit accept.

Beck smiles.

"Shouldn't you be sleeping?" I yell.

"I was, but I wanted to see how it went!"

I pull the phone back, so Dad falls into frame.

"George!" Beck yells.

Dad waves wildly. "You should have seen her up there! She was a showstopper!"

Eye roll. I bring the phone back in. "Beck, the roses—you are mad! I could barely hold them!"

"I'm glad they got to you." He smirks. "Wish I could have delivered them myself."

"Where'd your dad go? Put him back on."

Huh?

I pass the phone to Dad but hover close to eavesdrop.

"George! Two weeks from now, I've got a race at Zandvoort. My dad's coming, but Mum and the kids can't make it. I'd love to have you out for it."

My heart explodes. I move closer.

"Oh, Beck!" Dad says, taken aback. "I would love to come!"

"It's on then!" Beck says. "We've got the arrangements to get there. I'll give Soph the details. Come and have a good time."

Dad's nodding his head, speechless.

"Now go and enjoy the party!" Beck waves. "I'll ring you tomorrow after quali, Soph."

I blow Beck a kiss.

He ends the call. I can't believe it.

I grab Dad's arm. "Dad! You're coming to Zandvoort!"

I've never seen Dad this excited; he's ordered us champagne for a toast. *We already have arrangements to get there.* That means one thing: *the jet.*

The more I think about Dad and James meeting, the more I picture a destined friendship. I wave to Alice, who's walking in, giggling arm in arm with Evelyn. Alice nods and heads in our direction. Their friendship is endearing.

"Sophie!" Evelyn smiles. "I told Ella, I'll have your pieces cleaned and sent to you."

"I was going to ask if you would mind me wearing one of the pieces to a race?"

Evelyn's face lights up. "Oh, the top from your second look would be fantastic!" Alice says.

"I was thinking the same."

I nudge Dad. "Dad, this is Evelyn Edwards, the designer."

Dad takes Evelyn's hand. How have I never noticed Evelyn doesn't wear a wedding ring? The champagne he ordered us is set on the counter in front of him. Dad's fixated as he moves a glass of champagne into Evelyn's hand. Alice flashes me a look and raises her eyebrows. I move beside Alice and watch them clink glasses, enthralled. I've never seen Dad interact with a woman outside the office.

"I guess I'll order my own champagne!" I giggle quietly to Alice.

"I saw your headline last week," Alice says.

I roll my eyes.

"*Yeah...*" I say. "That was quite shocking."

Alice beams. "You're making a name for yourself, love."

Ella had to sit up front with the driver. My roses take up the whole middle of the backseat.

"I believe Miss Evelyn had eyes for George," Carmen says.

"Or was it the other way around?" Ella says, snappily typing on her phone.

"I'm—not sure how I feel about that…" I say.

I've never seen Dad flirt with *anyone*.

"I told her I'd wear the top from my set to a race. Qatar should be warm enough."

Carmen nods. "That would be perfect for the desert!"

"Deary me!" Ella shrieks. "I just got us invited to the costume party of all costume parties!" She whips her head around. "Last weekend in October! Our own table, and we can invite whoever we want!"

"Fabulous!" Carmen cheers.

My hand flies to my purse for my phone.

Ella gasps. "What a killer theme." She spins back around. *"Angels and demons."*

I open the calendar app and relief floods over me. *It's an off week.* My stomach dances. Beck might even be able to come.

***

I stop the alarm as quick as possible. I reach down to the floor for my laptop and pull it into bed. 7:01 a.m.. It's time to tune in to the qualifying broadcast from Japan.

I jump as my door creaks open.

"Sophie, what are you doing?"

Carmen stands in the doorway.

"I'm watching qualifying. Did I wake you?"

"No, I want to see!" Carmen closes the door behind her.

She stops at my dresser and shifts the vase on top. Not even a quarter of the roses fit in any vase we had. Using almost every glass in the cabinet, we now have twelve small bouquets scattered throughout the apartment.

"It's the second round, five drivers have already been knocked out."

Carmen climbs into bed next to me.

I point to the black car coming into the pit lane. "That's Ana's fiancé, Ren!"

The broadcast moves to a red car starting a flying lap.

"Is that Beck?" Carmen asks.

"No, that's Luca."

The broadcast hovers above turn eighteen.

I smile. "*There's* Beck."

Beck crosses the finish line, clocking in his first attempt. *WRI* moves up one position in the standings.

"Beck's in sixth?" Carmen asks.

"Yes, but he'll go again and try to get a better lap." I point to the elimination zone line on the standings.

"He can't fall below this line, or he won't progress to the third round."

Carmen shakes her head. "I can't wait to watch from the track!"

"I forgot to tell you!" I squeal.

"What?"

"Beck invited my dad to Zandvoort last night. He called at the after-party."

"Stop!" Carmen shrieks. "You *must* bring your dad to Oliver's show!"

"Absolutely! I'll be the girl that brings her dad to an EDM show."

Carmen laughs. "It's Amsterdam—*anything* goes."

Crap. I'm already running behind, but I haven't talked to Beck since last night. I accept his FaceTime and lean the phone against the mirror. I need to be hands free.

I step back and make sure the towel around me is secure. I would die if Charlie's around, and I gave an accidental show.

Beck's face fills the screen. His eyes grow when he notices my ensemble.

"Soph, don't do this to me."

I giggle. "I have to be ready in twenty minutes. *I'm terribly late!*"

Beck folds his lips together. "*Mhm.*"

Focus, Sophie. I grab my eyeliner and start the meticulous process.

"P4!" I cheer.

"You watched?"

"In bed! Carmen watched the second round with me."

Beck sighs. "I need my surprise dessert about now."

"That's just pitiful—no one got you something sweet?"

"Then I need Sophie for dessert after that."

I veer off my eyeliner trail. *I could go for a three-course meal of him myself.*

Beck smiles, pleased with himself.

"When do I get to see you?" I ask.

"I'll be at headquarters all week, but I just got off the phone with Mum and Dad. They'd like us to come out next weekend, to their house. Would you like that?"

I smile.

"I'd love that. I'm staying at Dad's Friday for his birthday!"

"Perfect. I'll pick you up Saturday morning and drive us out there," he says.

I pull back from the mirror. "Speaking of plans, I'm going to a costume party, and I need a date. It's here in Paris on the twenty-eighth of October."

Beck clicks around on his screen and grins.

"That's an off week."

"*I know.*" I waggle my eyebrows. "And you've never been to our place here."

"I suppose I've got to be your date, then."

I smile. "I want to invite Ren and Ana. Tommy can come too. We have a whole table to fill."

"Tommy might want to bring someone."

I stop. "*Oh?*"

"Emma," Beck says.

"Are they talking again?"

"Yes—well, sort of," he says.

I remember Emma's name from the blog. I'd love to meet her.

"Tell Tommy to bring her! I'll tell Ana."

I lean in close to the camera and drop the towel around me. "I've got to be going..." I wink. "Need to find some clothes to put on."

Beck bites his finger, staring at the screen intently.

I blow him a kiss and hang up.

A text arrives immediately after.

That was unfair.

I message back.

> Go to sleep

> Goodnight, my Sophie.

My Sophie. I melt. Okay, stop. I must focus and fix this eyeliner.

5:30 a.m. I do the math in my half-lucid brain for a third time. It's 1:30 p.m. in Suzuka, half an hour before *lights out* for the Japanese Grand Prix.I prepare my eyes for the blast of light before opening my phone. I turn the screen brightness down and type a message to Beck:

> Knock 'em dead!!!

I'd be in the garage by now, watching the action of the cars being taken to the start line before the national anthem. Soon, I'd get to give Beck his good luck kiss. *I should be there.* I've never been homesick in my own bed. How can I miss him this much already? Our last kiss in Singapore wasn't even a week ago yet, but it feels like forever.

If I stay here, *I will fall back asleep.* I throw the comforter back and use my phone for light. Somehow, I remembered to put my laptop on the charger last night. I scoop it up and grab the fluffy robe hanging on the back of my door. The sky is still the usual dark gray glow of Paris at night. I tiptoe through the living room and add the fluffy blanket on the sofa to my collection. I flip the latch on the French door and open it slowly.

Cool air sneaks up the sleeves of my robe. I step out and quietly close the door. I sit back into the single chair that fits on our tiny balcony. I cover my legs with the blanket and open my laptop. The livestream connects for the final few minutes of the prerace broadcast. It's not the garage, but this isn't the worst race-watching setup. Beyond the glowing screen and the ornate black iron railing of our balcony, dreamy Parisian rooftops stretch down our street. I open Instagram and capture my race-watching setup. I type a message over the photo for my story.

Cheering half a world away!

It's unbelievable. Three races and two fashion weeks have taken me to a new level. My follower count has tipped over twenty thousand. I click my tagged photos. My rose picture was reposted to several gossip accounts almost immediately after the show Friday. I open the tagged photo and expand the comments.

She flies all over the world for Beck and he can't even come to her show?

I shake my head.

Obviously, he isn't that into her.
He's racing, you twit! It's the Japanese Grand Prix.

Ha! That's hilarious. That's not even one of Ella's finsta accounts.

The sun is up, the birds are chirping, and Beck is going to make the podium. *I hate this.* It's not the same without my headset. I'm dying to hear what Beck and Coop are shouting back and forth. I need my dedicated onboard view. He's having a phenomenal drive but getting minimal airtime due to the battling in the midfield. This is the second time the broadcast has panned to Luca, watching from the garage. Luca retired from the race in lap fourteen when he, Leo and Wit collided in turn nine.

At this point, I'm *bitter*. This track is awesome, and Beck is set to get third. The broadcast jumps to Beck. Out of turn two, he heads for the high-speed squiggle turns that run parallel to the main straight.

"Here's Beckham Wright's final pass through the Esses! After that early incident took Luca out, all eyes shifted to Beck to bring home as many points as possible for team Furio.

"And again! The Makellos will be on defense with the MACH of Tommy Young."

The broadcast cuts to Ren defending his position in fourth as he and Tommy rip out of turn one. The broadcast jumps to Beck's onboard; I grip the edge of the screen as his speedometer nears 315 km/h. The track flashes by underneath him at the overpass ahead of turn fifteen. My leg's bouncing the laptop.

"And Beckham Wright will join Elijah and Geoff, taking that final spot on the podium!"

The broadcast flashes Furio's team radio.

"Is that really the chequered flag?" Beck cries out.

"Indeed, Beck. Stellar drive!" Coop yells.

It's P3. My heart aches.

Beck's out of the car. He throws his arms around Coop, and Charlie's slapping the top of his helmet. *How did I miss this?*

His helmet is off. I want to reach through the screen and touch him. His eyes are absolutely dazzling. Beck sets his helmet down and takes the microphone.

"Beck, you left Singapore hungry for redemption. What was your mindset today before the race?"

"That mistake in quali last week really crushed me. Qualifying obviously went better yesterday, but I still felt like I had to make it up to the team."

"Well, you certainly made up for it! Third place, fastest lap, it's your fourth time on the podium this season. When can we expect your inaugural race win?"

Beck chuckles. *"I knew that was coming! We've got four races left; I'd like to get it done this season."*

"After Luca's incident, what kept you from cracking under the pressure to perform?"

"The team did nothing but encourage that I could do it. The car was strong, our pace was on par with Valor and I was ready to fight."

He won't be able to read this text for hours, but I'm sending it anyway.

P3 AND fastest lap?!
I can't believe I missed this one! Never again.

CHAPTER 23

HIT ME

I TURN ON THE landing for the last flight of stairs. The way a day with nothing planned used to depress me—*oh, how life has changed*. I've fully embraced these quiet last few days. Fashion week's ending perfectly co-incided with an off week in the race schedule. *I have a minute to breathe again.* Pierre's on the phone at the front desk as I spring off the last step and wave.

Two more days, and I get to see Beck, starting with a visit to his family's home for lunch.

I push through the lobby doors, excited to get outside and do some-thing trivial—my old running route. I make my way down the block and pull up my favorite Oliver-curated playlist. Music pumps through my *RIMI* headphones. I cross *Boulevard Saint-Germain* and take off at a comfortable jogging pace. The first few months we lived here, I did this run multiple times a week. South from our place until I can cut across the Luxembourg Gardens. That was in my previous pace of life. That was *before Beck.*

I pick up my pace, crossing *Rue de Vaugirard*. The music stops from an incoming text notification. I reach the other side of the street, and the song picks back up. I run along the garden fencing. Another notification interrupts the song, completely throwing off my rhythm, immediately followed by another, then another. *You've got to be kidding me.* The song picks back up a few steps ahead of the west entrance. I turn into the gardens and slow to a walk. *Time to silence this ringer.* I pull my phone from my leggings pocket; the *Roomie Trio* group chat has four new messages. I pause the music and click the thread. Sandwiched between screenshots and a link, Ella's all-caps text jumps off the page and stops me dead in my tracks.

WHO LEAKED THIS TO THE PRESS???

My vision tunnels. I scroll up to the first screenshot. It's an article from the British tabloid, *The Scoop.*

Scandal before the Paddock! The latest girl on the grid with ties to Beckham Wright—juicy past exposed.

The world screeches into slow motion. *Please no.* I click the article link. My professional headshot loads. The next picture loads, and sheer panic cuts through me. I gulp. Fredrick's in a suit and tie, photographed speaking at a conference. I check the heading; the story was posted forty-two minutes ago.

Sources close to the situation say prior to dating Wright, Sophie Collins was a financial protégé of her father, London financier, George Collins. Her career at a prestigious financial firm in London was terminated after a workplace romance with a senior executive was brought to light. Both parties were terminated and were said to have left quietly.

In the following months, another (this time C-suite) executive left the same firm in the midst of a nasty public divorce, following cheating allegations. Questions have now arisen whether these allegations involved a fling with the same junior employee. Sophie is now seen trackside, supporting her latest catch, Formula One driver, Beckham Wright.

My heartbeat echoes, pulsating in my ears. I thought I'd escaped it, but here it is, rearing its ugly head, crushing me like a sledgehammer. A text from Alice drops down. I glance at the preview.

> Remember Sophie, there is no such thing as bad pre…

My phone vibrates violently. I nearly drop it from the jump scare; it's Beck on FaceTime. *I'm going to be sick.* I stare at the screen and let it ring. My heart knocks in my chest. For once, I can't stand to be face to face with him.

He's calling because he's seen this, right? *Of course he is, you idiot.* Can I decline and call him back? *Damn you,* modern technology! The visual context *will* help me better read his reaction. I take a deep breath and hit accept. It connects instantly and Beck smiles. I swallow and try to muster up what I can.

"Soph—you alright?"

Fuck. Don't be nice to me. He's on the move, passing through glass doors and heading outside. Can he see the lack of color on my face? *Breathe.*

"I-I'm guessing you saw *The Scoop* article?"

Beck stops and sits down; the camera goes still. Blue sky canvases behind him.

Beck shakes his head. "Sophie, I'm not interested in hearing about this from some sleazy tabloid. I'd rather hear it from you when you're ready."

The smile threw me off; his words sink in. I guess the time is as good as ever. I take another deep breath.

"Was this the messy relationship you spoke of?"

I nod slowly.

"I haven't seen it all, but from what I've read, they have the first part of the story right."

Beck raises his eyebrows.

I shuffle my feet to the edge of the pebble path—my legs suddenly the weight of concrete cylinders. I continue, "Fredrick was my mentor when I was an intern. He became a VP by the time I graduated. When I was hired on, I was placed on his team... that's when our relationship grew to—more than just colleagues..."Beck's face doesn't change.

"And this was found out?"

I nod. "Eventually."

"How long did that go on?"

I gulp. "We were together, *in secret*, for almost two years."

His eyes widen. *It does sound horrible.*

I exhale. "Anyway, we were fired pretty much on the spot, and he moved to New York four days later. As for the other part of the story, none of that is true; I had nothing to do with that man's divorce."

Beck's face changes. He looks away from the screen.

"This happened at the start of *this* year?"

I nod. "The first week of January."

His eyes come back to the screen.

"That's why you left finance and moved?"

"The girls were the only ones that knew about us, and they were already looking at places in Paris, so I jumped onboard and ran away with them."

Beck stares for several seconds. "Would he have been the one to leak this?"

"No." I shake my head. "He would never do that." My mind takes off. I don't know where it came from, but I know the first place I'll be checking. We left quickly. I'm sure there were mumblings around the office, but it wasn't widely known *until now.*

"Has he reached out to you? Do you think this has gotten to him?"

Ha! I haven't heard from Fredrick since the day he left for New York.

"If it has…he hasn't said anything."

Beck pauses, shifting his focus away from the screen again.

"You think you'd still be with him if you weren't caught?"

His words crash into me. Beck's eyes flick back to the screen.

"No, Beck. It was completely out of line—it wasn't healthy. Looking back now, it was a blessing being outed."

Forget the words. It's his eyes. I can see it now—he's worried. A pit pierces my stomach. *Why* does this have to be over the phone? I don't want to know the answer, but I have to ask.

"Has your camp said anything?" I ask.

Beck sighs. "Said anything? No—but they were the ones who sent it to me."

Fuck.

I turn to face the trees. "I'm sorry I didn't tell you sooner."

"There's nothing to be sorry for, Sophie. You are being honest with me now." He pauses. "That's all I can ask for."

Really? I chew my bottom lip. How is he this levelheaded? Maybe this isn't the end of the world?

His face is serious as his eyes penetrate the screen.

"You sure you're over him?"

It's a dagger to the heart.

"*Completely*. Beck, what we have—our relationship—I've never been so sure of anything...*or anyone...*"

A smile creeps over his lips. He lets out a long sigh.

"I just need it to be Saturday already."

The pit in my stomach drops further. *His parents' house.*

"You still want me to come...to your mum and dads?" I ask shakily.

Beck raises an eyebrow. "I'm not going without you. You're coming whether you like it or not."

After we hang up, I pull my headphones down and abandon the run. All things considered, the call went better than expected. I turn back to the west gate and scan the rest of the article. Beyond the first part, it's complete rubbish. His picture's there, but Fredrick's name isn't included anywhere in the piece. *Hopefully, that means he'll never see it.* I'm gutted Beck's name was included, and even more gutted *dad's* name was used. *How embarrassing.*

My excitement at visiting the Wright's home has been shattered. I'm queasy even thinking about it. What will his parents think? Will they have seen the headline? My mind sends me over a cliff. *What if Mia sees it?* Ten minutes ago, I was on such a high, now I've crash-landed.

I swing open the front door. Ella and Carmen stare back at me. Ella's laptop is open on the counter in front of them. Their faces resemble guilty kids caught searching something inappropriate on a school computer.

Carmen swallows. "Have you heard from Beck?"

"Yes." I kick the door shut behind me.

"What did he say about it?" she asks nervously.

I rest my elbows on the counter across from them. I cradle my forehead in my hands and stare into the stone pattern of the countertop.

"He wanted to know the story...so I told him everything."

"*Shit...*" Ella says.

I close my eyes.

"Was he mad?" Carmen says.

I tilt my head up. "Mad? *No...*" I pause. "But maybe worse than mad—he was acting worried that I'm still hung up on Fredrick."

I push back and walk around the counter. "Despite *that*, the conversation went *reasonably* well."

I stop between Ella and Carmen and lean in over their shoulders. The *Lights Out Ladies* gossip page stares back at me. Just as I suspected, there was a new post yesterday:

Major Sophie tea!

"I had a feeling," I say, retreating to the couch. I flop down on my back and fold my arms over my face. "Read it to me, please."

Ella begins.

"*A friend of mine who works finance in London dropped a bombshell on me. Sophie's dad is a well-known private equity magnate in London. Just so happens Sophie also previously worked in finance but was fired in January after she was caught sneaking around with her boss.*"

Alright. Accurate.

"Do you want the comments?" Ella asks.

"*Hit me,*" I mutter.

"That's one way to climb the corporate ladder. What a slut."

"Wait, she's a nepo baby? Like we need another reason to hate her."

"The timeline adds up. Sophie posted a photo from a business trip in Zurich on January fifth. She's in a post a week later, apartment hunting in Paris with Ella Humphrey."

"This is good... Like tabloid good. 1,000 points to Gryffindor."

"Well that pretty much confirms it," I say. "Send it through a tip line and get it in print for morning. Must be a slow news day."

How nice of them to add in the attempt to connect dots between me and Mr. C-suite's public divorce.

"How could they have that kind of detail? It had to have come from one of those brats you worked with," Carmen says.

I shrug. It doesn't matter who said it. The thought certainly takes me back to that morning in Zurich. I'll never forget the shock on Lenny's face when she turned around mid knock. She was outside my hotel room absurdly early that morning, hoping I'd run her through some numbers again. If only I'd paid attention to my phone, I would have seen her request. There she stood, watching me exiting Fredrick's room across the hall. I was half-asleep, but the instant we locked eyes, I froze. Her eyes jumped from me to him, standing in only his briefs in the doorway.

I knew there'd be repercussions...but I thought *at least I had Fredrick.* Now we could be together openly. We wouldn't have to hide any longer. He'd told me he loved me—but I realized four days later I wasn't enough. He'd come to say his final goodbye.

Ella's stool squeaks as she spins around. "Mum texted asking how you are."

"Managing," I say.

That reminds me, I never opened Alice's text. I uncover my face and grab my phone. It's the message sentiment I'd predicted.

> Remember Sophie, there is no such thing as bad press. Call me if you need to talk.

I know you're the professional, Alice, but I'm sure Shannon isn't saying the same. This has to be the very definition of *bad press.*

40K followers. My following has doubled in a day, thanks to the tabloid. Ella smiles.

"That's not something to be proud of," I say.

"Just trying to look at the bright side. Stuart's thrilled." Ella shrugs.

She unzips the garment bags that were delivered.

It's our *Eden Eves* pieces from the show. Seeing the pale blue set lightens my mood for half a second, but the nerves in my stomach take notice. The intrusive thoughts quickly squeeze the life from the happy notion.

I'm taking the noon train to London to be with Dad for his birthday. Some gift I've surprised him with this year: his name in a tabloid. I finally called him yesterday afternoon, after I sent myself into a full-blown panic attack. I invented multiple doomsday scenarios for how the tabloid could impact *his* career. Dad immediately put my mind at ease. *"I'm a celebrity around here!"* He was loving the attention. Everyone around me seemed to have a positive outlook on the tabloid. Even Ana tried assuring me no one reads the tabloids, and only idiots *believe* everything they read in the tabloids.

The scent in *Mille Doux Baisers* is overpoweringly sweet; it's making my stomach turn. The patisserie attendant's busy putting together an ornate basket of goodies. I asked to be crafted the biggest bundle possible. The surprise treat basket will be my shield. I'll hide behind it as long as possible when I arrive at the Wright's tomorrow. Four tiny red tables sit along the shoppe's windows outside. I wonder which spot James picked when he proposed.

My phone buzzes in my hand—*it's Ana.*

"Sophie!" she shouts.

"Hi, Ana."

"David messaged me," Ana says, skipping salutations. "He asked if I would do an interview with him Thursday."

"He probably wants to congratulate you, Ana! I think you should do it!"

"I told him I would think about it, but only if you can do the interview with me."

Show my face after the tabloid? Guess I've got nothing more to lose.

"I mean—I'll stand there with you, but you're doing the talking!"

"I'm nervous to put myself back out there..."

"Ana, you deserve to celebrate your engagement publicly, *if* that's what you want."

The attendant waves. *Crap.*

"Ana, I've got to go, my baskets ready. My advice—say yes."

I'll look ridiculous on the train. The basket is massive; beautifully wrapped in clear cellophane. A ribbon bearing the shop's name is tied in a blue bow around the handle. *It's perfect.* An arriving patron holds the door open for me and my colossal shield. The fresh air is a warm welcome, though butter and sugar still linger in my nostrils after I hit the sidewalk. My phone pings with a text message. I'm proud Ana's even considering an interview. Maybe she confirmed with David. I transfer the basket to my left arm and pull my phone from my purse.

I freeze. Fredrick's name shows on the message notification. A hand touches my back as someone steers around my abrupt stop. I step aside. I might need to sit down for this, but the café seats outside the shop are all occupied. I take a deep breath and open the message.

Soph, it's Fredrick. I hope you're doing well. I think about you often and the way we left things. I've seen glimpses of you on a few of the race broadcasts. It makes me happy to see you happy again. I'm glad you've found someone who can show you off the way you deserve to be. I also saw your name in the tabloids this week. I hope you're not in too much trouble.

It's like hearing from a ghost. I start from the top and read the message again. For months, I longed to hear from Fredrick. All the feelings I had for him now seem like a lifetime ago. A life I no longer recognize.

CHAPTER 24

A Sunday Roast

"You know I've never gotten this many calls on my birthday," Dad jokes, turning around at the stove. "Received another one this morning."

I narrow my eyes. "Tell me, did any of those calls *not* include some form of inquiry about the article?"

Dad sticks his tongue out.

I don't deserve how kind he's being about the whole ordeal.

"I should be the one cooking you breakfast."

"No, you need to sit there and relax. I've never seen you so jittery."

I jump as my phone vibrates against the counter. *Jesus, Sophie.* I click Beck's message.

Come out front. I have a surprise.

"Beck's here!" I shriek.

I scoot off the stool and knock my arm against the toast plate. It spins across the counter. Dad shoots me a look and chuckles. I slam my hand down on the plate to stop its clanging.

The chill on the front steps sends goosebumps up my legs. I take a deep breath; I shouldn't be this nervous. I finally get to see Beck. The chirping birds are drowned out by a boisterous grumble of an engine approaching.

A flash of red invades the green serenity of the front gardens this Saturday morning.

No. Way. Beck turns into the drive in a glossy, bright red Ferrari. I spot his smile through the windshield. The door opens behind me. The powerful growl of the engine made its way to inside to Dad's ears. Beck turns the car off and gets out.

Holy shit.

"My name's in the paper, and now a Ferrari shows up in my drive? The neighbors are going to think I'm having my midlife crisis, Beck!" Dad shouts.

I take a deep breath. *You did not just say that.*

"Happy birthday, George!" Beck pushes the door closed.

"It's a loaner for the weekend. Thought it would be fun to take out to Mum and Dad's."

Beck's eyes shift to me. Dad's presence might be the only thing keeping me from tackling Beck and taking him right here in the garden.

I sail down the steps and throw my arms around Beck. I relish in his scent, the solidness of his chest and the strength of his arms around me. *I missed this.* Dad whistles, finishing a lap around the car. "Is this a *Roma*?" he asks.

"Dad, did you leave the stove on?"

"Oh, shoot!" Dad takes off jogging. "Come on in, Beck!" he shouts, jumping up the steps.

Beck's grip around me loosens. Our eyes lock and I linger; drinking him in. His fingers comb into my hair before he closes in, drawing me to his lips.

Thankfully, Dad's keeping the jokes about his new claim to fame at a minimum. He's busy chatting with Beck about all the details of the

Dutch Grand Prix. Our breakfast is only slightly burned from the Ferrari distraction. I try to force down what I can, but the nerves are relentless.

As we head out, the cellophane around the basket squeaks against my forearms.

"Do we even have a boot?"

Beck waves me to the back of the car. *There is a little boot!* Beck takes the basket off my hands.

"Mum's going to go bananas when she sees this."

I smile. At least I have one thing going for me today. Thank heavens my shield fits in the surprise chariot. I open the passenger door and am instantly met with the aroma of rich leather. I sink down into the camel leather seat. The interior is almost as erotic as the exterior. Pristine stitching and red trim details. This is *hot*. How long is this drive? Am I expected to keep my hands to myself while *Beck's* driving *this*?

Beck backs into the street and clicks the car into drive. I wave at Dad, waving like a maniac on the front steps. The car purrs forward. Beck brings the back of my hand to his lips. He keeps my hand in his, resting under his chin.

"I don't want you to be nervous," he says.

That's impossible.

"You're sure you want me to come—with everything..."

Beck stops the car at the end of the street and turns to me.

His eyes are intense. "Sophie, this changes nothing. Everyone has stuff in their past."

Beck puts my hand back in my lap and puts both of his hands on the steering wheel. He checks both directions several times then smiles. I'm pushed into the seat as he floors it, making a sharp right turn. The engine roars and my heart races. Now, my smile matches his.

The streets turn to highways and the engine of the car truly comes to life. Beck heads west out of the city. I listen as he fervently gives the lowdown of everything I missed during the Japanese Grand Prix. We head southwest, and the knots in my stomach loosen. Soon enough, everything is green.

Thirty minutes later, Beck exits the highway, and the nerves start building again. He turns onto a small country lane cutting through the forest. I gasp as he accelerates, maneuvering the Ferrari through the bends of the road. *It's a rush.*

"There it is," Beck says, nodding to the right.

Across a few acres of open pasture, a modest house sits in front of an expansive grove of trees. He slows along the black iron fencing that outlines the property. A smooth drive winds its way through the pasture to the house. *It's beautiful out here.*

As we pull closer, details of the charming two-story cottage are revealed. Pastel chalk scribbles cover the drive. Ivy clings to most of the second story and every window has an open shutter. A small gray barn sits before the tree line. It's a house a picture-perfect family would dwell in—the very definition of the *Wrights.*

The red front door swings open, and Mia steps out on the front stoop. Louie's little face peeks out from a sliver in the doorway. Beck stops the car and powers down the engine. He reaches for the door handle then stops. He turns and gives me a final reassuring smile. I pull in a whale's share of air and grab the door handle. I need my woven armor *now.* That will ease my heart palpitations.

I meet Beck at the boot and eagerly reach for the bakery basket. I cradle it against my stomach in both arms.

"Sophie, what's that?" Mia calls.

"It's a surprise for your mum!"

Louie bolts out of the sliver in the door. He rushes down the steps, giggling, and collides with Beck on the sidewalk.

Louie clings to Beck's legs.

"What's up, big man!" Beck says, patting his back.

Elizabeth steps out onto the stoop, beaming ear to ear. She wears another shift dress with a scalloped trim apron around her waist. *Could she be any more perfect?* I'd bet money she's never had her name anywhere close to the tabloids.

Beck reaches for the basket; I reluctantly hand it over. I am a warrior without armor.

I step up onto the stoop into Elizabeth's arms.

"Oh, darling Sophie! Welcome! Welcome!" Elizabeth says, kissing my cheeks. A weight's been lifted off my chest. Her presence is so warm, and her hugs have the same effect as Dad's—*instant comfort.*

Her eyes are drawn to the basket.

"What is this?" she says excitedly, reaching for Beck. She grabs the ribbon on the handle and her jaw drops.

"Ah!" Elizabeth squeals. "It's our patisserie!"

"I found it." I smile. "It was even lovelier than you described."

Elizabeth takes the basket from Beck and waves us in. "Come! Come inside!"

No one blinked an eye at the chariot we arrived in; must be a typical car when your son is an F1 driver. Beck's hand meets my back and he guides me into the foyer. The charm inside matches the exterior. A rich mahogany staircase with a patterned runner lines one side of the foyer. Framed photos clutter the wall, trailing the length of the staircase. It screams happy family; it smells as divine as a kitchen at Christmas.

A pot covers every burner on the stove in front of James. Colorful cookbooks are crammed into a nook at the end of the kitchen island.

James turns around mid stir. "Hey, stranger!" He's wearing an apron himself and brings the spoon with him to hug me. The duration of the hug has me suspicious. *They know.*

"James, look what Sophie brought me from Paris!" Elizabeth points to the text on the ribbon of the basket.

James squints. "Sophie, thank you!" He smiles. "You've saved me a trip to Paris!"

Beck's eyes travel around the state of the kitchen. "What are we having, Mum?"

"Sunday roast—*on a Saturday.*" Elizabeth laughs. "We will eat in an hour or so. Would you like something now?"

"George had breakfast for us when I picked Sophie up."

"Why didn't you bring him out?!" James asks back at the stove.

"You should see how much gear he's ordered for the race," I say. "I've never seen him this excited." "Oh gosh, we have so much he could've worn!" Elizabeth says.

James turns around again. "Does your dad golf?"

"Not as much as he'd like."

"Ah! Next time, you must bring him!" James says.

Mia tugs at my hand. "Sophie, come with me. I'll give you the tour!"

I pause halfway up the stairs and gaze at the plethora of photos.

Mia points to a gold frame. "This is the day I was adopted."

Beck is just a boy, and Mia's a tiny baby. Next to the gold frame is a photo of the three of them. Baby Beck and a *very* young James and Elizabeth. The child star photo is a few steps up. Beck in a blue and white racing suit, holding a helmet and a trophy that's half his size. His smile is so big it's making his eyes nearly close. *What a cutie.*

"That was the first karting race Beck ever won!"

I follow Mia up the remainder of the stairs.

"That's Mum and Dad's room," she says, passing a sage-colored bedroom. She points across the hall to a room erupting with toys and lined with football posters.

"That's Louie's messy room."

Mia stops at the next door. "This was Beck's room, but now it's where Grandma stays when she visits."

I peer inside. There is a small bed, desk and dresser. One of the walls holds three floating shelves overcrowded with trophies, medals and plaques of all sizes. You couldn't fit another award if you tried. I smile. The room is almost as simple as his place in the city.

"And best for last—my room!" Mia squeals.

She waves me across the hall to a white and baby-pink striped dream room. She stands proudly at the foot of the bed as I take a full pass around the room.

Ornate white furniture holds every girly trinket and figurine imaginable. Lace edge curtains frame both windows. A pink pouf sits in front of a small vanity covered in nail polish and makeup.

"I love it, Mia!"

"Is this the finale of the grand tour?" Elizabeth says, walking in.

Mia rolls her eyes.

Elizabeth sits down on the furry pink blanket across Mia's bed.

I point to the gray barn outside Mia's window. "What's out there?"

"That's the stables—*pardon*, the *empty* stables," Mia answers.

Elizabeth smiles.

"But not for long," Mia adds. "I'm getting a horse for my birthday."

"We'll see about that," Elizabeth says.

I didn't know Ella as a child, but she's all I see when Mia opens her mouth.

I slip my foot out of my loafer under the table and put it to the cool stone of the back patio. Mum always talked about getting a house in the country like this. I imagine Beck was out on the expansive grounds more than he was ever inside.

Elizabeth and James are at either end of the table. Across from me, Mia pushes the peas from her Sunday roast as close to the edge of her plate as she can get them. Louie chows down beside her, barely coming up for air. My hand is in Beck's lap; he's giving James the latest updates from his visit to headquarters.

Elizabeth sets her hand on the table. "Sophie, we need to talk about your show in Paris."

Relief sweeps over me. I was prepared for the worst possible *we need to talk about* topic.

I smile. "It went even better than London! I had so much more confidence this time."

Elizabeth lights up.

"Did you see the roses Beck sent?" I ask.

"We saw your picture with them!" Mia says.

Oh lord.

Elizabeth leans in closer,

"I'm not sure if you've made your travel plans yet, but we're all coming out for Abu Dhabi; you should come out with us!"

"Yeah!" Mia yells.

"Oh—I haven't made any plans yet. That would be great!"

Elizabeth pats my wrist.

"I'll have Beck get you our flight information."

I help Elizabeth clear the plates and follow her inside. In the kitchen, she hands me a stack of small blue and white dessert plates.

"I'm so glad you were there for Beck in Singapore," she says.

She turns and grabs fresh napkins.

"I still can't believe you did this," Elizabeth smiles, picking up the bakery basket.

I feel silly for being nervous. It was the perfect afternoon. The idyllic glimpse into Beck's childhood put the state of my life on the back burner.

"Leaving overfed, per usual," Beck says, kissing Elizabeth's cheek.

James releases me. "Can't wait to meet your dad! We're going to have a blast!"

Elizabeth gives James a look before pulling me in for a final hug. When she pulls back, she keeps me close.

"Don't let the tabloids ruin your shine, Sophie."

Her face is serious. My cheeks flood with heat.

"They're awful. They always have been," Elizabeth says.

I fold my lips inward. *I don't know what to say.*

"You don't have to explain yourself. Having things aired out in public is an unpleasant part of Beck's world."

Beck fires up the engine. He makes a three-point turn, avoiding the chalk masterpieces on the drive. My eyes sting. It's a confusing mix of relief and embarrassment. I wave to his family on the front stoop once more as we pull away. My mind's racing; that caught me off guard.

A few seconds pass and Beck slows the car to a stop.

"What are you doing?"

He's smiling wildly at the steering wheel. His eyes drift to me.

"You want to drive it?" he says.

What?

Beck clicks the car into park and unbuckles. "Take it to the end of the driveway."

I glance over my shoulder to make sure his family has gone back inside. My non-answer answers for me.

The engine purrs from the outside as we switch seats. My heart races, slipping in behind the wheel. I trace my finger around the bright yellow emblem in the center of the steering wheel. Beck leans over from the passenger seat and looks down at my feet.

"That's not going to work," Beck laughs.

Leaning over my lap, he pushes a button, and my seat glides forward.

Beck squeezes my knee. "That's better."

I squeak and grip my sweaty palms to the steering wheel.

"Okay, foot on the brake, put it in drive."

"I know what to do!"

"Okay!" he says, holding up his hands.

"It's just been a minute since I've driven anything," I giggle.

I click the switch into drive and move my foot to the gas. I squeal as the car jolts forward from the touchy gas pedal.

"Easy!" Beck says.

I've never been behind the wheel of something this powerful; it's exhilarating. I give the Ferrari a little gas and steer through the bends of the driveway.

"Nice cornering…" Beck praises.

I brake as the drive runs out and put it in park.

"That was *awesome*."

The Ferrari passes by the last bit of black iron fencing on the country lane.

"Did Mum say something to you?" Beck asks.

"Only that I didn't need to explain myself."

"I told them hardly any of the article was true, love," he says. "They understand."

I chew my bottom lip.

"Are you doing okay with it?" Beck asks.

No. I'm a mess.

"It brings up a lot of insecurities—I didn't realize, at the time, how much being someone's secret would wreck my confidence." I smile. "But then I met you and you made me come alive again. I'm more brave than I ever was."

"Was that the only relationship you've ever been in?"

I nod. "Dad jokes about it now, but I still feel like I failed him. He set me up for that job, and I was *quite good* at it. But I was playing with fire, and in an instant, I lost it all, and had to tell him everything."

"Sophie, your dad thinks you hung the moon."

He's right. Dad's never shown an ounce of disappointment. He reflected it back on himself; how did he miss it and did Mum's absence play a role? The unconditional love he's shown me in the midst of everything will never cease to amaze me.

Beck reaches for my hand. "*I still think you hung the moon.*"

I shake my head. "I guess I don't quite understand what you see in me?"

Beck smiles. "I see *everything.*"

My heart stutters. *Everything.* I stare at him, waiting for more.

"I see a bright person, who's courageous, a wonderful friend and has a huge heart. You're there for me for the fun stuff just as much as you're there when I choke in qualifying," he chuckles. "I see all that wrapped up in the most beautiful girl."

His words melt into me. I look down at my hand in his and debate whether now is the time to ask about his past.

"I'm quite different from Sabrina..." I say.

"You're completely different," he affirms.

That was fast. Hmm...

"Everyone online still gushes about you two. People were devastated when I showed up—they thought you were the perfect couple."

"Exactly. They *thought* it was perfect, but it was far from it."

"Did the media spin some story when you broke up?"

"Yes and no—there were rumors made up, of course. She'd just had her first big song, and it happened right after that."

"So, why did you split up?" I pry.

"It was a lot of things—I always felt that she liked me *because* I was a driver. She was chasing fame. She demanded we stay in the spotlight any chance we could get, and I didn't want that. I wanted to focus on driving. It was my first real season. I tried to be what she wanted, but in the end, I'm not that person."

"I didn't even know who you were," I laugh.

Beck's smile grows.

"And that's what I love about you—with you, it's so easy. I don't have to try to be someone I'm not." He interlaces his fingers into mine. "And you don't try to be perfect for me, you're yourself."

My heart thumps. That's what he *loves* about me?

"Your mum said something else…"

He glances over, interested.

"She invited me to fly out with your family for Abu Dhabi."

"I told you." Beck grins. "My parents *adore* you."

The next morning, Beck pulls a bowl out of the takeout bag and sets it in front of me. *Breakfast.* I climb up onto the stool at the counter in my panties and one of his hoodies. I worked up quite the appetite after the *activities* we partook in last night when we got back…*and again this morning*. I take the lid off the fruit and yogurt bowl.

Beck stands across the counter, picking through a massive breakfast bowl of his own. His hood's still pulled up over his head from when he picked up the food down the street. Maybe that's the vibe I should go for in the paddock this week, *a low profile*. Beck's phone rings. He lifts it from his pocket and glances at the screen before dropping it back in.

"Answer it," I say.

He stares at me and reaches back in his pocket. He accepts the call at the last second. Even with the phone to his ear, I can recognize Shannon's voice. Does she know her PR nightmare is present? He's holding the phone to his ear with his shoulder, still shoveling food into his mouth.

"Put it on speaker phone," I mouth silently.

He nods and puts his food down. He reaches for the phone and hits the speaker button. He sets his phone on the counter and picks his breakfast back up.

"I've just emailed you a few talking points for Thursday's lunch interview and question prep for the press conference," Shannon says.

Beck nods, staring down at the phone.

"And last, on the Sophie headlines..."

His eyes flash up at me. My heart stalls.

"...if you are asked about any of it, simply say, 'next question.'"

Shannon continues, "Beck, I obviously can't tell Sophie what to say or how to respond to things, but maybe she would take your guidance to heart. We need to stay out of the drama."

Shannon's words rip through my chest. Beck's eyes haven't left me.

"Beck?" Shannon says.

He lowers his eyes to the phone.

The drama? I get up from the counter and head for the bathroom before I accidentally say something out loud. I keep the door open, still in earshot of the call.

"Yes, ma'am," Beck responds.

"The tabloids seem to eat up anything that comes out about Sophie. Every time she's interviewed in the paddock, it's *always* something."

My ears ring.

"Sounds good. Thanks, Shannon."

I hear him walk out of the kitchen. My heart races, and the tears well up. Beck stops in the doorway,

"Come here," he says, holding his arms out.

I fall against his chest and bury my face in his neck.

"Drama...is that what the team thinks I am?"

His arms wrap around me. "To hell with what they think...I don't think that."

I shake my head. "I'm not good enough for you. You need someone perfect, and that's not me."

Beck pulls back and grasps onto my shoulders. "It is you."

I stare down at my feet and blink through the tears.

"...but I'm tarnishing your name, your image."

"Why? Because you had a relationship with someone you worked with?"

"And the rest of it—they think I broke up a marriage."

"But that's not true."

"It doesn't matter what's true. People read that and it sticks."

I take a deep breath. "I'm good at hiding. I understand if you don't want to be seen with me."

Beck tightens his grip on my shoulders. "Sophie, don't you ever say that."

I lift my gaze up to his.

"You could never do anything that would make me hide you."

CHAPTER 25

DADS IN THE WILD

I POINT DAD TO the middle row seat.

"Sit here. Beck and I will be behind you."

Dad plops down in the jet's second row in his new team quarter zip. James takes the seat across the aisle from Dad, behind Charlie. He lifts the lid off the small cooler he carried on over his shoulder. Five beers are squeezed inside.

"In case we get thirsty." James winks at Dad.

It's hardly eight a.m.

Beck turns down the aisle, smiling. He stops beside Dad and pulls out a pink lanyard from his pocket.

"For you, sir," Beck says.

Dad stares at the paddock pass as if he's been handed a golden ticket to the chocolate factory. A valid reaction. The paddock is pretty *magical.* I take my seat. Beck pulls up his hood and lays his head on my shoulder. *No private pod beats this.*

"I'm so glad you were able to come, George!" James says.

"I haven't done a boy's trip in years."

So, this is a dads' getaway trip. Dad won't be entirely off duty—who knows what nervous breakdown lies on his daughter's horizon?

"The invite was the highest honor. I haven't been to a race since I was out at Silverstone, when Soph was a baby," Dad says.

"Ah! Zandvoort's always a good time!" James grins.

"Well, Sophie's got us going to a show tonight," Dad says.

James turns to me.

"My roommate, Carmen—her boyfriend's a DJ. He has a show in Amsterdam."

"You're going?" James asks Dad.

"Oh, yeah!" Dad says cooly.

"I've got to come to this!" James says.

Beck lifts his head. "*Dad.*"

"Please join us!" I say.

"I'm there!" James smiles. "Tonight's the night to go out. Without Beck, we can take the train in."

"Dads in the wild for a night on the town?" Beck laughs. "You're brave."

His head returns to my shoulder.

I'm outnumbered; it's as if I'm not even here. Beck fell asleep ten minutes after takeoff. James cracks a beer and hands it across the aisle to Dad.

James turns and raises an eyebrow. "Soph?"

"No, thank you," I giggle.

Charlie also declines, though I sensed some hesitation.

I close my eyes and rest my head against Beck's, listening to the back and forth in front of us.

"Soph doesn't cause too much trouble?" Dad asks.

"No," Charlie says. "She actually keeps Beck's nerves down. It's translated well in the races."

My lips curl into a smile.

"Though he does now seem to be in a hurry to leave his workouts," Charlie laughs.

Ha! I wonder what response Shannon would give if Dad posed her that same question.

Zandvoort is breezy. Our hotel sits across the street from the North Sea coastline. Too cold for my cherry bikini, but I may have to convince Dad to get up early for a walk in the sand one morning. Charlie went straight to the track with Beck. Joe dropped Dad, James and me at the hotel. It's sunny but chilly. I lace up the white trainers I was sent last week. The jeans are mine, but the jumper was also gifted. I check the contents of my red Chanel again. My lanyard is fixed between the matching card holder and compact mirror that came in the gift box. I stuff my largest pair of sunglasses inside, though I'm doubtful they'll provide enough cover to dodge every prying eye.

"Come here." I wave to Dad. "We have to take our outfit of the day photo."

Dad steps beside me in the mirror outside the lift. He smooths his hair and adjusts his Furio zip jacket. *Stuart will love this.*

When we arrive at the track, James waves at the few cameras pointing our way. *Look! It's the golden retriever's scandalous girlfriend.* I slide my sunglasses on. I can't hide, but I can pretend. Dad glances nervously at the cameras then down at me.

"This is nothing," I say. "We're late. You should see how many cameras are out when the drivers arrive."

I step between James and Dad. In my fragile state, I feel protected between them in Beck's absence.

The childlike wonder on Dad's face as we walk through the paddock is lifting my mood. The setup is different here. The suites are not directly behind the garages. The main straight parallels the coastline. The turns are banked, carved into the sand dunes. I'm relieved to see our radiant red fortress again. The glass doors of the suite's entrance part.

James introduces Dad to some of the team members in the dining room. Dad's beside himself. The sliders part, and Beck and Luca step inside the suite.

Beck lights up, seeing my dad. "Welcome, George!"

Oh dear. Shannon's come in right behind them. I recoil. Shannon gives me a soft smile; I muster up as much of a grin as I can.

Dad's starry-eyed as Luca shakes his hand.

"Glad to have you," Luca says.

"My wife, Pippa, stayed back this week to rest."

"Sophie told me the happy news—congratulations," Dad says.

Luca smiles. "Thank you, sir."

Beck's finger hooks into my belt loop. He leans down to my ear. "You okay?" he asks quietly.

I exhale and smile. "Yeah. I'm going to go find Ana."

He nods. "Remember, Sophie, nothing's changed." His lips press into my temple. "Go have fun."

Beck gestures to Dad. "Come meet Coop and the boys in the garage. You can walk the track with us."

Dad's eyes double in size.

Back outside, Ana rushes toward me.

"Let's see it!" I squeal, grabbing her hand. The facets of the flawless diamond dance in the sun.

"My word, it's gorgeous!" I squeeze her tight. "I'm thrilled for you, Ana."

"Oh God, there's David," Ana says, releasing me. "Why did I agree to this?"

I gulp. David waves, walking toward us, cameraman in tow. I lift my hand nervously. *I've got to be brave for Ana.*

"It will be easy! Two minutes tops!" I encourage. "I saw Ren's bit from the press conference—just say what you want!"

Here I am asking Ana to be brave while my heart is in my throat. *David wouldn't ask me about the tabloid, right?*

David hands both Ana and me a microphone. He's set us up at the end of the paddock where it's quiet. I want to hand the microphone back; this is *Ana's show.* Ana looks like she could puke. I move the microphone from her right hand to her left.

"Oh right," Ana chuckles, glancing down at her sparkling diamond.

Cameraman gives us a thumbs up. Ana's hand is shaking.

"Ana, first of all congratulations on your engagement to Ren Enatsu," David says.

I clap with the microphone.

"Thank you," Ana says, nodding. She glances at me nervously.

"We haven't had an F1 wedding in quite some time. Have you already begun planning?" David asks.

"A little bit. We are looking at the possibility of having it over summer break next year."

David smiles. "I imagine there are only a few windows of time you can pull off a wedding given the race schedule."

"Yes, it will be busy, and Ren and I are trying to get everything sorted out before our move to Monaco in December."

"Very exciting," David says.

I smile and nod. *She's doing great!*

"I'm delighted to have you here today. It's rare that you speak to the media..." David states.

Where's he going with this question...?

"*Yeah...*" Ana hesitates. "I had a hard time my first season with everything that comes with being in the spotlight. I pulled back a bit. But seeing Sophie speak up and have fun with it has given me confidence to show my face a bit more this season."

My heart races.

"I've enjoyed watching your friendship grow; I see you two romping about the paddock week after week."

Ana looks at me. "She's really brought me out of my shell."

I could cry. Ana's actually smiling. She looks so confident.

Ana glances back at David. "Now we just have to get Beck and Ren on the same team," she laughs.

"It could very well happen one day!" David chuckles. "I look forward to talking again soon, Ana! I wish you luck with the wedding plans."

The cameraman lowers his gear.

My jaw drops, and Ana folds her lips together.

"Ana, you did amazing!"

"I couldn't have done it without you!"

"You did great," David agrees. "Can I get a photo?"

I wait for Ana's call, and much to my surprise, she nods. I put my arm around her and reach for her hand. I lift her hand out in front of us to show off the sparkler on her finger.

"This is *perfect*," David says behind his camera.

David and his cameraman are off to their next interview. He didn't say anything about the tabloid. Maybe he didn't see it, or *maybe he's doing me a favor.*

"I won't be in Qatar next week," Ana says. "My mother's made several appointments. Her last-ditch effort to convince me to have the wedding back home."

"That will be fun!"

Ana flashes me a look. *Not fun?*

"The party gives me the perfect reason to come back early," Ana says. "I was thinking—we need to be demons!"

Oh right, the costume party.

I grin. "I was leaning that direction. Might as well beat the gossip page and put the devil horns on myself."

Ana laughs.

"Apparently, Tommy is thinking about bringing his ex?"

"Oh?" Ana narrows her eyes. "Wait, which one?" she asks innocently.

Ha! Ana giggles.

"Emma...she's the most recent, right?"

Beck's already gone to bed in sleepy Zandvoort, but the streets of Amsterdam are just starting to come alive. The vibrant glow of the buzzing walks is reflected in the iconic canals. I hang up the phone. "Carmen's coming out to collect us."

Dad and James are already a few pints deep, vibing on the busy sidewalk outside the venue. They acted like a bunch of rowdy university kids on the train in.

I wave them over.

"Should we join the queue?" James asks.

I smirk. "I'm afraid we don't wait in lines."

They pick up their pace following me past the queue to the entrance.

"You made it!" Carmen says, leaning out of the door. "Follow me! He's about to come on!"

It's pitch black, and security personnel wave neon wands, directing us up the stairs. We park ourselves in a private standing section, hanging over the front right corner of the stage. I lean over the railing and look to the chaos on the floor.

"Wait here," Carmen says.

James and Dad bob their head to the beat of the preshow music. "VIPs!" James says excitedly. I shake my head; I brought not one but two dads to the party.

Carmen returns, holding four pints across her chest.

"Cheers!" Carmen yells, passing Dad and James a pint.

The few remaining stage lights go out and the crowd rallies.

Oliver walks out behind his tables; the light show begins, starting his suspenseful intro.

Dad and James sway behind us, pints in hand. They've got at least twenty years on anyone in here. By far the coolest dads in town.

Carmen smiles. "This is the first time they've met?"

I nod. "This morning, *instant chemistry*."

Oliver picks up the microphone. "What's up, Amsterdam!" The crowd erupts, and James whistles wildly.

Carmen glances at James. "I'm obsessed with him."

I giggle. I knew James was a good time, but he's on a whole other level this trip. The intro beat transitions to Ollie's first song. A rush floods through me as the bass vibrates my stomach. I dive back in time.

"What is it?" Carmen asks.

"This is the song." I smile. "It was the song playing when I first met Beck."

I turn on the faucet and brace for the cold.

"That'll wake you up!" Dad laughs.

I hold my breath and run my feet under the stream. The sticky sand trickles off my feet.

"Worth it!" I huff, breathing through the chills.

A break in the rain this morning was our first chance to get out for a walk on the beach. We're taking the jet back to London tonight postrace. The rain has been on and off all weekend. Hopefully, we'll get lucky for the race. Despite the weather, Luca and Beck managed to have decent results qualifying P4 and P5. I've managed to steer clear of Shannon as much as possible. It's easier here, given the distance between the garage and suite. Maybe I'm in my head, hyperaware, but there are double the eyes on me in the paddock.

Umbrellas are open at a café across the street. *een bakkie*—jackpot.

"Let's stop in there quickly."

I point to the *appeltaart* in the glass display case.

"Can I get one of these pie squares to-go?"

The attendant nods.

Dad holds up his fingers. "Let's do two of those."

He smiles. "We have to taste test it, right?"

"Is James your new best friend?" I tease.

Dad sits down next to me with the plated pie square.

"Pressure's on, Sophie." Dad winks. "You and Beck better work out."

The trauma bonding from Friday's hangover brought Dad and James even closer. Both were struggling after the night out at Oliver's show. Patrizio nursed them back to health, delivering multiple courses of mouthwatering sustenance.

I cut back into the pie square. "Beck will absolutely love this."

"Big dessert guy?" Dad asks.

"Yes, I try to surprise him with something at each race. He has a bigger sweet tooth than you."

Dad smiles. "You really like him, don't you?"

The question catches me off guard, so much so that I must look away. I sink my fork back into the *appeltaart*.

"Yeah...It almost scares me how much I like him."

"Julien loses the rear! *Oh!* And he's taken out Antoine Auclair with him. Big contact in turn three!"

The broadcast hovers over Julien's car, facing backward in the barrier in turn three. Antoine's front end is smashed into Julien's front left.

"Box! Box!" Coop calls over the radio.

Again? The weather couldn't be more erratic. Beck's already pit three times, switching between intermediates and slicks. But that's been everyone's race. I've never seen the pit lane so chaotic. *And here they come again.*

It's not the race Beck was hoping for, but Dad's loving every minute. Tommy stays out, holding third position. I'm excited for Tommy; he's had a lucky race. Beck enters the pit lane behind Alek and Elijah. Three cars come in behind Beck.

We've run enough rounds today—let's see pit four's speed. *Whirr! Whirr!* Beck's car hits the ground, and the pit timer flashes on the screen.

1.9 seconds. *No way!* Dad swipes his hands together. "That gave me goosebumps!"

The garage goes bonkers. Beck's car passes Elijah in the pit lane, stalling his release.

"Look out! Furio gains a position in the pit lane! Major pit for Beck as he sneaks past the Valor of Elijah Kaplan. He'll join the safety car behind Aleksandr Kholodov. Valor will be kicking themselves, but that's the risk you take with a mediocre pit stop when the guys next door are doing it in under two seconds!"

"Heh, heh!" Beck sneers over the radio. "Nice pit boys!"

James smacks Dad's palm in the air.

The evil laugh. Charlie shakes his head. WRI switches places with KAP on the standings. Beck rejoins the track behind Alek in seventh.

The debris from the collision has been cleared. The grid remains behind the safety car, starting lap 66/72. I continue exchanging worried looks with Charlie. We're both monitoring the migrating green patches on the radar.

"Safety car's ending, Beck," Coop reports. "Also, the rain should hold off."

"Should?" Beck says.

Please no. Beck's soft tyres stand no chance if it starts coming down again.

"We'll get five laps to race. Everyone's bunched up, trying to get the temperature back on those tyres…And Geoffrey restarts the pack! We are back racing at Zandvoort!"

The laps have run out. At the exit of turn twelve, Coop comes over the radio.

"Last lap, Beck."

"Oh, really? I lost count," Beck says, annoyed.

James laughs. Charlie shakes his head. The *sarcasm* in his voice.

"Everything you've got, Beck," Coop says.

I press my lips together. He's closed the gap.

Beck's DRS enables, and he flies down the main straight, chasing Alek.

"Beckham Wright tries the outside, and Alek pushes him wide. Beck dives for the inside, passing Aleksandr

Kholodov through turn one! Aggressive overtake for the Furio!"

"Major move, Beck!" Coop yells.

Beck's name moves up to sixth place, behind Luca.

Beck's onboard mimics a rollercoaster as he flies into the banking of turn three.

"And Makellos picks up their first win since Mexico City! Geoffrey Hahn is your winner of the Dutch Grand Prix! Followed by the home favorite Leo VanBelle! Tommy Young will get his first podium this season in that final spot."

Beck flies under the chequered flag.

"That's P6, Beck," Coop reports.

Beck sighs heavily over the radio. "We did what we could."

James comes down the aisle of the jet. He pumps his fist in the air. "Weekend warriors!"

Beck pauses mid chew. "You didn't want a bite, did you?"

"No," I giggle. "Dad and I split one this morning."

Beck scoops up the last of the *appeltaart* crumbs and pops them into his mouth.

James has a second wind from his nap in the car. He takes his seat across from Dad.

"You're not working tomorrow..." Dad asks.

James nods.

"You're the warrior," Dad laughs. "I took the day off to recover."

"It's rough, but you can make it back same day for the close races. I'll drop the kids off and give you a lift home."

Ha! *Kids.*

"We're staying at my place," Beck says.

I cringe. I'm sure Dad knows I stay with Beck, but I adjust in my seat nervously, anticipating his reaction. Thankfully, James doesn't shut up.

"We've got to get you out to the house for a golf weekend soon!" James continues.

"My diary's *always* open for eighteen."

Thirty minutes later, James draws an even deeper snore.

"Should I hit him?" Beck asks.

"No!" I giggle. "Let him sleep!"

I'm surprised Dad hasn't started up. They both dozed off shortly after takeoff.

Beck nods at Dad. "You think he had fun?"

"Beck, this was easily in the top five weekends of his life," I say.

Beck smiles.

"You've got Carmen hooked too. She sent a photo of her and Ollie in their Furio gear. They were in a suite by turn eleven."

"I wish I could have come to Oliver's show," Beck says. He nods at James. "I wish I could have watched *them* at the show!"

"Well, you saw the shape they were in on Friday," I laugh. "They were a *riot.*"

CHAPTER 26

TEASER

I'VE BEEN ARGUING WITH myself for a while over what time it is. I can't remember the last time I didn't wake up to an alarm. Beck's on his stomach. He must be knackered. We were asleep quite fast; I barely remember cuddling. I carefully lean over to the side table and stretch for my phone. *It's almost ten a.m.* My stomach growls. I slowly lift out of bed, careful not to wake him. I tiptoe across the room and open his bedroom door.

The bottoms of my feet stick to the concrete flooring. I pull the handle of the refrigerator. *Oh, Beck.* The empty shelves laugh in my face.

Beck calls my name. I shut the fridge and retrace my steps. His eyes are still closed, but he's flipped onto his back.

"Why did you leave?" Beck groans.

"I wanted to make you breakfast in bed..." I climb on top of him and straddle over his hips. "But ice is the only thing in the freezer and your only pan still has tags on it."

Beck smiles and slowly opens his eyes. *How does he wake up this sultry?*

"Is this what it would be like?" I ask.

"What? Waking up slow?"

I nod. I often think of what our routine will be when the season wraps. Beck pulls his hands from under the covers and grips around my butt cheeks.

"This is what it *will* be like—*for a few weeks.*" He smirks.

"No plans and no one to answer to."

I lean down and hover above his lips. "And what are we going to do with all this free time?"

"First, I need you, *then I'll feed you.*"

Beck reaches his lips to mine. He pulls my bottom lip between his, sucking it tortuously. I force my tongue into his mouth. His hand moves into my hair, pulling me even closer. I slowly move my hips back and forth on him. He's already rock hard under the comforter. I push harder against him, building the heat between my legs. Beck pushes me from his mouth and grabs the bottom of his T-shirt I slept in. I'm already panting as he pulls it over my head. Every muscle on his stomach flexes as he sits up. He glides his finger down the front of my panties and looks up at me, eyes blazing.

"I want those off."

My inner thighs tense. *I want nothing more.* His hands grip around my waist, and he shifts me off his lap, onto my back; hovering over me. His hand slips inside my panties, and his fingers curl, sliding up and down my clit.

His mouth falls open. "You're soaking wet."

"I—I, oh God!"

His fingers push inside of me before I can explain. Every nerve ending fires. He uses his other hand to pull my panties down. I slip my legs out while his fingers move vigorously in and out of me. I throw my head to the side and grip onto the comforter. His fingers leave, and my eyes flash open. My chest rises hard and fast.

"Why are you stopping?" I moan.

"Put your arms around me," he says.

I follow instructions and wrap my arms around the back of his neck. Beck lifts me off the bed. I wrap my legs around his waist, and he takes off for the bathroom. His hands are occupied, gripping under my bum. He pauses and steps on the ends of his pajama pants, pulling them off. His length springs free.

My cheeks push against the frigid glass of the shower door. Beck swats the shower handle and steps inside. Freezing water splashes over me as he carries me under the stream.

"Beck!" I squeal. My back meets the cold tile on the shower wall. His eyes are wild, fixated on my lips.

"Just wait," he says softly.

The spray from the stream warms up as his tongue dives into my mouth. I grip my legs tighter around him. The water is steaming. Beck's mouth leaves mine; he pulls his hips back and pushes inside of me. I gasp, inhaling the billowing steam as Beck thrusts into me, pinning me against the tile. I tip my head back and revel in the heaven that is him inside of me.

"Fuck! *Sophie!*" Beck's muscles shudder. His grip around my legs loosens, and he slows, finding his release. His head falls, resting on my chest. Heat sets in on the pressure points from the friction against the tile. Beck takes a deep breath and lifts his head, slowly lowering my feet back to the ground. My legs wobble, not ready to hold weight. I keep my arms around the back of his neck. He backs us under the stream of steaming water. My hair saturates and lengthens over my nipples. Beck lifts my chin; our eyes drink each other in. The charge resonating around us is amplified in the close quarters of the shower walls. Beck opens his mouth, and my heart flips, anticipating his words.

He's staring, and it feels like an eternity before he hesitates and closes his mouth. I lower my arms and turn around to face the stream. He presses his chest against my back; his arms come around me, and his hands rest on my stomach. Was he about to say something—*something groundbreaking?*

Beck leans back in his chair, surrendering to the feat of finishing every plate. He runs his hand over my thigh. There's not a spot on the table open for anything else he might order. The café is quiet, we've beaten the Monday lunch rush.

"Now what?" Beck smiles.

The ideas been ruminating for a bit. I grab my phone and open the maps app. I glance up to the waiter, who, for the third time, lingers studying Beck's face. The waiter gathers three of the plates. *He knows this isn't any ordinary patron.* I zoom in on the maps pin and hold my phone out.

"Next, will be costume shopping!" I exclaim.

This is quickly becoming one of my favorite days. The bell on the shop door jingles. I choke slightly from the overwhelming incense. The tiny shop is stuffed to the brim. Masks and costumes line the walls from floor to ceiling.

"We are after devils and demons," I mutter.

The quirky clerk behind the counter doesn't look up from his book. "Back left corner."

We proceed through the store, and a red sequined bodysuit hanging on the back wall, catches my eye. I push up on my tiptoes and retrieve it.

I slowly turn the bodysuit; *sequins would be fun*. Beck eyes my find. "We're definitely going evil?"

"I think evil will be a little more...unexpected?"

He hooks his fingers into my belt loops and pulls me toward him.

"Red *is* our color," he says ardently.

I gulp and glance at the front desk. "Should I wear a mask?"

I look up to where he's set his eye. He reaches for a gold horned eye mask from a shelf.

"I'll wear this with a suit." He smiles. "That was easy!"

Annoyingly easy.

I enter the sole fitting room with my options, and undress. I step into the bodysuit and pull the straps over my shoulders. I put my hands around my waist and run my fingers along the sequins to my hips. *It could work*. Beck's trainers appear below the fitting room curtain.

"I found something else," he says.

Beck's hand comes through the curtain holding a red plastic pitchfork.

"Okay, that's enough accessories," I laugh.

It's starting to come together: satin elbow-length gloves, a horned headband, a tail *and now a handheld weapon*.

"You can look now," I say.

I watch in the mirror as Beck pulls the curtain back a few centimeters. His eyes enlarge, fixating on my ass. He presses his lips together. His gaze drifts up my body, stopping at my eyes. Beck looks over his shoulder then rips back the curtain, stepping inside. I spin around as he shuts it behind him.

"Beck!" I squeal.

He puts his hand over my mouth.

"Do you understand what you do to me?" he asks.

My cheeks flush against his palm. His lips attack my neck, sending my body squirming.

After a few *slightly* inappropriate minutes in the fitting room, I manage to coax Beck to the register.

"Did you find everything you needed?" the clerk asks.

Ha! I clear my throat, avoiding eye contact. "Yes, thank you."

Beck smirks, looking aimlessly out the glass of the shop's door. I set my devilish finds on the counter with Beck's mask.

The three-way FaceTime connects. The sight of Carmen unclenches my jaw.

"Holy glam!"

Carmen winks as another brush is put to her face. Ella puts her hand to her forehead, shading her eyes. At least we are on the same continent—three roomies in three cities. I came to the flat while Beck went to train with Charlie. Ella's on our balcony in Paris, and Carmen is in Antwerp, getting glammed for the *European Open*.

"Enough avoiding the question—did you watch the video?"

"*Yes, Ella.*"

She raises an eyebrow.

"You think it's about Beck?" Carmen asks.

"Of course it is," Ella says. "I would want my ex back too if he returned to the scene with Sophie on his arm."

I roll my eyes. The video was posted last night on Sabrina's page. A song teaser with questionable lyrics. It *could* be about someone else, right? My mind wanders.

"Our costumes arrived, Carmen," Ella says.

Carmen's eyes light up. "I was thinking we should host preparty drinks at our place!"

"Fantastic idea! I'll have the car pick us up here."

"Soph? You like that plan?" Carmen asks.

What?

"Preparty drinks at our place?" Ella repeats.

"Yeah! Sounds great."

Did I miss anything else half listening?

When we hang up, I play the video on Sabrina's page a second time. She's humming while putting on mascara then starts singing.

"Didn't think that I would miss you until I saw you with her."

I'm clenching again. I pause the video and try to decode the caption.

In my feels lately, I've been writing...

The comments on the post have been shut off, making it even more mysterious. It could easily be about some other guy. Luckily, I know one place to get an outside opinion without going to Beck.

The *Lights Out Ladies* header flashes as the filter on my name applies to the posts. *Wow*. The page has upped its activity. Carmen's photo of us at Oliver's show in Amsterdam has fifty-five comments.

HOW did Beck not drop her after the tabloid?!
Sophie's unworthy. She goes to the races only to go out and party?
Look who's brave again.

It's Ana's interview with David. I'm standing there, beyond proud of her, smiling like an idiot.

Brave, only when her yappy sidekick is next to her
This wedding will be like watching a car crash.
Three carats on your finger, giving you some confidence, aye? Better keep up with the diet. It'd be a shame to have to resize that ring.

My blood jumps from a simmer to a boil. How dare these people? I scroll down and find a teaser post.

!!PSA!! Sabrina wants her man back!!!! Beck x Sab!
...And the post comments have been shut off. That didn't take long.
Beck and Sab BOTH still follow each other!
Click here for the deep dive.

My tap-happy fingers have never clicked faster. A TikTok video loads.

10 reasons why Beckham Wright is using Sophie to get Sabrina Kaufman back!

Why do I do this to myself? I slam the laptop lid closed.

CHAPTER 27

DESERT RACER

DATING BECK HAS EXPOSED me to lots of firsts, today's experience included. I've never flown commercial with him, and I've never once required an escort through London Heathrow. The smooth jazz fades as we leave the civility of the private lounge. A security officer nods, holding the door open.

The fans are still waiting, and an escort team of three is holding back the traffic. Fifty phones lift and point in our direction and my cortisol censors flash red.

I leave Beck's side and step next to Charlie. We're escorted twenty steps from the lounge door to a descending escalator. Once my feet are planted, I turn back; Beck winks at me from the step above.

"I checked—from the bottom, we're only two gates down," Charlie states.

Twice as many people are crowding the first few gates of the terminal. All three escorts step off the escalator behind Beck. Another set of security guards hold back the fans, hovering around our gate. I stick with Charlie as Beck slowly moves along for selfies and signatures.

"Sophie!"

A girl in the crowd to my left calls my name. She's smiling, holding something out for me. I step her way and extend my hand. She sets a red and white beaded bracelet in my palm.

W-R-I 20 is spelled in letter beads. I'm taken aback. *It's adorable.*

"Take it!" She smiles. She lifts her wrist. A stack of similar bracelets line her forearm.

"Are you sure? Did you make this?"

She nods proudly. "Please, take it!"

Before I can say thank you, she departs, moving closer to where Beck is signing.

I stretch the bracelet over my hand and rest it at my wrist.

"You got a gift? Where do I get one?" Charlie jokes.

"Is it always this mad?"

"Sometimes we make it through fairly unnoticed. It only gets bad when someone sees us arrive and puts it on Twitter," Charlie says.

"Don't these people have flights of their own to catch?"

Charlie laughs. "They'll risk being late for an autograph."

Beck gives a final wave to the mob surrounding our gate before shaking the security guard's hand. I ready my boarding pass; Charlie scans his pass then enters the jet bridge.

Beck's hand slides around my back.

"Let's get out of here," he whispers.

Another first. A flight attendant directs me down the first aisle. She waves Beck past. He reappears in the second aisle across the 1-2-1 seat configuration in *first class.*

The divider screen between our seats slowly lowers. *I want to squeal.* Beck reaches his hand over and tickles behind my arm.

"You'll be okay over there?"

I peek over the separator between us. "You're quite far."

Beck points over my shoulder; to my left, an attendant hands me a glass of champagne. *This is too much.*

"What's that on your wrist?"

I rest my forearm between us. He runs his thumb over the letter beads on my new bracelet and smiles.

"A girl gave it to me at the gate. Charlie didn't get one."

Charlie pouts across the aisle from Beck.

I set my champagne down to retrieve the *RIMI* kit out of my backpack. I pull each of the travel kit items onto my lap.

Beck looks over the divider. "Where did you get that?"

"It's the travel company I told you about. I get the luggage next week."

"What are you going to listen to?"

"Oliver makes us playlists, or I listen to *ITK.*"

"Come again?"

"*In the Know.*" I smile. "It's a podcast...pop culture, fun things like that."

"I'm afraid I'm *not* very in the know," Beck laughs.

Did you know Sabrina is making new music?

He reaches over and takes the black silk eye mask. I open my phone camera and flip it into selfie mode. Beck stretches the mask and puts it over his head.

"If you're going to wear that, you have to be in the picture."

I hold up my phone; Beck leans closer and peeks his eyes out of the bottom of the mask. I lean my head against his and smile.

It's feed worthy. I open Instagram and create a new post.

Next stop Qatar!

The plane is quiet, and the cabin lights are dimmed. Charlie already has his feet kicked up. I don't want to rest—I want to soak up every minute of this flight with Beck.

After the race, I fly back to Paris, and he'll go to headquarters for the week. Beck pulls his hood up over his head. He picks up the remote and scans through the movie selection on the media screen.

"Should we watch something scary?" he whispers. "Get ready for the party?"

"You pick." I smile.

"We'll have to press play at the same time that way we can watch together."

"Romantic."

Beck laughs. "That's what Louie and I do."

My heart.

"Wait till you see this jacket I secured for the party."

"Already?" I ask. "I admire your enthusiasm."

"I've got a guy." He smirks.

Of course you do.

"Ren and Ana are doing *evil* with us. Ella showed me pictures from the party last year, it's over the top."

"That'll be such a posse...Ren, Tommy, Oliver, the girls."

I nod. "We're going to host everyone for drinks at our place before."

Beck flashes his eyebrows. "*Party in Paris.*"

He yawns; stretching his arms into the air. "In case I fall asleep, *I'll see you in the desert, baby.*"

"*Shh*," Beck instructs.

I squeeze my lips together to dull my voice. I swear he knows my body better than I've ever known it. Beck pulls out of me and flips the covers back. He slides his hand under my ass and flips me over. I push up onto my hands and knees. He grips my hips and dives back into me. I gasp as he grabs onto my ponytail, pulling my head back. *Oh*. I reach for the headboard; my fingers slip between it and the wall. There's pressure but no pain. All of my senses fade. Everything I should feel is diluted by the fire raging deep in my belly as he steadily thrusts in and out of me.

Beck slows; tightening his grip on my hip bones as he finds his release. He pulses inside of me, praising my name as my hearing returns. He falls onto his back, chest rising hard and fast.

"Shouldn't you be conserving your energy," I pant, lowering to my stomach.

We haven't been awake for half an hour yet.

"Gotta warm up somehow." He smirks.

I run my thumb over my red, tingling fingers.

"You think Charlie knows I slept here?"

"He might know—*now*." Beck says, amused. "I've got to shower—are you coming?"

"I can't move yet," I moan. I roll onto my back, intimately aware of the remnants of him inside me. I pull the sheet up under my chin and watch him move across the room naked.

Water spatters against stone; Beck peeks out at me through the crack of the bathroom door.

"I'll be there in a minute!" I giggle.

I reach for my phone on the nightstand. *Crap.*

> Look who was talking about you!!!

Three exclamation points? I can't think of a worse text to wake up to. My finger nervously clicks Ella's text notification. I must be hallucinating. The faces of Maggie and Julia stare back at me from the *In the Know* podcast set.

I glance at the bathroom door—Beck's only just started humming. He'll easily be another ten minutes.

I hit play.

"Speaking of tennis WAGs having a moment—this week we got served a teaser for some possible new music from Sabrina Kaufmann," Julia says.

"Love to see it!" Maggie nods.

"Well, let me tell you, since the teaser dropped, I am now F1's biggest fan..."

Maggie looks confused. *"Objection—relevance?"*

"It's not often that we talk about sports, but when it crosses over into pop culture, we're always interested. When Sabrina dropped her clip this week, I kept seeing comments of people guessing who the song is about. Everyone was commenting 'This is Beck coded,' ' This has to be about Beck,' yada yada yada. So, I went digging to find out who Beck is."

My heart races.

"Okay...?" Maggie says.

"Which jump-started the absolute rabbit hole I went down. Sabrina's ex-boyfriend is Beckham Wright, a Formula One driver. He's now dating a totally normal girl; she does some influencing, but she's not famous or anything. So, of course, I had to find out more about the girlfriends of these drivers." Julia pauses.

"Maggie, let me tell you—we thought we got a lot of hate? These girls get dragged through the mud."

"Really?" Maggie says.

"Yes, but anyway, back to the story. Beck's new girlfriend came along this year, and right out of the gate, she had a target on her back from the Sabrina fans. People roast her, but the girl has no filter. She has interviews where she flat-out calls people toxic."

Maggie smiles. *"That's amazing."*

Julia holds up her hand. *"There's more—she follows the podcast."*

"Oh my God, she's one of us?"

"Yes."

"We must get her on!" Maggie sings.

"I'll put out some feelers. The whole dynamic is so interesting, and my God, all the drivers are so hot and rich and sweaty it's fabulous."

The clip ends. My heart's pounding. I feel *validated*. This isn't any podcast—*this is our holy grail podcast*. Three exclamation marks were warranted. I open Instagram and tap the search on my followers list. I don't know how I missed it, but there it is:

In_The_Know_Podcast follows you.

My knuckles are white. "This part makes me quite nervous."

"For the second time tonight, it's lights out and away we go here at the Qatar Grand Prix!"

The mechanics cheer wildly. Both Luca and Beck have great reaction speeds off the start. The sixteen cars remaining in the race barrel down the straight to turn one. I suck in a deep breath and Pippa squeezes my wrist.

Beck and Luca pull into turn one, narrowly avoiding contact. The grid separates slightly as the cars pull from the apex of the turn. I exhale, and Pippa softens her grip.

She taps my *WRI* bracelet. "I love this."

I smile. "Does it ever get easier? Watching the first turn?"

Pippa ponders a moment. "After eight years—*it hasn't*." she laughs.

I haven't seen Pippa since Singapore; her bump has doubled in size.

Lights flood the circuit. The sky is black, and the desert outside the walls is moonless. I love it here. The track is a sparkling luxury oasis in the middle of a piping hot desert.

Only eight laps remain after the standing restart. Two drivers retired lap one after sustaining floor damage in the massive runoff outside the first turn. It was a fairly quiet race until Geoff and Alek made contact in the hairpin at turn six. Alek's MACH spun and ended up sideways along the barrier on the exit. The grid was called back to the pit lane while the marshals mended the barrier and cleared the debris.

As much as the incident was good for our race, I feel for Viktoria. I can't imagine the worry of watching your man smash into a barrier in an open wheel racecar. But Alek popped right up out of the cockpit without issue.

Coop comes over the radio. "Alright, Beck, team orders are let's go racing, but give each other space."

I nervously spin the bracelet on my wrist. Behind Beck, Tommy's in sixth in the remaining MACH. Elijah follows Leo to the final corner of turn sixteen. Ren holds third behind the Valors. I grit my teeth; Beck is right on Luca's tail.

"Will the Furios battle? Beck will have DRS to the finish! Here they go into turn sixteen!"

Pippa shakes her head; I've never seen a battle between Beck and Luca.
NEOW! NEOWWW!!
….. NEOWWW!

"It's a Valor one-two here in Qatar. Ren Enatsu brings home P3!"

Beck uses all of the grip to fly out of the exit of the corner down the main straight.

"And it's a Furio fight to the line!"

Beck's back wing opens, he pulls right out of the slipstream alongside Luca. They fly across the line together. Beck takes fifth, the nose of his car just behind Luca's front tyres. Fireworks crack in the black sky above the main straight.

Beck's lips are heavenly soft and salty. He steps back and grabs a towel off the shelf in his driver's room. He runs it over his face and up into his hair. His racing suit hangs around his waist. I step in front of the mirror on the back of the door. I'm in a daze. The over stimulation, the jet lag, the euphoria all commingling. I adjust my crop top and catch Beck staring in the mirror.

"Do you recognize this?" I ask.

Beck narrows his eyes, racking his brain.

"It's a piece I wore in the *Eden Eves* show."

Beck tosses the towel on the table and comes behind me. Heat radiates off his body. He picks up my wrist and turns my hand slowly, admiring my *WRI* bracelet. He brings my wrist to his lips and kisses it. Dropping our hands, he keeps ahold of my fingers. His sweaty head comes over my shoulder against my face. His eyes glimmer, and I raise my phone. Beck holds his tongue out, panting. I snap our picture in the mirror.

"A little *BTS.*" I smile. "*I love it.*"

Beck collapses onto the massage table against the wall.

With Beck tagged in the photo, who knows how many clicks this will get Evelyn. Maybe the photo will even get to my bracelet's creator.

I pocket my phone and open the cabinet. I pop the lid off the container, and glance over my shoulder. Beck perks up from the noise of the plastic. He sits up as I walk the surprise over. Even holding the container at an angle, the baklava is so sticky it stays in place.

"You first," he says, eyes smoldering.

I pull the baklava off the plastic with my thumb and index finger. I bite into the sugary square, my mouth waters from the rich honey flavor. I smile and move the rest to his lips. Beck bites the baklava out of my fingers. I pull my hand back, but he swiftly catches my wrist. My heart races, watching him chew. Beck holds onto my wrist until he swallows. I gasp as his tongue runs over my fingertips. The spark in his eyes fires every cylinder inside me as he sucks the remaining honey from my fingers.

379

CHAPTER 28
I Found a Hobby

Carmen's calling, *again*. I click ignore and put my phone in my pocket.

"Can't wait to see the photos!" Stuart calls.

I wave farewell and pull the *RIMI* roller bag out of his office. *I can't wait to see this bag on the jet next week.* My initials are engraved in the brass luggage tag attached to the top handle. I've been living out of my old suitcase for months. *Now* I have a matte sage hardshell beauty to travel with.

I hit the sidewalk outside and feel the wheels bump. I slow, passing two taxis on my right. I should grab a cab—I don't want to wear the wheels out!

I pull my phone out and return Carmen's call from the back of the cab.

"Hey, sorry. I was picking up something at the office."

"Sophie," Carmen says, worried.

The air leaves my lungs. *What now?*

"That gossip site," Carmen mutters. "Someone posted our address on it."

My mouth goes dry. "I'll be right there."

The cab slows to the curb. I scan the sidewalks before getting out. *How did someone get our address?* I drag the roller bag into the lobby. Carmen and Ella watch me from Pierre's desk.

"What the hell, Sophie?!" Ella says.

She holds her phone up. My heart slams in my chest. It's not the clearest photo, but it's me. I'm on the phone, coming out of our building without a care in the world. *Someone was watching me.*

I take Ella's phone and scroll up to read the heading.

I've found a "hobby", now that I know where Sophie lives

My insides shudder.

"What is wrong with people?!" Carmen says.

I expand the comments and gulp. It's the picture I posted from our balcony the morning I watched the Japanese Grand Prix.

Nice find! That looks to be the right neighborhood, assuming this picture is from her apartment.
It's an off week, and Sophie's in Paris. I wonder if we'll get any Beck in the wild sightings!

I shake my head and hand Ella's phone back.

"This is ridiculous."

I glance out the lobby doors, studying the random passersby. *What a nightmare.* I'm going to have to tell Beck.

I hate to bother Beck while he's at headquarters, but he insisted I ring him. He stares at me in the FaceTime as people pass by him through a hallway.

"Sophie, you need to go to a hotel," Beck demands. "*Now.*" *Maybe I shouldn't have told him.*

His face is stern. "I can't be there until tomorrow."

I shake my head. "Beck, that's crazy! We aren't leaving—*that's what they want!* They're only trying to scare me."

"Sophie," he warns.

"We have Pierre. It will be fine."

"Sophie," he says stiffly. "You don't know what kind of people could have that information now."

———

I close my eyes and exhale deeper into a child's pose. Beck's annoyed with me. The girls and I stayed at the apartment last night, and of course, nothing happened. Things were quiet as a mouse.

"Oliver bought a new white blazer, *and* he's wearing white trousers. I can see a trip to the cleaners in his future," Carmen says, rolling her eyes.

I sit back onto my mat and stretch my legs out in front of me. Class doesn't start for another five minutes.

"I haven't seen what Beck is wearing besides the mask we found in London."

"I can't wait to meet Ana!" Carmen says. "And Tommy's date!"

"*Emma.*" I smile. "I wonder if Ella will be jealous? She's the only one going *stag.*"

Carmen shrugs. "She wants her pick from the buffet of men at the party."

My eyes bulge.

Carmen holds up her hands. "Her words, not mine."

My phone lights up at the front of my mat. Carmen and I exchange a look. I lean forward to check the screen. It's a direct message from *In_The_Know_Podcast* podcast. My stomach drops. I snatch the phone and open the message.

Hello Sophie!
Each Monday, we have a guest interview segment at the end of our episode, and our guest this coming Monday has fallen through.
We received multiple requests to have you on for an interview, given the stories we've discussed on the show lately. Please let us know if you would be open to filming a short segment via video chat with us on Sunday!

My heart sprints. I turn my phone to Carmen. She leans closer and scans the message.

"Oh my God!" Carmen squeals. "Absolutely yes! Yes?"

I didn't *truly* expect to hear from them when they mentioned putting out "feelers." My mind races. Of course, it's a yes. I message them back:

I'd love to! Please send me the details for Sunday.

Why wouldn't I do it? I'll finally have a chance to clear up misconceptions from the tabloid and what's been said on the gossip site *on a huge platform*. I click their profile from the message. The podcast page alone has 1.5 *million* followers.

Yoga was Carmen's idea. It was supposed to be relaxing, but I couldn't get my head in the zone the entire flow. I'm too giddy thinking about the podcast. *Ella's going to freak.* The podcast page already tagged me in a promo on their story.

Drop us your question requests!
F1 WAG, Sophie Collins, will be our guest for Monday's interview segment!

We stopped by the market on our way home from the studio to grab a few more juice options for the preparty. I said yes to the podcast rather quickly; the gravity of the decision is setting in. It's exciting, but nerve-racking at the same time.

"I know what we forgot!" Carmen says at the checkout counter. "*Limes.* For the tequila."

I purse my lips then turn on my heel, heading back to the produce.

Carmen slows, nearing the intersection of our street. I match her pace and peer around the corner to our building's front lobby doors. *Nothing out of the ordinary.* Carmen hooks an arm through mine.

"This is silly," she laughs. "We're being paranoid."

"Mum said the podcast's a no-brainer. She *did,* however, agree with Beck about going to a hotel for the weekend," Ella says.

Carmen dumps out her bag from the market. The limes roll across the counter.

I roll my eyes. I am not forgoing hosting this party because of some dumb post.

"What's Beck going to say about the podcast?" Ella asks.

Were his ears ringing in Maranello? I pull my phone from my pocket, vibrating with his incoming call.

"Guess we'll see."

"Speaker phone!" Carmen whispers.

"Hello there," I answer.

I hit the speaker icon and set the phone on the counter.

"I've got some updates for next week," Beck says.

"Is everything okay for the race?"

Beck clears his throat. "Shannon and the team think it's best that you somewhat fly under the radar in Portugal. For your safety," he adds.

I glance up at Ella and Carmen, their eyes glued to the phone. I gulp. "You told Shannon about our address?"

"I mentioned it, yes."

My heart sinks... *Shannon thought I was drama before*. A podcast interview probably doesn't fall into the *fly under the radar* category. I take a deep breath; I have to tell him. I'll strike a compromise.

"I'll hideout in the paddock next week, but I'm doing an interview for *In the Know* podcast...I'm going to be their Monday guest interview..."

"*Sophie...*" Beck says, drawing my name out. "I don't think that's a good idea."

Ella grits her teeth. My breath quickens.

"It's a *great* idea! It's finally my chance to set the story straight! I've already said yes."

Beck groans. "Sophie, I think you should call and cancel. You have to ignore all the noise."

My hot-air balloon of excitement receives a pin prick. I bite my lip.

"I've got to run. I should be there by tenish," Beck says.

I remain silent.

"Sophie, think about it. I really don't think it's a good idea."

The call ends.

"Yikes," Carmen says.

As much as he wants me to, I *can't* cancel. I wasn't expecting that feedback from him. I wasn't expecting he would tell Shannon about our address though, either.

"That's a tough one," Ella says. "I understand where he's coming from, but I also see why you need to do it. It's our favorite podcast… you *have* to do it!"

I'm struggling with Beck's less than supportive reaction. It's too many conflicting feelings. Is it worth losing what I believe in? Standing up for myself? Standing up for Ana and the others?

I shake my head. "I'm not canceling. I have to do this for myself."

***

"It's been a while, hasn't it?" Beck says, hugging Carmen.

He takes a breath. "Those stairs!"

"They keep us humble," Ella laughs. "Did you meet Pierre?"

I chuckle. "He gave Beck a proper up-down."

Beck takes a few more steps across the herringbone floor. A garment bag is draped over his arm.

"This place is great," Beck says, turning around in the living room.

"It better be great for what we're paying," Ella jokes.

It's weird that he's never been here. How can he look more charming here than at the flat? Must be the Paris effect.

"I take it that's your demon ensemble?" Ella asks.

Beck smiles at me. "Soph wanted to go dark, so dark I went."

"Better than all white," Carmen laughs. "Oliver's going to be a wreck."

Beck flops down on my bed and rolls onto his back. It means the world that he came for this. I hang his bag on the hook on the back of my door and join him.

"What's the verdict? Did you think about canceling?"

I fold my lips. Having him in front of me makes it so much harder. *I can't do it for him?* No. *Stay strong, Sophie.*

"I'm sorry," I mutter. "But I can't cancel. You understand, right?"

I study his face. It hasn't changed, but he hasn't gotten up and left either.

He places his hand over mine. "I do. I know you want your voice heard. Just—don't say anything Shannon will pull her hair out over." He smiles.

"You didn't tell her, right?"

"God no!" he says quickly.

I smile—*he gets it.* I glance at his bag on the back of the door.

"Can I take a peek?" I ask.

His head shakes slowly. "It's a surprise."

Beck pulls me into his chest, and I nestle into my usual place in the nook of his arm.

Our hands swing between us. I've dreamed of taking Beck to *Café du Reve* for weeks. He enjoyed every crumb as much as I envisioned. We were those lovers in Paris, practically on top of each other at our table. Drinking in as much of each other as we were our coffees. We pivot, coming around the corner, and Beck stills. He stops our hands mid swing. The smile melts from his face. My eyes dart down the sidewalk. *Crap.*

Five people stare back, standing idle outside the lobby front doors. Beck continues apprehensively down the sidewalk and squeezes my hand. Our happy strut has vanished. The group's excitement builds as we get closer. I focus on the ground ahead, avoiding his *I told you so* eyes.

I pull my hand from his and nervously grab the cold handle on the front door. Beck quickly smiles for a photo with the giddy bunch of fans.

I whip the door open. Pierre stands staring behind his desk.

Beck nods at Pierre and quickly pulls my hand to the stairs.

On the first landing, Beck delivers the blow.

"We're leaving—*now*."

His statement punches me in the gut. I'll wait until we get upstairs for my backup before I put up any fight.

Carmen nervously peers down at the street from the living room windows.

"We can't stay here," Beck says. "This gets picked up, and the whole world is going to know your address."

"But our preparty! We're hosting everyone here!" I plead.

Ella breaks. "He's right, Soph. It will only get worse when the others arrive."

"Ren and Tommy are staying at the same hotel," Beck looks at me. "I'll call and see if I can get us a room."

Carmen smiles, and Ella nods her head. *They were supposed to be my backup.*

I'm crushed. I can't help but feel as if this is all my fault. The number of things we'll have to pack up is absurd. I toss the sequin bodysuit from my wardrobe onto my bed.

Beck walks in.

"All set," he says proudly.

I ignore him. I open my dresser drawer and throw the satin gloves to the growing pile on my comforter.

"Sophie, don't be upset."

I turn from the dresser. "I'm not upset," I lie. "I just didn't picture hosting everyone in a *hotel room*."

Beck catches my hips and pulls me under him. I'm fuming, and his smile is only making me madder.

"You're not hosting in a hotel *room*," he says. "I got us the *suite*."

I press my lips together.

"...two bedrooms, so Ella can stay in the other."

Now I feel like a proper brat.

CHAPTER 29
RED VELVET

Beck is in a trance.

"Do we have to go to this party?" he says slowly.

I keep my eyes locked with his and crown myself with the sparkly horned headband. I wink and turn to flash him the cheeky backside of the sequined bodysuit.

Beck runs his tongue over the bottom of his teeth. He's tantalizingly sexy, leaned back against the headboard in his white dress shirt and suspenders.

"You like?" I ask.

He takes a deep breath and hoists himself up.

"Soph, this costume..." He sucks in air, running his hands over the sequins around my waist. "I don't remember signing off on this..."

"Oh? You don't recall attacking me in the fitting room?" I tease.

"...*Torture*" he exhales.

I grab both of his black suspenders and pull our chests together. I hover against his lips. "Your turn," I whisper before pushing him away.

Beck shakes his head and walks to the garment bag hanging on the door frame. I turn my back and listen to the zipper unzip. I still haven't seen this surprise costume. A few seconds later, everything's quiet.

"I'm afraid I'm not worthy," Beck says.

I turn around and pull in a deep breath. *My word.* My eyes feast on my partner in evil; devilishly divine in a deep red velvet suit jacket.

Ana's disgusted. "Not only is that appalling, but it's also doxing!"

I take a sip of my vodka soda.

"I'm glad you left; there's no telling what people will do." Ana shakes her head.

I nod. I guess it all worked out. *The suite is fabulous.* The parlor separating the bedrooms on either side makes the perfect party gathering. Oliver and Carmen were able to get a room on the floor below. The walls must be reinforced; we've yet to receive a noise complaint from Oliver's blasting music.

"I missed you in the desert last week," I say.

"I should have come. No one tells you how dreadful wedding planning is," Ana says. "By the third venue, I told mom 'forget it, we're eloping,' and she started crying."

Beck returns his phone to his interior breast pocket. "Tommy's outside!" he yells.

Knocks don't stand a fighting chance against the blaring music.

Ella runs to the door.

"*You* went angel?" Ella shouts.

She holds the door open, and Tommy walks in, wearing a white suit with a bombshell blonde angel on his arm. *Emma.*

"Duh!" Tommy says. "I'm the most angelic."

Emma looks nervous. *I don't blame her; Ella's intimidating.*

"More angels?" Ana laughs. She leans in closer, "I love that we went demon."

I high five Ren; he went full-on red jacket *and* trousers. As cute as the angel costumes Ella and Carmen pulled together are, I'm emboldened in my red getup. *Though I'd prefer another drink or two before I step out in public like this.* I died and went to heaven when Beck debuted the red velvet jacket over his bow tie. I guess in this case, *I died and went to hell.*

Ella leads Emma straight to the bevvies. Tommy hugs me tightly. He gives Ren a playful punch to the shoulder.

"That red looks good on you, Ren. You sure about that *Mak* contract?" Tommy jokes.

Ha! Ren's got a few million reasons to be sure.

Emma's face sours from the shot Ella's force fed her. We lock eyes from across the room. She picks up two shot glasses Ella's refilled and steers my way.

I smile nervously.

Emma's gorgeous, *Ella level gorgeous.*

"I've wanted to meet you from the moment I saw your interview with David," Emma says.

"Which one?" I laugh.

"*Both*. The first one made me laugh, but the second one..." She pauses. "You're the only one who's ever been brave enough to speak out like that."

Emma leans in closer. "I *wish* I had the balls to say what you said."

Emma hands me a shot glass.

"Here's to the *WAGs*." She holds her shot glass up.

"And the former WAGs," I add. I glance at Tommy then back to her. "And *reinstated* WAGs?"

Emma smiles and clinks her glass to mine.

"Let's get a refill, Ella," Tommy yells. "I have a toast to make."

"Say no more!" Ella calls, happily refilling the shot glasses.

Beck tugs my devil tail.

"Your favorite," he says.

I shudder. I can already smell it.

"I'll do one with you for old time's sake." He smirks.

The tequila's been passed. Tommy holds up his shot glass.

"Valor's already run away with first place, *again*," Tommy shrugs. "And if Ren keeps racing like he is, Makellos has second pretty locked down. As for third," he says, bumping Beck. "May the best team take it."

Beck shakes his head. "Keep dreaming, mate!"

"Two more to go!" Ren yells.

I close my eyes and quiver as the tequila passes down my throat. I take a deep breath; when I open, Beck winks.

"You're getting better. I still remember your face that first shot we took together."

Carmen cranks the music back up and steps up onto the couch, assuming her favorite dancing platform. An already glossy-eyed Oliver bats at Carmen's sheer costume wings like a cat. *I think that's enough shots for Oliver.*

When Ella said she set up a car, she meant a limousine. Beck presses his hand on my bouncing knee. *What on earth did Ella get us invited to?* A dozen cameras flash, and a dozen more are waiting. A carpet runs up the stairs to a step-and-repeat before the entrance.

"Last sips!" Ella yells.

Crap. Beck and I are closest to the door. Beck's mask rests above his eyes on his forehead. *If he's not going to wear it, maybe I should.* I chug the remainder of my champagne. Carmen reaches for our glasses as a valet opens the door.

"Wait!" I yell frantically. "Where's my pitchfork?"

Carmen snatches it from Oliver and hands it over. I adjust my satin elbow length gloves and take it. Beck steps out and extends his hand for me. *Here we go.*

The cameras shift in our direction. Beck smiles and pulls me close. The volume dials up as the photographers start calling Beck's name. The rest of our party piles out of the limo, causing a tumultuous frenzy. I glance back at Ana; her eyes are on the ground. Ren and Tommy are beaming, waving at the cameras. *The A-list athletes have arrived.*

I ascend the carpeted stairs on Beck's arm; the liquid confidence has set in. Beck and I are first up for the step-and-repeat; *we look to die for.*

I glance up at Beck. "Do we smile?"

"No! We are demons. Give 'em *stone cold Sophie.*"

I bust out laughing as the couple ahead clear the backdrop.

An X marks the center of the photo. Beck drops my hand and wraps his arm around my waist. My sequins glimmer in the radiant light illuminating the step-and-repeat; the folds of Beck's velvet jacket glow in my peripheral. Cameras flash. I'm trying to keep a straight face, but I look up to check Beck's expression.

"Sophie," he says. "I just realized my mask is still on my forehead."

Beck loses it and doubles over, laughing.

***

We may have overdone the preparty. The first four buttons on Oliver's shirt are undone, and he's wearing Carmen's halo. Dancing with us girls, he has one foot up on the table, hip thrusting to the bumping music. Beyond the table, on the other couch, Beck, Ren and Tommy are entertained. A waitress replenishes our reserve with two fresh frosted liquor bottles as another collects three empties from our table.

"Is he always like this?" Emma yells.

"Ollie's always the drunkest girl at the party," I laugh.

Though Ana might give Oliver a run for his money tonight. Ana yanks her engagement ring off. She tries to force it on Carmen's finger. Ella grabs the ring and slips it on. Ella extends her hand out in front of her, and her jaw drops, admiring it. Ella turns and flashes her fingers at Ren. The strobe lights illuminate the diamond as she wiggles her fingers.

Beck's mouth falls open. Ren stops mid sentence and shakes his head. I throw my head back, laughing. I grab Ella and make sure the ring is transferred back to Ana's finger. The party is madness. If we didn't have our own table, we'd be lost in a sea of angels and demons. *Everyone* went all out. The costumes are over the top. I lost any sense of self-consciousness a while ago. My cheeks are numb; I can only feel the heat beneath them. Ella pulls me up onto the couch. The unsteady surface under my heels amplifies the alcohol's effects. I lock eyes with Beck across our table. Beck keeps talking with Tommy but doesn't break eye contact. *Let's play a game.* I turn my back to Beck and continue moving my hips. I glance back at him over my shoulder. His eyes are still fixated. Ella grabs my hands and lifts them over my head.

A man reaches for Ella's arm. A group of five hunky demons congregates around the back of our couch. My hand meets one's grasp; he's speaking, but I only see his lips moving.

Hands slip around my waist from behind; Beck's fingers dig into my stomach. I pull my hand from the man's grasp and squeal as Beck lifts me backward off the couch. My back falls against Beck's chest. His hands continue their descent, diving past my belly button. All the nerve endings fire between my legs. I spin around and meet his lips. My body jolts with a hiccup. Beck's lips curl into a smile. He firmly cups both of my sequined cheeks. I run my hands up the luxe velvet to his neck. My gloved fingers grip into his hair, allowing me to dive deeper into his mouth. I push my hips into him. Beck pulls his head back and brings his lips to my ear.

"*Easy*," he hisses. His breath sends chills down the side of my body. I lift my leg and wrap it around him ready to climb him like a tree when he catches my thigh. He floods my ear with a cautionary groan.

"You better calm down," he purrs. "Or *we are going to have to leave.*"

I gasp at the brightness of the unfamiliar room. My phone rattles on the nightstand. My heart races. I turn over and see Beck is sound asleep. *Thank God; we made it back to the hotel.* I grab my phone and accept Carmen's call.

"Is Oliver over there?" she grumbles.

Hmm. "Let me check."

My feet hit the floor and the wooziness sets in. My costume components are scattered about. I crack open the door of our room.

Oh dear.

"Affirmative. He's face down on the couch."

"Coming," Carmen says.

Beck stirs.

"Good morning, handsome devil." My voice cracks.

"Who's out there?" Beck squints.

"Who do you think?" I laugh.

"Get over here, you naughty thing."

"Naughty?" I blush and wrap my arms around my nakedness.

Beck raises an eyebrow. "You were an *animal* when we got back here…"

I gulp.

There's a knock on the door. I throw a robe on and tiptoe through the living room to let Carmen inside.

Two room service carts greet me. I clutch the robe closed at my chest. "*Oh!* I'm sorry. Come on in."

I hold the door open for the service man. *Shit.* The suite is in shambles, and Oliver's passed out on the couch.

Ella's door opens. She stumbles out and hands the service man a tip. Carmen nearly takes out the leaving man when she storms through the front door.

"I told him not to get our own room!" Carmen yells.

"*Dude,*" Oliver groans.

"Seriously, volume down, Carmen," Ella says, pouring herself a glass of champagne. She tops off her glass with a drop of juice. The smell of the champagne makes my stomach twist.

"Good morning, Beck!" Ella sings.

"Good morning, angels!" Beck laughs.

Ella gestures at the spread on the service cart. "Come one, come all."

Beck slips his hand around my waist. I reach for a toast wedge. I've got to get my mind right before the interview at three. Carmen pours herself a champagne.

Oliver sits up slowly.

"You good, mate?" Beck asks.

Oliver's still in half of last night's suit; pink mystery stains run down the front of his white shirt.

"Did your jacket even make it home?" Carmen asks.

"I'm lucky I made it home, okay?" Oliver groans.

"But you didn't—I slept in our room alone!" Carmen scolds.

Beck can't contain himself watching them bicker.

"It's okay, Oliver. My pitchfork didn't make it home either," I giggle.

Even with the last-minute change of venue, our party pregame was a success. The party itself was epic—*the parts I remember*. I scoop my legs under me and curl up next to Beck on the couch opposite Oliver. I bite into the buttery toast and chew with the minuscule moisture in my mouth. I text Ana to come to our suite for the regrouping feast. I wonder what shape she's in this morning.

"You girls need to stay here again tonight," Beck instructs.

Ella's eyes shoot to me. The anxiety of reality hits home. The party's over and our guests would be leaving soon, Beck included.

"Oliver, move in with us. I'll snuggle with Ella tonight," I say.

A door closes in Ella's room.

"What was that?" Carmen asks.

Ella squeezes her eyes shut and smiles.

"Filipe?" Ella says, opening an eye. "I think that's his name?"

Beck laughs. "That's what you were calling him last night."

I had the pleasure of meeting Filipe before he left. I might remember his face from last night, but I can't be certain. I secured a meeting room on the lobby floor of the hotel. I didn't trust Carmen, Oliver and Ella to keep quiet in our suite. Especially after the third room service delivery of champagne showed up. I had one mimosa to cut the hangover anxiety before I showered and got into serious interview mode.

I hover my mouse over my laptop battery icon—81 percent. *It's time. There's no going back.* Over the years, I've listened to hours of *In the Know* episodes. I've watched countless interview segments. I can do this.

I try to dull my starstruck smile, *but this is wild.* I press my thighs together under the table.

Maggie smiles. "We have submitted questions and some questions of our own."

"Nothing crazy—no bombshells," Julia adds. "We'll keep it easy and fun, okay?"

I nod. I let them know discussing the posting of our address was off limits. I made that promise to Beck before he left.

I could pinch myself. I adjust the computer angle ever so slightly. Maggie and Julia fidget in their seats then still.

"Alright! We're going to start recording now," Julia says.

I smile and watch their faces light up for the intro.

"Welcome back to *In the Know* podcast!" Maggie says.

"After causing some noise this season, F1's newest WAG, Sophie Collins, is joining us from across the pond! Welcome, Sophie!"

I wave at the camera. "Thank you for having me!"

"We had no idea so many of our listeners are fans of F1—I'm so glad we got this worked out. So, we're here to chitchat and get to know you a little bit better. Are you ready?" Julia asks.

"Let's do it!" I say.

Maggie picks up her iPad. "We had many questions submitted from our listeners, so let's start with the popular ones."

I nod.

"First question," Maggie says. "Let's set the record straight—how did you meet your boyfriend, Beckham Wright?"

Easy. "We met at a music festival in Mallorca."

"And did you know who he was?" Julia adds.

"I had no idea." I smile. "I thought he was a random, extremely handsome man. I knew what F1 was, but I didn't follow it in any way so—*no.*"

"Well, we only discovered what it was recently. Apparently, our husbands follow it. They knew who Beck was when we said we were interviewing you."

Julia pipes in. "You also didn't know what a WAG was," she laughs. "But you were a finance girlie—you know more important acronyms like EBITA."

Ha! "Yes," I laugh. "I'll never live that one down I'm afraid."

"Okay, question two," Maggie continues. "What is your favorite thing about being a WAG?"

Even easier. "My favorite thing is obviously my relationship with Beck."

They swoon.

Why am I smiling so stupidly only saying his name?

"He's amazing; we have a blast traveling and simply being together," I say. "But I've also met some wonderful people like Ana, another *WAG.* She's one of my best friends now."

"Ana's the one that recently got engaged, right?" Maggie asks.

"Yes!"

"Is it hard having to travel that often?" Julia asks.

"With influencing, *no* because I don't have a normal work schedule. It was only hard, the first few races being between fashion weeks...I didn't sleep much that month."

"Speaking of fashion weeks, you walked in a show!" Julia's face lights up. "Had you ever done that?"

I shake my head. "No. I was terrified, but honestly, it was brilliant. I got to walk with my best friend, Ella, in the *Eden Eves* show in London and Paris. Ella's mum is best friends with the designer."

Hope Evelyn's okay with the name drop...

"I love that picture of you backstage with the roses," Julia says. "Okay, switching gears. What would you say is the *hardest* thing about being a WAG?"

My heart rate picks up. *This is it.*

"The crazy things people say." I pause. "I mean, I don't really care what people say about me, but when they go after my friends—that's when I can't keep my mouth shut."

"You received some backlash after you called out toxic fans during an interview..." Julia reads.

"There was a tabloid piece written about *one thing* I said in a broader interview. I was talking about how amazing the fan base of the sport is, but I mentioned a toxic side of the fandom does exist." I shrug. "And unfortunately, groups like that sometimes have the loudest voices."

"They're just jealous," Maggie says.

"Maybe that's part of it, but some of these people are *unhinged.*"

Maggie throws her head back, laughing.

"If you are dedicated to creating entire blogs bashing us—you have too much time on your hands. I'm not asking for people to be nice; I'm asking for basic human decency."

"There's a snark page for this podcast too," Julia says.

"That was our favorite part of that one interview you did...what did you say?"

"*Perhaps get a hobby*," Maggie chuckles.

So, these hate pages are a common thing?

"Do you think you've had it harder than most?" Julia asks.

Easy.

"Not even close. The things I've seen and learned that have happened to other girls are horrible. I think I just *respond* to it, and it drives people nuts."

Maggie nods. "None of the other WAGs really speak much with the media…"

Because they're smart.

"I take interviews because if I don't, people make their own assumptions. At the end of the day, I'm really a normal, everyday girl. But if all I knew about myself is what is written in gossip pages and tabloids, I probably wouldn't like me either!"

Julia smiles. "Well, we like you and our fanbase was really excited for your interview."

My stomach flutters. "Thank you."

"Okay, don't kill us; we are recording, so we can clip this if we have to," Julia laughs.

I gulp.

"Did Beck know about the *'career ending relationship saga'* before the story was leaked?"

"You don't have to clip that." I smile. "He didn't know *all* of the details."

Their eyes widen.

"Really? Did that cause an issue?"

"Not an issue, but it certainly led to a conversation where I told him the full and *true story* and that was that."

"Did the tabloid get the story right?"

"Some of it—" I pause. "I was young and dumb. I'm sure I'm not the first person to have a workplace romance gone wrong. However, he was *not* married. The other parts of the article attempting to tie me to the divorce of another executive—was absolutely false."

"So, besides the colleague being your superior, this is a nothing burger?" Maggie asks.

"Exactly."

Julia scowls. "The media can be so vile."

"It's astounding, I…" I stop.

Julia smiles. "What were you going to say?"

"I don't want to get in trouble."

"Let it out!" Maggie yells.

I shake my head. "I find it hypocritical. The media touts mental health, but then the same tabloid proudly prints hearsay rumors that can send people spiraling."

Maggie nods her head.

Julia continues. "Staying on the topic of spiraling and past relationships, this was by far the most popular question: Do you think Sabrina Kaufmann's new song is a nod to Beck?"

My heart pounds. "Maybe it is, maybe it isn't? Beck's not the only person she's dated. I don't know why all of the speculation insinuates it's about Beck."

Julia grins. "*It's about Beck.*"

I smile back and shrug.

"And where will Beck be racing this week?"

"This week's race is in Portugal."

"Well, we look forward to staying in touch and up to date with you and Beck, the races, the outfits, all of the things," Maggie says.

"And next time we do this, you'll have to come here to the studio in New York!" Julia concludes.

When the video call ends, my head rushes. I close my laptop lid. The interview goes live tomorrow when their usual episode wraps. I push back from the table and stand up. *I did it.* It went better than I imagined. My voice will be heard—*the truth will be heard.*

CHAPTER 30

FALLOUT

"Sophie, what's wrong?" Ella says.

I read Beck's text again.

> I haven't had time to watch the interview yet, but Shannon isn't happy.

I hand my phone to Ella. The podcast only went live an hour ago—Shannon found it that fast?

Ella furrows her eyebrows. "*What?*" Ella passes my phone to Carmen. "You sounded great."

"You didn't say anything worse than what you've said in interviews with David," Ella huffs.

Carmen hands my phone back. I go on the defensive and start typing.

I erase my reply. I'm not sure how to respond. *I'm thinking about it too much*. I text him back.

> I was well behaved! I didn't say anything that would get me in trouble.

Beck's typing bubble instantly appears. *Woah.*

I'll ring you at 6.

———

Clips of the podcast interview have started popping up on social media. For the first time, I'm receiving overwhelming praise and supportive messages. I feel proud, validated and *vindicated.* Every message I read leaves me more confused why Shannon would have a negative reaction. A reaction that warranted expressing her concerns to Beck.

Beck's calling. My heart rate picks up—he's early. It's barely 5:30. And why is he calling when he can FaceTime?

"Sophie?" Beck answers.

"Yes?"

"Where are you?" he asks.

His tone is short and serious.

My heart jumps to my throat. "Walking to the market. We moved back to our place."

He sighs heavily.

"We can't hideout in a hotel forever, Beck."

"Sophie, why didn't you show me that page?" Beck asks.

I freeze. A few seconds of silence pass before I speak. "I mean, I've mentioned it...but there are horrible things written there—why would I show you that?"

"Sophie, there are death threats posted there—threatening *you.*"

Death threats? That's a new level of delusion. Threats are news to me; but I haven't visited the page since our address unveiling.

"I spoke with the PR team," Beck continues. "...They think you should sit this one out."

I stop dead in my tracks. Blood rushes to my head.

"Sophie, I hate that I'm saying this, but I think they're right."

The walls are moving, closing in around me. My heart sinks to the pit in my stomach. The lump forming in my throat curbs any response. Even if I could speak, I don't know what I would say.

"Sophie, I just want to protect you," Beck says.

Why does he keep saying my name like that? I swallow hard and muster up the words.

"How can you protect me if we're not together?" I choke.

Beck sighs. "By taking a step back and avoiding adding anymore fuel to the fire."

Now I'm mad. These are Shannon's words spilling out of his mouth. *I'm the fuel on the fire.*

"Beck, don't you see? This is what they want! These people want to drive us apart."

"That's not happening, Sophie—I think we need to take a step back and let everything settle down. I need to focus. The team really wants a win this season." He pauses. "Let's have you sit this one out."

I'm in shock, I'm spiraling. I need an out.

"Well, *good luck*," I say curtly, my blood boiling.

"People are threatening your life, Sophie. It's not okay. It's gone too far."

He's never used this tone of voice with me.

"I am not putting you in situations that will compromise your safety."

My safety? What's safer than a private jet? The paddock couldn't be any more of a fortress than it already is. This is about shutting me up.

"You said you'd never hide me..."

"I'm willing to go back on my word if it means I'm protecting you."

"I can't believe this. What do you want me to do? Hole up inside and be silent?"

"I don't know!" Beck yells.

I gulp.

"I don't know what to tell you! I told you the podcast was a bad idea!"

He's never yelled at me. The first tear spills over the floodgate and streams down my cheek.

"Sophie—" he says, coming back calmly. "I have to go."

I pull the phone from my ear and end the call.

All the oxygen has left my body. I step to the side of the sidewalk to put a hand on the building. I'm going to be sick. The mix of emotions searing inside is making my head spin.

I swing the front door open harder than intended. Ella shoots up from the couch. Red eyes and empty arms provide the distress signal.

"What happened?" Ella runs over. "Did Beck call?"

She grabs the door and closes it.

The tears build again as I prepare my reply.

"Beck said I'm going to sit out this race," I choke. "Apparently, there are death threats directed at me online."

"What?" Ella says, shocked.

She pulls out her phone, and I walk with her to the couch.

Ella shakes her head. "He must have found the page," she says, putting her phone in my lap.

It's the most recent post on the gossip blog. A screenshot of the podcast interview, with the header *"Kill the bitch."*

At this point, I'm not even interested in entertaining the comments.

"I think Shannon found it and showed him," I mutter.

"Sophie, seeing this probably freaked him out! *Understandably*," Ella says.

My head throbs.

"Do you regret it? The podcast?"

"No, of course not. Everything I said was warranted."

"Completely!"

Would I have done it if I knew this would be the fallout? That question isn't fair.

"Beck's under so much pressure, and I'm just—*complicating*—things and adding on to his stress."

Ella puts her arm around me.

I replay the conversation in my head a few times. I'm getting stuck at *we need to take a step back.* What did he mean by that? Did he mean a step back *from our relationship*?

"If you're not going to the race, then you're coming with me to Cannes. The *Beurre* shoot is Friday."

I close my eyes. *I cannot go to Cannes, Ella; I'm going to be in Portugal for the race...*But I'm not.

"I'll call. They'll be more than happy to have another girl," Ella says, attempting to comfort me.

Carmen leaves tomorrow, and with Ella gone, I will be stuck here alone. The thought is unnerving.

"Even if they say no, I'm coming to watch. I have to get out of here."

Ella nods her head. "The brand is cool. Paulo, the photographer, is a friend of Mum's, and he's awesome. We'll take the train down Thursday," she says.

My tears stop until I walk into my room and see the *RIMI* luggage. A few outfit ideas for Portugal already sit on top, including my cherry bikini, *just in case*. My eyes are on fire. I grab the bikini and scoop up the outfits. *Fuck. The luggage.* I throw the Portugal paddock looks out of sight, into my wardrobe. *How* am I going to break the news to Stuart that my grand ideas for the *RIMI* luggage posts will no longer be happening? I hope he hasn't communicated the ideas with the brand. I have to tell him, but I know all too well I won't be able to get through that call right now.

I type out a message instead:

> Stuart, I'm afraid I will not
> be going to the race in Portugal.
> I'm going to Cannes with Ella for
> the *Beurre* swim photoshoot.
> If they'll have me, I will participate
> in the shoot. I'll get photos with the
> luggage on the train. I'm sorry for the
> late notice and change of plans.

Fresh tears well up, finishing the last sentence. I hit send. *I feel so stupid.* I was over the top excited last week during our meeting, explaining my plans for the luggage posts. I went on and on about how great the bags would look inside and outside of Beck's pristine private jet. Now, *I'm humiliated.* I wipe the tears angrily from my cheeks. My phone rings. *It's Stuart.*

"The podcast put you right over the edge," Ella says.

"Edge of what? A cliff?"

"No," she snaps. "You just tipped over 100k followers."

My. I never imagined this day would come. I certainly didn't imagine I'd feel this way *if* ever I reached that milestone.

"I wonder how many of them are here to hate follow," I mutter.

"Jokes on them—*a follower is a follower*." Ella shrugs. "They only make you more attractive to new deals."

Radio silence. It's been two days since my call with Beck. I was supposed to take the train to London yesterday. *We should have landed in Portugal by now*. I keep trying to convince myself that Beck's training with Charlie, doing something dull, but I'm incapable of believing my own lies. *Everyone is taking Beck's side*. I get more agitated with each passing hour. Even when I called Dad yesterday to cancel our dinner plans, I was met with *"He's just trying to protect you, darling."*

Ana totally freaked when I explained why I wouldn't be seeing her tonight at the group dinner we'd planned in Portugal. *"It's for the best, Sophie. These people are scary."* I'm praying Beck still shows up for dinner. Ana can provide me intel on his state of mind.

It's been fifty-two hours, but who's counting? If Beck wanted me to stay quiet, then quiet I'll remain. That includes not speaking to him. If I'm riding the bench this week, what is he thinking for next week? It's the final race of the season. I'm supposed to fly to Abu Dhabi with his family. Elizabeth has a whole trip planned. *What do his parents know?*

According to Ana's last text, the group dinner's commenced. All original attendees minus *one*. But her text is from two hours ago. *Are they still there? What did everyone think when Beck walked in solo?* The knot in my stomach tightens. *What will the team think when my headset hangs untouched in the garage all weekend?*

I toss and turn in bed, falling in and out of sleep. When I hadn't heard anything by eleven p.m. I turned my phone face down. I promised myself I wouldn't look at it again. *No news is good news, right?* Even face down, the small ring of illumination taunts me each time the screen lights up. I squeeze my eyes shut.

But what if it's Beck? I flip over and stare at the phone. 4:03 glows on the clock face. *What if he can't sleep either?* I grab my phone; I've lost the battle. I squint at the screen and instantly regret it. Hundreds of tag notifications send me straight into fight or flight. I open Instagram, and it's the first post in my feed: a photo of Beck and Sabrina together in Portugal. My heart sinks. *There's no word from Beck.*

CHAPTER 31

THIS FEELS WRONG

I'M WAITING UNTIL SEVEN to wake Ella up with the news. I have twelve minutes. In the last hours, I've found the photo reposted on multiple gossip pages. Several other blurry photos from bystanders have come out. Sabrina originally posted the main photo to her page late last night. I've looked at it one hundred times at this point; it's her and Beck with the caption:

Speak of the devil!

Each comment added below the photo delivers another gut punch. No matter what I read, it's what I'm *not reading* that makes me sicker. Beck must know I've seen the photo, and yet he's said nothing.

6:50. *Fuck it,* close enough.

I open Ella's door quietly and tiptoe to her bed. I pull the comforter back and carefully climb in.

"What's wrong?" Her eyes open slowly. "You still haven't heard from him?"

"No, but Sabrina posted this last night."

I flip my screen to her.

Ella scoots up and reaches for her glasses. She grabs my phone. I lay back on her pillows and wrap my arms over my face.

"What the hell?! She's in—wait, where is the race?"

"Portugal."

The cage of my arms isn't dark enough. I squeeze my eyes shut. *How did I so willingly open my heart again?* I was naïve to think Fredrick wouldn't leave me, and I was naïve to think Beck wouldn't break my heart.

"Okay, before we start making assumptions, Sabrina's *from* Portugal...they are in public; it seems they are just at a restaurant?"

"There's more," I say.

"More? More what?"

"Pictures—they're easy to find. Blurry, but people saw them *outside* the restaurant." I gulp. "What if they left together?"

"If they left together, there would be evidence," Ella says.

"Sophie, think of the scenario—Sabrina saw him out and asked for a photo. You know Beck, he's not going to say no. It's entirely platonic. They are just standing there."

I have the picture memorized. "But where's his other hand?" I whine.

Ella doesn't answer. I uncover my face.

"Why would he do that?" I cry.

Ella zooms in on the picture, studying hard.

"I've never gone this long without speaking to him," I say.

I wait a few more hours before calling Ana. First, I send her Sabrina's photo. As soon as the message shows *read,* I call.

"Sophie, I don't understand what's happening here," Ana says.

"This is from dinner last night, right?"

"It's the restaurant," Ana confirms. "Ren and I left before Tommy and Beck. This must have happened after?"

My heart sinks. *My trusted source wasn't present for the incident.*

"Tommy's not in any of the photos," I say.

"I'm guessing you still haven't talked to him?" Ana asks softly.

"No," I choke, barely getting the word out.

"Well, Beck definitely was off at dinner. He wasn't his normal smiley self. He stayed pretty quiet."

Is it possible he's as miserable as I am?

"He didn't say anything about me?"

"No. All they talked about was the race—it was so boring!"

Ha! I can picture Ana sitting at the boys' table, bored out of her mind.

"Sophie, I'm sure that picture was incredibly hard to see, but…"

"You don't think anything happened?" I interrupt her.

"Of course not, Sophie. Beck wouldn't do that to you," Ana says.

"I'm about to walk in. I miss you. Also, who am I, walking in the main paddock entrance?"

God, I wish I was there.

"I'm proud of you, Ana."

Anger completely overshadows sadness. Some scum of the earth must have pulled the night shift. The photo of Beck and Sabrina is the top headline of *The Scoop*.

Rumors swirling about a potential reunion of Portuguese popstar, Sabrina Kaufmann, and F1 driver, Beckham Wright.

The two were spotted together Wednesday night in Portugal ahead of this weekend's Portuguese Grand Prix. Many speculate Kaufmann's latest song teaser is an ode to the former couple's split last summer.

The gossip page must be *eating* this up. Thank God for this Cannes trip distraction, *semi* holding space in my mind. When Stuart called Monday, I promised I'd try to get a usable photo on the train with the *RIMI* roller bag for the campaign. He was sweet, trying to calm me down while I spilled my guts, explaining why the bag wouldn't get its proper picture on the jet. I can't believe I actually cried over the phone to my agent. He had to be uncomfortably overwhelmed. He reassured me a photo from the train would be just as good, another attempt by him to calm me down. We've grown closer with how busy I've gotten. This meltdown is sure to get us to hugging terms. Since I'll be in Paris, Stuart canceled our video call next week. He wants me in the office first thing Monday for a "*surprise.*" Monday seems dauntingly far away, but I'm in no hurry or state of mind for surprises.

"Sophie, this is great. You actually look happy!" Ella smiles behind her phone.

Getting the *RIMI* photo is the only driving force behind my attempt to look presentable today. My eyes were dark and sullen this morning. I bit the bullet and put on a full face of makeup, did my hair, and begrudgingly put on my cutest travel set. That's how desperate I am to make this photo live up to half the hype I'd originally planned for it.

I squeeze the life out of the *RIMI* bag handle. The station's packed.

"Yes or no—did you get something usable?" I huff.

"Yes!" Ella laughs.

Hallelujah. I bend forward to gather my hair. I pull it up into a ponytail on top of my head.

"I love this train," Ella says. "I got us the good seats."

She's making all attempts to lighten my mood, and I love her for it. I sit down and pull a hoodie over my travel set.

"Yes, yes, you did," I say, scooting closer to her. I pull the hood up and lay my head on her shoulder. Ella reaches into her purse and pulls out a pair of sunglasses for me. Instantly, my aching eyes get a soothing hug from the darkness of the shades.

My eyes flicker open. *Woah.*

I take off the sunglasses and blink quickly. "How long was I out?"

"At least an hour," Ella says. "I dozed off a bit myself."

Not shocking. I maybe slept two hours last night. I scoot forward in my seat and stretch my back.

"What did I miss?"

"Nothing, I'm just doom scrolling," Ella says.

"Anything interesting?" I ask.

She gives me a hesitating glance.

"It looks like Beck isn't taking media day lightly," she admits.

It's David's account, and per usual, he's made a compilation of the drivers arriving at the paddock. The video switches from Qian and Eduardo to Beck. My heart slams against my ribs. *Beck looks furious.* He doesn't blink an eye or stop once at the congregation of fans calling his name outside the gates. His eyes are empty, a pair of headphones hug around his neck. Beck walks through the swipe gates, and the cameras call for him. He doesn't smile, doesn't wave; he reaches for the headphones and puts them over his ears. Charlie jogs up behind him, catching up. The clip skips to Leo arriving. I fold my lips. Ella pulls her phone back. His usual demeanor has completely shifted. *I'm shocked.* He didn't even give David a nod.

"Another account said Beck's taking fines for backing out of some interviews today." Ella studies me. "Sophie, maybe you should reach out to him."

Hell no.

I shake my head. "He's going to have to take the lead on that."

Ella nods then smiles. "Let me show you some of the shoot details!"

I take a deep breath from the whiplash of the abrupt shift in conversation.

"Yes, let's see it then," I say.

Ella spoke with the brand Wednesday; they were elated to have me participate in the shoot. I'm guessing my new 100k follower milestone had something to do with that.

Ella flips through the pages of the detail kit the brand sent.

"It'll be chilly, but the shoot should go fairly fast. There are only five of us," Ella says.

It's a campaign for *Beurre's* new resort collection. The fabric is a whimsical watercolor blue cherub pattern. She flips the page to the different swimwear styles, *both men's and women's.*

I swallow. "There are guys?"

"Yes, there were two on the call sheet."

I scan the women's styles. One is a tasteful bikini with a balconette top, then an asymmetrical one piece with cutouts. My eyes bulge. The last style is a skimpy triangle top bikini and *thong bottom.*

"*Uh*...I call not wearing the thong," I say.

Ella smiles. "Don't worry, I'll wear that one unless the other girl wants to."

The photoshoot isn't paid, but the brand's putting us up like kings on *la Croisette;* one block from the Carlton. I drag my bag inside the sky-blue sea view room.

"How *romantic,*" I say, spotting the king bed. "We can snuggle."

"Snuggle?" Ella laughs. "I won't be able to find you! That bed is huge!"

I open the Juliette balcony doors and inhale the magic fragrance of the French Riviera. The breeze hits my skin. Beck doesn't even know I'm here. *He doesn't even care.*

"Chilly!" I say, closing the doors.

Ella points across the street. "Let's bundle up and get dinner at the beach club."

I pull my hands into my sleeves and wrap myself in a bear hug.

"I can't imagine being outside in a bikini tomorrow morning."

It's cold, maybe only ten degrees. I ate what I could, but I'm on day four of this pit in my stomach that won't subside. Ella snakes her hand into my elbow and huddles against me as we walk to the end of the dock.

"I wonder if they'll want us in the water at all?" Ella says, worried. The thought makes me shudder.

"You have to go first, that way I can watch."

"I'll ask to go first, but Paulo will give you lots of instruction."

Good. *I don't have a clue what I'm doing.*

The last planks of the dock near; it's quiet and peaceful.

The water ahead reflects the golden tones of the sunset. But the city behind is cast in pink.

"I don't know which way to look," I say.

Ella detaches; the warmth of her body heat at my right side fades.

"Smile," she says, holding up her phone.

Ella flips the camera around and leans into me, taking a selfie of us with the Cannes backdrop.

I already know the answer, but I ask anyway. "Do you want me to get your picture?"

"Duh!" Ella squeals.

In the past, I would have never offered. I would have rolled my eyes at the endless task of becoming her photographer.

"Thank you for bringing me here." My voice cracks. "I don't know what I would do without you."

She puts her arms around me and holds me tight. I squeeze my eyes shut; holding back the tears. No, really, *what would I do without her?* I'll take her photo for the next hour if she wants.

I pull the plush comforter under my chin and scoot my hips next to Ella. I still have a chill from our *al fresco* dinner and time on the dock.

"I'll set an alarm for us," Ella says.

I plugged my phone in across the room. Without it next to me, I can't be tempted to do some doom scrolling of my own if I wake up in the middle of the night. *I need sleep.* Our call time for hair and makeup is five a.m.

Ella sets two alarms then continues posting our photos from the dock. Maybe if Beck sees her story, he'll call. She scrolls down her feed, a flash of red flies by.

"Wait, go back!"

She slides her finger back up. It's a video clip from the paddock.

A rare sight, an angry Beckham Wright at media day ahead of the Portuguese Grand Prix.

My heart strikes at Beck's clipped, one-word answers. His face is dull, and aggravated. The ever-present sparkle in his eyes is nowhere to be found. He turns and walks off as another media correspondent flocks to his side. Shannon walks beside Beck. Whoever's phone is recording Beck is struggling to keep up with his pace. *"Would you care to comment on the headlines this week?"*

"Next question," Shannon murmurs.

Beck glares at the camera. I thought for a second, he was about to swat the phone out of his face.

"Are any outside factors going to affect your race this weekend?"

Beck opens his mouth to respond but turns away and walks into the suite. The clip ends.

———

Paulo flicks his hand at me. "Oh, darling, you'll be perfect!"

The minute he arrived, the volume in the room went up twenty decibels. *This is the kind of energy I need.* I've got enough salt spray in my hair to garnish a flight of margaritas. Theresa, the other model, takes my place in the hair and makeup chair.

Beurre's brand representatives brought a breakfast spread into the room. The laminated pastries taunt me. I yank my gaze off the reminders of *him* and move to the fruit. *No cherries.* I rip off a small sprig of grapes and set them in the middle of my empty plate.

I join Ella and Paulo, who are excitedly catching up, and force the grapes down one by one. The door opens, and a rolling rack of the styles is pushed in. *Please let me have first pick.*

One of the bikini's has half as much material as the other. I gulp. The brand rep glances at Ella and I and pulls the thong and triangle top.

"Ella, I think we'll have you in this style…"

Oh, thank God.

Ella gladly steps forward, agreeing. "*Perfect.* I'm a little more well-endowed up front than Sophie."

I die.

The rep pulls the next style.

"Sophie, we'll put you in this."

Relief sweeps over me. I stand up and take the balconette and full-coverage bottoms.

I can count two of my ribs on each side. This is what five days of anxiety does to me. I turn in the mirror on the back of the bathroom door. The bikini's gorgeous, and my salty *all-day-at-the-beach* frizzy hair and natural makeup looks authentic, *even for November.* There's commotion outside the door. *The male models are here.* I put my robe over the bikini and take a deep breath.

Outside the bathroom, I nervously shake hands with Reggie after meeting Colin. Their chiseled abs peek out of their open robes. My brain isn't firing on all cylinders; I can barely keep up with the small talk. I don't know why their presence is making me this uncomfortable. Thankfully, Ella and Theresa are chatting the boys up.

Twenty minutes later, I pick up my sandals and step into the crisp sand. Instantly, my legs break out in chills. The professionals disrobe, Theresa doesn't seem to notice it's a nippy eight degrees. The guys are ripped—Reggie looks like he could curl me with one arm. I begrudgingly untie my robe. I toss the robe onto a beach chair with Ella's.

I fold my arms over my chest as tight as possible. Ella and I exchange a look, silently screaming as we follow Paulo and the others to the water's edge.

"Can I go first?" Ella asks.

Paulo nods.

Oh, good. I can watch her. Wait! That means she'll get back to her robe first. Now I'm jealous!

"Let's do Ella and Colin together. Sophie, you'll be with Reggie," Paulo says, camera in hand.

My stomach twists.

Ella's a goddess. She doesn't need Paulo's direction; she's a natural. I shouldn't be shocked with how many times I've taken her picture. She's unafraid to let her hands wonder over Colin's carved chest. Colin's loving every minute. Ella kicks it up a notch and turns around to face Colin. His hand comes to her ass. I swallow, and the panic builds. *What was I thinking?*

"Alright, we got it!" Paulo yells.

He rests his camera and turns to Reggie and me.

"Let's get you two on the loungers."

Ella and Colin run back up the beach to our pile of robes.

Paulo pops open the white umbrella in the center of a pair of pale yellow and white striped loungers in the sand.

"Sophie, I'll have you lay down on your stomach and put your feet up crossed behind you."

I climb onto the lounger, taking his instruction. I slowly lower my stomach to the frigid fabric.

"Prop up on your elbows," Paulo says. "Perfect!"

Paulo leans over me adjusting the back of my hair.

"Reggie, lay back on the one beside her, and let's do one arm behind your head. *Show off those muscles!*"

Reggie's abs flex as he reclines back in front of me. I stare down to my hands and run my fingernail over the fabric of the chair.

"Eyes on each other," Paulo instructs. "Reggie, pull your other hand through the bottom of Sophie's hair."

I cringe. My eyes float up to Reggie's. I try not to blush or pull away.

Reggie gazes down at me with sultry eyes and reaches his fingers into the hair that's over my shoulder. I try not to wince. *It feels so wrong.*

"Yes, just there!" Paulo calls out.

Ella cat calls.

I feel sick. This is absolutely killing me. *I just want Beck.*

"Alright, now, Sophie, turn your head and look back at me..." Paulo says.

I turn over my shoulder and Paulo clicks away.

"Beautiful, we got it!" he says, resting his camera. I bolt up.

Paulo looks at the water then back to me.

"Don't hate me," he says. "I want a shot walking out of the water."

What!

Reggie smiles at me. "We got this."

Ella didn't have to get in the water!

I shiver, stopping at the water's edge.

"The sooner we get in, the sooner we get out," Reggie laughs.

He's right—just get it over with. Real models put up with far worse than this. I take a step; my feet fully submerge in the surf. *Holy shit.* I take a deep breath and push on. Reggie walks in beside me. I get up to my knees and stop. The rolling waves splash water up my thighs. Reggie holds his hand out. "You got it?"

I quickly press on, pretending I didn't see his extended hand. I bounce off my toes, jumping as the next wave oscillates.

"That's good!" Paulo yells from the beach.

My toes are numb.

"Now turn around and walk forward together."

The water covers my thighs; Reggie turns and reaches for me. His hand rests around my waist. I tense, arching my back.

Reggie quickly pulls his hand back, noticing my *overreaction.* "Sorry!" he says.

"No, it's okay," I reassure him.

Chill out, Sophie. It's only modeling. I extend my arm out for Reggie.

I suck in air, losing my breath every time water splashes up my back. Reggie and I step toward the beach as gracefully as possible, switching from looking at each other to looking at Paulo.

I scream as an unexpected wave slams into us, splashing up my shoulders. I lose my footing and start to fall. Reggie's hands catch around my stomach. My heart pounds at my near face-plant into the frigid water.

"That was perfect!" Paulo yells from the beach. "Now get out of there! Theresa, you're next!"

Reggie straightens me up. "You okay?"

I'm shaking, and Reggie's arms are still holding me. I take a few breaths before I burst out laughing.

He joins my laughter. "Come on, let's get out of here."

We take off running for the beach.

"Thank you for grabbing me. That could have ended terribly," I say, reaching for my robe.

"You would be the one to face-plant," Ella teases. "Thank God you were out there with her, Reggie," she says, batting her eyes at him.

I pull a pair of jeans out of my suitcase.

"Did you get Paulo's email? He sent sneak peeks we can post!" Ella says.

I button the jeans around my waist. *I need to eat.* These are not usually this loose.

I grab my phone off the charger, and my heart aches. There's no word from Beck. I open the attachment in Paulo's email. He sent four photos. I zoom in on the group shot the five of us took at the end of the shoot. *This guy knows what he's doing.* The photo's stunning. I swipe to one of Theresa in the water. Such a trooper—*she laid down in the surf.* I swipe to the next. Ella and Colin resemble a steamy couple.

"Oh my God, Ella, your ass!"

"Nice booty shot, yeah?" She smiles proudly.

I swipe to the last photo. It's Reggie and me in the water, captured perfectly a second after the near face-plant. His hands are gripped around my stomach. My eyes are closed, my mouth is open playfully. The shot is effective and candid, Reggie's staring straight at the camera, smiling as the water splashes around us. My heart takes off, saving the photo. I open my text thread with Beck. His last message was from Monday when he said he'd call at six. I swipe out and open Instagram. I upload mine and Reggie's photo to my story. I add a text overlay and tag the brand.

Launching soon: the Resort Collection by Beurre Swim

I'm being petty, and I don't care. *I want to hurt him.* I would tag Reggie, but I don't know his handle. I submit the post.

The sun has come out; it's pleasant now that we are properly dressed. I sip my mojito next to Ella at lunch with the brand and the other models. I'm actually looking forward to eating. The *Beurre* reps are thrilled with the photos Paulo captured. Ella dominates the conversation at the table. The way Collin's eyeing Ella, he won't be leaving without her number.

My phone buzzes in my lap. I lean back and tilt my phone up under the table. Adrenaline explodes. *It's Beck.* I glance around the table nervously before scooting further back in my seat. I look back to my lap and open his message.

I know what you're doing, Sophie.

My eyes jerk back up to the conversation happening at the table. My heart pounds. I look back down and reread the text again. I swipe out of the text.

Beckham_Wright20 is the latest view on my Instagram story. Every fuse inside me blows. I posted *that* photo to get a rise out of Beck, but he wasn't playing my game. How dare he have the audacity to reprimand me? I bump Ella's thigh and reopen his text.

Ella leans toward me as I punch out a reply.

Funny, I don't have any idea what you're doing.

I hit send without a second of hesitation and tilt the phone her way.

Ella's eyes widen. "Ouch, Sophie!"

I scoot forward and grab my mojito. I suck down three large gulps. *So what?* He thinks I'm being childish, posting that photo? After his radio silence? After *his* picture with Sab came out? *The audacity.* First practice should be over. Maybe he's in his driver's room. I move my phone into my purse. *Be present.* I force a smile and jump into the conversation at the table.

CHAPTER 32

GRAB THE POPCORN

PIERRE SMILES. "HOW'D IT go, ladies?"

"We slayed," Ella says. "We'll be working for them again."

Yes, the photoshoot exceeded expectations. It was the distraction I needed, *but it's over*. I try not to act hurried, but qualifying started thirty minutes ago. I steer my roller bag to the stairs.

"Did we miss anything here?" I ask. *Any unwanted solicitors?*

Pierre shakes his head. "It's been quiet. But now that you girls are back…"

"Hope you enjoyed the quiet while it lasted," Ella smirks.

"Carmen should be getting in soon enough, as well." She blows a kiss to Pierre.

I grip the handle of my bag behind my back and start hauling it up the stairs. Beck's returned to radio silence. He never replied yesterday, which made me even more angry. Having slept on it, my rage has left the chat; the blues have moved back in. I put myself on the verge of tears, thinking what a dark place the world would be without friends like Ella and Carmen. Both of my security blankets would be by my side tonight.

I dart to my room to plug in my laptop. By the time the battery allows the computer to fire up, Q2 is over. Beck set the third fastest lap. I turn the volume to the lowest setting and set my laptop on my dresser. I don't know why I care to watch when Beck doesn't even care to speak to me or try to explain himself.

I find random tasks to keep busy. I glance at the standings every time I come in and out of the room while unpacking. Half paying attention, half pretending like I'm not paying attention. My *RIMI* roller is empty. There's a minute left in Q3. Beck's sitting in fifth on an out lap, coming around for a final flying attempt. I turn up the volume.

"Stellar lap from Elijah Kaplan! He'll knock Luca Lombardo to second. It won't be enough for Ren Enatsu—that lap only brings him up to fourth! One Valor's still on the track on a flying lap, and here comes Beckham Wright, already outpacing his Furio counterpart through sector one. Beck's repeatedly struggled in the final round of qualifying, but he's looked unstoppable today."

The clock's up. The middle of the standings shift. Leo and Beck are the only dots remaining on the track outline. Leo's dot moves through the final corner; Beck has two turns left before he reaches the main straight.

"Can Leo shake things up at the top? And...It's only good enough for P2! Elijah still holding onto pole position!"

Luca's name drops to third place. The broadcast pans to Beck, cresting the small hill out of the final turn.

"Beck is absolutely *flying*. Will he break into the top three?"

The broadcast pans to the eruption of the team in the Furio garage.

"And it's a mighty lap! Forget top three! It's the top spot! By three-hundredths of a second, Beckham Wright takes his first pole position of the season!"

My heart sinks. WRI shoots past ENA, LOM, VAN and KAP to the top of the standings. I slam the laptop lid closed. *I can't believe I'm not there.* The celebrations happening in the garage—I squeeze my eyes shut, holding in the tears. I'd give anything to hear the messages flying between Beck and Coop on the team radio. I open my eyes. *I need air.*

I exit my room for the balcony as Carmen plows through the front door. Three bottles of wine are cradled in her left arm. *God love her.*

Carmen glances down at the bottles.

"I—thought we could use these…"

I rush to the door and hold it open as Carmen pulls in her luggage. She sets the bottles down on the counter and throws her arms around me. *The flood gates burst.* And Carmen doesn't let go.

"What are you looking at?" I hiccup then press my lips together.

Ella lowers her phone and hesitates.

"*What* are you looking at?" I repeat.

Ella swallows. "The pictures—from last weekend are in."

"From the party," Carmen says.

I wince and refill my glass.

We haven't had a Roomie Trio wine night in months; *it was past due.* Wine glugs into my glass. I take a substantial gulp then return to my place beside them on the couch.

Carmen sighs. "Ana and Ren are so cute."

"Her ring is *goals.* You should have tried it on," Ella says.

Ella swipes to the next photo. I tip my glass for another sip, anticipating the inevitable.

"Look, Ollie's MIA jacket!" Carmen laughs. She zooms in on her and Oliver. "How was his shirt already that dirty?" She shakes her head. "At least his eyes are open."

Ella swipes to the next photo and I take a spear to the heart. My bottom lip quivers. I pull the neckline of my T-shirt up over my nose.

Carmen puts her hand on my leg. "Everything's going to work itself out, Sophie. *Don't worry.*"

I stare at the photo; Beck and I are pure bliss. How can so much change in a week's time? Ella swipes to the next photo.

The cork squeaks as Carmen lifts it from the third bottle. She picks up the first bottle lying on its side and flips it upside down above her glass. A small stream pours out. *Carmen knows all the tricks.* She lays the second bottle on its side to gather the residuals.

My head is floaty; my cheeks are hot. Ella's going on and on, recapping the *Beurre* shoot. Colin's been texting her, asking when he can take her out. I drift off into my own world. I've been strong; I haven't looked at the gossip blog since Monday. The wine encourages me. *Now's the time.*

Start your engines ladies, look who Beck's cuddled up with in Portugal!

I scowl. Beck and Sab's photo post has *two hundred* comments.

Finally, Sophie's gone! Fastest to rise, are always hardest to fall. Calling it now—Beck and Sab are getting back together, if they haven't already started hooking up again.

My heart skips. There's a photo of Sabrina in one of the Paddock clubs.

Sabrina was at quali today in Portugal! She was a guest of another team, but we all know who she was watching!

I collapse the post. It isn't the first time the thought has crossed my mind, but seeing other people say it hits different.

Beck and I are over, aren't we?

I scroll down the page. Surely, if Beck and Sab shared another *moment,* I'd find the evidence here.

Grab the popcorn, Sophie's self-destructing

It's mine and Reggie's photo that someone screenshot of my story.

Can someone tell her she's not a model?
Who's this guy?
Bitter much?
Sophie's not at the race?
No. Assuming Ella Humphrey's stories are current, she was in Cannes with Ella.

Carmen brings the bottle out of the kitchen with her. I close out of the blog back to the gossip account's Instagram page. *Why am I spiraling? Have I learned nothing? Nothing* on that page should shock me.

Carmen hovers over me. She grabs my empty glass to refill it.

"Sophie, what are you doing?!" she scolds.

I drop my phone, trying to click the screen off. It slams face down on the herringbone. *I'm caught.*

"Self-sabotaging," I answer honestly.

"Give me your phone, Sophie. I'm blocking all of these gossip accounts," Carmen says.

My head rushes as I lean down to retrieve my phone from the floor. I trade Carmen my phone for my refill. She sits down next to me and starts her spree. She searches high and low, blocking every F1 gossip account she can find. I've counted ten before I lose track. The wine is working.

CHAPTER 33

HALO

HOW IS MY HEAD still throbbing? I grimace at the tiny pools of deep red staining the base of our glasses. The three empty bottles on the counter turn my stomach. I fill my water glass for the third time and chug it. Wine night got the best of me, but at least it knocked me out. My reality isn't a bad dream I can wake up from—Beck's starting the race P1, *and I'm not there*.

"Where's Ella?" Carmen asks. She squints, still trying to wake up from her second nap today.

"She went to her mum's."

Carmen collects our wine glasses and moves them into the sink. "Thank God I didn't get that fourth bottle."

I lie back on the couch with my laptop and unmute the broadcast. The formation lap is starting. I turn the volume down to the lowest setting.

"You want me to watch with you?" Carmen asks.

I glance at her.

She smiles. "Let me brush my teeth again. I still only taste wine."

Carmen walks back into her room and my phone pings—*it's James*.

I nervously click his message. It's a selfie of him and Charlie in the garage.

> Wish you were here, Sophie!

What?! The aloofness of the message doesn't make me feel better or worse—only more confused. My heart aches. When did James get there...what does he know? *What does he not know?* James was not supposed to be at the race.

Beck's car pulls down the main straight to the 1st grid position. Nineteen cars take their place behind him. I'd give anything to be in the garage. If only he wanted me there. The red lights illuminate one by one. I take a deep breath and exhale as the lights go out. Beck's car lurches forward.

"It's lights out and away we go!

"Great launch off the line for Beckham Wright! He holds the lead, staying ahead of the two Valors. Leo veers left, taking the outside into turn one..."

Elijah slams into the back right of Beck's car. I gasp as his car lifts off the ground.

"...*Big contact!*"

Beck's car smashes into navy, barrel rolling over the top of Leo's Valor on his left. Debris flies as Beck's car slams to the ground right side up.

"Chaos in Turn one! "

Beck, Elijah and Leo's cars screech to a halt in the gravel runoff outside the track. The red flag banner flashes on the screen.

I throw my laptop off my lap; it slams onto the table. I grip the edge of the couch.

"We've got a red flag! That's a nasty crash! Both Valors are out! Beck's Furio's out..."

The broadcast hovers over Beck's car, but there's too much dust kicked up to see anything. My heart punches.

Carmen runs out of her room.

"Sophie, what's wrong?!"

I can't take my eyes off the screen.

"Oh my God! Is that Beck?" Carmen says.

The broadcast flips to Beck's onboard camera. The wishbone shaped halo surrounding his cockpit is intact. The dust settles outside his car. The broadcast shifts to Coop at the island in the garage.

Coop's radio message displays:

"Beck, are you okay?"

There's no answer. Only static.

"Beck. Check in."

Carmen grabs my wrist. I'm shaking. Down to my bones, *shaking*. The cameras move back to the crash site. Leo's out of his car, running across the gravel to Beck. With the dust settled, a third of Beck's car is missing; vaporized from the impact.

Beck pulls his head forward and groans, "I'm okay..."

His radio message echoes in my ears. His hands are moving, trying to detach the steering wheel. Leo throws his helmet off as he reaches Beck's car. Leo reaches over the halo into the cockpit. The medical team closes in on the crash site.

The footage flashes inside the garage. The whole team has their hands over their mouths, eyes glued to the screens. The camera pans to James and Charlie. All the blood has drained from James's face.

"Beck confirms with his engineer he's okay. Both Valor drivers are up and out of their cars at Beck's side. Race control has called everyone back to the pits."

The broadcast cuts back to the crash site. Beck's out of the car. The white number twenty on the back of his racing suit makes it more real. Two people are on either side of him, helping him to the medical van. Elijah and Leo walk alongside. I push up from the couch. Carmen mutes the broadcast. I push my door open and frantically pace in my room. I don't know what to do. *Why did I come in here?* I must call James. I rush back out to the living room. Carmen's on her feet, holding my phone out.

"It's your dad," she says.

The screen's lit up with his call. He must have been watching the race. I grab the phone and accept the call. I can't control my breathing as I put the phone to my ear.

My bottom lip quivers. "*Dad?*" I barely get the word out.

"Sophie? Darling—"

I lose it. I close my eyes and collapse onto the couch.

"Sophie, he'll be okay. He's up and moving…" Dad continues talking, but I'm not comprehending. My thoughts are pandemonium. Carmen's arms come around me.

I glance back at the muted broadcast on the table. The debris field is massive, sweeping clear across the width of turn one. The footage flips to the drivers back in the garage; out of their cars. Luca looks crushed; Tommy's face is haunted. I don't know when, but Dad's stopped talking. He sits on the other end of the phone with me in my silence.

Of course he won't answer, but I want to leave a message at least. I take a deep breath before the beep; *I can make it through this.*

"James…it's Sophie. I'm—I'm just calling to make sure Beck is okay. I feel helpless and sick that I'm not there to do something. Not that I can…*I just*…want to make sure everything is okay. Don't worry about calling me back, just make sure he's okay for me."

I whip the phone from my ear and quickly hang up before my sobs are recorded. I face-plant into the pillows on my bed. My head is throbbing. I hate myself. I hate this feeling. My hand buzzes. I snap my head up. *It's Ana.*

"Sophie! Are you okay?"

"I can't believe I'm not there, Ana," I cry.

"Beck will be fine, Sophie. He's so strong, and the cars have droves of safety measures."

I sob harder.

"They're only taking him to the hospital to get him checked out for good measure."

I turn over to my side and see my *WRI* bracelet. It's sitting on the nightstand, staring at me.

"I shut off the broadcast. What's happening?" I sniffle.

"The race restarted. I just stepped out of the garage for a moment. They showed Beck and his dad leaving with Charlie in an ambulance."

I swallow hard. "I couldn't keep my mouth shut, could I—*I could have been there for him—*"

"Sophie, you were speaking up for all of us—don't ever regret that," Ana says. "You don't know how much that meant to me."

Speaking up got me in this position.

"Text me if you hear anything, or if you don't...text me anyway. I miss you."

"I will. Get back in there," I say. "Love you, Ana."

I've never had this many emotions battle at one time. From sad to mad, hurt to confused, spiteful to full of regret...*now panic and worry*. I never thought I would experience a state of hell like I did the week I was fired, *now that seems like child's play*. Forget the pictures, forget the argument. The only thing that matters now is that Beck is okay. He has to be okay.

Beck, help is coming!

Silence of radio static.

Beck, check in, Beck?

More static and silence.

Beck?

I jolt awake, feeling the instant release of my jaw. I try to catch my breath and blink quickly, gathering my surroundings. Ella's asleep next to me. Carmen must have updated her when she came home. It's dark and my heart's still racing. *It was only a dream*. The crushing reality stays true: I wasn't there for Beck when he needed me.

I reach for my phone. James texted several hours ago.

Sophie, thank you for calling. Beck is doing well; he was released from the hospital. We are trying to fly back to London this evening.

CHAPTER 34

HOUSE OF CARDS

IN THE BOWELS OF my sleeplessness, I'd decided as long as Beck is okay, *nothing else matters*. Though it would crush me, I could accept our relationship being over so long as he's uninjured. I think they call this the bargaining state of grief. No additional news came from James, and there was no word from Beck. Even though Ella was asleep, it helped not being alone overnight.

I can feel it standing at the window; the first truly cold snap has arrived. I dig in the far end of my wardrobe for my quilted Burberry and pull it on over my jumper, skirt and tights. My meeting with Stuart is at eight a.m. I'm wobbly and lightheaded. My heart rate remains elevated, coffee isn't a good idea.

Carmen smiles. "You look lovely, Soph!" The girls watch me nervously for fear I will fall apart the moment they ask me something. I shakily fill a glass of water.

"I tried." I shrug. "I feel like I need to save face a bit."

"If we miss you, we should be back right after lunch," Ella says gently.

I nod. I put the glass to my lips and take a small sip. The spectrum of emotions I've endured the last few days has wrecked my body. I've already struck a deal with myself: make it through this meeting, and I'm allowed to come straight back to bed.

At the final landing, I pop the collar of my coat around my neck, as if it will keep me safe and help hold me together. Pierre looks up from his desk; his eyes are sad.

"Oh, Sophie," he says.

No, please don't do this. I push off the last step. Pierre comes around the front of the desk with his arms open. *One of the girls must have spoken to him.*

Pierre pats my back. Of course, I appreciate it, but any and all forms of affection instantly break me. I pull away after a few seconds and blink quickly, holding back the tears.

"Where are you going, Sophie?" Pierre asks worryingly.

"The office." I swallow. "I have one meeting then I'll be right back."

I just have to make it through this meeting. I push the door open into the wind. The cold air smacks my face and stings the extra moisture at my eyes. I bury my chin in my coat collar and head for the office.

I was right. Stuart and I are now on hugging terms. A hug, which I managed to make it through without choking up. He's impressed with the *RIMI* photos Ella took in the station. Or he's a good actor, pretending to be impressed for my sake. Maybe he's avoiding another meltdown. We aren't on breaking down in my boss's office terms yet, *only over the phone.* Regardless, Stuart's started a story board to brainstorm the posting schedule for the *RIMI* content. He spins away from his computer, turning back to me.

I hand my phone across the desk. "Paulo sent another batch from the *Beurre* shoot."

I lean back into my chair and count the pencils in the mug on his desk. Anything to keep my mind moving. Stuart swipes through the photos and shakes his head. He looks up at me.

"Sophie, you say you're not a model, but these pictures!"

I hold up my hands. "It was the photographer. I had no idea what I was doing."

"Well, I might just have to start putting your name in the hat for more modeling oppies." He smiles.

Stuart hands my phone back. He appears pleased, like we've checked all the meeting boxes. *Can I go back to my bed now?*

"Enough shop talk," he says, raising his eyebrows. "Are you ready for your surprise?"

My stomach churns. I'd forgotten the surprise he mentioned last week.

I nod nervously.

Stuart leans over and opens his desk drawer. He straightens up and sets a shiny spectacle in front of me on the desk.

It's a miniature golden trophy. *100k Club* is engraved into a plaque at the base.

An impossible smile takes over my face; the trophy is *adorable.*

"100k followers is a big milestone," he says.

I stare at the illuminated spots on the cup.

"Now that you're over that threshold, you're supposed to move to another agent," he says slowly.

I glance up at him.

"But I've made a request to keep you, if that's okay."

I shake my head. "I don't want anyone else. Please let me know if there's something I can do."

I did it. I made it through the meeting. I made it through without crying. *Small victories.* I step into the lift and stare at my 100k trophy. I'm holding it in both hands as if it's an Olympic gold medal. The lift stops and a man gets in with me. He gives me a nod, eyeing the trophy before turning around.

This isn't a participation trophy—I *earned* this. Through sweat and tears and every hard day I pushed through the bullshit, *I earned it.* The doors part at ground level, and I pull my collar up in preparation for the cold.

My lift mate steps out. I smile at him as he holds the door for me to exit.

The cold blast hits my face. I bury my chin into my neckline. I round the corner and knock into the back of a man. I bounce backward, almost dropping my precious trophy. I glance up to apologize, and Beck spins around. My body turns to Jell-O. Even dark and tired, his eyes are as beautiful as ever, *searing into me.*

His mouth opens. "*Sophie.*"

The sound of his voice undoes me.

I shake my head. "Beck, what are you doing here?"

He takes his hands out of his pockets. It's as if he's moving in slow motion. He steps toward me and rests his hands on my shoulders. His touch is the wind that demolishes the house of cards holding me together. Before my head hits his chest, *I lose it.* All of the sadness, anger and anxiety empties from my eyes with no off switch. Beck holds me tightly against him. I force my eyes shut, overcome with emotion.

I pull back, desperately needing to look into his eyes to ensure this is truly happening. Beck resists. I put my hand on his chest and tilt my head up. It's him. Beck stares down at me like he's found the one person in the universe that understands the pain he's feeling.

"*Y—your* crash," I mutter, barely getting the words out.

"I'm fine," he says, guiding my head back against his chest.

His other hand reaches for mine, still grasping my trophy. "What's that?" he says, touching the base.

"My trophy," I whimper.

He tips my chin up with his finger and our eyes meet again. He cradles the side of my face in his hand.

"I can't believe I wasn't there," I cry.

His gaze shifts as he watches a tear slide down my cheek. He moves his thumb, catching it before it falls further.

"I know. That's not going to happen again," he says. "I was wrong. I shouldn't have pushed you away."

The tears fall full force. *It's too much.* There isn't room left inside me to hold another emotion. It's everything I've been dying to hear for the past week.

Beck brings his other hand to my face, and he rests his forehead against mine.

"Sophie, *I love you.*"

My eyes flash open.

"I need you to know that," he says.

I close my eyes as he brings our lips together. I'm weightless, floating through the air, absorbing every passing millisecond. I wrap my arms around the back of his neck and kiss him as if he produces the only air my lungs will accept.

CHAPTER 35

STICKY

ALL REASON WENT OUT the window the moment Beck said those three words. I reach down and clasp my fingers into his hair. His tongue's working magic between my thighs. If he doesn't stop, I'll be leaving the atmosphere without him. I grasp for his shoulders—I need him inside me *now*. He pulls his head up and crawls over me, bringing one of my legs over his shoulder. His eyes are blazing. I reach my mouth for his, but fall back as he pushes inside me, instantly sending my body to the moon.

"There's my girl," he groans.

I don't have words. I fight through my spiral, trying to move. I wrap my shaking leg around him and snake my hands under his armpits. I dig my fingers into the top of his shoulders, pulling him *deeper into me*. It's sweaty, it's sticky, it's *explosive*. It's all over in less than two minutes.

Beck collapses onto me; his cheek rests between my breasts. A layer of sweaty dew blankets both of us. Our breathing syncs, as we catch our breath together. *What just happened?* My chest is strained under the weight of his head. I open my eyes. The door didn't fully shut. *Crap.* I need to collect my clothes—they didn't all come off in here. Surely none are outside in the hall; we did make it as far as the front door, *right?* I scoop his head up and shimmy out from under his weight. Beck collapses back into a puddle on the bed. One of his shoes got caught in the doorway. I tiptoe out of my room and into the bathroom to quickly clean myself up. *Phew,* no one is here. A trail of clothes stretches through the living room. I pick up each article and hold it against my skin. *We just missed the girls*; the wax in the candle on the coffee table is still partially liquid. My coat's in a pile in the entryway. I turn the knob and peek outside the front door. My keys clang, hanging in the lock outside. *Good.* Nothing came off in the hallway. I fish my hand around the front of the door and pull my keys from the lock.

I push the door shut and smile, thinking back ten minutes ago when we burst into the lobby. Pierre jumped up, clapping his hands. *"You found her!"* There was no time for chatting. We were on a mission; a mission to remove our clothes as quickly as time allowed. I never knew I could get up the stairs that fast. I kick Beck's shoe out of the doorway and swat my door closed.

He's still in a puddle, his bare ass exposed. I drop our clothes to the floor and crawl back into bed with him. I lay my head next to his on the pillow. His eyes are closed. I take a moment and study him. When I left this bed this morning, I wasn't certain I'd ever get to see him again. *Now I need answers.*

"How did you know where I was?" I whisper.

Beck's eyes flutter open. *"Pierre."* A soft smile graces his lips. "And Ella has you GPS tracked."

My eyes trail over the silhouette of his shoulder blades. I reach out and trace my finger along his skin.

"Are you okay?" I swallow, holding back the tears.

"I'm okay," he says. "My back is a little out of whack."

"You went to the hospital?"

"Only as a precaution. Thank God for the halo."

I swallow. "...It was quite scary to watch."

"Yeah, I've kind of blocked it out but I've seen the replay several times."

Beck puts his hand on top of mine and smiles. "Were you watching from the beach?"

I'm not smiling. *Those are fighting words.*

"No. We came home Saturday."

"Your photos were beautiful," he says.

Oh, you want to go there?

"Your photo was—*nostalgic.*"

His smile fades. "Sophie, it meant nothing. I happened to run into her leaving dinner."

"I know." I pause. *I know that now.* "It was still hard to see...considering there was *no* communication happening between us."

He takes a deep breath and flips onto his back.

"When I saw all the grief you've been given online, I felt quite guilty. It's because of me—our relationship."

"And yet, I don't care—it's all worth it to me. *You* are worth it."

His eyes are misty. "Sophie, I'm never too busy to hear about these things."

I let that sink in. I was scared to bother him with something so ridiculous and unimportant, *but that's what having someone is all about.*

"I'm sorry. I should have told you how bad it was."

He leans to my nightstand then rolls back over. He's running the beads of the *WRI* bracelet through his fingers. He turns his head and stares deeply into my eyes.

"Will you come to Abu Dhabi?" he says. "I really want you there."

Ha!

"Want me there? You *need* me there. Look at what happens when I'm not in the garage!"

Beck chuckles and puts his hand over his eyes. "God, I missed you."

After finally rousing ourselves from bed, I hand Beck his jeans.

"What exactly was your plan in coming here?"

He sits down at the foot of my bed and pushes his foot through the leg.

"It was either show up and try to convince you to still come this week. Or show up and keep pushing our flight back *until* I convinced you to come."

He stands up, buttoning his jeans. He walks toward me bare-chested, staring down at me like he could pounce again at any second.

I narrow my eyes. "Both of those options have the same outcome."

He smiles. "I didn't want to think of a scenario in which you said no."

I shift my eyes to the floor, turning away in time to hide my satisfaction. I lift my bag off the floor and pull out my mini trophy.

"We still have to be careful," he says. "I don't want any media approaching you at the race."

So, hide the fact that I'm even there?

I catch myself mid eye roll.

"Wait—you said *our* flight?" I ask.

Beck nods. "Dad won't leave my side. He and Charlie are taking the jet back to Milan with me. We fly out with the team tonight."

I set the trophy on my nightstand. "Your dad is here?"

"He stayed at the airport."

My heart skips. "Pit stop in Paris?"

Beck grabs my hips and pulls me under his lips.

"I told him I'd be as quick as possible. I should get going," he says.

I run my palms up his chest. *Already?*

"Are you okay going with Mum? Sticking to the original plan?"

I hesitate. "What do your parents know?"

"They know everything, Sophie."

I had a feeling. At least the pressure's off me to explain anything to Elizabeth. *Amazing how quickly circumstances can change.* My lips curl.

"What is it?"

"Nothing." My smile grows.

He raises an eyebrow, displeased.

I sigh. "Everything in the world—feels right again."

Beck's eyes sparkle.

"I love you, Sophie."

My heart swells. *He said it again.* I push up to meet his lips, avoiding a response. Surely, he can feel it? How can a statement so beautiful be so terrifying at the same time? I love him with everything I have in me, but I'm scared. Once I say it out loud, the genie can't go back in the bottle.

CHAPTER 36
HOW'S BUSINESS?

I STEP ONTO THE escalator and answer Ella's FaceTime.

"Sophie, what's going on?" Ella says.

"*Hi.*" I smile.

"Beck called me *three times.* I sent him your location. I hope that was okay?" Ella takes notice of my surroundings. "Wait, where are you?"

I gave into my urge to leave for London early. I step off the escalator and onto the platform.

"I'm in the station—Ella, he showed up outside the office."

"What?!" Ella screams. Carmen jumps into the frame.

"He showed up and we...we worked it out." I blush. "I'm going to Abu Dhabi."

"Oh my God!" Carmen screams. She steps back from the screen.

"I knew it would all work out," Ella says, shaking her head. "We love you; he loves you! Keep us posted!"

"He does..." I nod. "He even said so..."

Ella's jaw drops, she glances back at a pacing Carmen.

"You've got Carmen crying!" Ella laughs.

Carmen waves her hands at her face. "I'm sorry!" she yells. "I'm just so happy!"

I take my seat and wait for the aisle to clear. I lean out and snap a picture of my *RIMI* bag in the overhead rack. I type out a message to Stuart:

> It's me again. Hold off on the RIMI plans. I'll be getting an airplane shot with this beauty after all.

I click on Ana's message thread and get a text out before the train pulls out of the station.

> Ana, he showed up in Paris

I put my phone away and sit back. All I need now is a hug from Dad after I give him a proper update.

Jo's heels click on the tile in the lobby.

"Sophie, we weren't expecting you." She smiles.

"Last-minute visit I'm afraid—is he busy?"

"He's finishing up a call. I'll take you up."

Jo swipes her badge at the gate. The security clerk behind the reception counter buzzes me in. I roll my suitcase behind me.

Jo's been Dad's assistant for as long as I can remember. She must be seventy at this point. She was so upset at Mum's funeral, people assumed she was a family member. Jo adored my mother and always reminds me how much I resemble her. She reminds me again as we take the lift to the twenty-first floor.

My roller bag wheels bump along the seams in the floor. Not sure if it's Jo's clicking heels, my rolling suitcase or my overly casual outfit that turns every head. We make our way past the junior colleagues, sitting in open cubes in the center of the floor. A glimpse into my old life of fancy pantsuits and the grind of a junior finance associate. The fluorescent lighting gives way to the natural light coming from the outer glass offices.

We round the corner of the cube maze.

"He's still using the open-door approachable model?"

Jo laughs. "Some things never change."

Jo stops outside the corner office. Dad's leaned back in his chair, facing the floor to ceiling glass windows. He's clicking the top of a pen, nodding to the call on his headset.

"He should be just a few more minutes," Jo whispers.

She pats my back then retreats down the hall. I quietly roll my bag inside and take a seat in one of the chairs facing his desk. Dad leans forward and spins his chair around. His eyes bulge, half happy to see me, half taken aback with my surprise visit.

I sink back into the chair and rest my arms on the armrests. Just like old times when I'd come after school and pretend play "business meeting." Dad didn't have a corner office back then; he was on a much lower floor. His view's gotten substantially better with each ladder rung he's climbed. *Have I seen this office before?* He's got a killer panoramic view of the Thames. No matter how substantial the office upgrade is, the same framed pictures of me make it onto his desk. *I have seen this office.* Once.

This was the office Dad moved into that morning, ten months ago, when I was called into HR.

Within five minutes of arriving that Monday after Zurich, I got the call. I walked to HR knowing fully I'd be leaving with an escort. I was in such a state of shock, I left the building and walked the five blocks to Dad's office. I didn't cry, I didn't say a word. I was dead silent until Jo brought me to this very office. There were boxes of Dad's things still on a waiting dolly. Dad knew immediately something was wrong. That might be the only time he's closed his door.

I smile. For the first time, I can think about that day without getting a pit in my stomach. If I hadn't blown up my career, I never would have packed a bag and run off to Paris. I never would have said *what the hell* and dove into influencing. I never would have been on that trip in Spain. *I never would have met Beck.*

"Sounds good," Dad says. He puts his hand to his headset. "Cheers."

I snap out of it.

Dad takes off the headset, smiling. "Well—this is unexpected."

I adjust in my seat and get into character. I fold my hands and place them on his desk. "Can you squeeze in a rather important business meeting?"

His face turns serious. He glances at his computer then back to me, fully in character. "I think I have ten minutes," he says in a stern voice.

He breaks.

Dad pushes back from his desk; I stand up for a George Collins hug. *This is why I came straight from the train.*

I retake my seat. "For real, do you have a minute?"

"For my daughter, I have all the time in the world."

I take a deep breath.

"You'll never guess who was waiting outside my eight a.m. this morning..."

Dad's elated. He slowly shakes his head as I recount the morning's events. Beck's grand gesture pit stop, the words that came out of his mouth, the invite that still stands. *I skip over the part where we sprinted upstairs.*

"I'm glad you'll get to be there for Beck, especially given his crash."

I nod. "He wants me there, but he wants me to lay low." I pause. "No pictures, no media, *no walking in with him.*"

"Those threats really scared him, Sophie. He's likely getting guidance from his PR team too."

Ha! *Shannon will be dreading my arrival.*

"That's the only part I'm still struggling with, him wanting to *hide* me."

"Not hide you, Sophie. He only wants to protect you. I raised you to stand up for yourself, and I've been so proud you've used your voice, but sometimes, you have to pick and choose your battles."

I nod. *I'm not surrendering, but I can lower my weapons this time.*

"I can fly under the radar for him." I smile. "At the end of the day, I'm just happy to be there."

My eye catches a large glass service award under one of Dad's monitors.

"How's business?" I say 180-ing the conversation.

Dad narrows his eyes. "The fund is thriving. We're on track to record the best Q4 we've had in years."

I raise an eyebrow. "*Impressive.*"

I smile down at my purse. I'd turned around and grabbed it off my nightstand before I left.

"I've also been *thriving* in my *career*—I hit a big milestone last week."

"Oh?" Dad says, interested. "Does that get you some kind of promotion? A raise?"

"No," I say. "But it did get me this."

I reach down into my purse for the trophy and set it on the desk in front of him.

Dad lights up and moves his glasses to the top of his head. He picks up the trophy to read the engraving.

"100k!" he says excitedly. "Well, this sounds deserving of a celebratory dinner at the club!"

CHAPTER 37

MAGIC CARPETS

I HANG UP THE phone and wave to Elizabeth. The Wright's SUV pulls to the curb. In typical Beck's parents' fashion, Elizabeth insisted on picking me up for the airport, even though it meant an absurdly unreasonable detour.

Elizabeth kisses my cheeks. "Was that Beck?"

My expression's a dead giveaway. He's only four hours ahead; he called to say goodnight.

"I'm truly happy to see you, Sophie."

I set my bag in the trunk, and Mia waves over the backseat.

Elizabeth closes the hatch. "You're a saint for coming with me. I'll be needing a wine on the plane."

I slide into the passenger seat, then turn around and wave at Louie. Elizabeth clicks off the flashers and steers from the curb.

She exhales deeply. "*My*, I'm glad you're coming."

"Me too!" Mia yells.

"Has your week been well?" Elizabeth asks.

I glance at her and smile. "Better than last week."

"Beck's an idiot," Mia sasses.

"Mia!" Elizabeth snaps. "Language!"

Louie giggles. I can't help but join him.

Elizabeth smiles. "Sophie, don't provoke her."

Mia huffs. "Who takes a picture with their ex-girlfriend?!"

"What did we talk about?" Elizabeth says glaring at Mia in the rearview mirror.

I smile—I should have called Mia last week in the depths of my grief.

Heathrow looks different when you don't require a security escort.

Arriving at our gate, Mia flips the luggage tag on my bag. "You didn't have this suitcase in Milan."

Sheesh, she misses nothing.

"It's new," I say. "I'm working with a luggage brand."

"Do you need me to take your picture?!"

"Let's—wait until *after the race...*" I nod. "I promised your brother I'd keep a low profile."

Mia rolls her eyes.

Louie looks up at Elizabeth. "Why aren't we sitting down?"

"We'll be sitting down for the next seven hours, love."

"Will there be a TV like the Italy plane?" he asks.

"Yes, you'll have your very own TV."

Louie's eyes light up. "Can we watch *Alladin* again?"

"We'll have to see if they have that," Elizabeth says. "I'm going to run to the restroom one last time. Do you want to come or stay here with Sophie?"

Louie glances up at me and reaches for my hand.

My heart melts.

"What are we going to watch?" Mia asks.

"I'm sure we can watch a few different things."

Louie's eyes drift up to mine. "Do you believe in magic carpets?"

"No, Louie, those aren't real," Mia says.

His smile drops; he looks to his feet, embarrassed. I run my thumb over his hand. Louie perks up.

I lean down. "I'll leave our window shade open," I whisper to him. "I'll let you know if I see any magic carpets."

Across the aisle, Elizabeth takes a sip of her wine.

"Thank you for coming with me," she sighs.

"Of course," I say.

"James was adamant about traveling with Beck. I said 'Charlie isn't enough? You have to ditch your wife?'" she laughs.

"I wasn't going to ditch; I was looking forward to this."

"Mia's dead set on going to *Ferrari World* after she saw Beck and Luca there."

I smile. "We should go!"

She takes another sip. "You're not getting me on that rollercoaster…"

Elizabeth leans against the headrest,

"I'm sorry I didn't ring you Sunday. I didn't want to meddle in your and Beck's business—but *I should have meddled.*"

I spin the stem of my wine glass.

"It's okay. I didn't have as many words as I had *tears.*"

"Beck's been banged around before, but he's never had a wreck like that. I can't wait to squeeze him."

Me too.

Elizabeth finishes her last sip of wine. "I'm going to try and get some rest. Wake me up if you can't sleep, and we'll get more wine." She winks.

"*Goodnight.*"

Though the mother figure void in my life can never be filled, people like Elizabeth and Alice make the void much smaller. *Princess Diaries* is still playing on mine and Mia's media screens. Mia approved the selection when I told her the main character's name was also Mia. *I wish I was tired.* A few quiet days at the flat did wonders. I needed it after the hell week I survived. I think I completed some form of exorcism by going to yoga three mornings in a row.

I open my phone. It's still on the team's Instagram page. Beck and Luca look jovial together at their event in the theme park. It would be a fun outing; for our few days stay after the race while Beck participates in post season testing. I can't wait to be with him. This plane sure feels like a *magic carpet.*

I click my home feed, and a blurry picture sits at the top. My heart flutters. *Carmen missed a gossip account.* The post is several days old. It's Beck and James…shopping? I swipe through the carousel of secretly captured images.

Excuse the photo quality—a follower in Milan spotted Beck and his father yesterday. The pair went into *Giuseppina Milano*, a local luxury jewelry store. The shop quickly locked their doors, and an attendant brought a display piece into a private room. Thirty minutes later, Beck walked out with a bag.

I swallow and expand the comment thread.

Rumor has it Beck and Sophie are still together…she was spotted with his mum at Heathrow earlier.
Please don't tell me it's a ring…

"They should be done with practice debrief anytime now."

Charlie smiles. "Glad to have you back, Sophie."

"Is Beck—how is he doing?" I stutter.

"He was brilliant. Beck's always done well here; he had his debut at this track."

My rock. Unshaken from the crash. I'm afraid I'll be a bundle of nerves for second practice. Charlie looks over my shoulder.

I gasp as Beck's arms snake around me; his chest meets my back.

Charlie sneaks past us.

Beck's lips touch the top of my ear, and I melt.

"*Now*," he says. "All is right in the world again."

No. Don't cry, Sophie! I squeeze his hands at my stomach. *You are my world.*

I turn to face him.

"We got here as fast as we could. I'm sorry I missed first practice."

Beck holds my face in his hands. His hair is unruly, and his eyes gleam. "You're here now. That's all that matters."

I take a deep breath as he brings me to his lips. The kiss is swift, leaving me wanting more. Charlie waits in the doorway of his driver's room.

My cheeks flush. "Well, I'll get on my way."

"Before you go"—Beck grabs my hand—"Shannon would like to talk to you."

I gulp.

Beck smiles. "Don't worry."

Patrizio sets a bowl of cherries in front of me and Louie in the lounge. Louie reaches for one.

"Careful, there's a seed in the middle," I say.

Louie inspects the cherry then pops it into his mouth.

A hand meets my shoulder. The voice startles me.

Shannon peers down at me. "Sophie, do you have a few minutes to chat?"

I take a seat at the table. The huddle space too closely resembles an interrogation room. Shannon closes the door then pulls out the chair across from me.

"How are you doing?" she asks, taking her seat.

Um? "I'm great, thank you—I"

"You're quite brave," she cuts me off. "The way you've handled everything."

She looks sympathetic. Is this woman complimenting me? *Now I'm truly gobsmacked.*

"What you've experienced is unacceptable. I want you to know the entire team not only supports you and Beck's relationship, but we support you as an individual."

I stare down at my fingers twisting in my lap.

"I...I don't know what to say. That means a lot."

Shannon smiles.

"About the podcast and the interviews—I promise, I don't try to be a thorn in your side."

I glance up and Shannon listens.

"The things I've seen," I continue. "It would have haunted me to not speak up."

"I understand why you did it."

Wow.

Shannon crosses her legs. "As you can tell, this race is *very* high profile."

I nod.

"A special guest will be joining us in the garage. There also will be double the number of cameras following us Sunday," she warns. "We'll have you use the side entrance with Beck's family for the rest of the weekend."

Yes, I know my role. I'll remain invisible.

Golden hour. I refrain from speeding too far ahead of Elizabeth and the kids. It takes everything in me to walk to the garage at a normal pace. I can hardly contain myself, reaching for my headset.

Pippa turns from our station in the garage. A man's next to her, speaking with Luca.

"It's good to have you back," Pippa says, kissing my cheeks.

Luca smiles.

"Congratulations on your win last week," I say.

"I had to get it for Beck," Luca says. "Sophie, this is Franco Morelli, my former teammate."

The special guest. Franco takes my hand. Deep lines run across his forehead. This is the legend Beck's always comparing himself to.

"It's an honor to meet you," I say.

Coop waves excitedly from the pit wall, speaking with Beck. It's hard to keep my emotions at bay. The last time I saw Coop's face was when he was checking on Beck, calling his name over the radio. I've always admired the engineers and mechanics, but now I see them with a whole new layer of appreciation. They built Beck a car so sound, he walked away from that crash uninjured.

Beck joins us in the garage. Holding his helmet, he leans over the displays and brings his arm around me.

I grip onto his racing suit and his lips touch my ear. "It means the world that you're here," he whispers.

He retreats.

"This is your track, Beck," Franco says, patting Beck firmly on the back.

Beck chuckles. "We'll see what we can do!"

He winks at me before turning around to put his racing cap on.

My heart races as Beck's waved out of the garage. Luca's tires squeak, pulling out after him. I watch the onboard nervously. Beck descends into the pit lane exit, turning left into a tunnel beneath the track.

"He better not wreck again," Mia says.

"Mia!" Elizabeth scolds.

James laughs.

"What? No one wants to see that again—it was scary!" Mia says.

I twist my lips.

James takes notice, and puts his arm around my shoulders.

"Beck was great in first practice," Pippa assures.

I force a smile, but my stomach is in knots. I pull my headset over my ears.

"Both Furios strong throughout first practice. Beck hasn't shown an inkling of hesitation after the scary incident in Portugal last week. He mentioned in Thursday's press conference that this circuit holds a special place in his heart, ever since he answered the call and stepped in for Franco Morelli three years ago. Quite spe-

cial, as Morelli watches from the garage with the team this weekend.”

Beck pulls out of turn five. I exhale, finally releasing the breath I've been holding.

Pippa's hand rests on her bump, and she brings her other hand to my arm.

"See? It's like nothing ever happened," she says.

I'm glued to Beck's onboard. His speedometer hits 315 km/h, flying down the massive straight.

"He's *fearless*," I whisper.

CHAPTER 38
EVERYTHING.

I'M BEWITCHED, BEING BACK in Beck's *anything is possible* world. Beck's car moves along the floodlit circuit. He disappears for half a second under the sparkling purple lights of the hotel straddling the track.

"...And it will be P4 for Luca Lombardo!"

My heart skips. I clap along with the rest of the garage. The mechanics embrace. Luca's name moves to fourth, and Tommy's name moves up to sixth place beneath Elijah. For the second weekend in a row, Beck's out-qualified Luca. Franco smacks James's hand. It's P3 for Beck.

"And that will conclude the final qualifying session of the season. Ren Enatsu takes pole position followed by the world champion in second. The Furios split the Valors in P3 and P4..."

I flip the light off in the bathroom. The breeze coming off Yas Bay gently sways the palm trees surrounding the glowing pool in front of the hotel.

My phone lights up; Dad's sent a photo.

Saw Beck qualied P3!

Dad's seated outside, holding a glass of wine. I study the photo. That's not the club—*is he at a bar?* A woman's hand rests on the table.

Did you take Jo for a drink?

No.

My heart skips.

Whose hand is that?

His message bubble flashes as he types.

Evelyn Edwards.

What?! My phone vibrates as a FaceTime from Beck comes through. *Is this a date? Is Dad alone with her?* I blink quickly to gather myself and accept the call. Beck's moving.

"Can I come see you?" Beck says.

"Yes? Is everything alright?" I ask nervously.

He smiles. "I'm outside."

He knocks at the door and hangs up.

"Charlie's going to kill me, but I wanted to come say goodnight," Beck says, pushing inside.

His hands are in the pocket of his hoodie.

"What's wrong? You look like you've seen a ghost."

I shake my head. "My dad…he's—*he's on a date?*"

"A date? With?"

"Evelyn, the designer I walked for…"

"Good for George!"

I nod. "Dad doesn't go on dates; he doesn't go anywhere but the office…*anyway.*" I smile. "How long can you stay?"

"Just a minute, but I have to show you something," he turns, heading further into my room.

"Sit down." Beck nods.

I lower onto the foot of the bed. His eyes are focused and intense. He pulls his hands from the front pocket of his hoodie. *Giuseppina Milano* is imprinted in gold leaf on a small rectangular box.

My heart skips.

"Beck, what is that?"

He stares down at the box. "I told myself I was going to wait until after the race, but I can't wait any longer."

He lifts the lid from the box. A strand of chunky, sparkling diamonds lies against navy velvet. I gasp.

"I know you have your race bracelet, but I wanted to get you a special one."

Beck unhooks the strand from the clips in the velvet.

"Since the day we met—you've been such a light in my life. You've traveled for months to support me…"

Beck pulls both ends of the bracelet around my wrist and clicks the clasp together. The bracelet slack hangs heavy.

His eyes flash up. "*You're my everything, Sophie.*"

I stare at the diamonds dripping around my wrist. *This must have cost a fortune!*

I shake my head. "Beck, this is too much."

"No, it's not," he says. "Not for you."

It's mesmerizing. The stones radiate with the slightest movement.

"Beck, it's absolutely gorgeous."

"There's something else." He pauses.

I lift my eyes.

"I filmed something Thursday—*an announcement.* It'll be released tomorrow morning."

I swallow, waiting with bated breath.

A grin shoots across his face. "I've signed a contract extension with the team."

My heart soars. I spring up and throw my arms around him.

His fingers spread out on my back. I close my eyes. *Is it possible to share this many surreal moments with one person?*

"You deserve it," I whisper. I squeeze him tighter. "A million times over—*you earned it.*"

Beck's lips graze my neck. "It's a dream come true," he says. He softly kisses up my jawline then pulls back. "But it is still a secret—" Beck smiles. "*Until tomorrow.*"

I lay back into the pillows.

"Did you know Franco would be here?"

Beck nods. "He usually comes out for a race or two every year. He fancies keeping tabs on things."

Beck pulls the comforter up to my chest and kisses my forehead.

"I'm sad the season will be over; it went so fast."

Beck smiles. "Baby, that was only half a season."

Oh right.

"I wish you could stay and—snuggle," I say.

Among other things.

He sighs. "Tomorrow night, we snuggle for eternity."

I pull my hands out on top of the comforter and stare at the stones around my wrist.

"Go to sleep, Sophie," he says. "But I can't stop looking at it!"

I never want to take it off.

I've kept up my end of the bargain; I haven't posted a single thing since we arrived. I've stayed tucked into the garage or inside the suite all weekend. I can't wait to call the girls tonight with all of the updates. I wanted to call last night, but I couldn't risk the bracelet giving away Beck's big announcement.

The bracelet came off to shower but went back on the moment I stepped out. I slept in it, frantically feeling for it every time I woke up during the night. I tilt my wrist slowly from side to side. It's even more beautiful than it was last night. I lift my lanyard and spray my chest with perfume. My new accessory upped the ante. It's red on red for the final race. I slip the beaded *WRI* bracelet on my other wrist, and I pull Mum's bag over my shoulder. The red leather sits beside the red *House of CB* mini I've been saving.

Maggie and Julia's tangent gets interrupted. I still owe them an update; they messaged me days ago in the midst of the fallout. Beck's sent a message. I pause *In the Know* and click the notification. *It's the announcement.* The video was cross-posted by Beck and the team's page fifteen minutes ago. I press play. A text from Ana drops down in all caps.

JUST SAW THE NEWS!!!!

The camera pans around Beck then pulls in close to his face. His eyes sparkle.

"I'm excited to announce I'll be staying on with team Furio." The video flashes to Beck and Luca walking toward each other in their racing suits. They meet and shake hands before the clip ends.

Over one hundred comments already sit below the post. The top comment catches my eye.

Contract is rumored to be a 2-year extension $12 million a year.

My jaw drops, and my eyes shift to the diamonds around my wrist. There's a knock on the door. I put my phone in my purse and step into my heeled sandals.

Mia's mouth drops open.

"You look like a movie star!" she squeals. Her eyes shoot to my wrist and double in size.

Behind her, James lights up. *He's seen this piece before.*

"I knew he wouldn't be able to wait," James says.

Elizabeth holds my arm, admiring the bracelet as we walk to the lift.

Mia finds the bracelet on my other arm.

"I like this one too!" she says, scooting the letter beads on my wrist.

I slip the *WRI* bracelet off. "You should wear this one today, Mia!"

She happily slides it on as the lift opens.

"We could have a craft day with Sophie and make more bracelets over break!" Elizabeth says.

Mia looks up at me. "Can we?"

James laughs. "Only if you make one for me!"

Beck's pacing on the phone in the lobby. Charlie's all smiles. Louie runs and attaches to Beck's leg. Two black SUVs wait outside in the drive. Beck waves me over. Louie keeps hold around the back of Beck's leg. Louie's other hand grabs onto the bottom of my dress.

Beck puts his arm around me and pulls the phone from his ear; putting it on speaker.

"...Another season together, mate. Where we throwin' down tonight?" Tommy says.

"You tell me, man," Beck says. He winks. "Sophie wants bottle service."

"Is she there?" Tommy asks.

"Hi Tommy," I giggle.

"That's a given, Soph. Don't worry, I'll be scheming." Tommy says.

"Alright, I'll see you out there." Beck smiles. "Cheers."

"Cheers, mate."

"Look how cute Sophie looks today!" Mia squeals.

Beck pockets his phone. "She always looks this cute."

Mia holds up her wrist. "Sophie's letting me wear her other bracelet today!"

Elizabeth kisses Beck's cheeks. "We have so much celebrating to do!"

The lobby door's part for Shannon. She moves her sunglasses to the top of her head.

"Luca's just arrived," Shannon says. "There's a media storm waiting for us at the main gate."

Shannon turns to me. "Go ahead and ride with us. Charlie and I will get out with Beck. Joe can bring you to the side entrance after."

I nod.

Beck ushers me into the first SUV. James, Elizabeth and the kids pile into the matching one behind. Joe smiles from the front seat. I take the window; Beck sits between Shannon and I in the backseat. As Joe pulls out of the drive, Beck takes a deep breath and pulls my hand into his lap. Even though it's only a few minutes ride to the track, it means the world that Shannon invited me to ride along. Beck runs his finger along the diamonds on my wrist.

"I loved the end of the video," I say.

Beck chuckles. "We had to reshoot that so many times. Luca and I couldn't keep a straight face."

"Ana says congratulations," I say. "She's waiting for me with her parents at the side gate."

"Oh boy! Ren will have the future in laws in the audience?"

I nod.

"Goodness," Shannon sighs.

I look out the windshield. Joe turns into the main gate drop off. *My word.* I've never seen this many waiting cameras. They know the team's car. Joe puts the SUV in park.

"Ready?" Shannon smiles at Beck.

Beck nods.

Charlie opens the front door; noise floods in. Charlie steps out in his red team polo, confirming the media's excitement. I recoil closer to the window.

Charlie opens the back door for Shannon. Beck takes another deep breath and squeezes my hand.

"I'll see you soon." He presses his lips to my temple.

Beck scoots out of the backseat. The moment his feet hit the ground; his name resounds.

Beck gives me a final nod and pushes the door shut.

He turns away from the car, heading for the swipe gates behind Charlie and Shannon. Even with the door closed, the clamor behind the lenses is loud and clear.

"All eyes on Beck today," Joe says, shifting into drive. The car slowly starts to pull away. Beck's saunter stops before the swipe gates. He stands there for a second then turns around.

"Wait!" I yell.

Joe hits the brakes and whips his head around.

Beck's striding back toward the car. Charlie and Shannon watch beyond the gates.

"Did he forget something?" Joe says.

I search beside me and on the floor of the backseat.

"There's nothing here," I say frantically.

My heart races. Beck's eyes fix on the car.

The backseat door opens. A smile stretches across Beck's face. He reaches his hand inside. "Come here, Sophie."

What? I stare back at him. Time screeches to slow motion. The echo of my heartbeat dulls the noise outside the car.

Beck reaches further into the backseat. I set my hand in his and scoot across the seats to the doorway. My sandals meet the ground; Beck pulls me toward him. The car door slams, jolting time back up to speed. Beck doesn't say a word; he takes my hand, confidently pressing back toward the gates. I float next to him, my heart pumping pure adrenaline.

Stepping through the scanner, Beck drops my hand. His eyes stay fixed on me while the media relentlessly demands his attention. I reach down for the pass on my lanyard and shakily hold it to the scanner. The scanner beeps, accepting my badge. Ten meters ahead, Shannon's watching us. I retake Beck's hand and step beside him. He's unwavering. Somehow, my feet are moving. A smile takes over my face. Beck's not hiding me, *he's making a statement.* My breath is so heavy, I can't comprehend the demands surrounding us.

Does he realize how much this means to me? The cameras pivot as we pass by. Beck's eyes drift down to me, and he slows his pace. *Why are we stopping?* A wild grin takes over his lips. *I know that face.* He comes to a complete stop and raises my hand. My bracelet slides from my wrist and comes to a rest at my forearm. The sun hits every diamond facet, making it sparkle as if it's battery powered. Beck's eyes sear into me as he brings the back of my hand to his lips. *It's out of body.* we're surrounded, and yet he's the only person here. I shake my head slowly; there's only one thing left to say, one thing echoing through my whole body. I can't hold it back this time.

"*I love you, Beck.*"

The declaration departs my lips, igniting a supernova in his eyes.

"I know you do," he whispers.

My heart soars. Beck lowers our hands, and we continue onward. Beck waves, finally acknowledging the media. I wish he could see the way he smiles; I wish he could feel what his smile does to me. I look to the lenses on my right and beam. David cheerfully nods behind his camera. I lift my hand and give him a wave. This is Beck's moment—he didn't need me, but he *wants* me by his side. We have something to be proud of. We have something worth fighting for, something worth showing off no matter the consequences. I believe it now more than ever; *I am his everything.* And in his world of *anything is possible,* maybe we are the perfect formula.

Playlist

The songs of Formula Love:

Acknowledgments

First and foremost, thank *you* for reading this book. Whether you are a seasoned F1 fan or newly obsessed, I hope you enjoyed Sophie and Beck's story. This sport has a special way of capturing people's hearts—don't be surprised if you quickly go from watching races to *attending races*.

For as long as I can remember, I have been making up fictional characters and creating scenes, watching them play out over and over in my head. Some of these characters have been with me for over ten years. Only recently did I discover this isn't how everyone "daydreams." I want to thank my friends and family for encouraging me to start writing these "stories" down. Once I started, I couldn't stop. If you haven't seen me in a year, now you know why! One hundred thousand words came easily (and Sophie and Beck's story still isn't over!).

A huge thank you to my brilliant editors at EJL Editing. You have taught me so much, and I truly appreciate your patience, enthusiasm, and feedback during each round of revisions, editing, and formatting! And finally, thank you to my proofreader at Brandee Paschall Books LLC.

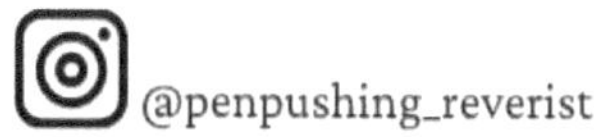

www.ingramcontent.com/pod-product-compliance
Lightning Source LLC
Chambersburg PA
CBHW022015300726
48970CB00003B/901